# The Teeth of Giants

Gordon Wallis

# Contents

# 1

# Chapter One: Many Years Back. The Bush War. Inyanga Mountains, Rhodesia (Zimbabwe) / Mozambique Border

The old Mercedes Unimog lurched violently and spluttered diesel fumes as it ground over the rocks on the mountain pass. The young soldier manning the twin-mounted 7.62 mm MAG machine guns hung on to the grips to avoid being thrown onto the steel floor behind the cab. He couldn't have been more than seventeen years old. A recent conscript to the Rhodesian Light Infantry, his gaze shifted from left to right constantly. Occasionally he glanced nervously down to where Johannes Kriel and I sat casually smoking cigarettes. Cap set at a jaunty angle the young man was desperately portraying a bravado immediately given away by his eyes. I had seen this look a thousand times before. It was one of pure unadulterated fear. It was obvious that the road had not seen a vehicle for years. On three occasions Hannes and I had to disembark to remove boulders that had fallen into the rutted [and], eroded trail. Above us, a perfect blue sky spread across the green vista of the mountains to the left and the yellowed lower lands of Mozambique to the right. I watched Hannes as he took a drink of water from his camouflaged bottle. His eyes were closed as he drank, and he kept them that way as he screwed the green top back on the bottle. His head nodded slightly to the broken rhythm of the vehicle. Hannes Kriel was humming to himself. I had no idea what song it was, but I had seen him do this whenever he was bored or at rest. He was in his 'happy place' and I had no reason to disturb him.

It was half an hour later when the truck finally came to a stop. Hannes and I stood up to look around. Through the dusty back window of the cab, I saw the driver's assistant had laid a map out and was pointing at the spot where we had stopped. Without turning the engine off the driver turned in his seat and gave us the thumbs-up signal. We had arrived at our drop-off point.

"Ready Hannes?" I asked over the rumbling engine.

"Ya, let's go," he replied in his heavy Afrikaans accent.

Strapping on our rucksacks and retrieving our rifles Hannes and I moved to the rear of the vehicle past the young soldier at the mounted MAGs. Contrary to orders he muttered,

"Good luck guys."

"Thanks. See you tomorrow," I replied cheerfully.

The young soldier was under no illusions as to who we were. I met Hannes on the first day of training for the Selous Scouts. At almost seven feet tall his massive bulk towered above me. His protruding forehead and thick ginger beard gave him the look of a Neanderthal. For all his immense size Johannes Kriel was as fast and deadly as the best of them. There was also a gentle side to Hannes Kriel which few knew about. The soft hazel eyes set in the sunburnt face were the giveaway and I knew him well enough to understand this.

We jumped from the rear of the truck and immediately headed left down the rugged mountainside towards the invisible line of the Mozambique border. The fresh mountain air was sweet and cool, and we broke into a slow trot as we descended. The brief was clear. Aerial reconnaissance had indicated the presence of an insurgent camp near the Mozambican town of Catandica. We were to infiltrate the camp, ascertain the number of insurgents, and draw clear maps of the layout and access to the base with a view to a future ground strike. This had to be done in twenty-four hours. The same truck that connection. Hannes and I squatted in the tall grass for cover and watched in silence for any movement. There was none. We moved off to the right staying crouched in the grass as we went. We arrived at the far corner of the base to see the guard still passed out leaning on the mast of the light as he had been before. His AK47 rifle and an empty plastic five-litre container lay next to him.

We passed the perimeter of the camp by forty metres before making a left turn towards the access road the beer truck had used. Realising we were exposed we crossed the sandy road as quickly as possible to get to the tall grass beyond. Once we were in cover, we stopped again to look for any movement. Seeing nothing we continued our progress silently through the trees up the right. Tension mounted as we approached the upper right corner of the base.

From our lookout on the hill, we had been unable to see this area clearly and we had no idea if the sentry was in a similar condition to the rest. When we got there, there was no guard present although two plastic bottles were lying on the ground near the mast. Hannes and I looked at each other for answers but could only conclude that whoever had been there was either drunk, missing, or both. We decided to move on in the darkness behind the camp towards the vehicles and the administration block. Eventually, we passed the armouries and arrived at the point opposite the thatched building. Behind it was a radio mast, three civilian pickup trucks, one Russian-made seven-tonne lorry with a wheel missing and two double-barrelled anti-aircraft guns. From where we were, they looked like early Soviet ZPU-2 towed units. These were old weapons but extremely effective nonetheless and their very existence was a crucial piece of intelligence. Hannes and I crouched in the darkness whilst I wrote down what we had seen. Satisfied we had seen enough we cut back on our path towards the armouries or storerooms we had passed earlier. There were three small buildings placed in a row with brick walls and corrugated iron roofs. It was clear their contents were of vital importance. The doors to these buildings were to the front facing the camp but they each had small ventilation spaces to the rear. Hannes and I crouched in the darkness contemplating how best to inspect them. After a few minutes of studying them, we decided that Hannes would attempt to look in through the ventilation space to the rear of each building while I would circle the front to do the same. This would be by far the most dangerous part of our mission, and we would be exposed to the full glare of the lights. We decided that we would start with the building closest to the administration block, take a quick look and retreat to the cover of darkness. We would then repeat this for the final two buildings and our mission would be complete. We would be over the hill and on our way back to the border well before sunrise.

"Are you ready?" I whispered.

"Ya, let's go," he replied.

I watched as he made his way across the dusty soil quickly and silently to the shadows of the corrugated roof at the rear of the first building. There was no sound or movement and soon I heard the signal I had been waiting for. The whistle of the Nightjar sounded softly from the back of the building. It was time to move. I quickly made the crossing to the left of the building and stood flat against the wall in the shadow of the roof. All around was brightly lit although quiet and deserted. I moved slowly in this position towards the front pausing to poke my head around the corner to check for trouble. Seeing nothing I made the turn and looked to my right at the front of the building. There were no windows, only two large steel doors that were bolted shut with heavy padlocks. Above these were two small ventilation holes similar to the ones at the rear.

There was no way I would be able to look into them, but I was certain that Hannes would already have done so given his height. Keeping my back to the wall and scanning the area in front of me I made my way to the corner of the building and around to where Hannes stood in the darkness. We gave each other the all-clear signal and scurried back to the cover of darkness at the back of the camp.

"Did you get a look in?" I whispered.

"I did. Standard RPGs, 60 MM mortars, assault rifles and ammo."

We moved to our left in line with the second building and repeated the process. The results were the same. It was when we aligned ourselves with the third building and paused to assess the situation that I felt the first twinge of unease. I have no idea what brought it on. Perhaps it was an instinctive premonition of trouble ahead but as I watched Hannes cross to the rear of the last building there was a cold sliding feeling in my stomach. Regardless, upon hearing the soothing whistle of the Nightjar I crossed the sandy soil to the left-hand side of the building and stood with my back to the wall. All was clear around me but still, there was the fear that something was not quite right. Silently I shuffled to my right towards the front corner of the building. It was as I turned to face the front of the building that I saw the empty five-litre bottle lying near the steel doors. Crouched and hidden in the shadows of the doorway was the figure of a man. Upon seeing me he leapt to his feet and raised his AK47.

"Ndiani?" he said loudly. Shona for 'Who is there?'

A thousand thoughts shot through my mind as I silently turned back around the corner. I knew then what it was that had been bothering me. The missing sentry from the far corner of the camp. It was surely him.

"Ndiani?" he shouted this time.

My rifle was of no use to me. Although my face was blacked out, he was clearly alarmed and would certainly come around the corner at any moment. I drew my knife as I waited.

"Enoch Walaza," I said trying to buy time.

Sweat formed on my face as I contemplated my next move. I knew Hannes would have heard this outburst and would be taking action as well.

I slung my rifle behind my back, hid the knife up my sleeve and turned around the corner once again. The man stood there clearly alarmed, his AK47 at the ready.

"Ndino reva aiwa isva," I said quietly with my hands raised. 'I mean no harm.'

He looked at me with wide confused eyes. As I spoke, I saw the mountainous figure of Hannes come up silently behind the man. His left arm flashed around the man's chest while his right hand, like a huge bunch of bananas, completely covered his face. There was a brief, muffled grunt before I heard his neck break. It sounded just like the branch of a tree snapping. The man's body shook violently in Hannes' grip and his right hand tightened on the trigger of his weapon as he died. Three shots rang out in quick succession before his arm slackened. The bullets ricocheted off the wall of the building sending sharp chips of brick and mortar into my face. The sound of the shots split the night leaving my ears ringing. I lurched forward to catch the weapon before it fell. Instinctively we moved back towards the darkness with Hannes carrying the dead man like a rag doll. There was no reason or time to talk. We needed to get away and do so immediately. When we arrived in the cover of the darkness behind the camp, I gave the signal for Hannes to follow me back along the route we had taken. With the man's body slung over Hannes' shoulder in a fireman's lift, we started. Already there were sounds of alarm and shouting. The slumbering camp was coming alive quickly. I wiped the blood from my right eye as we rounded the corner of the parade ground in the darkness. To our right all was confusion, mainly centred in front of the administration building. A group of around one hundred men in various stages of undress had gathered and loud angry orders were being barked out by a drunken senior officer. I stopped when I heard a dull thud and a gasp from behind me. Hannes had tripped on a rock and both he and the dead man had taken a tumble. We crouched in the darkness sweating and panting heavily. Ahead of us, to the right, the corner guard had woken from his slumber and was racing towards the administration block rifle in hand. Seeing a gap ahead we quickly got to our feet and proceeded cautiously in the moonlight. The edge of the camp and the base of the hill were forty metres away from us. There was no doubt Hannes could easily carry the man's body up and over the hill where it would not be discovered for some time. By then we would be far away through the minefield, approaching our rendezvous in the safety of the mountains. It was as we approached the corner of the camp that the siren sounded. The noise from the camp became a cacophony of confusion with lights and torches appearing everywhere. I paused and glanced at Hannes who stood panting behind me. We had run out of time. Soon the entire camp and surrounds would be swarming with rabid drunken insurgents. There would be trackers with spotlights sent out immediately and I knew we would stand little chance of escape. I pointed towards the line of thatched wall structures at the front of the camp.

"The latrines, Hannes. Let's go"

Staying in the darkness we moved at an angle that would prevent us from being seen by the crowd at the centre of the camp. We arrived at the third structure from the end. Crouching down I quickly parted the grass wall and crawled inside. The moonlight shone through the open top revealing a floor of wooden poles set across a three-metre trench. Positioned at a height of half a metre and running the length of the latrine was a single wooden pole that would act as a seat for the user. The structure would accommodate six people at a time. I turned back to the hole I had made in the grass wall. Hannes had laid the dead man on the ground with his head and shoulders facing me. I pulled the body through and dropped it into the trench behind the pole. It landed in the liquid muck below with a soft slapping sound. The man with the megaphone started issuing frantic orders as Hannes shifted his colossal frame through the hole I had made. Once he was through, I quickly closed the hole by pulling the grass back into place. By then there were thudding footfalls and confused shouting all around us. Silently I glanced at Hannes, his eyes were wide and alarmed. I pointed to the trench behind the pole and mouthed the words.

"Down, now!"

Carefully, using the raised pole, we lowered ourselves down into the stinking darkness. The semi-liquid sludge was physically hot and came up to our waists. There was sufficient light from the opening behind the pole to see the body of the dead man was still not fully submerged. I pulled it through the darkness towards the corner of the trench under the pole floor. Above us all around were the sounds of people running and shouting. After a while, my eyes became accustomed to the darkness as thin slivers of moonlight shone between the poles above. The trench was three metres long and two metres wide. The wooden poles above us stretched one and a half metres until they ended being supported from underneath by a cross beam. Hannes and I stood in the far-right corner under the poles. Above the putrid liquid waste were rough earth walls. Already the stinking liquid had permeated our boots and clothing completely. Knowing we would be there for some time, I decided I needed to improve our situation. Slowly I waded across to the far side of the trench and during a lull in the activity around, I removed one of the poles from the rough floor above. When I returned to where Hannes stood, I removed my knife and began digging into the earth walls above the sludge to create a ledge on which to sit.

The panic and chaos above continued as I worked but my efforts had a calming effect on me. Half an hour later I managed to slot the pole into place and Hannes and I raised ourselves onto it. Still, our legs dangled in the fetid liquid below. In the dim light, I turned to look at Hannes. His eyes were wide, and he constantly looked at the poles above. I turned my gaze and saw the face of the dead man lying below me.

His body was submerged but his face stared upwards, eyes and mouth open. A look of frozen terror on his face. I removed his rifle from my shoulder and placed it on top of where his shoulders were submerged. With my right foot, I slowly pushed him down and his face disappeared beneath the stinking dark liquid with a soft bubbling sound.

The shouting and searching abated around 5.00am although there were still the sounds of people moving around above. As the daylight started to filter through so did the flies. They came in great swarms and settled on every surface above the steaming liquid. Hannes and I sat with our eyes closed leaning against the earth walls of the latrine. We blocked one ear with one hand while cupping our noses and mouths with the other. The buzzing sound was deafening, and the insects crawled on every surface of exposed skin. At 6.00 am a siren sounded near the administration building and we heard the camp come alive. The man with the megaphone began barking orders and soon after our little hideaway had its first visitors. The home-brewed beer had caused a common and terrible side effect on the men. Everyone who had drunk it woke up with a severe case of explosive diarrhoea. The men rushed in groups of five into the latrine above us and groaned as they vacated their cramping bowels not half a metre from where we sat. We were literally in a shower of shit. Thankfully we remained undiscovered where we sat as both Hannes and I knew that if we were to be found, the consequences would be far more appalling.

The heat started to come in waves along with more flies and the occasional rat at around 9.00 am. The men in the camp above were being put through a gruelling training day of marching and singing. They were being punished by their superiors for the previous night's excesses and for the missing sentry who lay submerged with his gun beneath us. Every few minutes an exhausted man would burst into the latrine above and either vomit, defecate, or both. It was at around midday that I saw the first cracks appear in Johannes Kriel. As I sat with my eyes closed, I started feeling the pole on which we sat begin to shake. I turned, to see him staring down at the stinking pool of liquid below. The dead man's upper body had risen and his grotesque, shit-covered face was looking up at us. Hannes stared at the spectacle with wide eyes and his entire body shook violently. I gripped his arm firmly.

"Hannes!" I whispered.

There was no response. With my right foot, I gently pushed the body down, so it was once again submerged.

"Hannes!" I growled between clenched teeth.

He turned to face me with wide unseeing eyes.

"Think of the tune Hannes," I said "The song you always hum to yourself. Close your eyes and think of the song!"

He nodded back at me jerkily and closed his eyes. He began to nod his head and hum to himself quietly. After a few minutes, the shaking subsided and Johannes Kriel was calm again. It was clear the abject horror of our situation was too much for him and he had been on the brink of a nervous breakdown. I couldn't blame him either. I let out a sigh of relief, closed my eyes and tried to remain focused on my goal of leaving that hell hole.

The relentless marching and singing continued throughout the day. Although I had become accustomed to the stench, I preferred to keep my eyes closed to my surroundings. In my mind, I wished myself away to a happier place and time from my youth. Occasionally I would glance at Hannes who by then appeared to be in some kind of trance with his song. I was under no illusions that we were still in an extremely dangerous position and the risk of us being discovered was a very real possibility. The drill on the parade ground above ended at 4.00 pm and the great swarms of maddening insects began to dissipate gradually. I nudged Hannes who turned to look at me calmly.

"Two o'clock we leave," I whispered.

He nodded his approval and gave me the thumbs-up sign before returning to his trance-like state. In the fading light, I got off my seat and waded to the far side of the trench to retrieve another thin pole. I used this to wedge the dead man's body beneath the surface of the liquid to prevent him from being found for a good while. After doing this I returned to my seat, closed my eyes, and waited. The camp fell silent at around 10.00 pm that night. The only visitor being the occasional rat. The temptation to bolt and run was overwhelming, but I was acutely aware that a sentry would be in position not fifty metres from where we sat.

At 1.45 am I opened my eyes to assess the situation. The moonlight shone in through the rear of the latrine and all around was dead silent. I knew we were about to embark on the single most dangerous part of our mission. I felt a bizarre reluctance to leave our safe little cocoon of excrement. Putting that firmly out of my mind I nudged Hannes gently.

"Time to go," I whispered.

Our lower bodies were cramped and stiff from being seated for so many hours, but we waded quietly to the far side of the trench and slowly lifted ourselves out using the raised pole seat.

Once again, I parted the grass at the rear of the latrine and crawled out. I paused for a moment to look and listen for any sign of danger. I could not see the guard from where I was, but I knew full well that he would be there. I signalled Hannes to come through which he did quickly and silently. Ahead of us was the darkness and safety of the hill from which we had viewed the camp the previous night. We were both desperate to get going but we purposely stayed where we were for five minutes in case of a patrol. Eventually, I closed the opening in the grass barrier, and we made our way carefully towards the base of the hill. I glanced once towards the base of the tower light at the corner of the camp. Sure enough, the guard was there albeit fast asleep leaning on its base. Slowly and with great care we began the climb to the top of the hill not once pausing to look back. By the light of the moon, we avoided all the loose rock and boulders on our ascent until finally, we stopped at the summit to look down.

"Let's get the fuck out of here," I said.

"Yes, let's do that," said Hannes.

We walked all through the night only stopping once to wash at the Pungwe River. The sun had risen by the time we approached the minefield, and we passed without incident near the rocky outcrop through which we had come. By midday, we had crossed the invisible border and had climbed up once again into the sweet cool air of the Inyanga mountains. The old Mercedes Unimog was parked on the rocky pass where it had dropped us. The young trooper who had been manning the twin MAG machine guns got the fright of his life at the sight of Hannes and me approaching.

"Jesus! You guys are a bit late?" he said as we climbed into the back of the vehicle.

"Ya," I replied as Hannes and I took our position on the steel floor behind the cab.

"Ran into a few problems. Nothing serious."

# 2

## Chapter Two: London, Present Day

I awoke to the usual sounds of my North London flat. With one eye open I reached for the glass of water and took a long drink. After a minute of lying motionless, I swung my legs off the bed and stared at the pack of cigarettes that lay on the bedside table next to me. *Don't do it, Green*. I cursed softly, stood up and walked to the bathroom to shower and shave. Afterwards, wrapped in my towel, I finally lit a cigarette and went into the kitchen to make a cup of coffee. With the hot cup in hand, I walked into the lounge, turned on the television and opened the curtains. I shook my head in disgust at the sight before me. From five floors up the scene was bleak and grey. North London in mid-March with an Arctic chill descending. I stood sipping coffee staring at the desolate windswept urban decay below. With a sigh, I returned to my desk to sit and smoke while watching the news headlines. The stories were the usual dreary bullshit that I saw every day, so I decided to browse my emails to see what the day had in store for me. One of the potential jobs grabbed my attention immediately. Thirty-seven-year-old Damon Mountford from Bethnal Green had claimed disability after he had been knocked from a moped on the high street. The insurance company had suspected fraud as he had an extensive criminal record and was also rumoured to be still actively coaching the local kickboxing club. I took a sip of coffee as I looked carefully at his picture. His hair was peroxided and stood up in gelled spikes. He had an arrogant pinched face and wore earrings on both ears.

"I'll get you, Mr Mountford," I said under my breath.

My contemplation was disturbed by an unusual report from the news reader. Immediately I stopped and focussed on the television screen.

"A well-known Zimbabwean ivory trade investigator who pioneered efforts to combat elephant and rhino poaching has been killed in the Mana Pools National Park in Zimbabwe. Johannes Kriel, 51, died after being shot by suspected poachers two days ago. His wife, Teresa, found his body. Mr Kriel, who had led global investigations into illegal wildlife trading since the 1980s was a charismatic and familiar sight at conservation conferences. Initial reports suggest that police believe the murder was part of a botched robbery but there are also concerns that the murder may have been related to Mr Kriel's work. A spokesman for the charity Save The Elephants has expressed shock and grief at his untimely passing."

I sat in stunned silence for the duration of the report. The picture of the man that came up briefly certainly looked like my old friend Hannes albeit thinner and without a beard.

Floods of forgotten memories washed over me as I googled the report with slightly shaky hands. The pictures and articles that came up confirmed my worst fears. There was no doubt it was Hannes. The gentle eyes and tall frame were the giveaway. A wave of sad nostalgia swept over me as I remembered our ill-fated mission to the base at Catandica in Mozambique. We had formed a very special bond that night all those years ago and this sudden unexpected news had touched a raw nerve deep inside me. Next, I went to Facebook and searched. As I suspected there was no page for Johannes Kriel but there was one for his wife Teresa. I browsed the many photographs some of which were of their family and kids growing up enjoying holidays in the bush. Hannes had had two boys who were now in their mid-twenties. There were hundreds of posts from friends sending their condolences. It appeared the family were well known and dearly loved in Zimbabwe. I felt a deep pang of guilt that I had neglected to try to stay in touch with him. The break I had made with the country of my birth in 1980 had been sudden and final. I began typing a message to Teresa Kriel.

'Dear Teresa, you don't know me, but I was in the Army with Hannes many years ago. We had a very special bond and I wanted to tell you how sorry I am for your loss.

Sincerely, Jason Green'

I hit the enter button and sat back to think. It was not thirty seconds later that a reply popped up on my screen.

'Dear Jason. Thank you for your message. I cannot tell you how devastated we are at the loss of Hannes. He spoke fondly of you so often and always wondered where you ended up after the war. There will be a memorial at Highlands Presbyterian Church in Harare on Wednesday at 11.30 am. Thanks again for making contact. Teresa'

I read the message five times over while drumming my fingers on the desk. Eventually, I got up and took my coffee and a cigarette over to the window to think. I was suddenly overcome by great sadness and a feeling of isolation. My old friend had died thousands of miles away in the Zambezi Valley he loved. Somewhere in the distance, a siren sounded and below me, in the street, a woman screamed at her delinquent child who was refusing to go to the nearby preschool. *Fuck it Green. You have to go.* With my mind made up I returned to my laptop and began to search for flights. I ended up settling for the Ethiopian Airways flight that evening from Heathrow. There would be a three-hour stop-over in Addis Ababa then I would connect directly to Harare. It would give me around twenty-four hours to rest before the memorial service. I left the ticket open as I hadn't been there in so long, I thought I might do some travelling afterwards. I then booked a Toyota Land Cruiser to hire and a plush-looking lodge in the leafy suburb of Glen Lorne. Satisfied, I sat back and lit another cigarette.

My sadness was mixed with excitement now at the prospect of returning to the country of my birth. I called the case supervisor at the insurance company to inform her I would be unable to take on any new jobs for the time being. Next, I dressed and started packing my bags. As usual, I packed my work kit out of the force of habit. I paused to look at the Christmas present I had bought for myself but never used. The drone had cost £1,600.00 but it had been too cold and I had been too busy to use it. It had remained forgotten in my cupboard. I decided that after the memorial I might do some travelling so I removed the expensive machine from its box and packed it in the bag. Next, I called my cleaner. I told her not to bother coming in until I phoned on my return. I spent the rest of the day cleaning up the flat and browsing the internet for possible places to visit in Zimbabwe after the memorial. It seemed that despite Mugabe's ruinous rule. tourism was flourishing in my home country and there were plenty of high-end lodges and resorts scattered all over the country. At 5.00 pm. I did a final check of my luggage and then headed out to Seven Sisters tube station. The frigid blast of air took my breath away as I made my way down the open walkway towards the lift. As usual, the lift smelt of urine and I held my breath as it descended. The sun was setting as I made my way from the building towards the main road that led to the station. A group of noisy, foul-mouthed kids were jumping on the rubbish bins to the left of the building. I wrapped my jacket tightly around me and walked with purpose through the freezing wind up the rapidly darkening street.

I picked up a newspaper outside the station and started reading it as I took the escalator down into the humid bowels of North London. The train arrived after five minutes, and I managed to find a seat beside my bags so I could keep an eye on them during the journey to Heathrow. The train filled as we neared central London and the seat next to me was taken by a young man carrying a takeaway box meal from McDonalds. His jeans were halfway down his waist exposing most of his red underwear as he sat. He wore Bluetooth headphones through which I could hear loud rap music. He proceeded to noisily eat his burger and chips while intermittently slurping his Coke through a plastic straw right next to me. *Fucking idiot*. I hated the tube. Thankfully, he soon left, and I could read my newspaper in peace.

By the time I arrived at Heathrow, I was more than ready for a smoke, so I hurried out of the station into the frozen night air to do just that. The wind howled as I huddled in my jacket. After a few minutes, I left to make my way into the building to check-in. That process followed by security took half an hour and finally, I was through to the duty-free area. I made my way to the nearest bar and ordered a whisky. After my drink arrived, I turned to look around.

The bar was busy but there was an unoccupied table in the far corner, I made my way over and sat down. Sitting at the table nearby was an elderly American couple who had just ordered some dinner.

"I can't wait to get home to some real American food," said the overweight woman loudly.

"Not long now," replied the husband as he browsed his phone.

I shook my head and took a sip of the drink. An hour later I made my way to the departure gate to get my flight. The aircraft was boarding when I arrived and the crowd shuffled forward, documents at the ready. The plane was a clean modern Dreamliner, and I took the window seat I had booked in Economy class. After loading the aircraft began its pushback and taxi to the runway while the safety procedures showed on the screens to the rear of the seats. I watched the freezing drizzle and the lights of the airport from my window. Soon after that, the giant aircraft accelerated and took off leaving it all behind. I was feeling a mixture of excitement and sadness at the time. Once the plane had reached cruising altitude the crew began to serve dinner and drinks. I ordered the chicken with a lager and bottled water to drink. The food was edible, and I swallowed a strong sleeping tablet with the beer. Afterwards, I adjusted my seat and began to watch a movie. Within half an hour the effects of the sleeping tablet kicked in and I drifted off into a deep dreamless sleep.

I woke feeling stiff and uncomfortable seven hours later as the plane descended into Addis Ababa. To my left were the rolling green mountains of Ethiopia in the morning sunlight. After landing we filed out of the aircraft and into a bus that took us to the main terminal. The place was more like a factory than an airport with thousands of people of all nationalities milling around waiting for their flights. Feeling groggy I found a coffee shop and eventually managed to get the lazy and disinterested staff to serve me a cup. I sat in silence watching the world go by for two hours until it was time to head to check in for the flight to Harare. The queue to the gate was chaotic and unorganized but eventually, we boarded the aircraft and took off for Harare. I was still drugged by the sleeping pill and fell asleep almost immediately. The three and a half hours flight time flew by, and I woke as we were coming into land. From the window, I looked out at the granite outcrops and the lush green countryside of Zimbabwe in the late rainy season.

The sleeping tablet had done its job and I was feeling refreshed if a little stiff. The aircraft landed and taxied to the new main terminal which had not been there when I left all those years ago. Eventually, we filed out of the plane and into the glass-sided gangway that led to the terminal. The sun shone brightly, and the air was warm and slightly humid. I was acutely aware of the portrait of Robert Mugabe staring down at me ominously as I entered the building.

We made our way down to the immigration desks where I was made to queue for twenty minutes and pay fifty dollars for my visa despite having been born there. Once I had completed that I headed to the baggage reclaim with the other passengers. My main bag was already out and I retrieved it quickly. One of my worries was the drone I was carrying, and I noticed that everyone was being made to put their luggage through an X-ray machine near the exit. Sensing this might pose a problem I removed it from my bag and pocketed it before leaving. The drone, although powerful, was small and had foldable arms and easily fitted into a jacket pocket. My bags went through the machine without a problem, and I walked out of the exit looking for the car hire rep who was due to meet me. I found him holding a sign that bore my name near the exit to the building. He accompanied me outside briefly as I wanted to have a cigarette. I stood there basking in the afternoon sunshine and made small talk with him as I smoked. Once I was satisfied, we went back into the building and to the car hire offices to complete the formalities. This was quick and hassle free and within fifteen minutes I was led out to their yard to find my vehicle. The Toyota Land Cruiser was dark blue in colour and was fitted with off-road tyres. I thanked the rep as he handed me the keys. The interior of the cab smelled new and looked clean. It would suit my purpose well. The sun shone brightly as I drove out of the airport complex, and I had to put the air conditioning on. Although the vehicle was fitted with Satnav I decided to try and find my way to the lodge without it. I saw the impressive skyline of Harare on the horizon as I drove, and the memories began to flood back in. Although the road was new, I recognized the buildings I passed, and I knew precisely where to take the right turn that would lead me to the northern suburbs. I found myself amazed at my instinctive sense of direction as I drove. The only thing of note was that the streets were slightly unkempt and littered. Otherwise, they were pretty much as I had left them all those years ago. On the way to my lodge, I decided to drive past the house I had grown up in. Although now behind a tall wall and electric gate I managed to get a glimpse of it from the running board of the vehicle when I stopped briefly outside. It looked exactly as I remembered it in the late afternoon sunshine only it seemed a little smaller. Two young kids were running around the swimming pool and diving in just like I had done as a child. The sight brought on a sense of melancholy that stayed with me through the afternoon.

The lodge I had booked was plush and well-fitted. The tropical gardens which my room overlooked were immaculate and the host was pleasant and helpful. I unpacked my bags and took a shower after which I sat by the pool to watch the sunset and have a few beers. I ordered a dinner of fillet steak and gratin dauphinoise to be served out by the pool. I sat in the cool African evening and watched the stars while listening to the cicadas in the garden. By 9.00 pm. the food and drink had caused me to feel exhausted, so I retired to my room to relax and watch a movie. Before long I fell into a deep sleep. I dreamt of the ill-fated mission to Catandica with Hannes and re-lived every terrible moment of it. Despite my nocturnal horrors, I awoke feeling fresh and invigorated the following morning.

I took a half-hour run through the suburb of Glen Lorne followed by a swim at the lodge and a shower in my room. After a full English breakfast served by the pool, I browsed the internet looking for places to go the following day. I decided I would take the five-hour drive to Bulawayo and stay in a lodge at the Matopos Hills before making my way through the Hwange National Park and onward to Victoria Falls. The thought of the trip lifted my spirits on what was a rather sad day. *Just go and pay your respects, Green. Once that's done you can get on with your trip.* At 10.40am. I dressed for the service. The day was getting hotter by the hour and there were ominous grey and black storm clouds gathering on the horizon behind the hills. The drive to the church was simple as I knew exactly where it was. I arrived to find the car park packed full of vehicles and I had to turn down a side road to find a parking spot. I crossed the main road on foot and made my way into the churchyard. There was a large group of people slowly filing into the church. I kept to the back of the crowd not wanting to meet or speak to anyone. It was then I noticed something unusual. At the far end of the car park to the right were two black men in suits wearing dark sunglasses. Their suits, although expensive, were light in colour and they appeared somehow out of place showing no inclination to enter the church building. Instead, they stood and observed proceedings from a distance whilst leaning on a new twin-cab pickup truck with no number plates. From behind my sunglasses, I watched them feeling slightly puzzled that they would be there. I was also sure that I saw the bulge of concealed handguns under their jackets. I put the two men out of my mind as I entered the church building and took a seat on a bench at the rear. The church was filled with people of all races. There were at least ten game rangers in uniform sitting towards the middle of the building. It seemed my friend Hannes had been an extremely popular figure in Zimbabwe. The service was a sad occasion with hymns being sung and eulogies given by friends and family. When it had finished a choir sang 'Morning has broken' as the family made their way out of the church. I felt a stab of guilt and sadness as I watched Teresa and her sons walk past me in tears.

Gradually the church began to empty with people stopping to commiserate with the family standing near the exit. *You go pay your condolences and get the fuck out of here Green*. I was one of the last people to leave the building and approached the two sons first. I was struck by how tall they were and how much they looked like Hannes.

"Sorry for your loss," I said to both, shaking their hands.

Next, I moved on to speak to Teresa Kriel who was very distraught and was being tended to by a friend. I took her hand and spoke.

"Hi, Teresa, you don't know me, my name is Jason Green. I came from..."

"Oh my God you're Jason!" she interrupted, a look of frightened desperation on her face "Hannes spoke about you all the time. Oh, thank you, thank you for coming."

Her hand shook nervously in mine.

"Please, please stay a bit longer," she pleaded. "There's something I need to talk to you about. There is tea being served in the courtyard. Please stay for a while and I'll find you there. Please!"

I was taken aback by the sense of urgency in her voice and face. Immediately I put it down to grief and shock.

"Of course," I said. "I'll be there."

It was the last thing I wanted or needed. I had paid my respects to my old friend and was desperate to leave. I hated funerals and I needed to get on the road. However, it was a plea I could not ignore so I made my way out of the church building and into the burning sunshine. Some of the crowds were leaving while others were making their way to the courtyard area for the tea. Out of the corner of my eye, I noticed the two men in suits at the far side of the car park. They were still standing there watching proceedings, talking quietly.

Again, their presence gave me a slightly uneasy feeling, but I put it out of my mind and followed the crowd into the courtyard. The tea and coffee and snacks were being served to the left-hand side of the courtyard. In the centre was a raised fishpond with water lilies and a fountain. I made my way to the linen-covered table that was serving coffee. Standing next to me as I poured was a large man with a wizened sunburnt face. He delved into his pocket and withdrew a silver hip flask from which he poured a liberal tot of whisky into his cup.

"Good idea," I said under my breath.

He raised his eyebrow surreptitiously signalling his willingness to share to which I quickly offered my cup. The man poured a substantial shot.

"Cheers," I said quietly.

I turned around to look at the crowd. Teresa Kriel was surrounded by friends, but she constantly turned to look at me to make sure I was there. I nodded once to acknowledge my presence and walked to a quiet corner to drink my coffee. I stood alone wondering what it was she wanted to talk to me about.

After a few minutes, she excused herself from her friends and made her way over to where I stood. With shaking hands and a look of desperation on her face, she pulled me into the corridor that led to the church office. Once we were alone, she spoke.

"Oh my God Jason you have no idea how glad I am that you came. There are people after me, after my family!" she said on the brink of tears.

"What's going on?" I asked.

"You know Hannes was involved in anti-poaching and elephant conservation," she said.

"Yes, I know that."

"Well for the past year, he has been involved in some top-secret investigation and was unable to tell *even me* what he was doing. He said it was far too dangerous for me to know *anything* about it. He was murdered, Jason. Murdered! The police said it was a robbery that went wrong but it just doesn't add up. He was afraid for us all. Me, our kids."

She held my elbows tightly as she spoke looking up at me.

"They've been following me since we got back from the Zambezi Valley. Did you see the men outside?"

"I did notice two strange men hanging around yes," I replied.

"That's them!" she said. "We had a robbery at the house last night. They left the TVs, the speakers, the safe, everything! They took only the laptop computer. They are after Hannes' work! I'm leaving with the boys this afternoon and flying to Port Elizabeth in South Africa. They are after us! We'll be safe there."

I shook my head not knowing what she wanted me to do.

"Hannes trusted you with his life Jason. I know it's been a long time, but I need to give you something. He would have wanted it that way. Please, please take it."

"Take what?" I asked.

She began to frantically rummage in her large cloth handbag and brought out an external hard drive which she pushed forcefully into my right hand. I knew of course that she was bereaved and upset but it was starting to become clear to me that she was frightened as well.

"What is this?" I asked.

"That is Hannes' work, Jason. He made a point of telling me that what he was working on was far too sensitive and dangerous to simply leave on the laptop. He told me that if ever anything was to happen to him that I was to keep this hard drive safe and give it to someone outside the country whom he trusted. There is no one he trusted more than you Jason. The laptop they took last night had nothing on it. Nothing. Hannes was far too careful. Anything of any importance is on that hard drive."

"What do *you* think it's all about Teresa?" I asked.

"It's something to do with the ivory trade. That's all I know. Now I have to get myself and my family out of here. Thank you for doing this, Jason. I know Hannes would have wanted it this way".

"Okay. I'll look at it for you," I said resignedly.

After I had pocketed the hard drive, she held my hands and looked up at me with tears in her eyes.

"Thank you, Jason" she whispered before moving off in a hurry.

I walked back out into the sunlight of the courtyard to see her busily talking to her sons and friends. These were not the rantings of a mad woman. She was clearly alarmed. *Time to get out of here Green. Fucking hell.* I left the courtyard and walked into the car park. As I walked, I was once again aware of the two men standing near the pickup truck to my left. They hadn't moved in all the time I had been there and stood in silence trying to appear casual but all the while watching the proceedings carefully. As I left the church premises and crossed the busy road to get to my vehicle I reflected on the strange events of the day. I decided to put it out of my mind until I got back to my lodge and was able to take a look at what was actually on the hard drive. My plan of leaving for Bulawayo would have to wait till the following day. As I took the left turn onto the main road towards the lodge, I noticed one of the men in dark glasses had walked to the exit gate of the church. He stood there watching my vehicle while smoking a cigarette. I glanced back through the rear-view mirror to see him casually flick the butt into the ditch as I drove away.

# 3

## Chapter Three: Messages from the Dead

Ten minutes later I arrived and parked at the lodge in the warm afternoon sun. Feeling puzzled and intrigued I flipped open my laptop on the teak desk and plugged in the hard drive from Teresa Kriel. I was not surprised at all to find the data was password protected. *Fuck. What now?* I started with the obvious family names, birth dates and similar. No luck. I continued for fifteen minutes idly inputting various familiar words and terms all to no avail. Eventually, I stood up, grabbed a beer from the mini bar and walked to the sliding doors of my room to look out into the garden. As I stood there smoking, I watched a family of African Weaver Birds tending to their nest in a nearby palm tree. My mind went back to that terrible ill-fated mission in Mozambique with my late friend Hannes. A few password ideas popped into my mind, and I headed back to my computer to give them a try. 'Catandica' no luck. 'Mozambique' nothing. 'Selous Scouts'. Password incorrect. With a deep sigh, I sat back in my chair and turned to look at the garden once again. Dark storm clouds were gathering beyond the green hills in the distance. I took a deep draw of the beer as I watched the male Weaver Bird arrive at his nest with a thin strand of palm frond. *What password would you use Hannes?* An idea came to me suddenly and I leant forward and typed in the words 'Pamwe Chete' the motto of our unit in the army. Instantly the screen changed and in front of me were one hundred and eighty-six separate document and video files.

"Hannes, you fucking beauty," I said under my breath.

I was in. I put the beer to one side and started looking at the files individually from the top down. To say the information was 'hot' was an understatement. It appeared to be the culmination of a three-year investigation conducted by Hannes into the illegal poaching of elephants in the Lower Zambezi and the subsequent export of raw ivory both through Harare Airport and through the Forbes border post in the city of Mutare on the Mozambique border. Each document contained names, dates, photographs, and numbered shipments of raw ivory. The amount of detailed information in each file was staggering and I realised quickly that I would need many hours, if not days to take it all in. I perused each document quickly so as not to get bogged down by too much detail. The information appeared to document the methods and locations used by the actual poachers, followed by the trail and transportation of the raw ivory to either Harare or Beira in Mozambique. Included were names, phone numbers and addresses of those supposedly involved from the lowly paid individuals at the bottom end of the organization right up to high-ranking government officials and the companies and individuals at the top in China. I sat back in my chair and took a sip of beer as I stared at the screen. *What did you get yourself into here Hannes? This is a fucking can of worms if I ever saw one.*

The documents went on to describe the packing of the ivory in factories in Beira and the methods used to conceal it, along with the procedure for bribes at the port of Beira to enable the containers that held the shipments to be loaded without discovery onto ships to the Far East. Feeling overwhelmed I skipped the bulk of the documents that Hannes had so methodically compiled and clicked on the last one at the bottom of the list. The document was titled 'Report to The World Wildlife Fund Annual Forum on the organized poaching of Elephants in the Zambezi Valley and subsequent illegal export of ivory to the Far East by Mr Johannes Kriel. Geneva, Switzerland.' The date of the report which was to be presented in person was June that year. In three months. My friend had toiled for three years to make that presentation and his dream had been violently and abruptly halted by his murder. His life's work had been stolen from him. His wife Teresa was right.

My mind went back to the two individuals I had seen at the memorial that morning. There was no doubt in my mind they were after the hard drive and the information held on it. I was sitting on a very valuable and dangerous piece of property. I finished my beer and took the hard drive and my laptop to the car. I placed both under the front seat and headed out to find a replacement hard drive. I would set it up with random password-protected files and use it as a dummy in case of a visit from the two men. The drive to the shopping centre took fifteen minutes and I was careful to keep an eye on my rear-view mirror in case I was being followed. I bought a similar hard drive and headed back to the lodge again watching for any vehicle that might be following. Thankfully, I saw nothing, and I went straight to my room to continue studying the files on the original hard drive. Using the password, I decided to look at one of the first files titled 'Lower Zambezi Operation'. I spent the next hour poring over the document which was incredibly detailed and long. It primarily described a particularly ruthless individual by the name of Dixon Mayuni who was based on the Zambian side of the lower Zambezi near the mouth of the Kafue River. Hannes had described him as playing a major role in the poaching on the Zimbabwe side of the river. His role was the supply of cyanide, guns and ammunition to a team of poachers that he would bring across the river once a week to carry out their activities. The drop-off would happen every Friday night without fail. The practice of using cyanide for elephant poaching was relatively new, silent and especially cruel. The poachers would travel inland by night to remote watering holes and contaminate the water with the deadly white powder. Any animal who drank from that particular source was condemned to a horrendous and agonizing death. Hannes went on to intimate that not only elephants were affected but many other buffalo, buck and big cats as well. The slaughter did not end there either. as the carcasses of the dead animals were then eaten by scavengers such as Hyenas and African Vultures. They too would be poisoned and suffer a slow and painful death and the ecosystem permanently damaged.

Three days after poisoning the pool the poachers would return with Mr Mayuni to harvest the spoils. The tusks were indiscriminately hacked from the skulls of the dead animals with axes. Any other carrion of value such as Lion or Leopard was also carried back across the river for processing. The flesh would be boiled off the carcasses in great steel vats on bush fires to produce clean bones which have a high value in Chinese medicine. Although Hannes had documented the operation with cold accuracy and precision there was no escaping the fact that it made sickening reading. Dixon Mayuni, a Zimbabwean by birth, was an albino with a fearsome reputation on both the Zimbabwean and Zambian side of the border. Hannes had documented two cases of first-degree murder he was wanted in connection with in Zimbabwe. He had fled to Zambia four years previously but had continued his activities and poaching excursions from his bush camp near the Kafue River. According to the document he was both loathed and feared by those he employed. There were four photographs, taken from a distance, of the man himself. Dressed in faded camouflage the man was tall and thin. He wore a wide-brimmed bush hat to protect his pale skin from the scorching sun of the Zambezi Valley. The photographs showed him with a group of men walking through the African bush carrying AK47 rifles. Although clearly taken with a zoom lens, Dixon Mayuni was pictured turning back to look at the camera as he walked. His thin pale white face clearly different from his dark-skinned compatriots. The document ended with a chilling note from Hannes. 'I am fully aware that Mr Mayuni, through his network, has first-hand knowledge of this investigation and my activities in the Zambezi Valley. In the past three years, I have received more death threats than I can count and sincerely hope that after my report is made in Geneva Interpol will step in to deal with this criminal even if he is on the bottom rungs of this ladder of evil. He and all the others above him mentioned in this report must be made to answer for their crimes. I took a deep breath and sat back in my chair as I took it all in. *Jesus Christ Hannes. You went and got yourself killed, didn't you?* I stood up, grabbed another beer and went to stand at the sliding doors once again. I watched the Weaver birds in the fading afternoon light as I drank. My mind was spinning with what I had read. There was no doubt I was in real danger simply because I had possession of the files on the hard drive. Powerful people wanted that information, and it was clear they would stop at nothing to get it. One thing was certain. I would make sure that Hannes' report would be delivered and presented to the Word Wildlife Fund Forum in Geneva later that year. It would be the least I could do for my old friend.

With my mind made up I returned to the desk and plugged in the replacement hard drive. From my laptop, I downloaded and copied a few hundred random files from the internet. The process took me half an hour and once done I installed password protection on the whole lot of them. I had no doubt that should the goons get their hands on the hard drive they would spend some time trying to hack it and would be bitterly disappointed to find I had duped them.

Finished, I sat back and unplugged it from my laptop. *Probably won't happen, Green, but is a good precaution anyway.* The sun had set and beyond the sliding doors, the lush tropical garden was cloaked in darkness. I pocketed the original hard drive and locked my room leaving both my laptop and the dummy hard drive on the teak desk. I made my way to the parked vehicle down the tastefully lit garden path. The evening was pleasantly cool and out in the distance, I heard the familiar, cooing sound of the Fiery Necked Nightjar. The vehicle was in darkness, and I stepped unseen to the rear and opened the compartment that housed the spare wheel. I placed the hard drive safely within it and returned to my room.

There were only a few other guests, and they were dining near the pool. I left my room as I had before and walked to find a table nearby for dinner. The prime Zimbabwean fillet steak was washed down with several glasses of good South African red wine. Afterwards, I sat back and took in the African night as I drank coffee. The sound of the cicadas blended with the croak of a nearby frog and the Nightjar. *You keep the hard drive safe, and you can continue your trip, Green. It's unlikely they will know where it is or who you are. Should be fine.* Half an hour later I made my way back to my room to find it exactly as I had left it. After a shower, I locked the sliding door from the inside and drew the long curtains closed. I briefly checked my emails and the news on the internet before turning on the television and lying down on the bed. As I flicked through the channels my mind went to the goons from the memorial and how I had seen them watch me drive away in the rear-view mirror. I dropped the remote on the crisp white duvet and stared at the replacement hard drive on the teak desk.

"Better do something," I said under my breath. "Just in case."

I became conscious a few minutes later. There was an intense throbbing pain to the right of my head and with my eyes still closed I slowly raised my right hand to investigate it. My hair was wet and slippery with blood.

"Bastards," I said under my breath as I lay there.

A few minutes later the throbbing pain had subsided enough for me to lift myself from the bed. I groaned as I pushed myself up to reach for the bedside light. The light was blinding me and I collapsed once again onto the now blood-soaked duvet. I lay for a few minutes as I tried to stop the bleeding with a pillow. Eventually, I was able to get up and stumble to the bathroom. I stood unsteadily in the shower and washed the blood from my hair and shoulders. There was a frantic knocking on the sliding doors as I walked back into the bedroom with a white towel around my waist.

"Come in," I said loudly.

As I spoke the throbbing became worse and I stood there with my eyes closed as the manager of the lodge came in with the night guard.

"Oh my God!" said the manager as he saw the blood-stained duvet. "Are you okay Mr Green?"

"I'm fine," I said quietly. "They hit me on the head."

The night guard stood shaking with fear, his eyes like saucers as he looked at me apologetically.

"I'm very sorry sir," he said, "they came with a gun, and they said they would shoot me"

"I know. Don't worry about it," I replied.

I turned to the manager.

"Prepare my bill now, please. I'm leaving," I said quietly.

"Mr Green I'm so..."

"Just get the fucking bill, will you?" I barked in annoyance. "No police, just the bill."

Both men looked back at me with worried fearful eyes.

"Yes, sir," said the manager as he ushered the night guard from the room.

I turned towards the dressing table to pack my bag and get my clothes. The surface was smeared with blood, saliva and mucus from the man's face. *I got you good you fucker.* The bleeding above my ear had stopped as I dressed and packed my bags. The laptop and the dummy hard drive were gone but I wasn't too worried about the computer. I could replace it easily and there was nothing on it of any importance. The manager returned with the bill and the card machine as I got ready to leave. Sensing my anger, he kept the conversation to a minimum and I swiped the amount quickly and made my way to my vehicle. I dumped my bags on the back seat and got into the front to start the engine. I revved the vehicle hard as I drove towards the electric gate. It opened promptly and I drove out of the lodge and took a right turn towards the city.

It was 3.00am. dark and the roads were empty as I drove. With my head still thumping I looked around and watched the rear-view mirror as I drove. *They are gone, Green. Long gone.* I was right, there was no sign of any vehicles on the road let alone any following me. The drive to the city centre took fifteen minutes. I drove to the Crown Plaza Hotel and parked my vehicle in the underground parking lot to avoid it being seen. I retrieved the original hard drive from the spare wheel compartment and headed up to the reception. It was 3.45am. by the time I checked into my room on the fourteenth floor and poured a whisky from the minibar. I was tired. Tired, sore and angry. I stood near the huge bay windows of the room and stared down at the lights of the sleeping city below. The words the man had spoken were ringing in my mind.

"You are very lucky my friend. Mr Kriel was not as lucky as you."

This confirmed that my old friend Hannes had been murdered. There was no doubt. Teresa had been right. The horizon to the East had started turning a golden yellow colour by the time I lay on the bed to rest. The acid of the drink and the pain in my head exacerbated the caustic anger I was feeling, and it was a full half hour before I drifted off to a troubled sleep. In my dreams I repeatedly saw the face of the albino poacher from the Zambezi Valley, Dixon Mayuni. At around 8.00am. in the morning I accidentally turned onto my right side. The pain from my cut and swollen head woke me with a start. I lay there with my eyes closed as I gently massaged the tender area around the cut. *Yes, Mr Mayuni. I believe you killed my friend. I have an appointment with you...*

# 5

## Chapter Five: The Zambezi Valley

I opened my eyes to bright daylight streaming through the bay windows. I was feeling exhausted, but it was time to move. After a shower and shave I headed down to the reception to check out. While there I called the car hire company to instruct them to collect the Land Cruiser from the hotel car park and bill my credit card for the hire. The vehicle was known to whoever had sent the goons to my room and there was no way I would risk moving around in it again. After paying the hotel bill I ate a quick breakfast in the restaurant and had the receptionist call a taxi. It arrived promptly and I told the driver to take me to the nearest car hire company. The journey took less than five minutes and I walked into the office and ordered a new Land Cruiser. The four-by-four vehicle would be necessary for the journey I had in mind. By 10.00am. I packed my bags into the new vehicle and drove out of the yard and into the busy Harare traffic. The morning was both hot and bright and I dug my sunglasses from my bag as I drove to dull the glare that stung my eyes and exacerbated the ache on the right-hand side of my head. My aim was to get out of the city as soon as possible but I needed to buy a new laptop on the way. I drove to the plush shopping centre which I had visited the previous day to buy the dummy hard drive. As a precaution, I pocketed the valuable device before entering the shops. The new laptop was the exact model that had been taken by the men and I swiped my credit card to buy it and walked back to the parked vehicle. I drove to the nearest service station and bought a six-pack of bottled water and washed down three painkillers with one of them. As I headed north out of the city, I watched the rear-view mirror for any sign of a following vehicle. There was nothing and I decided that I was probably being a little paranoid. Eventually,

Lower Zambezi Valley. One particularly harrowing clip showed a family of Elephants that had been recently shot and their tusks hacked out. Two baby Elephants had been left alive as they had no value to the poachers and were seen in a highly confused and distressed state nudging their dead mothers with their feet and trunks trying to revive them. There was no doubt as to the identity of the person taking the video. It was my old friend Hannes Kriel. I heard his unmistakable accent as he filmed.

"Unbelievable," he said repeatedly "Unbelievable."

Hearing his voice was like hearing a ghost from my past. I sat back and stared at the screen feeling angry and worried. *I'm going to find you Mr Mayuni. I'm going to find you.* I was suddenly snapped out of my brooding melancholy by the sound of the drums from the dining area. Outside the rain had stopped and the sun was starting to break through the clouds. The visibility was good, and the trees and lawns glistened with moisture. I closed the laptop and walked to Andrew and Shirley's house with the hard drive in my hand.

"Morning, Jason. Hope you slept well?" said the old man.

"Very well thanks. I wanted to ask if you could put this in the safe again," I said.

"Sure, no problem," he said as he took it inside. "You better go for breakfast your boat driver is ready."

"Thanks very much," I said turning to walk across the lawn to the dining area.

Even at that early hour, the sun was fierce on the back of my neck as I walked. I ate a full English breakfast under the thatched roof while watching a pod of Hippos fifty metres from the camp. In the distance on the Zambian side, I watched as a group of women risked their lives by washing their clothes in the river. I was fully aware that the great river was teeming with man-eating crocodiles, and I shook my head as I drank a second cup of coffee. Afterwards, I walked back to my chalet in the bright sunshine to get ready to leave. I packed a couple of bottles of water in the day bag along with the drone and applied some sunscreen to my exposed skin. I hung a small pair of binoculars and my camera around my neck and locked the grille doors of the chalet on my way out. I put my sunglasses on and crossed the lawn to the firepit and the stairs that led down the riverbank to the jetty. There were three fishing boats moored with one being attended to by a thin black man in a cap and dark glasses. His skin was extremely dark due to the nature of his job and his perfect white teeth gleamed as he smiled and greeted me.

"Good morning, sir, my name is Amos, and I will be your driver today."

"Morning, Amos, my name is Jason," I said.

"You have no fishing equipment, sir, are you not going for tigers? They are on the bite now," he said referring to the vicious African Tiger Fish so popular with anglers.

"Not this time Amos," I said, "I'm more interested in birdwatching."

"Ah! Okay, sir but if you change your mind."

I put my bag down and sat on one of the swivel seats at the front of the boat as Amos finished filling the tanks with petrol.

"Where would you like to go, sir?" he asked politely.

"I would like to have a look around the mouth of the Kafue River," I said.

"Certainly, sir we can go down there but it is illegal to enter the river or to stop on the Zambian side".

"Yes," I said, "I don't want to get off the boat. I would like to take a look is all".

Ten metres from the boat a young one and a half metre crocodile surfaced ominously in the shallow water and looked at us.

comfortable in the shade leaning against the Baobab tree and lifted the left control stick to take the drone up. Instantly it rose to a height of ten metres still facing the river. The shade allowed me to view the screen without glare and I continued to raise it to a height of thirty metres. From that height, I could see over the island and saw the mouth of the river in the distance ahead. Still, I could hear the machine clearly and I wanted to be sure that it would pass over the area I wanted to cover unheard. I raised the drone until the screen showed it was hovering at a height of sixty metres. I closed my eyes and listened. Had I not known it was there I would have been unaware of it. I stepped out of the shade to look up at the aircraft. Squinting in the sun I saw it as a silent speck hovering in the blue sky above me. I walked back into the shade and sent it up further to an altitude of seventy metres. I looked into the screen and saw the landscape of the Zambezi River and the Zambian bush and escarpment as clear as day in front of me. Feeling confident that it would be silent and invisible at that altitude I pushed the right-hand stick on the controller forward and sent it on its way across the river towards the mouth of the Kafue. The flight range of the aircraft was five kilometres so I knew it would easily handle the distance to my target area. There was also little or no chance of any interference in such a remote location. The flight across the river took less than five minutes. I adjusted the tilt of the camera until it was facing directly downwards. On the screen, I could see the entire mouth of the river below the aircraft. I continued flying up the Kafue for another six hundred metres and then stopped. I planned to move within a grid system from six hundred metres on either side of the river and work back towards the mouth taking photographs every fifty metres.

The GPS showed the exact location, altitude, and distance so I had exact coordinates to work with. Keeping the aircraft facing north I moved the right-hand stick on the controller and watched the screen as the drone moved away from the river and over the thick bush below. Once I was six hundred metres in, I pushed the button to the front left of the controller and it responded by making a loud clicking sound like that of an old-fashioned camera. Satisfied. I moved the drone to the right for fifty metres and repeated the process until I had once again reached the bank of the Kafue River. I moved the drone over to the right and did the same on the other side. Once I had reached six hundred metres on the other side, I brought the drone back towards me for fifty metres and repeated the process once again.

It was when I had taken forty-eight photographs that the controller bleeped its first battery warning. I had a good idea of where the aircraft was, but I decided to use the 'Home' button to be on the safe side. Instantly the aircraft's GPS kicked in and I saw the bush below moving rapidly as the drone returned to the exact spot it had taken off from. Five minutes later I heard the drone descending above me. I walked out into the sunlight and flicked the controller back to manual to land. By my calculations with the two remaining batteries, I would be able to cover the area working back to the mouth of the river completely. If Dixon Mayuni's camp was indeed where Hannes had said in his report, I would surely have a clear idea of its *exact* location. Sweat was forming on my arms and face as I replaced the spent battery and took off for the next flight. Apart from a near miss with an overly curious Fish Eagle, the flight went off well and I got the next forty-eight photographs without any hassle. It was on the third and final flight that I started running into problems. The wind had picked up in the valley and there were numerous warnings on the controller that the fact that the aircraft was fighting this high-altitude wind would affect the usual battery life of twenty-five minutes. In the end, I managed to get thirty-five photographs in all before the second battery warning sounded and fearful of the important data on the memory card, I brought the drone back. Just before landing, I took one more photograph at altitude of the Zimbabwe side of the river so that I might identify the drop-off point that Mayuni used on his frequent trips to the Zimbabwe side. The drone landed safely near me, and I carried it back to my spot in the shade. Leaving the memory card in place I folded the arms on the aircraft away and packed everything back in my bag.

I spent the next thirty minutes sitting in the shade listening to the sound of the bush. From the buzzing of insects to the cry of the Fish Eagle and the quarrelsome grunting of the hippos, I was reminded that the entire valley was alive. Soon enough I heard the boat motor approaching and I got up to watch it arrive. Amos was gliding through the shallows towards the tree branch with a relieved smile on his face. I climbed down the sandy bank and got onto the boat.

"Everything okay sir?" he asked with a smile.

"Yes, all good thanks, Amos" I replied "I think let's get back to camp now".

The sun was blazing out on the river, and we passed a herd of elephants near the pump house on the Zimbabwe side. Eventually, we arrived at the jetty, and I slipped Amos a twenty-dollar note as a tip.

"Will you be needing the boat again today sir?" he asked.

"I might want to go out again," I replied. "So, if you could wait on standby?"

He agreed and I made my way up the stairs to the green grass and cool shade of the camp. It was time to find Mr Dixon Mayuni.

# 7

## Chapter Seven: Needle in A Haystack

The inside of the chalet was cooler under the thatch roof. I turned on the overhead fan and sat at the desk to boot up the laptop. Once done it was an easy job to remove the memory card from the drone and insert it into the computer. Sure enough, one hundred and thirty-one JPEG files were showing on the card. *Time to get to work, Green.* I started with the first photograph I had taken. The quality and resolution of the 4K image was impressive and I was able to zoom in easily and keep the clarity. I carefully examined the picture for any sign of human habitation. The image showed nothing but dense bush. Slowly and methodically, I examined each image carefully zooming in to each one. At the end of the first row of the grid, I sat back and took a deep breath. Outside the staff had connected the sprinklers to quench the grass from the burning heat of the day. The repetitive sound of the water squirting combined with the blanket of warm air that surrounded me made me yawn. I got up and made myself a cup of coffee. Staying in the shade of the thatched roof I went to stand by the grille door of the chalet to drink it and smoke. Through the heat haze, I could see the greenery on the other side of the river and the mountains of the Zambian escarpment in the distance. *Hannes wouldn't make a mistake, Green. He said in the report that Mayuni's camp was there. It must be there.* With the caffeine boosting my energy I returned to the laptop to continue. It was on the second row of the grid of images that I picked up the first sign of human activity. It was only after zooming in that I saw the overgrown track. It crossed from left to right going towards the Kafue and although faint I clearly saw the log of a cut tree in the image. It was not a path that a vehicle could have taken but more of a footpath through the bush. The second image confirmed my suspicions and I continued to zoom in and follow the track across the grid until finally I saw the bank of the Kafue River. Once again, I zoomed into the image and found yet another clear sign. It would have been impossible to see from ground level but hidden deep in the tall reeds on the left bank of the river was the unmistakable long dark shape of a dugout canoe. The next picture showed the right-hand bank of the river and again there was a clear indication of a footpath heading into the bush. It was as I was zooming out that I saw the motorboat. Like the canoe, it was cleverly hidden in the reeds of a small tributary but when I zoomed in, I could clearly see the shape of a boat with a motor. It was covered with camouflage webbing, but the glint of the propeller was clear to see in the sunlight. *On to something here Green*. I logged the coordinates of the boat and went on to the next picture. Again, it was mainly thick bush, but the pathway was visible upon zooming in. I followed the path for the next three photographs, but it was on the fourth that I had my eureka moment. In the centre of the picture nestled amongst the trees was a clearing. Near the top was the clear image of the thatched roof of a mud hut. Five metres from that I saw the blackened soil and ash of the remnants of a cooking fire. Laid out on a small bush nearby and clearly visible were four khaki shirts and other clothing. *I see you Mr Mayuni. I see you now.* On the right-hand side of the clearing was what looked like a series of shiny metallic objects stacked together.

Puzzled, I zoomed in on this until I realized what I was looking at. The picture came up as clear as day. I was looking at sixteen twenty-litre drums on a pallet. *Cyanide. Containers of cyanide powder. They must be. Murdering bastard!* I zoomed out a bit to look at the general layout of the camp. To the left of the clearing near the pathway were two large dark circular objects. Once again, I zoomed in to take a closer look at the image. Around each object was an area of blackened soil. *Pots, large steel cooking pots for boiling the flesh away from Lion and Leopard bones.* It was exactly as Hannes had said in his report. In the centre of the clearing was a tattered and faded green tarpaulin held down by rocks on four corners. Printed on the tarpaulin was the emblem of a dragon. Clearly, something of value was being stored beneath it or it simply wouldn't be there. Once again, I zoomed in on the canvas and it became clear. A hole in the top left of the material revealed it. The curved white and cream stick-like objects that were visible through the hole in the tarpaulin were ivory tusks. There was no telling how many there were but there was now absolutely no doubt in my mind. I was looking at the camp of Mr Dixon Mayuni. I logged the coordinates of the camp and carried on looking through each image the drone had captured. Apart from the small and cleverly hidden camp, the entire area was untouched, thick, virgin bush. The last image was the one I had taken before landing the drone on the Zimbabwe side. The image was familiar as it showed the clearing around the giant Baobab tree I had sheltered under while flying. Further downstream about fifty metres from where I had sat was a gulley that cut into the steep bank for roughly fifteen metres. I had been totally oblivious to it earlier, but it was clearly visible from four hundred feet up. Seeing nothing of interest anywhere else in the image I decided to zoom in and look. As the image expanded, I saw the clear signs that humans had been there. Above the gulley near a tree facing the river was a small area of grey and blackened soil. It was the ashes of a campfire. Not far from this was an area of disturbed soil through which something glinted in the sunlight. There was no way of telling what it was, but I assumed it was some kind of tin can or some other metallic object. I could only imagine it was some kind of rubbish dump. The gulley was clear and filled with water. It would serve as the perfect spot to moor a small motorboat and to drop and collect people. I was certain that I was looking at the point from which Mr Mayuni would launch his poaching operations on the Zimbabwe side. This was the spot where he would deliver the armed men and the cyanide drums. This was also the spot where he would collect the spoils of his murderous trade. The very spoils I had seen hidden under the tarpaulin at his bush camp on the other side of the river.

I sat back in the chair to take it all in. Everything Hannes had said in his report was accurate and true. His killer, Dixon Mayuni, was close by. I got up and made my way out of the chalet and across the lawn to Shirley and Andrew's house. After a bit of small talk, I asked for the hard drive. Shirley retrieved it from the safe and I walked back to the chalet and plugged it into the laptop. I typed in the password and brought up the report titled 'Lower Zambezi Operation' I skimmed through it looking for the piece of information I sought. Soon enough I found it. 'The drop off would take place every Friday night without fail.'

I glanced at the time and date on the screen of my computer. The memorial service had been on Wednesday. Today was Friday. Hannes had been right about everything so far, so I had no reason to doubt it. Dixon Mayuni and his band of merry men would be coming across the river that very night. With my mind spinning I drummed my fingers on the desk and stared blankly out at the lawns of the camp. I got up and took a walk to the drop-off to the riverbank. I sat on the grass and stared out across the river towards the Zambian side. The afternoon was stifling hot, and the sun burned my skin pleasantly as I sat thinking. *What can you do Green? One unarmed man against a group of murdering poachers with guns and cyanide. What the fuck can you do? Nothing*. I sat there rolling this over and over in my mind. The anger I felt towards Mr Mayuni and the entire operation was real and it burned in my gut, but I realized the single most valuable thing I could do was to make sure Hannes' report was presented to the forum in Geneva. *You already have the aerial photographs of the camp and the landing. Combine those with the rest of the information on the hard drive and the whole thing will blow up*. I took my eyes off the river and looked down at the green grass beside me. I picked up a dried twig and rolled it between my fingers as I thought. *But you have the night vision goggles and the Astroscope zoom lens on the camera. You could easily get more evidence. Current evidence. Proof*. I was suddenly disturbed by the sound of branches snapping to my left. I turned to see the family of Elephants I had seen the previous evening. They were slowly approaching the camp from upstream moving slowly through the trees. I marvelled at their dignified and graceful movements and their tight family unit. My mind went back to the harrowing video clip of the baby Elephants confused and distressed at the horrific killing of their herd. For some unknown reason, I felt a strange duty of care for the animals of the valley. I put the twig into the corner of my mouth and chewed it lightly. *Fuck it. I'm going*.

# 8

## Chapter Eight: Savage Kingdom

It was 4.00pm. by the time I was fully prepared to leave. I had given the hard drive back to Shirley and Andrew and told them I would be walking through the bush downstream that afternoon. At first, there was a bit of resistance to this idea, but I explained that silence was important for birdwatching and that I was aware of the dangers, having been born in Africa. In my bag were two bottles of water, the night vision goggles, the camera with the Astroscope night lens and a packet of homemade biltong from Shirley. Around my neck, to keep up appearances, were the binoculars and around my waist under my shorts, my knife in its sheath. Once again, the air was tinged with an ethereal orange colour as the sun made its way down towards the Zambian escarpment. I left the camp quietly giving a wave to the security guard as I left and made my way downstream near the riverbank. The grass gave way to the sandy soil of the valley floor and the bush became thicker as the human pathways gave way to animal tracks. I felt a buzz of excitement mixed with expectation as I walked around the giant ant hills and under the spreading canopies of Mopani, Acacia and Fig trees. All the while I kept the river in view not wanting to venture too far into the bush for fear of predators such as Lion or Leopard. The chance of running into either was real and expected and I wanted to keep an escape route to the water an option even with the ever-present danger of Crocodiles and Hippos. I was aware that the average walking speed was roughly five kilometres an hour which would mean, with obstacles, it would take me about an hour and twenty minutes to cover the ten kilometres to the Baobab tree opposite the Kafue River. I broke into a slow trot all the while scanning the bush around me for any movement of animals.

The afternoon was still and hot and apart from the birdsong and chattering of Vervet Monkeys in the trees above, everything was quiet. I found my pace after a few minutes and easily jumped over the narrow gullies and slipways that led to the river. After ten minutes I came out on an open flood plain which was covered in knee-high green grass. Ahead of me a herd of fifteen Cape Buffalo were grazing near the bank of the river. Scattered around them were several Impalas. They raised their heads in alarm as they sensed my arrival. Dotted around the waterlogged plain were a few dark ponds with white lilies decorating the surfaces. Knowing these were havens for Crocodiles and needing to keep a good distance between myself and the foul-tempered Buffalo, I cut away to my right to stay on the dry ground. This detour added at least a kilometre to my journey and by the time I arrived at the abandoned pump house, I was panting heavily and dripping with sweat. The old building was crumbling and surrounded by thick reeds. Once again, I had to cut inland to pick my way around it. As I crossed a muddy gulley in the thick bush, I saw the unmistakable spoor of a large female Lion. It was a stark reminder that death lurked everywhere around, and I paused, to gauge my surroundings before moving on.

Eventually, I came up onto dry clear land and I paused to look through the binoculars at my surroundings. In the distance downstream I saw the giant Baobab. The light was just beginning to fade, and I knew that I would need to move fast to get there before the darkness set in. I knew the moon was nearly full and would rise around 7.45pm. It would allow me to take a slow walk safely back to camp later. I continued my run along the bank of the river only slowing down occasionally to divert around an area of thick thorn bush or a wide gulley. I passed at least five pods of hippos wallowing in the river on the way. Some were slowly making their way to the bank to start their nighttime grazing. I reminded myself to be wary of the giant animals on my return. The adults were as big as a small car, and I knew full well that stepping between a mother hippo and her juvenile was a surefire way to get killed. With my breathing heavy and steady I continued the run. The sun had gone, and twilight had set in by the time I arrived exhausted, dripping with sweat, and panting heavily at the clearing around the Baobab. I sat on the sand against its gnarled trunk and drank a litre of water from one of the bottles in the bag. Once I had caught my breath, I took a walk to the drop-off to the riverbank. Using the binoculars, I scanned the Zambian side for any sign of movement. There was nothing. The dark powerful waters of the Zambezi had taken on the colour of gun metal in the fading light. Its silence belied the terrible dangers it held in its depths. Using the last of the light I tracked back along the route I had used on the way in until I found the last gulley I had crossed. I reached down into it and pulled out a handful of sticky black mud which I used to blacken the exposed skin on my legs, arms, and face. It smelt of rotten vegetation and animal dung, but it would do the job perfectly. The light had gone completely by the time I got back to the Baobab tree and sat down to wait.

Up above, the Milky Way began to show in a great clear swathe across the sky and the sounds of the African night increased. I removed the night vision goggles from the bag and pulled them over my eyes to take a look. Instantly the scene in front of me was illuminated in a dull green monochrome light. I had not had much occasion to use them, but they had proved useful a few times in the past. After taking a good look around for any movement of animals I made my way carefully downstream towards the gulley that I suspected was the landing point for Mr Mayuni and his band of poachers. Through the goggles, the stars above were astonishing in their clarity almost to the point of being too bright. Even from forty metres away, there was no mistaking the gulley I had seen from the aerial photograph. The glint of light I had seen in the picture turned out to be several tin cans carelessly buried under the sand and the fireplace was also clear to see. It was the perfect spot at which to moor a boat and make drop-offs and collections. A few metres ahead of me upstream from the gulley stood a large flat-top Acacia tree. Its thick trunk had created a mound of soil around its base, and I decided that if there were any visitors that night that I would use it as a spot from which to take the photographic evidence. Seeing no need to venture further I turned back to take my seat at the base of the Baobab and wait. There was a warm quiet breeze coming up the river and I sat in silence occasionally pulling the night vision goggles over my eyes to check for animals.

Apart from the odd gurgle of water from the river and the distant hoot of an owl, the night was silent. I pulled the bag of biltong and a bottle of water from my bag and ate. It was game biltong, perfectly spiced Impala steak and I sat eating the thin sticks of cured meat for the next hour. It was 8.00pm. when I got up and took a walk to the riverbank to look and listen for any sign of Dixon Mayuni and his crew. The moon had risen by then so there was no need for the goggles. The surrounding bush had taken on a grey hue while the surface of the river glistened silver. Across the water, there was only darkness and silence. Feeling perplexed and doubtful I walked back to my seat at the base of the Baobab to bide my time. I spent the next two hours sitting under the canopy of the Baobab listening to the sounds of the night. On more than three occasions I heard rustling and movement in the bush behind me but thankfully no animals emerged.

It was at 10.15pm. that I heard the boat motor starting on the Zambian side of the river. The driver wisely kept the revs low but there was no mistaking the distinct sound of the small outboard engine in the distance. Immediately I felt a surge of adrenalin tingling in my limbs. *I hear you Mr Mayuni.* I retrieved the camera from my bag and checked the Astroscope night lens. Its picture showed even better than the goggles with a bright green monochrome view of the surrounding bush. Finally, I checked that the camera was on silent, and the powerful zoom lens was working. All the equipment was functioning perfectly. With the droning sound of the motor growing louder I got up and walked to the mound of earth beneath the flat top Acacia tree. I lay on my stomach on the sand beneath it and tested the zoom lens once again. The foliage above created a large circle of complete darkness under which I lay in wait. Propping myself up on my elbows I scanned the gulley below with the camera. The view was near perfect with only the bottom part of the gulley being obscured by the drop off. The sound of the boat motor grew louder as the boat neared the Zimbabwe side. For a moment I thought I might have misjudged their landing point as the sound seemed to come from my immediate left. It was with great relief that I heard the motor cut back and saw the boat silently drift into the water-filled gulley in front of me. There were four men in the boat, but their features were obscured by the darkness of the overhanging bush. With excitement and adrenalin buzzing through my body I pulled the goggles over my eyes. The two men near the front of the boat got off on the far side of the gulley. One of them tied a rope to a protruding branch to secure the craft while the other positioned himself alongside it to help with the offloading. The two men sitting in the middle of the boat began handing bags of supplies to the men on the bank. I removed the goggles, raised the camera, and zoomed into the scene in front of me. I snapped six clear pictures of the operation as it happened. Next to be offloaded were the guns. I spotted four AK47 assault rifles, an ancient British 303 and several handguns being handed from the boat to the waiting men. They worked silently and efficiently in the dim light of the moon under the overhanging branches. To my great frustration, the rear of the boat was lower than the rest of it due to the weight of the motor and the fuel tanks and I could not get a clear view of the driver.

They spoke in hushed voices that I could not quite hear from where I lay. Last to be offloaded was a metal twenty-litre drum with a handle and screw cap to the top. On the side of the container was a white sticker with the universal symbol for a deadly poison. The skull and crossbones were as clear as day through the zoom lens as was the word printed beneath. 'Cyanide' *Oh yes. That's what I came for. Now I just need a picture of you Mr Mayuni. Come on, get off the boat*. With the weight of the load having been removed, the rear of the craft had dropped further below my line of sight as had the driver. The other men were clearly black and were dressed in tattered rags, unlike the pictures I had seen of Dixon Mayuni who was an albino with a thin face who wore khaki bush clothes. I was certain it was Mayuni who was the driver of the boat, and it was him who I wanted to photograph so desperately. I needed only to move a few metres forward to clear the mound of earth and I would have a clear line of sight to the rear of the boat and the driver. The darkness from the canopy above would prevent me from being seen and the soft sandy soil would ensure I would move unheard. Slowly I got up on one knee and moved forward crouched down as far as I could. Suddenly I heard the motor of the boat start again and I realized I might miss my opportunity to photograph Mayuni.

There were still many metres of darkness ahead of me, so I quickened my pace to get the shot. I will never know whether the pitfall trap was built for animals or humans, but it was expertly made and totally invisible even in the daylight as I had completely missed it earlier. My left foot broke the surface of dried reeds and hessian covered with soil and I fell the four feet to the rack of metal spikes below with a thunderous crash. Instantly a bolt of white-hot pain shot up my left leg and swirled around my groin area before rocketing into my skull like a shot of lightning. One of the twenty-five-centimetre spikes had pierced my shoe and gone through the area to the front of the arch of my left foot. The weight of my fall had ensured it travelled straight through the foot and its tip now protruded a clear fifteen centimetres out of the top of the shoe. I yelled in agony and shock as I desperately tried to back up and away to the rear of the trap to find a handhold from which to pull myself out. Around me was a confused mess of dried broken reeds and choking dust. I became aware of shouting and confusion in the gulley below and within seconds there were three powerful torch beams focused on the area around me. My first instinct was to get away and once I found a handhold behind me, I forced myself up into a sitting position at the edge of the trap. The action of lifting myself up pulled the spike in my foot at an awkward angle and once again I yelled with agony. Once seated I used my right foot to find the base of the spikes. They were attached to a thick piece of flat bar that had been buried in the soil at the bottom of the trap. I looked up briefly to see the torch beams whipping wildly around as the men rushed around the gulley towards me. Using my right foot, I found the flat bar near my injured foot and held it fast as I pulled the fifteen centimetres of sharpened round bar back through my left foot. Once again, a bolt of white-hot pain exploded in my brain like a firework. Once the foot was free, I glanced up and ahead of me. There was more shouting and confusion as the beams of the torches rounded the gulley and came towards me. I turned over on my front and brought my right leg up to stand.

Already my left foot was warm and soaked with sticky blood within the shoe. Gasping with pain I hobbled desperately off into the darkness heading upstream. The left-hand side of my body was becoming increasingly numb with every step as I tried my best to put minimum weight on the injured foot. Behind me came the rumble of footfalls and the manic swinging of torch beams as my pursuers rapidly gained ground. The gunshots came in fast random bursts. Two of them passed my left ear so close, that the air was displaced, and my hearing turned to a high-pitched whistle. The next shot hit my back above my right shoulder blade and spun me around like a gyroscope. I landed face up, winded, bewildered and wide-eyed in the sand. Within seconds they were on me, and I was blinded by the beams of the torches. Rough quick hands quickly ripped the camera and binoculars from my neck as the blood formed warm pools at my shoulder and foot. Still blinded by the torches and unable to speak from the shock I was turned over onto my front and my wrists bound with a length of thick wire. It cut into my flesh, and I felt the burning sensation of the blood being cut off in my fingers. Slowly my senses began to return as they turned me over onto my side and began frantically rummaging through my pockets. I kicked at one of them violently with my right foot, the blow connecting with the side of his knee. The man yelled and fell to the floor instantly. In the torchlight, I could see he was middle-aged and dressed in the filthy, ragged clothing of a desperately poor man. One of the other men slapped me across my face as punishment. The blow stunned me further and seeing it was now futile I stopped my struggling. In the distance near the gulley, I saw the dark figure of a man approaching with a paraffin lamp. He was tall and held it high to spread as much light around as possible. The men around me stood and were silent as he approached.

"Well, well, well," he said softly in perfect English. "What do we have here?"

I blinked the dust from my eyes and spat out a mouthful of sand as I strained to see the man's face. The man handed the hissing lamp to one of the others and knelt on one knee beside me. I smelt the man before I saw his face. It was a pungent mix of body odour and sour milk. He wore long dirty khaki trousers, and his pale exposed arms were dotted with the crusty weeping sores associated with albinism and overexposure to the sun. The thin emaciated face smiled at me and there were large gaps between his yellow teeth.

"Mr. Man," he said, "although you took great precautions to fly your camera high this afternoon I saw it from the forest."

The man laughed and I smelt the overpowering rot of corruption on his breath.

"Hold the lamp closer!" he shouted to the others.

His narrowed eyes were a malevolent pink colour, the lids surrounded by tiny clumps of yellow mucus. With a bony hand, he pulled me over onto my front and poked a finger into the soaking bullet hole in my shoulder. I screamed in agony as he turned me back onto my side. The sweat poured from my face, and I blinked again to clear my eyes.

"This is a dead man" he said as he licked the blood from his finger "Put him in the boat. It will be much easier to throw him in the river than to bury him here."

One of the men cautiously grabbed my feet while the other gripped me under my arms.

"Rot in hell, you murdering piece of shit," I whispered as I was lifted from the dirt.

"Yes Mr. Man," said the albino. "I'm sure I will, but you will be there first to greet me, no?"

Two of the men broke into raucous laughter while the one with the injured knee hobbled along silently. The journey down to the gulley was excruciating but I gritted my teeth and squeezed my eyes closed as we moved. My body was tossed into the front of the boat from a height of one metre. I landed on the thick fibreglass, head and shoulders first and the blow knocked the wind from my lungs for thirty seconds. When my breath finally returned it came in great whooping sobs. Mayuni climbed carefully into the boat near the steering wheel at the stern and told the injured man to get in after him. The other two were instructed in Shona to remain and continue with their poaching mission. The motor gurgled into life as the two men onshore pushed us out into the shallows of the Zambezi. Mayuni and the injured man mumbled together as the boat made its way out towards the Zambian side. The interior of the boat was filthy and stank of rotten flesh from the tusks and animal carcasses it had carried. I lay still with my head towards the bow and my back facing the port side of the boat. I could see both men clearly in the moonlight. I began to feel for the twisted wire that bound my wrists behind my back. In their haste, the men had left the two ends exposed and I was able to reach them with the fingers of my right hand. Slowly I began to twist the wires behind my back. The ends were sharp and one of them pierced the skin on my thumb, but I persevered until I felt the blood flow once again followed by intense pins and needles from the obstructed veins. Mayuni pushed the throttle forward and the boat gained speed as we neared the deep water at the centre of the river. Finally, I removed the twisted wire from my wrists completely and laid it quietly on the fibreglass hull behind me. My body was freezing cold from shock, and I shivered as I lay in silence watching the men. The injured man sitting between Mayuni and myself had put his gun down on the deck behind him and was gently massaging his knee. Mayuni was not as careless and had propped his AK47 up behind the steering console where he sat.

I could clearly see the barrel protruding from the top. It was when I saw Mayuni peering over the side of the boat and pulling back on the throttle that I decided to make my move. There was no doubt in my mind that we were now in the middle of the river, and he had chosen the spot at which to throw me overboard. It was my deepest yearning wish to take Mayuni with me, but I knew he would get me first with the rifle, so it had to be the injured man seated between us. Despite the bleeding and the pain, I leapt towards him with a sudden animal snarl. His eyes were wide and terrified in the moonlight, and he wailed as I pulled him overboard by his shirt. Once in the water, I held his frantic flailing body between myself and the boat. The current was overwhelming and within seconds we were ten metres away and gaining as we drifted downstream.

"Maaaiweeeee!" the man screamed as his arms flapped uselessly around.

He was clearly a non-swimmer. The last thing I saw was Mayuni standing in the boat in the moonlight as he raised the assault rifle and pointed it in our direction. I quickly pulled myself underwater and pushed the man's body away from me. The bullets made a curious 'choo, choo' sound in rapid succession as they hit the water around me. One of them must have hit the drowning man as there was a meaty thud in the blind chaos of swirling water and sound. With my lungs burning I forced myself deeper underwater with my arms and allowed the current to carry me away. After what seemed an eternity, I stopped fighting and allowed my body to drift to the surface once again. Gasping for air I opened my eyes to see the great drape of the Milky Way above. I realised I was facing downstream, so I quickly lifted my head and looked around for any sign of Mayuni and the boat. Apart from the fading sound of the outboard motor, there was nothing. The force of the current was immense, and I felt it pulling me, at great speed downstream. I twisted my aching and broken body in the water to look towards the Zimbabwe side of the river. In the distance, I saw the grey outline of the bank and the trees moving past at a steady pace. The vast expanse of water between us seemed impossible, especially given the state I was in. Nevertheless, I began pulling at the water with my left arm and kicking with my right foot in a desperate effort to close the gap between me and the moving horizon. After four solid minutes of acutely searing pain and effort, I stopped in the water to gauge my progress. It appeared to me that apart from being swept several hundreds of metres downstream my efforts had come to nothing at all. If anything, the bank and tree line seemed further away. My body was starting to feel weakened and cold from the blood loss and shock and I started feeling lightheaded and sleepy. I resolved to lie face up in the water and allow the current to take me downstream for a while as I rested. I lay in that position, eyes closed in a dreamlike state for a good ten minutes until I lifted my head in sudden panic. Ahead of me the great river curved to the right and it appeared the deep channel I was drifting in was edging towards the Zimbabwe side at the curve.

The trees were closer and appeared to be moving faster and faster as I travelled. With renewed energy, I began pulling and kicking at the water as I had done before. Once again it seemed my efforts were in vain, and I allowed myself to go with the flow. It was when I was a few hundred metres from the bend in the river I became aware of the island. It seemed small and inconsequential at the time but as I was swept nearer, I realized there was only a gap of perhaps twenty metres between it and the bank. From where I was it looked like it was only a few metres wide and covered with some sort of low-growing vegetation, but it grew larger as I travelled downstream. Soon enough I realized that the deep channel I was being carried in would flow directly to the left of the island and if I missed it there was a very good chance I would once again be swept out into the middle of the river to drown or die. Desperately I began kicking and pulling at the current with my good limbs which felt like lead. After thirty seconds of gruelling effort, I felt the current begin to slow around me as I left the faster-flowing water and began to drift comfortably towards the island. Soon I felt the blessed crunch of river sand under my hands as I glided neatly into the shallows at the head of the island. I crawled slowly through the water on all fours before collapsing in a heap on my stomach with my legs still in the shallow water. I lay there sobbing with relief on the sand for a good minute before I raised my head to look at my surroundings in the moonlight. The island was low and covered with a thick mat of reeds. To my right, not twenty metres away across a deep channel was the bank of the Zimbabwe side of the river. Overcome with exhaustion and gratitude I closed my eyes and rested my head on my right hand as I thanked my lucky stars for the very fact that I was alive. *Jesus Christ Green. Maybe you will survive this night after all.* Although I was aware of the blood loss from the gunshot wound in my shoulder and the hole in my foot, the shock and fatigue were kicking in and I felt my mind drifting off to the soothing gurgles of the river and the peaceful melodies of the African night. The Crocodile struck with inconceivable ferocity. It must have been three metres long and its jaw a foot wide at the widest point. Having been drawn in from the silent depths by the smell of blood its jaws clamped down on the calf of my injured left leg with unimaginable force. The hideous creature wasted no time and immediately began its death roll as it dragged my semi-conscious body back into the water. Once again, my body was spun around like a gyroscope with my flailing arms slapping the wet sand repeatedly as I was dragged backwards. Instantly my world was turned into an ear-splitting mess of confusion and terror. My vision flicked between the moon and the darkness of the water every second and it was a while before I knew what was actually happening. After what must have been ten rolls I had been pulled back into the shallows and the primitive animal started the violent thrashing from left to right. A movement enhanced by its powerful tail and designed to tear the flesh and limbs from its prey. I reached into the side of my shorts and found the sheath of my knife which the poachers had failed to take off me. No sooner had I removed the eight-inch blade, the creature resumed its death roll all the while dragging me deeper and deeper into the water. In some dark recess of my mind, I knew there would be only one more opportunity to end the horror.

I pulled my body into a foetal position and rode the waves of anguish and confusion until it stopped once again. With my left hand, I felt the snout of the great beast still clamped to my calf and ran my fingers up to the protruding knob of its eye. I slammed the blade into the thick-plated skull with my right hand and it penetrated to the hilt. Instantly the creature stopped moving, its massive jaws still locked onto my leg. My vision began fading and I felt a far greater force pulling the creature and me away. Although I did not realise it at the time, it had pulled me back into the deep channel. Its long tail now acting as a weighted keel drawing me into the depths. Leaving the knife, I gripped the jaws of the dead creature and pried them apart away from my leg. The brain damage it had suffered had caused its jaw muscles to contract and it took many seconds to free myself from the razor-sharp rows of teeth. My ears were bursting with sharp stabbing pain from the water pressure by the time I had freed myself and floated slowly to the surface. My face broke the surface and I saw the moon above, but I have no recollection of what happened afterwards. I awoke sprawled and face down in the sand on the very same island the crocodile had taken me from. The effort of lifting my head to look around was tiring. My entire body was numbed and shivering with cold. I looked down to see my legs were in the water as they had been when the crocodile had attacked. With a sudden surge of terror, I dragged myself up the sand towards the reeds. When I finally arrived, I found the reeds were soft and bent easily under my weight. I pulled my body into a foetal position and blacked out immediately. I awoke in the moonlight, hours later, to the bellowing, roaring sound of Lions calling to each other on the bank nearby. This alarming and ominous sound was soon followed by the manic and insane laughter of a pack of Hyenas. Their footfalls, rumbling nearby, were a stark warning that predators would be around, and my nightmare was far from over. I glanced down at the water and noticed a thick line of pebbles that had been washed onto the sand by the current. Seeing them as my only possible form of defence I pulled myself out of the nest of reeds and down towards the water. I gathered as many of the smooth rocks as I could and placed them into the bottom of my shirt which acted like a sack. From there I clawed my way back up to the hollow I had created in the reeds to await the next ordeal.

Before long there was a great crashing sound of water nearby. Something big and heavy had come through the channel and onto the island. I looked up to see the enormous silhouette of a Cape Buffalo walking towards me through the reeds. A lone Buffalo was one of the most feared animals in Africa and I watched it silently as it raised its nose to catch my scent on the air. Its horns spanned three feet or more in the moonlight and I was fully aware that they could toss a man high into the air. The great beast stopped twenty feet away from me and carefully folded its legs. With a huffing sound, It lay in the reeds and stared at me as it casually chewed on the grass. I pulled the shirt from my back and using a stick I wound the material around my ruined left leg to slow the bleeding. It was a matter of minutes before I passed out once again. I was awoken by an intense itching all over my body. I opened my eyes to find the sun was just breaking the horizon and my body was covered in red ants.

Having forgotten the Buffalo, I quickly began to brush them from my skin. The movement startled the massive beast which was still lying in the reeds nearby. It leapt to its feet with an indignant snort and crashed through the channel of water back to the riverbank. I realised then that in safeguarding itself, the animal had guarded me through the night. Five minutes later I heard outboard motors upriver. Eventually, I saw two boats coming around the bend in the river towards me. I immediately recognized one of them as belonging to my camp and I saw the tall figure of the old man Andrew standing at the wheel with a pair of binoculars held to his eyes. He soon saw me waving and both boats raced towards me. Andrew's boat crunched onto the sand below me. He and another worker climbed out and rushed towards me.

"What the hell happened to you?" he snarled.

"You don't want to know," I whispered. "I need a hospital now."

9

# Chapter Nine: Sister of Mercy

After the journey upstream Andrew and the staff wasted no time in loading me into the back seat of his own Land Cruiser. My only request was that they safeguard my laptop and the hard drive which they promised to do. The journey to the small tourist town of Kariba at the dam wall of the lake by the same name took exactly two hours. The journey was a miserable one mainly because Andrew insisted on speeding around the many sharp bends on the road down to the town. Shirley had obviously phoned ahead as the staff were waiting to receive me. I was unceremoniously dumped on a worn hospital trolley and taken immediately to an operating room with broken tiles and peeling green paint on the walls. Although threadbare, the room looked clean and smelt strongly of antiseptic. The nurses began by cleaning the wounds to my left leg and I gritted my teeth in pain. It was then I heard Andrew's voice outside the room. He was obviously talking to the doctor on duty and was demanding that I be given morphine. The doctor replied that the hospital did not have any stocks of the drug, but it was readily available in the privately-owned pharmacy next door.

"Just get everything you need dammit!" he shouted "This man is seriously injured! I will guarantee payment in full!"

There was a flurry of activity as the doctor called one of the nurses and instructed the rest of them to wait. Ten minutes later they returned with a trolley full of drugs and equipment. A drip was positioned nearby, a cannula line inserted into my arm and then finally the morphine injection. The drug took effect in a series of warm soothing waves. First to fade was the pain followed by my thought patterns which slowly drifted into calming randomness. My last memory was that of the doctor and nurses surrounding me and the bright theatre light above shining into my face like the warm African sun. I awoke slowly much later that day as the sun was making its way down towards the outline of the mountain outside the window. I looked around the room to find I was alone. The walls of the room were painted in the same green paint which was faded and peeling leaving areas of white plaster beneath. Surrounding the outside of the window was the rusted frame of a grenade screen. A bygone from the war days. Above me hung the dirty and tattered remains of a mosquito net. Cautiously I moved my left leg a little to check how it felt. Immediately I was overwhelmed by an intense and painful itching that covered the entire leg up to the knee. I lifted my head to see the leg was dressed in bandages and raised slightly on a wooden ramp. The rest of my body was covered in an old threadbare sheet. My mouth was dust dry, and I looked around for water. The old steel shelves on either side of me were bare.

"Hello!" my voice was parched and croaky "Hello?"

The swinging door banged open, and Andrew and a nurse walked in.

"Finally! You're awake," said Andrew.

"Please can I have some water?" I whispered.

The nurse busied herself to my left as Andrew walked around and stood between me and the window.

"They removed the bullet from your shoulder," he said loudly. "Lucky it was a small firearm. A .22 mm pistol by the look of it. Your leg is another story. What the hell happened Jason? How did you end up so far downriver?"

I had to think before I made my reply. The nurse walked up to my left side and handed me a battered tin cup of water. Before answering Andrew, I quickly emptied it. In the process, I spilt some water on my neck and chest. The nurse wiped it away with a small white towel and went back to whatever she was doing to my left.

"Poachers," I said quietly, not wanting to say too much "They must have been poachers. They came on a boat. I fell into a pit trap, and I got shot trying to escape. They threw me in the river."

Andrew's forehead creased in frustration and anger.

"But..." he said.

We were disturbed by a loud knock on the door. Two uniformed policemen were standing there, clutching files and papers. They had obviously walked to the hospital as their faces were glistening with sweat. The nurse to my left suddenly started into a loud tirade in the local Shona dialect.

"Out! Get out! The doctor has told you this man can only be interviewed once he has recovered. Come back tomorrow!"

The wide-eyed and chastened officers retreated into the gloom of the corridor and the door closed once again.

"They're going to ask you a lot more questions than I, you know that?" Andrew said.

"There isn't much more to tell, Andrew" I replied resignedly.

"Hmmm," he nodded. "Well, you're bloody lucky to be alive is all I can say. I must go back to Chirundu. I'll be back here tomorrow morning. Can I bring you anything?"

"Um, my bags, shoes and my phone please," I said.

"I don't think you'll be needing your shoes for a while," he said. "There's a bloody great hole through your foot and as for your leg .......!"

I looked down towards the bandages.

"Please keep that hard drive safe, Andrew," I said. "That's the most important thing I have to ask."

His craggy face softened as he looked at me.

"Of course. Now I've told the staff here to look after you. I organized this private room. You really don't want to see the other wards. Everything costs money as the government hospitals don't have any drugs, but I have bought morphine and fresh dressings. I'll see you at around 11.00am. tomorrow. I'll ask Shirley what I can bring to make you as comfortable as possible."

"Thanks very much, Andrew," I replied as he walked out of the room.

Once again, I shifted my left leg slightly to see how it felt and again there was terrible itching and deep pain. The nurse who had told the police officers to leave walked up to me on the left-hand side of the bed.

"You must keep your leg still please, Sir" she said in a loud clear voice with a strong Shona accent.

She was young and had a stern look on her round moonlike face, but I could see her bright clear eyes were soft and caring.

"How is the leg?" I asked hopefully.

"Your leg is seriously injured and there is a risk of infection. That is why I ask you to please keep it still. The doctor will be through to speak to you soon."

She stopped to look at me.

"What is your name?" I asked.

Immediately her face lit up and the faux stern look was replaced by a beaming smile of perfectly white teeth.

"My name is Sister Mercy Chavunduka. Please do as I say, Mr Green."

I grunted and turned to look out of the window once again. The Kariba Hospital was situated on the outskirts of the town and the bush on the nearby hills was as wild as any in the Zambezi Valley. In the distance at the foot of the mountains, a group of barefoot children were kicking a soccer ball around on a dusty rural pitch. I could just hear their joyful yells in the distance. The setting sun created a red aura around them as they played. With the shock and morphine still running through me, I began to drift off to sleep. I was awoken in the twilight of early evening by a thin bespectacled man in a white coat.

"Mr Green wake up, please," he said.

I moaned as I opened my eyes. My entire left leg was alive and buzzing with an intense itching and a deep gnawing pain.

"My leg," were my first words.

"Good evening, Mr Green. Yes, your leg was badly injured. We had to put in fifty-six stitches and then there is the injury to your foot. Any wound from a Crocodile attack carries a high risk of infection due to the millions of bacteria found in the mouth of the animal. We have you on a high dosage of antibiotics but the itching you speak of is entirely expected. You must keep your leg still and allow the drugs to do their job."

"It's unbearable," I said quietly.

"It will get better with time and rest. In the meantime, you must eat and sleep. Mr Andrew from Chirundu has purchased some drugs for the pain. I will have the nurse administer some after you have eaten. You are a very lucky man. See you tomorrow, Mr Green."

His words were no comfort, and I closed my eyes to ride the waves of agony and torment. It was half an hour later when the nurse Mercy Chavunduka came back. I had no idea she had entered until I felt the cool wet towel wipe the sweat from my face and neck.

I opened my eyes to see her looking down at me with a stern look on her face.

"It is time to eat, Mr Green," she said.

"I'm not hungry. The doctor said you had some morphine, please give me some. I need it." I replied.

"Of course, I will but first you will eat" she replied. "Here,"

She handed me a battered metal plate with a portion of rice and beef stew. With sweat streaming from my temples and the overwhelming discomfort of my injuries, I forced myself to swallow most of the stew and half of the rice. When I was finished, I laid my head back and sighed with exhaustion.

"Good food, eh?" she said cheerfully.

"Superb," I replied, eyes closed.

Suddenly there was a loud buzzing sound above me. I opened my eyes to see she had turned on the lights and one of them was faulty and flickered noisily.

"Are you going to leave that light making that noise all night?" I growled.

"No Mr Green, you are going to sleep. I am going home, but first I am going to give you the injection you have been waiting for."

"About fucking time," I said under my breath.

"Hey! Hey! I will not have language like that in here Mr Green!" she scolded.

I realized it was a battle I would not win. I turned my head and looked out of the window into the night. Turning back, I saw a broomstick hovering above, beside the tattered mosquito net.

"What the hell are you doing now?" I asked quietly.

"Mr Andrew has bought you a new mosquito net. You are very lucky, Mr Green."

I continued to gaze out into the darkness as the old net was removed from its hook in the ceiling and a fresh one put in its place.

After a while, she came to stand near me once again.

"Now, Mr Green. Here is your injection," she said as she drew the clear liquid from the small rubber-capped bottle with a fresh syringe.

The sting of the needle in my arm was an immense blessing and soon after the familiar waves of relief and calm washed over me in soothing ever-increasing swells. I looked up to see her holding the bottle of morphine up to the light.

"Ten milligrams administered at 8.00pm. three doses remaining in the bottle." She said the words under her breath as she wrote the information on a tattered file attached to the bottom of the bed.

I watched as she untied the mosquito net and pulled it around the four corners of the bed. Lastly, she walked up to my left and parted the netting to check on me.

"I think you are now ready to sleep, Mr Green," she said as she mopped the sweat from my temples.

"Thank you, Mercy," I mumbled in a euphoric half-stupor.

Soon after, the lights stopped buzzing and the room was dark and silent. In my dreams, I saw the smiling encrusted face of Dixon Mayuni in the light of a lamp. The gaps between his teeth were wide and sneering. In the flickering light, his jaws and teeth morphed into those of a crocodile which snapped viciously as they came towards me.

# 10

## Chapter Ten: Baboon on My Back

It was 3.00am. when I was once again awoken by the fiery buzzing itching of my leg and the dull ache in my shoulder. The back of my head was soaking wet with sweat on the pillow and my arms felt weak as I parted the mosquito net to reach the water on the shelf nearby. The movement caused my discomfort to increase, and I let out a loud moan as I stretched for the cup. Outside the window, the mountains were a towering light grey mass in the moonlight and the cicadas were chirping constantly. The room was dark and feverishly hot. For the first time in over twenty-four hours, I felt the need to urinate. There was a door on the opposite side of the room which I assumed was the en-suite bathroom and I lay still as I contemplated how to get there. Eventually, the need became overwhelming and combined with the extreme discomfort and sweaty conditions I gave in and decided to call for a nurse. After five attempts I heard a shuffling in the corridor and the door swung open noisily. The lights were turned on to reveal a massively obese woman wearing a dirty nurse's uniform that was stretched to almost bursting around her rolling frame. She stood, unsteady on her feet, under the flickering light and rubbed her eyes with pudgy hands that protruded from the colossal glistening brown sausages that were her arms.

"What do you want? Everyone is sleeping here!" she hissed with genuine malice.

"I would like to go to the toilet please," I said evenly.

"Ahhhhhh!" she exclaimed in annoyance as she shuffled her gargantuan frame towards the shelves to my left.

When she finally reached the shelf, she removed an ancient, dented bedpan and tossed it carelessly onto the mosquito net near my hip.

"There! Go!" she grunted, and I smelt the unmistakable sour aroma of home-brewed beer, on her breath.

"No!" I said firmly. "I want crutches. Get me some crutches please, and hurry."

She stared at me unsteadily through bloodshot eyes that were set deep into her distended and enraged face. Eventually, she snorted indignantly and shuffled off again to the shelving unit to my left. She returned with a battered set of aluminium crutches. The tops had long since lost their padding and were bound with filthy strips of bandage and fixed with bicycle tyre inner tube.

"Mmmm!" she said as she held them out far enough to ensure I would have to stretch to the point of nearly falling out of the bed to reach them.

As I reached, I noticed the name tag pinned to her mountainous chest. 'Sister Anna Chimene' She stood there, duck-footed and watched with great pleasure as I slowly swung my legs from the bed and positioned myself to stand with the crutches. The rush of blood to my leg caused it to come alive with a furious burning pain and my shoulder throbbed and ached deeply as I slowly stood up. With the sweat pouring from every pore, I made the sluggish journey towards the door on the opposite side of the room. I felt her contemptuous glare as I pushed the door open with my right hand.

"Is there a light in here?" I shouted in annoyance.

"No lights!" came the reply.

It took a few seconds for my eyes to adjust to the darkness but eventually, I made out the shape of the toilet. With great relief, I stood and relieved myself unsteadily with the crutches still under my arms. It was on my return that I took the fall. The rubber at the base of the right crutch was worn and the metal slid on the tile beneath. I broke the fall with my right arm and managed to keep my injured leg raised but the wind was knocked out of me, and I groaned as I turned onto my back on the floor.

"Fucking hell!" I growled when I got my breath back.

I opened my eyes to see the woman's body shuddering with mirth as she held a podgy hand to her mouth to stifle her amusement.

"Do you think this is a fucking joke?" I shouted as I slowly brought myself to a standing position using the good crutch.

She made a loud clucking sound and sucked air through her teeth in annoyance as she began to waddle towards me.

"No, no you just stay there thank you," I whispered through gritted teeth.

My body was soaked with sweat, and I was panting heavily by the time I finally parted the mosquito net and lay down.

"There is a bottle of morphine up there," I said with my eyes closed. "I would like some now, please. I am in great pain."

I opened my eyes to see the huge woman heaving herself toward the shelf to my left. I heard her rustling through the contents of a steel tray.

"There is nothing," she replied loudly.

"What? Look again! Read the file at the bottom of the bed. There are at least three doses left. It was written down by the previous nurse."

"I said there is nothing! Look!" she bellowed as she tilted the tray towards me.

Sure enough, the bottle was gone...and I was in no doubt as to who had taken it.

"You stole it. I know you did" I whispered.

"Hehe!" she laughed again. "I am not the one!"

*Fucking thieving bitch!* I closed my eyes as the huge woman shuffled towards the door and turned the lights off. I heard her shoes scraping the tiles as she made her way down the corridor. Her feet never left the ground as she went. I spent the next five hours in abject misery riding the waves of fevered agony from my leg and shoulder. The night was sweltering and dead still and the pain that emanated from my left leg seemed to concentrate in the very bones and travel up to my groin where it swirled constantly like fire. The sound of the cicadas was amplified in my brain, and I lay fully conscious with my eyes screwed up tightly. To say it was the lowest point in my life would be an understatement and during the crescendos of anguish, I focussed my anger on one thing and one thing only. Dixon Mayuni.

It was 8.00am. when I heard the door open. I opened my eyes, and the daylight startled me briefly. I turned to see the nurse from the previous day, Sister Mercy Chavunduka, frowning at me as she drew the mosquito net from around the bed.

"What happened, Mr Green?" she said with concern.

"There was a nurse here last night. She was drunk and I'm sure she stole the morphine," I whispered.

"Ahh!" she exclaimed loudly as she rummaged in the tray near the bed.

"Listen Mercy," I said. "That old man from Chirundu is coming back here this morning and will be bringing my cash and belongings. Please go and get something for the pain.

Some Morphine. Explain to the pharmacy that it will be paid for in full this morning. I am not going anywhere as you know."

She touched my forehead with the back of her hand as she mopped the sweat from my face and neck.

"This is terrible," she said shaking her head. "You are burning up. Okay, let me go now."

She returned ten minutes later with fresh syringes and an identical bottle to the one from the previous day. I watched in desperation as she removed the needle and drew the clear liquid from the bottle. The pin prick in my arm was an immediate respite from the horrors of the previous hours. Instantly the room cooled down and the colours softened. The dreadful ache in the core of my lower body dissipated and I felt serenity return to my world. Sister Mercy busied herself around me humming to herself as I drifted off into a deep dreamless sleep.

I awoke at 11:00 a.m. to the sound of Andrew talking to the doctor outside the room. Both he and the doctor entered the room together.

"Jesus!" said Andrew "Looks like you had a rough night."

"I've had better," I said.

The doctor took my temperature and removed the bandages from my wounds. I gritted my teeth as he pulled the long bloody cotton plugs from the holes in my foot and shoulder with glittering steel forceps. Sister Mercy assisted him as the wounds were re-dressed. I waited till both had left the room before I spoke.

"Andrew, you have to get me out of here. This place is a fucking hell hole. I have international health insurance. They will fly me to Johannesburg or wherever. I can't stay here."

"Hmm, I know," he said as he took a seat near the window.

"I'll speak to the doctor again. In the meantime, I have brought your bags and wallet. I've also organized a secure trunk and a padlock. I hear there was an unfortunate incident last night."

"More than fucking unfortunate," I replied.

Andrew pulled the wallet from my bag and handed it to me. I extracted my BUPA global healthcare card and handed it to him.

"Call the number on this card and explain what has happened. They will evacuate me. Please Andrew," I said.

"Okay," he grunted as he stood once again "Let me see what I can do."

As he left, the doctor and Sister Mercy walked back into the room.

"Time to change your dressings, Mr. Green," she said cheerfully.

I gritted my teeth as they went about the work of swabbing the stitches and replacing the cotton plugs into the open wounds from the spike and the bullet. Finally, the doctor left and once again I was given the shot of morphine, I craved by Sister Mercy.

"Sleep now," she said gently as she wiped the sweat from my forehead.

Once again, the soothing waves of relief washed around me...and I drifted into a hallucinatory but happy stupor. I came to at around 3:00 pm that afternoon as Andrew and the doctor walked through the door. The heat of the day was easing, and I could hear the children playing soccer in the distance through the window.

"Good afternoon, Mr. Green," said the doctor as he removed his spectacles. "Mr Andrew from Chirundu has arranged for you to be evacuated to a private clinic in Lusaka,

Zambia, but I have told them you must remain here for another two nights at least. Your injuries are such that it would be unwise to move you until then."

I looked at Andrew with wide eyes. He responded by shaking his head and opening his hands in a gesture of helplessness.

"Two more nights," I said out loud.

"That is correct Mr Green," said the doctor. "We will do our best to make you as comfortable as possible,"

"Well, you can start by firing that drunken thieving bitch of a nurse from last night," I said quietly.

"We have reported that, Jason," said Andrew. "You won't be seeing her again."

The door opened and Sister Mercy walked in carrying a steel trunk with a latch on the front.

"This is for your belongings, Mr. Green," she said as she placed it near the bed to my right.

"And here are your padlock and keys," handing me a sealed package.

Andrew busied himself placing my belongings in the trunk as I opened the packet that contained the lock. I kept my wallet and the three keys at my side and handed the lock to Andrew.

"What about your wallet?" said Andrew.

"I'll keep it with me for now," I replied.

Andrew locked the trunk and stood up as the doctor and Sister Mercy left the room.

"Well Jason," he said "It looks like you'll be leaving here Tuesday morning. I'll be here at 8.00 am. sharp with your computer and your hard drive. I'm sorry I couldn't get you out faster, but you know... Doctor's orders."

The prospects of another two nights in there were daunting, to say the least.

"I appreciate everything you've done Andrew," I said as I shook his hand. "Thank you."

The two police officers from the previous day arrived as Andrew left. This time they were a little humbler and both removed their caps and introduced themselves before taking seats near the window to my right. The interview lasted an hour, and I was as vague as possible telling them that I was simply a tourist who was interested in the bird life of the Zambezi Valley and that the men who had attacked me had come on a boat from the Zambian side. The fact that I was immobile and unable to pinpoint the exact location was clearly frustrating them, but I kept the story as simple as possible and promised to assist them further after my recovery. This eventually, seemed to satisfy them and they left after I was made to sign a handwritten statement on a tatty piece of newsprint. By then the pain and itching had returned and I called for Sister Mercy to administer some more morphine. She walked into the room carrying a tray of food that turned out to be the same stew and rice as the previous day.

"You will have nothing until you eat, Mr. Green," she said sternly as she handed me the food.

This time I finished all the food and she beamed at me as I handed her the empty tray.

"Ah! You are hungry today," she said in her strong Shona accent.

"Listen, Mercy," I said quietly "This might sound unusual, but I would like you to get me some more drugs for the pain. I would hate for what happened last night to repeat itself and I really don't want to run out either."

She immediately looked towards the door nervously.

"I have cash, and everything will be kept safely in the trunk. How much is each bottle of morphine?" I asked.

"Forty dollars," she replied.

"Here," I said as I removed five crisp $100.00 bills from my wallet. "Get me ten bottles and you keep the change".

"Mr Green," she said as she stared at the money in my hand.

"Mercy, please. I *really* don't want to run out and I will return any that is not used".

She shook her head as she took the cash.

"Okay, Mr. Green, but this is not our normal procedure."

"I know, I know, but trust me and it will be safe," I said.

It was a blatant lie. Without realising it I was starting to show the traits of a drug addict. Such was the pain and my craving for its relief.

"Oh, Mercy," I said as she turned to make her way to the door. "Get a bunch of syringes as well."

Finally, I was left alone staring out at the orange light of the afternoon. I watched as an African Hornbill landed in a nearby Mopani tree, its curved beak bright yellow against the grey and silver bark of the tree.

I sighed as I stared at it in silence. *What a mess Green. What a fucking mess.* Mercy returned ten minutes later with a brown paper bag containing the ten bottles and a handful of syringes. I leaned over the right-hand side of the bed and locked it all away safely before pocketing the keys. By then the pain had returned in earnest and the injection, when it came, was a truly blessed relief and I retreated into my private world of quiet blissful stupor. I was awakened an hour later by the sound of a branch snapping nearby. With the morphine still coursing through my veins, I opened my eyelids slowly to see an Elephant had walked under a large Mopani tree nearby. I knew that they were plentiful around the town of Kariba and were free to roam wherever they chose so it came as no great surprise to see one right outside the government hospital. I stared at it in drugged fascination as it moved slowly on the dusty sun-baked ground. Its juvenile tusks were only half a metre long, but it stood huge against the tree in the orange light. At one stage it turned its head and, in my drug-addled mind I was sure it was looking at me with its big hazel eye. *So many people are trying to kill you* I thought as I drifted back to sleep.

It was dark by the time I awoke and the corridor outside the room was quiet. I called for a nurse hoping not to see Sister Anna Chimene from the previous night. Thankfully there was a different nurse on duty and although she was morose and silent, she administered the shot of morphine quickly and left me in peace. It was 3.00am. when I next woke up and the room was hot, dark, and quiet. I pulled the keys from my pocket and leaned over the right-hand side of the bed to access the trunk. It opened on the first attempt, and I rummaged through my bag and retrieved my head torch.

I strapped it to my head and turned it on. Next, I pulled out the bag of morphine and syringes. I lay back and stared at one of the bottles turning it slowly in my hand. The burning itch and aching had returned by then and I glanced briefly at the door as I weighed up my options. I removed a needle from one of the sealed packs and placed it on one of the new syringes. Slowly and carefully, I drew ten millilitres of the clear fluid from the rubber top of the bottle. I depressed the plunger till I saw a fine squirt of the liquid in the torch light. I adjusted the torch and looked for a vein on my left arm. The process was quickly over, and I managed to get the trunk and its contents locked away safely before the familiar waves of calm washed over me and I drifted away once again.

It was daylight when I woke up and Mercy had returned to work. For the first time in days, I felt hungry, and I managed to eat a breakfast of boiled eggs and toast with tea. I spent the day in a vicious cycle of acute discomfort and appeasement with every dose of the drug. The doctor made his rounds and expressed satisfaction with the state of my wounds. Even the change of dressings was manageable and before I knew it, it was dinner time albeit with the same stew and rice as the previous days. That night I dosed myself three times with the morphine and I felt no guilt whatsoever.

Instead, there was a feeling of smug satisfaction that I had enough of a stash of the drug to last for weeks. I had no idea that I had become a true addict. Andrew arrived as promised the following morning and brought my laptop and the hard drive with him. I unlocked the trunk and keeping the paper bag of syringes and morphine hidden, I placed them in my bag. We spent the next hour in quiet conversation as we waited for the vehicle from the private clinic in Lusaka to arrive. It was 9.00am. sharp when the medics from Mercer Clinic in Lusaka arrived. They were dressed in immaculate white uniforms and were quietly efficient in their preparations. The local doctor came in and officially signed me over to the two medics who had brought in a modern stretcher from their vehicle. I gave my passport to them so they could take care of the border crossing into Zambia.

"Well, Andrew," I said. "Looks like I'm out of here. Thank you for everything. You saved my life."

"Take care of yourself, Jason," he said as he shook my hand.

At that moment Sister Mercy walked into the room.

"Time for your injection before you go, Mr. Green."

I sat up and was helped onto the new stretcher as she prepared the shot. She administered it with a knowing look on her face.

"You were very kind, Mercy. Thank you," I said as the drug took effect.

"Hmm," she said. "Wishing you the best. Mr Green."

Before I knew it the stretcher was moving, and the sight of the ancient, stained ceiling tiles blurred my vision as I was moved from the room through the darkened corridors towards the exit. The bright sunlight blinded me as the stretcher left the building and I lifted my left arm to shade my eyes from the glare. The ambulance was a brand new and shiny import from the UK. It was fitted with state-of-the-art medical equipment and the two medics wasted no time in tilting the back of the mattress and turning on the air conditioning to make me comfortable. My bags were brought in, and I made a point of securing the one that contained the hard drive and the morphine nearby. One of the medics attached a fresh drip to the cannula insertion in my arm. Soon enough, the engine was started, and we were off. The road to the border post at the Kariba dam wall was winding and it took twenty minutes to get there. As we drove, I stared in a state of drugged lethargy, out of a gap in the window at the massive lake that stretched out below the road. The exit procedures at the border post were taken care of quickly by the medics.

Apparently, medical emergencies had priority over all other traffic, and it was only necessary for an immigration official to confirm my identity and my passport was stamped. We crossed the dam wall and arrived at the Zambian border within a few minutes. Once again, the fact that I was in an ambulance seemed to do the trick and we were cleared to leave within thirty minutes. The drive from the border to The Mercer Clinic in Lusaka took exactly two hours. I spent the time in and out of consciousness in the pleasant cool of the air conditioning. When we arrived, the medics kept the stretcher back in the upright position as they removed it from the ambulance. The gardens were lush, green and tropical and there was a fishpond and a huge ornamental rockery near the wall.

The Mercer Clinic had obviously been purpose-built with no expense spared. The building had three floors and a modern grey façade with tinted windows. I saw that there were split-unit air conditioners outside every room. My stretcher was wheeled through a set of dark automatic glass doors into a stylish reception area where the medics immediately checked me into the facility. Within minutes I was wheeled into a room on the ground floor that was cool, bright, and spotlessly clean. Coming from an impoverished government hospital in Zimbabwe, the difference between the two was staggering. The bed was fitted with a remote control for adjusting it and surrounding it were all manner of modern ECG machines and similar. Opposite the bed near the door to the en-suite bathroom there was a large flat-screen television on the wall and beneath it stood a table with fresh cut roses in a vase. To the right of the bed, near the tinted window were two comfortable easy chairs and a table with more flowers. The medics were joined by two more nurses, again dressed in immaculate white uniforms. Although they tried to assist me, I managed the move from the stretcher to the bed myself, albeit a little unsteadily.

"Please could you bring my bags in from the ambulance immediately" I asked one of the medics.

"Certainly, Mr Green," he replied politely.

I lay back on the comfortable memory foam of the mattress. The sheets were cool and crisp to the touch, and I quickly found the remote control to tilt the back of the bed up into a sitting position. My bags arrived and I first checked for both the hard drive and the packet of morphine and syringes. Both were there. *Good.* One of the medics offered to unpack my bags and put the contents in a cupboard in the corner of the room.

"Are there keys for those cupboards?" I asked.

"Yes sir, you may keep the keys to secure your property although it is not necessary here," he said.

"Don't worry about unpacking them but please lock them up and give me the key," I replied.

The man did as I asked and handed me the small set of keys which I pocketed.

"Doctor Preuss will be in shortly to take a look at you, Mr Green. Meantime we are going to clean your wounds," said one of the nurses.

"That's fine," I replied.

I turned on the television as they worked. They did so with gentle professionalism and before long they were finished. The two nurses left the room and I lay alone feeling satisfied I had finally gotten into a modern and sophisticated facility. The aching and itching had returned but I decided to tolerate it until the doctor had visited. Soon enough the door opened and in walked a tall heavily built white woman in her sixties. She wore a grey suit and around her thick neck hung a stethoscope. Her grey hair was cropped short and on her bulbous nose, she wore a pair of horn-rimmed spectacles.

"Now then. My name is Doctor Preuss," she said quickly in a German accent as she glanced at my file. "Mr Jason Green. Bullet wound to the shoulder, a severe puncture wound to left foot and multiple lacerations to lower left leg. Good grief! You have been in the wars!"

"You could say that" I replied quietly.

# 11

# Chapter Eleven: Lusaka

Dr. Preuss made her inspection of my wounds and expressed satisfaction with the healing process. She gave the instruction for a shot of morphine to be administered and for the dressings to be changed. As I was able to move around alone, I was given a set of crutches so I could get myself to and from the bathroom. I was also given a small fridge that contained all manner of fresh fruit juices and bottled water. After everything was completed, I spent the afternoon happily dozing and watching television. At 6.30pm. as I was watching the sun setting through the tinted window one of the nurses brought in my dinner. The difference between the two hospitals was incredible. For a starter, there was pickled fish pate and crispy toast followed by a main course of perfectly cooked roast beef with potatoes, three vegetables and gravy. For dessert, there was a choice of crème caramel or chocolate ice cream followed by tea or coffee. My appetite had returned and after I had finished the meal it was cleared away and a bowl of fresh fruit was placed on the side table near the bed. *This place is like a hotel.* I thought. *Beats the NHS any day.* It was 8.30pm. when a nurse walked in to administer some more morphine. I noted with mild alarm that the prescribed dosage had been reduced to eight millilitres. I questioned this as she swabbed my arm before the shot.

"Doctor's orders, Mr. Green," said the nurse with a smile.

Despite the reduced dose it had the desired effect and I slumped back on the bed happily and fumbled with the remote control for the television as the lights were turned down.

It was 11.30pm. when I awoke in darkness. The automatic sleep timer on the television must have turned it off. I felt the surface of the table to my right for my head torch and strapped it to my head. All was quiet around me and I looked towards the cupboards where my bags were stored. With my right hand, I felt in my pocket for the keys. They were there. The crawling irritation in my leg and the deep aching in my shoulder had returned and I looked around the room as I weighed up my options. After ten minutes of indecision, the scales were tipped once again. *Fuck it., I'll give myself one shot.* Slowly and quietly, I made my way over to the cupboards using the crutches. I retrieved the bottle I had used the night before and a fresh syringe and made my way back to the bed. I attached the needle to the syringe in the light of the head torch and held the tiny bottle upside down to draw the precious liquid. Once I had withdrawn exactly ten millilitres, I placed the bottle on the bedside table and tapped my left arm. The needle was a centimetre from my arm when the doors burst open, and the lights were turned on. Dr. Preuss was accompanied by two nurses who rushed towards me and quickly grabbed both the bottle and the syringe.

"What are you doing Mr Green?" she shouted. her face red with rage.

She took the bottle of morphine from the nurse and shook it in my face.

"Where did you get this?" she demanded in her German accent.

*Busted, Green.* I sat back resignedly and took a deep breath.

"I got it in Kariba," I said quietly.

Dr Preuss was bristling.

"Nurse, I want you to search his belongings thoroughly while I am here and give me anything that is not allowed here. Do it now!"

I pulled the set of keys from my pocket and handed them to the nurse who immediately went to the cupboard.

"We have cameras in every room Mr Green and our patients are monitored twenty-four hours a day. What you were attempting to do is strictly against our rules at The Mercer Clinic! What on earth were you thinking?"

"I am in pain," I said in a calm voice which belied my own growing fury.

"This is absolutely no excuse Mr Green!" she yelled as she walked around to the bottom of the bed and pulled up my file. "Your next dose of pain medication is due at 1.00 a.m.!"

I looked at my watch as the nurse handed her the brown paper bag of morphine and syringes that she had retrieved from the cupboard. She looked once at the contents and shook her head in disgust.

"You will wait until then. Good night, Mr Green!" she said as they all walked towards the door.

"Leave the light on, please. I need to use the bathroom," I said.

They left the room and I lay on the bed staring bitterly at my bandages. I swung my legs slowly from the bed and grabbed the crutches as I sat up. The increased pressure of the blood in my leg doubled my discomfort to the point where it felt like there were thousands of biting ants crawling over it. I did my best to put it out of my mind as I made my way slowly and carefully to the bathroom.

I flicked the light switch and made my way to the basin. I placed the crutches against the wall and turned the cold tap to full flow. Using my left hand as support on the sink I bent over and splashed my face repeatedly with the cool water. Leaving the tap running

I slowly lifted my head until I faced the mirror on the cabinet in front of me. I hated the person that stared back at me. My hair was matted and untidy. The unshaven cheeks were sunken and there were greasy purple marks beneath my eyes. *Look what he has done to you, Green. Turned you into a fucking junkie! What he did to Hannes. What he is doing right now.* Without thinking I clenched my right fist and drew it slowly behind me as I stared at the mirror.

"Fucker!!!" I screamed as I slammed my fist into the mirror repeatedly.

The glass shattered immediately and fell onto the basin and floor in shards. Still, I punched savagely, again and again at the woodwork of the cabinet until it too disintegrated into a bloody dusty mess of particle board and screws. Suddenly I was gripped firmly by both arms and pulled away from the mess. My hand was badly injured and dripped blood continuously as I was led back through the door towards the bed. There was panicked shouting all around and I lay with my teeth gritted and my eyes closed as the nurses attended to my hand. I heard the furious voice of Dr. Preuss instructing the nurses to administer sedatives and morphine and when I felt the needle in my arm it couldn't have come sooner.

6.30 a.m. and I woke slowly from the sedatives. For the first time in many days, I felt human again. The irritation and pain had now subsided, and I felt a certain clarity of mind. I looked down at my bandaged fist and shook my head at the astonishing events of the past ten days. With my left hand, I felt the long stubble on my chin which firmed my resolve. *Clean yourself up, Green. Right now.* Using the crutches, I crossed the room and retrieved my ablution bag from the cupboard. During the night the mess I had made in the bathroom had been cleaned up. I spent the next fifteen minutes washing and shaving in the bathroom and on the way back to the bed I collected my laptop to catch up with some work. Before I settled, I poured a glass of fruit juice and then positioned the table to enable me to work. I found the free WIFI immediately and set about dealing with the many emails that had built up. There was a number from my case supervisor asking what had happened to me. I replied simply saying I had been involved in an accident and could be away for a while yet. The freelance nature of my work with the insurance company allowed me such freedom. After I was finished, I turned on the television news as I browsed the internet.

Dr. Preuss walked in with a nurse at 7.45 a.m. on the dot.

"Oh!" she said with a surprised look on her face. "You look a lot better, Mr. Green".

"Thank you," I replied. "I feel better."

She examined my wounds and once again expressed satisfaction with the healing.

"You are due some pain medication after breakfast at 8.30 Mr Green," she said sternly. "I hope that is agreeable?"

"That will be fine, thank you," I said staring at my computer screen.

The breakfast consisted of muesli and fruit followed by bacon, eggs, sausages, and toast. I wolfed down the lot and this was noted in my file by the nurse. The morphine shot, although welcome when it came, reminded me of the dreadful cycle I had been caught in. The dosage had been reduced to seven millilitres, but it was enough to send me into a dreamlike state for the next three hours.

I came to at 12:00 noon and reached for the glass of fruit juice near the bed. Once again, I felt rejuvenated and stronger. I pressed the buzzer near the bed to summon a nurse. She arrived promptly and I asked if she would get the hard drive from my bag in the cupboard. I spent the rest of the day thoroughly engrossed in the many files of Hannes' reports. It made for fascinating but disturbing reading. I concentrated on the second section which dealt mainly with the transport of the ivory from Mayuni's base in Zambia to the port of Beira in Mozambique. The amount of intelligence he had gathered was staggering and it listed transport companies, corrupt border officials, illegal crossing points and clearing agents etc. The lists were unending, and I realised that during the weeks it would take for me to recover fully I would be kept very busy indeed.

It was 4.00pm. when I asked Dr. Preuss if I would be allowed to venture out into the gardens on my crutches. She refused this outright but promised that if my injuries continued to heal as they were, I would be permitted to venture out the next day in a wheelchair. By that stage, my head was spinning with all the information I had read from the hard drive. I decided to put it away and watch television as I waited for dinner. The time passed quickly, and I was comfortable in my surroundings. Soon after an excellent dinner of roast chicken, the nurse arrived with my early evening shot of morphine. By that stage, I was indifferent to it but it did help to alleviate the pain of the change of dressing.

Later that night I felt better still and busied myself re-packing my bags and putting my dirty laundry away for washing. I found myself becoming faster on the crutches and at one stage I put my head around the door to look outside. Instantly a nurse appeared and scolded me with a waving finger.

I obediently retreated to my bed and chose a film to watch on the television. The nurse arrived on cue at 1:00 a.m. with my morphine shot. The seven millilitres did the trick and I fell soundly asleep until 6.30am. in the morning. The sun had risen so I could see billowing grey thunder clouds in the distance through the tinted windows. As I had done the previous day, I took myself to the bathroom to wash and shave. When I was finished, I looked at myself in the recently replaced mirror cabinet above the basin. The dark marks under my eyes had disappeared and the colour was returning to my face. *Good*. Dr. Preuss was true to her word and that day I ventured out into the garden twice for two hours at a time. Although I was wheeled out on a chair, I was able to get up and walk around the fishponds using the crutches. That afternoon I stood near the pond and watched as the ominous black clouds piled up in the distance and the deep rumbles of thunder and lightning grew nearer the city. The afternoon was dark and humid, and the rain had started to fall when the nurse finally called me to go back to my room.

My health and strength were improving steadily and that night I spent another three hours studying the files on the hard drive. By the time I had finished, I was exhausted, and the nurse arrived once again at 1:00 am. to give me my shot. I followed the routines of the clinic and obeyed the rules for the next four nights. Over that period my dosage of morphine was reduced to three millilitres administered twice daily. It was on the fifth night that I refused the shot and opted to sleep without any sedative whatsoever. In that period, I had gained unlimited access to the gardens under my own steam on the crutches and I spent many hours working on my laptop at a chair and table under a Giant Mahogany tree. Its thick green foliage provided good cover from the fierce African sun. On a few occasions, I was visited by a family of Vervet Monkeys that had come in over the perimeter wall. I tossed them peanuts and fruit and watched as they raced back into the branches above to eat as they stared down at me with their startled expressions.

In my mind, I had formulated a plan but to carry it out I needed to be fully fit once again. My shoulder had healed to the point where they no longer changed the dressing, and I was finally able to take a shower albeit with a plastic bag strapped to my leg. The itching on my leg had gone and on the many occasions I examined it, it was clear it was healing well. No longer were the many ugly stitches swollen, red and oozing. Instead, they were flat and even in colour. Of more worry was the puncture wound from the spike in the pitfall trap. On the few occasions I had tried to put weight on the foot it resulted in a deep, sharp, and intense pain that lingered for some time. I was assured by Dr. Preuss that in time this would disappear. It was two days later when I finally convinced the doctor that I should be released. It was reluctantly agreed on the condition that I visit the clinic every two days to have my leg and foot assessed. I wasted no time booking accommodation at a bush camp situated ten kilometres south of the city on the Kafue Road.

Ulrika Camp was set in a private game park and was popular with overland trucks and campers. The grounds were populated with Giraffe, Zebra and Impala and there were several thatched A-frame chalets set amongst the trees. I booked one of them for two weeks. I set about packing my bags as the receptionist called a taxi. The last thing I did was to do an online search for a hunting and fishing shop. As luck would have it there was one situated on the outskirts of the city in a mall on the Kafue Road. Desperate to get out of the clinic I wasted no time when the taxi arrived and walked out quickly on the crutches with the staff carrying my bags behind me. The taxi was small and cramped but by that stage, I didn't care a bit and I smiled to myself as we drove out the gate of The Mercer Clinic in the mid-day heat.

## 12

# Chapter Twelve: Ulrika Camp

The drive to the hunting outfitter's shop took twenty minutes through heavy traffic and by the time we arrived, I was wet with sweat. I grabbed the day bag that contained the hard drive and slung it over my shoulder as I reached into the back seat for the crutches.

"I'll be back soon," I said to the driver who nodded and thanked me.

The interior of the shop was air-conditioned and stocked to the roof with all manner of camping, hunting, and fishing equipment. An impressive range of hunting rifles was displayed at the rear of the glass sales counter, but I wasn't there for one of those.

"Can I help you sir?" asked the young sales assistant.

"I'm looking for a hunting knife," I replied pointing at the selection on display under the glass counter. "A big one."

The young man opened the cabinet and handed me the largest example he had. I pulled the blade from the leather sheath and turned it in my hand. The polished metal gleamed in the light and I saw my reflection on the surface. It felt balanced and heavy in my hand.

"This will do fine," I said still staring at the knife. "I'd like a sharpening stone and some honing oil as well please."

I put the knife back in its sheath as the young man fetched my order. Once I had paid, I bagged the lot. thanked him and made my way out into the fierce sun and the waiting taxi. The traffic on the Kafue Road was heavy and it took another twenty minutes to get to the gate of Ulrika Camp. We turned left onto a dirt road and travelled for a hundred metres until we arrived at a game fence and a small brick guard house with a boom. A sleepy-looking guard walked up to the driver's side of the vehicle and after a brief conversation, he made his way back to lift the boom so we could drive through. The smooth dirt road to the reception of the camp was two kilometres long and it wound its way through the dappled shade of a forest of Msasa and Mopani woodland. The surrounding grass was tall and green, but I noticed a few Impalas and Warthog grazing as we drove. The reception was a huge, thatched structure with brick walls painted with African designs set under the trees with a car park to the front. I left the driver sitting in the car as I made my way into the building to check in. The interior was dim and cool, and I noticed a bar area with a pool table and television to the right. On the high roof hung the flags of various countries and a barman stood diligently polishing glasses.

I rang a bell at the reception and immediately a door opened and an overweight white lady in her mid-sixties came out to greet me.

"Hi there," she said. "Are you Mr Green?"

"Hi. Yes, Jason Green, pleased to meet you," I said offering my hand while keeping the crutch under my arm.

"Welcome to Ulrika," she said as she peered over the reception desk at my leg. "What happened to you?"

"Oh, hunting accident," I replied. "Nothing serious."

"I've put you in chalet number five. It's the furthest from here and quite secluded but I'm worried now seeing as you're on crutches."

"That's perfectly fine," I said. "I need the exercise."

After the formalities I was given a set of keys on a string attached to a wooden plaque and one of the waiters walked with me to the waiting cab. To the left were a series of thatched A-frame chalets each set thirty metres apart stretching off into the woods.

"Yours is the last one, sir," said the waiter with a worried look on his face.

"That's fine," I said. "Let's go"

I told the driver to follow us, and we made our way down the track that led behind the buildings. I opened the back door to the small kitchen area of the chalet as the waiter busied himself collecting my bags from the car. The interior was dark and cool and there was a musty smell in the air as if the building had not been used in a while. I walked back to pay the waiting driver as the waiter made his way inside with the bags to open up. Once the driver had gone, I made my way back into the building to find the waiter had opened the double doors to the front and the building was filled with light and fresh air. Beyond the kitchenette, there was a rustic wooden lounge suite upholstered with green canvas cushions on a concrete floor. Scattered around were occasional tables made from rough wood and to the right was a workstation. To the left was the entrance to the shower and toilet and above was a deck where I imagined the bed would be. The stairs were wide and shallow so would be easy to navigate on the crutches.

I made my way through the lounge area and out to the deck at the front of the building. In front was a large grassy glade that stretched off to the tree line a hundred metres away. To my left a herd of Zebra stood with their heads bowed as they grazed the fresh green grass.

"Is it okay for you sir?" asked the young waiter with an expectant look on his face.

"Perfect," I said as I handed him a $10.00 note.

I spent the next hour unpacking my bags and having a look around the chalet. The upstairs area was small but clean and the bed had a much-needed mosquito net above it.

I set up my laptop at the workstation connected to the WIFI network and browsed the news. After being cooped up for so long in the hospital I soon grew impatient and shut down the computer. I grabbed my day bag and walked out on the deck to the front of the chalet. The open space and fresh air were invigorating and for the first time in ages, I felt unrestrained. I leaned back in my chair, closed my eyes, and allowed myself to soak up the rays of the warm African sun. My mind drifted as I sat for a good twenty minutes until the reason I was there slowly began to tug at my consciousness. Eventually, I sat forward, lit a cigarette, and stared across the tree line towards the South where I knew the Zambezi River flowed. *The time will come Green*. Half an hour later I grabbed the hard drive, locked the chalet, and made my way up the track towards the main reception area of the camp. By then I was able to move at some speed on the crutches and it only took a few minutes until I was once again greeted at the front desk by the owner.

"I was wondering if you had a safe. This hard drive has all my work on it," I said.

"Sure, Mr Green. I'll have that locked up no problem," she replied as I handed her the device.

I made my way back out to the car park to decide what to do. In the campsite to my right, an overland truck had arrived and there were a group of people setting up tents under the trees while trance music played softly from a sound system in the vehicle. There was no way I could spend the afternoon browsing the internet or sitting on the deck of the chalet. I had been cooped up for too long and my objective was to recover and get fit. I looked down the dirt road that led to the boom at the entrance to the camp. I knew it was at least two kilometres through the bush, but my mind was made up and I set off.

I started at a quick pace and put my left foot down lightly every five steps. The deep pain from the puncture wound was still there although it had lessened slightly. I realized it would be some time before I would be able to walk unaided.

By the time I had covered five hundred metres, I was sweating profusely and panting heavily. The crutches were chaffing under my arms and the handles were slippery in my hands, but I persevered in the humidity of the afternoon. My walking became rhythmic and repetitive as did the pain in my foot every five steps. I passed the one-kilometre mark totally oblivious of my surroundings as I blinked the sweat from my eyes. The pain became a point of focus in my mind as I went, which spurred me on towards my destination. With my head bowed I pushed and pushed looking only at the tufts of grass that marked the right-hand side of the bush road below. In my mind, I saw the face of Dixon Mayuni smiling at me with his gap-toothed grin. With every fifth step, the pain in my foot made the vision in my brain pulsate until it began to infuriate me. Faster and faster I went, grunting repeatedly and kicking up small clouds of red dust with each step. At one stage I thought I might collapse into the green grass but instead, I lifted my head and screwed up my eyes in the sunlight to see the small brick guard house and boom were only two hundred metres away.

Without slowing I pushed on totally oblivious as to how much I had exerted my weakened body. *Faster. Faster.* I repeated the word in my mind. I lifted my head to see I had almost crashed into the rough brick wall of the guard house. Almost sobbing with the effort of the exertion and the pain I threw the crutches violently into the dust and held up my left arm to lean my head against the wall. I stood there shakily on my right leg sucking in great whooping gulps of air until finally my breathing slowed. With my eyes closed I had no idea I wasn't alone.

"Your journey has been long and hard," said a voice.

I turned my head to see the guard who had lifted the boom for the taxi earlier. I had not noticed at the time, but he was an old man with a grey beard and a wrinkled wizened face. His clothes were scruffy and torn and he wore a pair of sandals he had made from old car tyres. He stood there looking at me with an open expression and a knowing look in his eye.

"You could say that" I replied.

The man reached inside the open door of the guard house and brought out a worn wooden stool fashioned in the style of the Batonka tribe of the Zambezi Valley. Without a word, he placed it near the wall where I stood for me to sit on. Keeping my left leg up

I swung around and gratefully sat down with my back against the dusty brick wall of the building. The old man once again reached into the hut and pulled out another stool. It stood about thirty-five centimetres high with a rounded seat and an intricately designed body. Years of wood smoke and constant use had given it a shiny black patina. The old man placed the stool near mine and sat.

We sat in silence staring out at the trees with the sun beginning its descent like a giant orange orb.

"You are going somewhere, but you are not ready yet," said the man without looking at me.

I turned my head and looked at him.

"I must be ready," I replied.

The old man reached down and pulled a strand of dried grass from the dusty soil. He put it in his mouth and sat back against the wall in silence. I resumed my study of the trees.

"A journey of a thousand miles begins with one step," he said quietly.

"And I have taken that step," I replied.

The old man nodded and reached into the door with his left arm. He retrieved an old glass Coca-Cola bottle that was filled with water. Without a word, he handed it to me. By then my mouth was bone dry and I took it gratefully and drank the warm liquid.

"Thank you Mdara," I said using the respectful Shona term for 'old man'.

The man reached into the pocket of his ancient jacket and pulled out a pouch of loose tobacco and newspaper with which to make a cigarette.

"No, here," I said as I pulled the pack of cigarettes from my own pocket.

The old man's smoky eyes lit up as he took one and we both sat back in silence to smoke. A few minutes later I stubbed out my cigarette and reached for the crutches that lay in the dust near my feet.

"I will see you again, Mdara, my name is Jason."

"Thank you," he replied. "My name is Jameson."

I took a much slower pace on the walk back to Ulrika camp and my chalet. For the first time in ages, I felt free and I knew my health was improving rapidly. I stopped numerous times to rest and take in my surroundings. The afternoon heat was waning, while birds were coming to life and chattering in the trees above. It was 4:00 p.m. by the time I opened the back door to the chalet and made my way to the front deck to watch the sunset. The grassy glade between the chalet and the tree line had come alive with animals. There were the Zebras from earlier along with a herd of Impala and a trio of Warthogs all grazing together. I pulled the sharpening stone from my bag and placed it on the table in front of me. Next, I opened the bottle of honing oil and squeezed ten drops of the viscous liquid onto the flat black surface of the stone. Using my thumb, I carefully worked the oil into the stone, so it covered all four corners. The blade of the hunting knife glowed bright yellow from the reflection of the setting sun as I turned it in my hand. Once again, I felt pleased with its substantial weight and balance. I held the blade at a shallow angle on the stone and began to sharpen it with a steady repetitive back-and-forth motion that covered the entire length of the stone. I repeated this motion ten times before turning the blade and doing the same with the other side. I found the process therapeutic, and it helped to focus my mind, so I repeated it time and time again until a full hour had passed. When I was done, I sat back, wiped the blade clean and lit a cigarette.

The heat of the day was gone with a cool breeze was blowing in from the south. I stared out at the tree line as I smoked and thought about the great river that flowed not far away. I thought about the pain and humiliation which I had suffered and the long road ahead. *When the time comes Green, it will be worth it.*

I nodded to myself as I stubbed out the cigarette and reached for the crutches. The Mercer Clinic had supplied me with several large plastic bags with which to cover the dressing on my leg when showering. I sat on the rustic couch inside the chalet as I secured one of them and then made my way to the bathroom to shower. The water from the pressure geyser was hot and it blasted over my body as I washed. When I was finished, I dressed and locked the front of the chalet from the inside before making my way through the kitchenette and out the back door. The surrounding bush was filled with the singing of the Cicadas as I made my way up the track towards the reception of Ulrika Camp. I arrived to find the reception empty and a few of the overlanders playing pool and drinking in the bar area. The lighting inside the massive, thatched building was dim and there was soft music playing through the speakers behind the bar. I nodded my greetings to the tourists and took a seat on a stool at the bar. There was a tall man in a worn white shirt and tie polishing a glass behind the counter.

"Good evening, sir, what can I get you?" he asked.

I glanced at the selection of drinks behind the bar and noticed an advert for the local Mozi Lager.

"Good evening," I replied pointing at the sign. "I'll have a cold one of those please".

The beer was served in a chilled glass, and I drank a full half pint before placing the glass on one of the bar mats. The beer was good and burned my throat pleasantly as it went down.

"Is it good, sir?" the barman asked with a smile.

"Not bad at all," I replied.

Over the next few hours, the rest of the tourists from the overland vehicle came in to join their friends. The music went up in volume and the pub had a festive atmosphere although I kept to myself in my corner of the bar. A waiter appeared with a menu, and I ordered a T-bone steak with chips and salad to be served where I sat. The food was good and went down with a glass of South African wine followed by another beer.

It was 9.00pm when I signed for the drinks and food and made my way out of the pub. The group of young overlanders were in fine form by then and I waved as I walked past them and out of the building. The music faded and the night was cool and quiet as I followed the track to my chalet. After brushing my teeth. I made my way a little unsteadily up the stairs and lay down gratefully on the bed under the mosquito net. I was asleep within minutes. I awoke the next morning at 6:00 a.m. feeling no ill effects from the previous evening's drinking. I put my left foot on the ground lightly as I sat up and was pleased to feel the usual pain had subsided. After a shower, I made my way back to the restaurant for a full English breakfast.

After the food, I made my way out through the back of the dining area to the pool. There were several tables set under nearby trees and I sat at one of them to have coffee and smoke a cigarette. I was feeling rejuvenated and strong so afterwards I decided to take the two-kilometre walk back to the gate to see the old guard I had met the previous day. I set out expecting the journey to be a repeat of that painful process. but I was pleasantly surprised to find I could put a fair amount of pressure on my left foot without too much discomfort. The journey passed quickly in the cool of the morning and I found old Jameson, sitting on his stool outside the guard house.

"Today is a better day Mr. Jason," he said with a toothless smile as he reached into the room to retrieve another stool.

"Much better Jameson," I said as I leant the crutches on the wall and sat. "Much better."

I pulled the pack of cigarettes from my pocket and offered the old man one of them. We sat once again in silence as we smoked and surveyed the trees. Finishing, I crushed out my cigarette, grabbed the crutches and stood.

"I will see you this afternoon Jameson," I said as I walked off.

"I will be here," he replied.

The walk back to the chalet was slow but painless and I spent a few hours attending to emails and browsing the news. At lunch time I made my way back to the bar and dining area of the main building and ordered a meal of Chicken Kiev with chips and salad. I ate alone outside at the pool area in the shade of the trees. There was no sign of the group of overlanders, and I imagined they were sleeping off a heavy night of drinking. Later that afternoon I took another long walk through the bush to the gate and sat with Jameson for an hour smoking. On the way back I was able to put more weight on my foot than ever and I arrived back at the chalet feeling satisfied.

Like the previous day, I sat on the deck and spent an hour meticulously sharpening the hunting knife. Once more it had the effect of focussing and calming my mind. That night I had dinner and beers in the pub as usual and retired to bed at around 10.00pm. I awoke the next morning feeling even stronger and I took the walk to see Jameson, using one crutch only and putting more and more weight on my foot as I went. After lunch, I took a taxi through the chaotic traffic of Lusaka to The Mercer Clinic where Dr. Preuss examined my foot. Finally, I was given the go-ahead to have the stitches taken out and to remove the dressing albeit with a stern warning to keep it dry and not put too much weight on it.

The dust and heat of the drive back to Ulrika did nothing to deflate my sense of enthusiasm as I realised that I was making real tangible progress and I would be able to put my plans into action sooner than I had anticipated. That afternoon I took the walk to the gate to visit Jameson who also expressed satisfaction with my progress.

I kept this steady and repetitive routine going for the next seven days with my mind singularly focused on my objective. There was nothing and no one that would stand in my way. It was early on a humid and cloudy Thursday morning that I set out from the chalet for the first time without the crutch. By then the wound had all but healed and there was only slight discomfort as I walked the familiar road through the forest. I found my friend Jameson sitting on his stool leaning against the guard house as usual. He nodded his approval as I approached and sat down.

"You are now ready, Mr. Jason," he said as I offered him a cigarette.

I lit our cigarettes, leant back against the brickwork, and exhaled.

"I am ready, Jameson," I replied.

# 13

# Chapter Thirteen: Dixon Mayuni

My mind was buzzing as I walked back through the forest to my chalet. When I arrived, I quickly browsed the internet for a good car hire company in Lusaka. After calling them to book a vehicle I made my way to the pool area to have breakfast and coffee. The clouds were clearing and the day growing hotter as I paid for my stay at the reception and thanked the staff for everything. I collected the hard drive and made my way back to the chalet to pack my bags. The taxi arrived as I placed a $100 note in an envelope and pocketed it. Leaving the crutches behind I picked up my bags and made my way out to the waiting vehicle.

"I need to get to Avis Rent-A-Car please," I said to the driver.

We made a U-turn and headed back down the track towards the road I had walked so many times in the last few days. I watched as my friend Jameson stood up from his stool as we approached the gate. Before he lifted the boom, I called him around to my side of the vehicle and handed him the money envelope along with a pack of cigarettes.

"This is for you Jameson," I said as he took the gift and pocketed it without looking in the envelope. "You have helped me a lot. Thank you."

"Kupedza nyota kuenda padziva, Mr Jason," he replied in Shona.

I looked the old man in the eye and nodded in understanding of the old African proverb.

"To quench thirst is to go to the pool," I said quietly.

He nodded at me and then walked off to lift the boom. The car lifted a cloud of dust behind us as we drove off towards the main tar road.

Five minutes later, on the outskirts of the city, I told the driver to pull over at a shopping mall on the right-hand side. I pocketed the hard drive, told the driver to wait for me and headed in to buy some supplies. I found a hardware shop that was stocked to the ceiling and told the assistant what I needed. He arrived shortly with a roll of twenty metres of soft baling wire and a pair of rubber-gripped wire cutters. I nodded in approval and made my way to the counter to pay. It was as I waited for the salesman to finish with a customer that I noticed the packet of child-safe sparklers in amongst some other fireworks on the shelf behind the till. When the salesman had finished with his customer, I placed my purchases on the counter and asked him to hand me the pack of sparklers.

They were standard Chinese-made examples, thirty centimetres long and coated with a grey powdery resin. The pack contained ten. An idea was forming in my mind.

"I'll take these as well please," I said placing them on the counter.

The sun was burning hot as I made my way out into the dusty car park to the taxi. I placed my purchases in my bag and told the driver to proceed. The traffic was heavy, so it was a full twenty minutes before I arrived at the car hire company. The back of my shirt was wet with sweat as I paid the driver and climbed out of the car with my bags. Thankfully the Toyota Land Cruiser I had booked was fitted with air conditioning and within forty minutes I found myself driving through the bush south on the Kafue Road towards Chirundu and the Zambezi River.

Two hours later after passing a few police roadblocks where I was asked for my driving license, I arrived at the ramshackle border town and saw the huge concrete bridge that crosses the great river into Zimbabwe. The lodge I had booked was situated ten kilometres downstream on the Zambian side and I soon found the dirt road that led there. The road was rough and passed through several dry riverbeds as it wound its way through the bush downstream. Occasionally it passed near the river, and I glanced at it frequently as the vehicle lurched over the tree roots and rocks. I arrived at the gate to Kiamba Lodge in the late afternoon as the heat of the day was subsiding. The guard saluted and opened the gate pointing me in the direction of the reception area. The lodge grounds were manicured with green lawns set amongst indigenous riverine trees. I parked the vehicle in the shade behind the attractive, main building which had a thatched roof. I was immediately struck by the heat and humidity of the afternoon as I locked the car and walked inside. Immediately a waiter approached me with a glass of chilled orange juice on a tray. I thanked him and drank it as I made my way to the front to take a look. The front of the building was open and there was a horizon pool that looked out at the impressive expanse of the Zambezi River below. I glanced downstream to the left to where I knew the Kafue River flowed and where Dixon Mayuni had his base. *Oh yes, I'll be seeing you soon.* I turned away and walked back into the cool of the building. It was tastefully decorated with tan leather lounge suites, locally woven rattan rugs and distressed furniture. At the centre of the lounge hung a huge chandelier on a chain and to the right was a dining area and bar with a view of the river outside. I made my way to the reception and admired the desk which was made from a giant slab of Mukwa. The manager appeared from a door to the left and greeted me warmly. He produced a pamphlet which showed the layout of the lodge and the accommodation. There was a series of seven thatched bungalow chalets each with river views away downstream. Immediately I pointed at the one furthest from the main building.

"I would like this one, if possible," I said.

"Certainly sir, we can put you in there."

"Another thing," I said. "How far is it to the mouth of the Kafue River from here?"

"That would be roughly four kilometres, sir," he replied.

"Is there road access there?" I asked.

"No sir, ours is the last lodge on this side of the river. From here it is all bush."

I nodded to myself.

"Okay, that's fine," I said.

"We will have someone help with your bags right away."

A porter appeared and we walked outside to the car park. The light had changed to that familiar orange glow of late-afternoon Zambezi Valley. I pulled the bags from the car, locked it and started off down a bricked pathway behind the other chalets. Eventually, we arrived and I was led around the front where the porter opened a giant glass sliding door into my accommodation. The room was well furnished with expensive fittings, air conditioning and a flat-screen television. Outside the front were four canvas-covered campaign chairs and a folding table made from teak. Three metres from my door the brick paving ended, and the land dropped away down to the banks of the mighty river itself.

"Very nice," I said handing the porter a $10.00 note.

After he had left, I set up my laptop at the table and connected to the Wi-Fi. While I waited for it to boot up, I found myself feeling uneasy, as if there was something I should be doing. I soon realized that I was in the habit of sharpening the hunting knife every evening at that exact time. I removed the knife and the sharpening stone from my bag and sat on one of the campaign chairs to start. The viscous honing oil squirted from the bottle, and I rubbed it into the surface of the stone with my thumb. So began my routine sharpening of the huge blade. The steady back-and-forth motion with each side had a calming effect on me. It was forty minutes later when I sat back and wiped the blade clean with a cloth. I lit a cigarette as I studied the edge. By then it was beyond razor sharp, and the red glow of the setting sun reflected on its surface. I replaced the blade in its sheath, put it on the table and sat back to think.

It was a Thursday, and I knew from bitter experience that Mr. Mayuni would be making his routine journey across the river to the Zimbabwe side to drop his men the following night. I knew I would have to make at least one journey to the Kafue River the next day.

With the hard drive in my pocket, I locked my room and headed back up the brick pathway to the main building of Kiamba Lodge. By the time I arrived at the bar area, there was a steady breeze blowing in and the setting sun had changed the dark green waters of the river into a molten red lava flow. The interior lighting was mellow and soft music played through hidden speakers. I drummed my fingers quietly on the surface of the bar as I waited for my beer. *Patience Green. The time is coming.* That night I dined on braised Impala with Irish champ washed down with a South African red wine. It was 8:30 p.m. by the time I walked back down the pathway to my room. The moon had risen, turning the surrounding bush to a curious spectral grey colour. In the distance, a pod of Hippos grunted noisily. I opened the sliding glass door to my room, adjusted the air conditioner to 22c and sat down to work.

I brought up the file that contained the aerial photographs of Mayuni's base that I had taken with the drone. My focus was not on the camp itself but rather the mouth of the river. At the point where the Kafue met the Zambezi it was at least 120 metres wide and flowing with considerable speed. I recalled seeing dugout canoes hidden in the reeds, so my focus was on that point. I found them two hundred metres upstream on the Kiamba side of the river. As long as they were still there, I would have no problem crossing the river to Mayuni's camp. After staring at the image for a few minutes I sat back, lit a cigarette and looked out at the river. *Tomorrow, Green.* I closed the laptop and lay on the crisp white duvet. The bed was firm but comfortable and I watched the moonlight play on the surface of the river for ten minutes until I fell asleep. In my dreams, I saw the scabbed face of Dixon Mayuni in the moonlight. Laughing, taunting, celebrating my death. Or at least what he thought was my death.

I awoke at 6:00 a.m. sharp and stood outside in the relative cool of the morning to smoke. The birds had come to life, and I noticed a few boats on the Zimbabwe side. No doubt keen fishermen from one of the camps there. The pod of Hippos grunted and snorted indignantly and below me, some unseen creature rustled the reeds and splashed the water near the bank. The river was waking up to a new day and so was I. After a shower, I made myself a coffee and sat out once again to plan my day. Regardless of there being no road access to the Kafue, I would have to get there to make sure the canoes were where I had seen them in the photographs. I decided I would once again play the role of the keen bird watcher and wander off into the bush alone. Taking the hard drive with me I walked to the main building of the lodge. An hour later having eaten a full English breakfast I dropped the hard drive with the manager and asked him to lock it up in the safe.

I told him I would be heading out into the bush to do some birdwatching. After a little protest, I convinced him that I was experienced enough to handle it and assured him I would be vigilant to any wild animals. It was 10.00am. and the heat of the day had set in with a vengeance when I set off downstream from my room with my binoculars and camera as my props. As the manager had said the bush was thick and there was no evidence whatsoever of human activity. I did my best to stay near the river but on more than a few occasions, I was forced to track inland to avoid deep gullies and impassable thickets of thorn bush. It was over an hour later when I came upon a giant ant hill that protruded three metres from the ground - long since abandoned by its makers. I stopped and crouched in the shade beneath it to have a cigarette. I imagined I had travelled at least two kilometres which would put me halfway to the mouth of the Kafue. The anthill would serve as a landmark from which to gauge my progress later. I crushed out the cigarette and pressed on through the bush.

The final two kilometres were even more difficult until I found a game trail that snaked along parallel to the river. From the tracks in the dust, I could see that it was frequented by Impala and other small buck. Thankfully there was no evidence of any big cats. The bush became thicker as I approached the confluence of the Kafue and the Zambezi, and I had to cut further inland as the track became impassable because of gullies and rivulets. Finally, in the full heat of the midday sun, the bush cleared to reveal the swift deep waters of the Kafue River in front of me. I crouched in the shade of a flat top Acacia tree and scanned the far side with the binoculars. I was craving a cigarette, but I decided I would wait until I had found what I was looking for and returned at least to the ant hill at the halfway point. I could see no evidence of any human activity but a glance at the mouth of the river to my right confirmed I was directly opposite Mayuni's camp. I knew from the aerial photographs that the dugout canoes I had seen were hidden on my side of the river approximately a hundred metres upstream. Slowly and carefully, I moved upstream in the cover of the bush. Occasionally I moved closer to the water and parted the reeds, but I found nothing. All the time I watched and listened for any movement; animal or human. I was more than aware of the real risk of a pitfall trap so if ever I was unsure of the surface ahead, I prodded it with a dried reed I had picked up.

I found a small clearing cleverly hidden in the hollow trunk of a giant Baobab tree. The inside was cool and smelt of tobacco and wood smoke. I scanned the compacted earth and saw a cigarette butt half buried in the dust. *Must be the crossing point*. To my right was a huge thorn bush with a tiny, man-made crawl space beneath it that led to the reeds near the river. My entire body was dripping with sweat as I slowly made my way through on my hands and knees. Eventually, I emerged at the reed bed on the other side where I stopped to listen. Apart from the gurgle of the river and the birds, there was no sound.

I wiped the sweat from my eyes and parted the reeds. *Bingo*. Lying in the shallow protected water in front of me lay three wooden dug-out canoes. Spread out on top of them was a mat of dried reeds but this effort at concealment had failed. They were exactly where the drone photographs had shown them to be. One of them had leaked and lay half submerged in the shallow water but the other two were floating proud and were completely dry inside. Lying in each of them were two crude paddles fashioned from branches. *Good*. Slowly and carefully, I turned around and made my way back through the crawl space to the hollow in the Baobab. I sat there in the cool shade for a few minutes as I planned the night ahead. *So far so good Green*. Eventually, I stood and started making my way back using the tracks I had made on the way. It made for faster progress as there was no guesswork navigating the various gullies and thickets of thorn bush. The sun was scorchingly hot above on the occasions I was in its direct light. It was forty minutes later that I found myself at the giant ant hill I had marked as the halfway point. Being mid-day there was no longer any shade afforded by it, so I made my way to a tall Kigelia sausage tree near the river to rest and smoke. There was a breeze blowing in from the south and although it felt more like a hair dryer it had the effect of drying the sweat from my clothes.

The walk back to Kiamba Lodge was long and tiresome in the heat but was once again made easier by my tracks and it was just before 2.00pm. when I arrived at the deck of my air-conditioned room. Once inside I slid the glass doors closed and drank a full two litres of water while staring out at the river. Afterwards, I took a shower being careful not to use any shampoo or soap. I knew from experience that Mayuni had long abandoned using personal hygiene products and I had no intention of giving my presence away by smelling as fresh as a daisy when I met him later that night. Instead, I chose to simply wash off the sweat and I stood with my eyes closed for ten minutes under the blast of 'cold' water from the shower head. Afterwards, I sat outside on the deck in a shaded area to smoke and plan the night ahead. When I was done, I crushed out the cigarette and made my way up the pathway to the main building to find the manager. I found him at the reception working on the computer.

"Good afternoon," I said. "I have a lot of work to do tonight so I was wondering if you could have my dinner brought to my room at 6.00pm?"

"Certainly sir," he replied. "Please make a choice from the menu and I will have the kitchen staff deliver it down to you then."

I thanked him and walked to the dining area to get a menu. Having made my choice, I walked back to the reception to place my order.

"I would like the fillet steak with pepper sauce please," I said. "Rare... oh, and a bottle of Nederburg Baronne as well."

The manager made a note of my order on a pad then looked up at me and smiled.

"I'll have that delivered down to you at 6.00pm sharp sir," he said.

I thanked him and made my way out past the pool to the pathway that led to my room. As I walked in the afternoon sun, I smiled to myself as I thought about my order. *Rare......Bloody even...* I spent the next two hours poring over the aerial photographs of Mayuni's hidden base. I studied the layout in minute detail, so I had a clear picture in my mind of the exact whereabouts of each part of it from the cyanide dump to the ivory store to the hut. In my mind, I pictured my approach from the river to the left of it. When I could study it no longer, I closed my laptop and went onto the deck to smoke and think. The breeze was still blowing in from the south albeit a little cooler than earlier in the day. Afterwards, I returned to the cool of my room to prepare the equipment I would take with me. On the bed, I laid the rolled-up coil of baling wire, the binoculars, a torch, the cutters, the pack of sparklers, a cigarette lighter and the hunting knife. I stared down at the grouped items and contemplated if I would need anything else. Deciding I would not, I packed them into my small day bag and placed it near the doors. I spent the next few hours pacing the room in frustrated anticipation.

Occasionally I stepped outside for a cigarette and sat glancing at my watch as I waited. Eventually, the hour arrived and at 6.00pm sharp, as the sun was starting to approach the tree line behind me, the waiter with the tray of food arrived. I thanked him and carried it inside as he made his way back up the pathway. I knew I had roughly forty minutes of light left so I quickly grabbed the bag, checked that no one was around and left. I headed downstream as I had done earlier in the day. It was easy enough to follow my tracks through the bush for the first thirty minutes, but it then became necessary to use the torch to navigate. The night was still, clammy and hot as I walked but my body and mind were buzzing with anticipation. My long overdue meeting with Mr Dixon Mayuni was finally going to happen and there was one thing I was certain of. He would pay for what he had done. Darkness descended soon after and without the light of the moon, the going was slow and tedious. Eventually, I arrived at the giant ant hill that marked the halfway point. I sat leaning against its base and lit a final cigarette. The moon showed on the horizon as I smoked and began its journey upwards. *Good*. Once again, I closed my eyes and pictured my approach to Mayuni's camp. My arms and legs tingled with adrenalin as the scene played out in my mind. Eventually, I opened my eyes and crushed out the cigarette. *Time to go, Green*. The moon cast a ghostly pale light over the sandy soil as I walked.

On more than one occasion there was a rustling in the nearby bushes and trees, but I persevered regardless. As I neared the mouth of the Kafue, I turned the torch off for my own safety and followed my tracks using the moonlight only. I arrived near the confluence just after 8.00 p.m. and found a place near a tree to wait with a view of both rivers. My body was once again wet with sweat, and I was panting lightly as I sat. The reflection of the moon cut a wavering, rippling swathe of silver across the water and the air was filled with the whistling of the cicadas and the occasional gurgling of the water. Each minute felt like an hour as I sat in silence waiting and watching but there was no movement. Half an hour passed by and feelings of doubt began to creep in and gnaw at my consciousness. *What if there would be no crossing that night? What if Mayuni had moved his camp? This could all be a waste of time.* I shifted in discomfort where I sat and tried to push these feelings from my mind, but they kept crawling back. *Fuck, I need a cigarette.* The murder of my friend Hannes, the slaughter of thousands of majestic animals and the horrific injuries I had personally suffered at the hands of this man; this organization; played on my mind as the minutes passed.

It was at 9.00pm. sharp when I heard the first attempt to start the outboard motor. The sound carried across the river clearly and there were three more attempts before the engine fired and gurgled quietly in idle. Instantly the hairs on the back of my neck stood up and I fought the urge to stand and look. The boat emerged from the reeds on the far side of the Kafue roughly a hundred metres from where I sat. There was no need to increase the revs as the current swung it around until it faced the Zambezi and it cruised quietly downstream. My breathing quickened as the vessel approached and I lifted the binoculars to take a closer look. It was plain to see in the moonlight that there were four men on board. Mayuni was obvious from his thin frame and pale blotchy skin. He stood at the wheel with his hand on the throttle. The other three men appeared to be packing bags and stacking large tins at the stern of the boat. *Cyanide.* I sat in electric silence as the boat passed forty metres from me and entered the confluence of the two great rivers. It was then that Mayuni pushed the throttle and swung the boat to his right to pass the island that lay ahead in the Zambezi. The sound of the motor faded as he passed the island and continued to the drop-off point on the Zimbabwe side where we had met that fateful night not so long ago. I used the opportunity to light a cigarette. The nicotine had a calming effect on me but still, my mind was ticking over at a thousand miles an hour. I sat nervously drumming the fingers of my left hand in the dust as I waited. *Will he return? Will he return alone?* It was exactly fifteen minutes later that I heard the outboard motor once again. I lifted the binoculars and watched for the boat. In the distance, I saw it round the island and power towards the Kafue River. As it drew closer it became obvious there was only one occupant. Dixon Mayuni flicked a cigarette into the water as he passed me and dropped the revs as he swung back towards the reed bed the boat had emerged from on the far side.

"Very good..." I said under my breath.

I felt my hatred coming alive and swelling inside me like a balloon as I watched the boat disappear into the reeds. The motor fell silent after thirty seconds and I knew it was time to go. As I stood, I felt the adrenalin coursing through my limbs. My legs and arms felt like coiled springs as I tracked back to find the route to the Baobab at the crossing point where the canoes lay in the reeds. I found my tracks almost by accident in a gap between the trees. The bush near the river was thicker and the moonlight was almost completely blocked out. Regardless I pressed on through the mottled gloom of the forest until I saw the ominous shape of the giant tree ahead. As I approached the hollow at the base of the trunk an owl screeched in the branches above and flew away to another tree. The noise caused a fresh wave of adrenalin to pump through my body and I felt a surge of energy in my limbs. When I reached the hollow, I got down onto my hands and knees and made my way toward the crawl space under the thorn bush. I moved by instinct as it was pitch black and on one occasion, I lost my direction and tore the skin beneath my right eye on a thorn. I emerged into the moonlight on the other side of the bush and dabbed at my face with the palm of my right hand. It came away bloody, but the wound was superficial and would quickly dry. Next, I parted the reeds to see the three dugout canoes were undisturbed where I had seen them earlier. I stood and moved forward until I was knee-deep in the black sticky mud of the riverbank. The moon had risen, and my surroundings were even more visible than before. I scooped a handful of foul-smelling, mud from the bank and with my eyes closed I carefully smeared it over the exposed skin of my face and neck.

I repeated the process with my arms and legs until I was sure I was fully blacked up. Next, I placed my bag in the canoe and began to push it slowly through the reeds to the flowing water of the Kafue. I slid my body into the canoe when I felt the tug of the main current. It swiftly pulled the front of the heavy boat around and I had to start paddling furiously to correct it. Soon enough I found my rhythm and began the journey across the river. I felt exposed in the moonlight as I made the crossing and the fact that the current was dragging me closer to the point where Mayuni had entered the reeds with his boat did nothing to quell my anxiety. Still, I pressed on pulling at the crude paddle harder and harder to make my landing as far upstream as I could.

After what seemed an eternity, the heavy canoe silently disappeared into the reeds at the far side of the river fifty metres upstream from where Mayuni had landed. I laid the paddle across the boat, closed my eyes and hung my head to listen for any signs of activity. There was nothing apart from the croak of a nearby frog. Carefully I lifted my body from the canoe and dragged it through the reeds towards the shallows. Ahead of me stood a tall Ilala Palm which would serve as a landmark for when and if I was to make my escape. After securing the canoe I waded through the reeds and mud to the bank of dry land. Once I arrived, I quickly crossed the open space to the cover of a thorn bush to rest and wait in the darkness. I was panting heavily, and I wiped a mixture of sweat, blood and mud from my right eye as I waited.

There was a warm breeze still blowing from the South and I pulled the pack of cigarettes from my pocket instinctively. I took a single cigarette out telling myself the wind would blow the smoke in the opposite direction of Mayuni's camp. *Don't be an idiot, Green. Later.* I placed the cigarette behind my left ear and put the pack in my bag. After a minute of sitting in silence and listening for any movement, I decided it was time to move. There was an area of open space that ran along the bank between the tree line and the reeds. Keeping nearer the tree line I began to walk downstream in the moonlight towards where I knew Mayuni had hidden his boat. Again, aware of the grave danger of a pitfall trap I picked up a dry reed and prodded the earth ahead of me regularly as I walked. It was slow going and my nerves were strained to breaking point as I went but still, I persevered. It was five minutes later that I saw the motorboat hidden deep in the reed beds to my right. Mayuni had draped a net of webbing and dried reeds over it but its shape was clear in the moonlight along with the pungent smell of petrol. Glancing to my left I saw the path that led to his camp. It wound uphill into the darkness through the trees and bushes. I knew full well that it lay hidden in the forest less than sixty metres from where I stood. Sensing danger I backed up twenty metres and ducked into the cover of darkness in the tree line. I crouched down on my haunches and quietly removed the hunting knife from the bag. I attached the leather sheath of the blade to the back of my belt and paused to listen. Apart from the soft rustle of dried leaves in the breeze and the whistling of the cicadas there was no sound. Sweat oozed from every pore on my body and my limbs itched from the caked mud and dust. *Time to go Green*. Once again, I left the sanctuary of the darkness and made my way back towards the path to the camp. Leaving the relative light of the clearing I started up the path through the dappled gloom.

My eyes swiftly became accustomed to the low light, and it was clear and easy enough to follow. I was still going painfully slowly, and my nerves were stretched to breaking point as I inched forward. It was when I had travelled thirty metres and the incline had levelled out that I first heard the music. There was no mistaking the tinny distorted guitars and repetitive beat. Dixon Mayuni had turned on a radio and was listening to the local Sungura music popular in Zimbabwe. After another ten metres, I saw the flames of the fire through the trees. Feeling exposed I moved off to my left into the cover of the trees and continued to inch further forward. It was after a few more metres it all became clear. Dixon Mayuni sat alone on a low stool near the fire with a five-litre plastic bottle of opaque beer between his feet. A small transistor radio had been placed near the entrance to his small hut and attached to a car battery. His work done for the day he sat in silence staring into the flames and drinking occasionally. Carefully I got down on all fours and lowered myself until I was lying flat with a clear view of the scene in front. My mental preparations and studying of the aerial photographs had paid off. It was as if I knew every inch of the entire camp. At the far side was a neat stack of twenty-litre metal drums. In the flickering light of the fire, I clearly saw the skull and crossbones label on each of them. *Cyanide*. Also, clearly visible was the ivory stash.

It was as I had seen it from the photographs under a tattered tarpaulin in the centre of the camp. What I had been unable to see from the photographs was the depth of it. The great pile stood nearly six feet tall, and I estimated there must have been at least a tonne of it. It was then that a breeze broke the stillness and for the first time I smelt the putrid stench of rotting flesh. I looked beyond the pile of ivory to see the two huge steel pots used to boil the flesh from the bones of big cats. They were blackened from flames and shiny with the fat of the dead beasts. In the darkness, I shook my head incredulous that anyone could live in such a foul and rancid environment. Totally oblivious, Dixon Mayuni sat staring into the flames of the fire drinking occasionally from the bottle. *Drink deep, my friend. Enjoy your Friday night. It's about to take a turn for the worse*. I watched as he pulled a pack of cigarettes from his pocket and lifted a glowing stick from the fire to light it. I felt a pang of envy as I watched the smoke curl and twist as he exhaled. I lay in silence for the next hour never once taking my eyes off him. In my mind I relived every shiver and spasm of pain I had suffered at his hands. My mind went back to my old friend Hannes who had been so brutally murdered and to the thousands of animals condemned to an agonizing death due to him. My hatred burned inside me like acid as my body itched and the mosquitoes buzzed around my ears. It was when Mayuni had almost finished the five litres of beer that he stumbled forward from his stool knocking the bottle over. Clearly drunk, he kicked it aside and rose unsteadily to his feet. Slowly he walked towards where I was lying, and I instinctively reached for the handle of the knife behind me. Dixon Mayuni paused ten metres from where I lay at the perimeter of his camp and staggered slightly as he undid the zip on his filthy jeans. His body swayed slightly as he relieved himself and once again, I was reminded of his foul smell. When he was done, he turned and lurched towards his mud hut turning the radio off as he arrived. He disappeared through the small doorway and after a few seconds, I saw the flicker of a candle from the inside. *Bedtime, my friend. Go to sleep.* For half an hour I lay motionless in the darkness as I watched the flickering light of the candle in the doorway.

When I was sure he had passed out I slowly got to my feet and approached the camp from the right. There was a woodpile near the fire, and I paused as I pulled a thick fifty-centimetre length of hardwood from the top of it. With the doorway in view, I crouched and paused to wait and watch. I pulled the binoculars from the bag and looked. It was as I had expected. Dixon Mayuni lay on his back in the hut with a candle in a bottle to his right. The white wax had dripped down and covered half of the bottle, but I expected that it would burn for another half hour at least. Leaning against the wall of the hut to his left was an AK-47 assault rifle. He was still fully dressed, and it appeared he lay on a dirty foam mattress with no bedding at all. To his right, near the candle, was a low Tonga stool like the one I had used with the old man Jameson in Lusaka. To his left near the mattress lay a large machete. With the heavy section of wood in my right hand I slowly crossed the abandoned camp towards the hut. When I arrived at the door, I squatted down on my haunches to look inside.

Immediately I was struck by a wall of indescribable stench. The memories of that terrible night on the Zimbabwe side of the river came rushing back as I breathed the foul mix of sour milk and extreme body odour. Dixon Mayuni lay still on his back snoring quietly in the candlelight. Silently I entered the hut and sat on the stool looking down at the man's face as he slept two feet from me. His pale skin was blotchy and scabbed and dried saliva and the opaque brew had formed in clumps at the corners of his mouth. I felt no pity as I sat staring at him. I noticed the crumpled pack of cigarettes that lay next to him, and it brought on an intense craving for myself. With my left hand, I felt above my ear and found the single cigarette I had put there earlier. My eyes never left Mayuni's face as I placed the cigarette in my mouth and reached into my pocket for the lighter. With the heavy log in my right hand, I brought the lighter to my face and flicked the spark wheel. The sound was louder than I had anticipated in the confines of the hut and as I drew on the lit cigarette Mayuni's eyes suddenly opened and stared at me with uncomprehending terror.

"Good evening," I said quietly.

Instantly the man beneath me attempted to reach the machete to his left and sit up at the same time. The move was futile as I brought the heavy log down onto his forehead violently. It landed with a heavy thud and slammed his head back into the filthy yellow foam of the mattress. His head sagged to the right and the blood flowed immediately from a deep horizontal split in the skin to the centre of his forehead. It gathered in a pool at his cheek on the mattress and looked black in the candlelight. Immediately I crushed out the cigarette and reached for the rolled-up length of wire and the cutters in the bag. Placing them on the dirty floor I reached forward with both arms and roughly flipped the man over, so he lay on his front. I grabbed both his arms, holding them together behind his back and bound them tightly with the wire. As I wound the wire tighter and tighter, one of the larger scabs on his wrist gave way and began to ooze a foul-smelling yellow liquid. It left my hands slippery, but I quickly wiped them on the mattress and continued the job.

When I was done with his arms, I used the cutters to clip the wire and moved onto his legs. I repeated the process just above his ankles winding again and again and finally twisting and folding the wire so escape would be completely impossible. Dixon Mayuni lay unconscious and silent as I worked but I was aware that he could wake at any time and would more than likely start howling. Frantically I looked around the interior of the hut for anything I could use to silence him. Inspiration came in the form of a dried-out cob of corn that had been discarded near the door. After clipping the wire to his ankles, I picked it up and studied it. Long since having been picked clean of any corn it was dry and rough to touch. *Perfect.* Using the wire again I bound one end of the cob tightly and repeatedly. This done I got off the stool and straddled the man's back on my knees. With my right hand, I held his forehead up from behind as I placed the cob in his mouth between his teeth as one would do with a bit for a horse.

I turned his head and pulling the wire hard, wrapped it from behind his head repeatedly around the other side of the cob. The wire pulled tighter and tighter, and I was sure at one stage I heard one of his teeth breaking. Now effectively gagged, Dixon Mayuni began to regain consciousness and started moaning softly. Unable to speak with the cob of corn firmly wedged in his jaws his muffled cries grew louder as he realised the seriousness of his situation. Reaching behind me I pulled the hunting knife from the leather sheath. Using my full weight, I kneeled with one leg on the back of his shins and the other on his thighs.

"I don't think you'll be setting foot in Zimbabwe again," I said as I brought the shiny blade down towards the Achilles tendon of his right leg.

Dixon Mayuni's thin body arched in agony as the blade sliced quickly through the thick tendon above his ankle. It made a curious popping sound like a syrup-covered tennis ball hitting a tiled wall. Blood flowed profusely from the deep wound and the foot flopped uselessly on the mattress.

"In fact, I don't think you'll be walking much at all," I said as I repeated the process on his left ankle.

Muffled screams of abject terror and agony filled the small space in the hut as I wiped the blade on the mattress and placed it in the sheath on my belt. I found my own stolen camera equipment lying in a pile of clothes next to the mattress and quickly put it in my bag. Wasting no time, I then stood and grabbed him by his jeans and his collar. I felt a twinge of pain in my lower back as I lifted him up and carried him out of the small doorway. Without pausing I straightened myself and made for the pathway that led through the bush to the hidden motorboat. As I left the moonlit camp and entered the dark of the pathway I glanced down at the man's ankles. His feet flopped uselessly and dripped a steady trail of dark blood in the dust. The frenzied, muffled howling continued, and the man twisted and arched his body repeatedly as I walked. My mouth was dry, and I was dripping with sweat as I arrived at the motorboat hidden in the reeds at the bank. I waded into the mud and threw Mayuni in like a sack of potatoes. He landed with a loud crash, and I heard the wind get knocked from his body. He squirmed on the floor of the stinking vessel as I climbed in and shone my torch on the motor. As it had done earlier, the motor took three attempts to start and with a squeeze of the bladder on the fuel line and a firm tug on the pull start rope, I managed to get it to idle. I jumped from the boat into the mud once again and pushed it out through the reeds into the river. The current pulled the stern around instantly and I had to quickly leap aboard at the bow. We had drifted for twenty metres by the time I made it to the steering wheel, and I wasted no time pushing the throttle and steering out into the main current and turning to face the Zambezi. The moon was bright overhead, and I could see my destination clearly in the waters ahead. The island lay not far from the mouth of The Kafue and I clearly remembered the dead tree stump in the river near the bank where I had seen the giant crocodile basking in the sun.

The current of the Zambezi was strong and fast and I had to push the throttle harder to fight it and get to the top of the thin strip of land. It was with relief that I saw the tree stump protruding from the dark water ten metres from the bank at the head of the island. Its bark had long since fallen away and the pale wood glowed silver in the moonlight. I dropped the revs to idle and rushed to the bow of the boat stepping over the writhing body of Dixon Mayuni as we approached. I glanced at the sand bank where I had seen the crocodile as I tied the boat to the tree stump. It was not there but I had no doubt it would be lurking nearby. With the boat secured I turned and lifted the body of Dixon Mayuni into a sitting position and leant him against the hull. His terrified eyes were wide and glowed yellow. His forehead was shiny with drying blood and a deep pool of it was forming around his useless feet. I sat opposite him, and we both stared at each other for a few seconds. The cob of corn wired into his jaws had distorted his face somewhat.

"I do recall a conversation I had with you not so long ago," I said quietly. "I told you to rot in hell and you said that I would be there first to meet you. Well, I beg to differ."

The man's eyes pleaded with me, and he shook his head frantically as I stood up and turned him round so that he once again lay face down on the floor of the boat. Being careful not to slip in the blood I lifted him from under his arms and held him in a standing position with my left hand. I pulled his bound arms up behind him with my right hand and slipped them over the top of the tree stump. The muffled screams became hysterical; almost rabid as I pushed his legs from the side of the boat. It took some manoeuvring and effort on my part but eventually, I lowered him into the water until it came up to his chest. I left him there, completely unable to move as I paused and took one last look at him.

"Goodbye, Mr. Mayuni," I said as I untied the rope and allowed the boat to drift away slowly.

Immediately I went to the motor and tried to start it. I never saw the crocodile attack, but I heard it as I pulled at the starter rope. It came a lot sooner than I expected. Drawn by the blood it must have started with his legs and a few seconds later Dixon Mayuni bit through the corn cob. The frenzied thrashing of the primitive animal and the blood-curdling screams of the man split the night. I suspect there may have been more than one crocodile because the screaming soon stopped and all I heard was the whipping and thrashing of tails in the boiling water. Finally, I got the motor started and I pulled away from the island and headed towards the Kafue. The reeds were still parted from where I had pushed the boat out and I pulled into them at some speed. The front of the boat crunched on the muddy sand, and I immediately cut the motor, jumped from the bow, and ran up the pathway to the camp. I spent a full hour carrying the tusks from the camp to the boat. As I had estimated, there was close to a tonne of them, and I was completely exhausted when I threw the last two of them onto the great pile in the boat.

I waded through the mud to the stern of the vessel and retrieved the fuel tank. It was still full, and I carefully opened it and walked around the hull as I poured the entire tank onto the tusks and into the bottom of the boat. When I was done, I threw the empty tank back in and retreated a good twenty metres upstream to rest. I sat in silence and lit a cigarette as I stared at the boat with its gruesome bloodstained cargo. When the cigarette was half finished, I opened the bag and pulled the packet of sparklers out. I took a single sparkler and pushed it carefully through the lit cigarette near the filter.

"That'll do," I said under my breath as I turned it in my hand.

I walked up to the boat and ran my left hand down the side of the hull until I felt a crack in the old fibreglass. With great care, I forced the wire at the base of the sparkler into the crack until it held firm. As soon as that was done, I pushed the boat back through the weeds into the main current of the Kafue. The weight of the tusks made it hard at first but eventually, I watched as it swung around in the current and began its journey. Wasting no time, I headed to the bank, retrieved my bag, and ran upstream to where I had left the dugout canoe. It was as I was paddling back across the river that I heard the massive explosion. I turned briefly to see the sky had turned yellow. Satisfied the job was done, I turned and pulled harder on the crude paddle.

# 14

# Chapter Fourteen: Beira, Mozambique

The mid-morning sun burnt the back of my neck, and I pulled my sunglasses over my eyes to counter the blinding glare from the concrete surface of the runway as I walked towards the plane. I had left Kiamba Lodge early in the morning following my 'appointment' with Dixon Mayuni and returned to Ulrika Camp in Lusaka. After booking the flight to Johannesburg for the following day I had slept for eight hours solid only waking at 6.00 pm in the evening. After a quiet dinner, I spent the night studying the second part of Hannes' report on my laptop. Imperial Dragon Trading was a huge company owned by a flamboyant Chinese businessman by the name of Charles Tang. The company had offices and warehouses in the port cities of Durban South Africa, Maputo and Beira in Mozambique, Dar Es Salaam in Tanzania, and Mombasa in Kenya. Their primary business was importing raw chemicals into Africa and the export of granite and hardwood. The focus of the report was, of course, ivory and it centred on the Mozambican city of Beira. My connecting flight there was booked for that afternoon from Johannesburg. The South African Airways flight was full, but it was a relief to step into the air-conditioned cool of the cabin. I spent the two-hour flight further studying the report in preparation for my arrival in Beira. Johannesburg Airport was busy but thankfully I moved straight into transit and made my connecting flight to Beira on time.

Two hours later I closed my laptop and looked out of the window as the plane descended into the outskirts of the port city. From above it appeared to be nothing but a sprawling waterlogged shanty town. A maze of muddy and littered dirt roads crisscrossed the lush green foliage of palm trees and overgrown grass. Rusted corrugated roofs covered the many thousands of dilapidated shacks and filthy buildings. Great pools of stagnant water filled the small fields between the buildings, and it appeared the whole area was close to being submerged. Eventually, the city and the coastline came into view, and I was relieved to see taller buildings and ordered streets. I gazed down at the gantry cranes, fuel storage tanks and shipping containers in the port as the plane banked around to face the airport. Three minutes later the plane touched down and I looked out at the tired 70's style facade of the airport building as we taxied to a halt.

Even at 3.30 pm the heat and humidity hit me like a tonne of bricks as I stepped out onto the stairway and walked down to the tarmac. The back of my shirt was damp with sweat by the time I entered the building and headed for the immigration section. The visa process took half an hour and after I handed over $50.00 a large sticker was placed on a single page of my passport, and I was in. Nearby at the baggage carousel, an elderly Indian man was causing a stir shouting that a large amount of cash was missing from his baggage. Thankfully I had the hard drive in my hand luggage and my main bag had been shrink-wrapped in Lusaka. I walked through customs with no hassle and found a short, coloured man in uniform holding a sign with my name on it.

"Senhor Green?" he asked as I approached him.

"That's me," I replied as he took my main bag.

"Your vehicle is ready, sir. If you would follow me, we need to fill in a few forms and you can go."

With the formalities completed, I followed the man out into the car park and to the waiting twin-cab Toyota Hilux pickup.

"Does this have air conditioning?" I asked as he handed me the keys.

"Yes sir. Obrigado, Senhor Green," he replied with a wave as he walked back to the airport.

I started the engine and waited for the interior to cool as I typed the name of my hotel into the Satnav. Although the grounds of the airport were clean and orderly, I was instantly shocked as I took the right turn that led to the main road to the city. Huge sections of tarmac were missing and there were water-filled potholes the size and depth of paddle pools. On either side of the road, where it existed, there was a sharp drop off of at least a foot and the roadsides were a sea of human chaos with tin shacks, market stalls and thousands of people milling around. Loud music blared on either side and young barefoot children ran around free dodging the many three-wheel auto rickshaws or tuk-tuk taxis. Great steaming piles of rotting vegetables and plastic waste lay in the sandy mud between the haphazard half-finished buildings, and it appeared that the entire area had never seen a coat of paint. Palm trees were everywhere as far as the eye could see. The traffic was painfully slow as the drivers dodged and weaved their way through the many obstacles in their paths. *Jesus Christ what a dump.* It took a good fifteen minutes to reach the main Beira Road which thankfully was a freshly tarred double-lane highway. I took the left turn under a flyover and headed towards the city.

Although the traffic moved faster, the road was full of haulage trucks, dilapidated cars, tuk-tuks and pedestrians. The sun glared in my rear-view mirror and on the many occasions I had to stop I was instantly approached by groups of begging street urchins who glared at the interior of the vehicle and held out their hands in the hope of a coin. On either side of the road were thousands of rusted tin shacks and badly built bungalows many of which had plastic sheeting on their roofs. Piles of empty beer crates, used tyres and planks lined the makeshift shop fronts and great tangled clumps of electrical wire hung from the decayed street poles. Everywhere I looked people were walking and milling around in the heat of the late afternoon.

The outskirts of the city were squalid, and the appalling poverty of the country was clear. Eventually, I entered what I assumed was the border of the city. The buildings grew taller, and I passed various shops, bars, and service stations on either side of the road. If anything, the chaotic traffic got worse as I left the highway and entered the maze of streets and roundabouts of the city. I passed a mixture of grim 1970s tower blocks and old Portuguese colonial relics as I dodged the sea of humanity and the potholes. Not one building appeared to have been painted in the last forty years. All exposed plaster or concrete was stained and blackened by decades of neglect. It appeared to me that the entire city was sinking in pools of dirty water and slowly decomposing in the humidity.

Eventually, I left the thick of the city and entered what appeared to be a more upmarket residential area. The Satnav showed I was near the sea and was in an area called Macuti. The streets were wider, and the buildings seemed better maintained. There was a lot less litter and the roads were relatively free of potholes. After a while, I took a left turn and drove North up the coast road. To my right was the beach which looked clean, and I could see the waves crashing into the yellow sand beyond. I passed the famous red and white lighthouse which I remembered from my youth and eventually, the Satnav informed me I had arrived at my destination. To my left was the Hotel Beira Sands. It was built in a Spanish style with cream-coloured walls and terracotta roof tiles. The individual double-storey villas were set near each other in lush, shaded tropical gardens with Japanese cycads and palm trees. Each villa had a private veranda with a view of the sea through the Casuarinas on my right. The place looked clean and secure. I drove through the security gate after being saluted by the security guard and parked the vehicle. After checking in I left the hard drive in the manager's safe and was escorted down a paved garden path to my villa by a porter who spoke no English at all. The room was like a sauna, and I wasted no time in setting the air conditioner to 22c. The ground floor consisted of an open-plan lounge and kitchen with a toilet to the side. The walls were finished with rough plaster painted in a Spanish style and the floors were polished terracotta tiles. There was an arched doorway with a wooden frame that led out to a small, enclosed veranda with a view of the ocean across the road. The upstairs area had a double bed with an en suite bathroom and another small veranda. The place was clean and tastefully fitted.

"Obrigado," I said to the porter as I handed him a tip.

I opened my laptop, connected to the internet, and turned on the television to watch the news. After ten minutes I opened the door and sat outside on the veranda to smoke. There was a steady breeze coming in from the ocean and the heat of the day had subsided somewhat. As I stared through the trees out to sea, I began to ruminate on the reason for my being there. Having taken care of Mayuni I no longer felt the same burning hatred as I had done although the murder of Hannes still weighed heavily on my mind.

The pain it had brought to his family had been clear. The blatant impunity that Imperial Dragon Trading operated with angered me and the wholesale slaughter of the Elephants and other animals could not go unchallenged. It was, after all, Hannes' life's work. It had cost him his life as it had very nearly done my own. The main priority was that the report was delivered, made public and the main players exposed. It was surely the most important evidence of organized wildlife crime with state collusion ever made. Not only would it expose the main players, but it would also uncover the corruption that allowed it. *So why are you here Green? What more can you do?* It was the same dilemma I had faced the evening before I decided to go downriver to photograph Mayuni and his men. *Surely you would be best delivering the report to Geneva and making sure it is published!* I sighed as I crushed out the cigarette and leaned back into the chair. Far out at sea, a supertanker moved slowly across the horizon. The sun had moved behind the building, and it cast a purple tinge on the edge of the clouds above the sea. Above me, to my left, the fronds of a palm tree rustled in the warm breeze. *You need a break, Green. You've been through a lot. Stay here for a week. Gather more evidence if possible and then go to Geneva with the report. Job done*. With that decided I stood up and stretched. My body ached from the stress of the past few days, and I knew I was exhausted both mentally and physically. I walked back into my villa and locked the door behind me. I was feeling hungry, so I took the walk back up to the reception where I found the manager sitting at his desk. To my disappointment, I was told the hotel offered breakfast only but that there was a pub/restaurant eight hundred metres down the beach. Feeling the need to stretch my legs I decided to walk. The guard acknowledged me with a nod as I left the front gate and crossed the road to the pedestrian walkway near the beach. The tide had come in and the waves crashed repetitively into the sand to my left as I walked. The beachfront avenue was lined with Casuarinas to the left and old colonial houses to the right. Some of them had been renovated and painted and it was clear to me that Macuti had once been an extremely upmarket suburb of Beira. The place had an understated charm and as I walked in the sea breeze breathing the smell of the Indian Ocean, I found myself relaxing for the first time in many weeks.

Charlie's restaurant was set on the beach behind a row of trees. There was a car park near the ablution blocks and beyond that was an open area neatly set with tables and a stage for live music. I crossed the concrete floor and walked into the main pub area. To the front was a long 'L' shaped bar with a dining area to the left. The place was clean, orderly, and well-decorated. Behind the well-stocked bar was a large flat-screen television that was tuned to a music channel. The sea breeze blew in gently through cleverly designed gaps in the wall. To my right, huddled in the corner, were two large Asian men in tight t-shirts and jeans. Both had their hair cut short and spiked with gel. Their muscular arms were covered in tattoos, and they scowled at me briefly as I pulled out a barstool. To my immediate left at the bar was an overweight middle-aged white man drinking coffee and watching the television.

"How're you doing?" he asked.

"Fine thanks," I replied.

"Can you recommend a good beer?"

"Has to be draft Manica," he replied. "We do it in pints."

"I guess I'll have one of those then," I said.

The man called the barman and made the order for me. As the beer was poured, he turned in his seat and offered his hand.

"Charlie Wilson," he said.

"Jason Green, nice to meet you," I replied as I shook his hand. "You the owner?" I asked.

"I am," he replied. "For my sins."

The lager was ice cold and served in a heavy frosted Heidelberg beer mug. It was refreshingly bitter, and it burned my throat pleasantly as it went down. In the dining area to the left was a group of white men eating an early dinner. The bar was empty, and the television was annoying me, so I thanked Charlie for the recommendation and moved to be alone on the far side. I sat there feeling relaxed, occasionally looking out to sea as I drank. The barman handed me a menu along with a fresh beer and a small plate of bar snacks. The Jalapeno peppers were delicious filled with cheese and deep-fried. *Perfect with a cold beer*. It was then I saw the lights of the old open-top Land Rover as it pulled into the car park. Through the trees, I saw the figure of a woman walking over the concrete towards the bar. Her powerful legs were long and tanned and she walked with quick confident strides past the tables and chairs outside. Over her broad shoulders, she wore a spotless white cotton shirt with long sleeves rolled up to just below her elbows. The shirt was loosely tucked into a pair of khaki shorts held up over her shapely waist by a thin leather belt. On her feet, she wore a pair of veldskoens or bush shoes with thin white socks just showing above the heels. She carried no handbag. It was only when she stepped into the full light of the bar that I saw her properly. She was slim and just under six foot tall and if she was wearing make-up it was not immediately apparent. I put her age in her mid-thirties. Unlike the rest of the patrons in the bar whose faces were either red, shiny, or both due to the heat and humidity, hers was perfectly dry and silky smooth. Her skin was a deep olive colour and her nose regal and thin below perfectly formed eyebrows.

Her dark auburn short-cut hair hung in loose natural curls and her neck was long and defined with prominent tendons. She had a delicate diamond-shaped face, but her jawline was strong and determined and her sizeable teeth were perfectly white when she flashed a smile at Charlie as she saw him. It was at that moment that the Asian men in the corner started shouting, laughing and gesticulating towards her from their seats at the far side of the bar. From where I sat it sounded like Chinese. She turned to face them with her hands on her hips.

"Vai al diavolo feccia!" she shouted back at them.

Her outburst was louder than I had expected, and it immediately answered my question. The woman was Italian. She turned back to the bar and collected the mug of beer the barman had poured. Charlie opened his hands in a conciliatory gesture, but she shook her head and walked towards where I sat with an angry frown on her forehead. She stopped suddenly two metres from where I sat and downed a full half pint of beer.

"Everything okay?" I said without thinking.

The woman put the mug back on the bar with force, wiped her mouth with the back of her left hand and turned to look at me. With the light behind her, I could see the outline of her upper body through the white cotton shirt. Her dark eyes were spellbinding, intense and fiery with anger.

"Everything is fine, thank you!" she said in a perfect English accent. "I can look after myself."

I raised my eyebrows and prepared to respond but it was too late. The woman lifted her beer mug from the bar and walked off to take a seat behind me. *Jesus, wasn't expecting that. Sorry I asked.* Feeling suitably admonished I shook my head and lifted the menu to make my choice for dinner. As I was ordering from the barman, I noticed the two Chinese men get up to leave. Both were unusually tall, and their torsos bulged with muscle. *Steroids perhaps?* One of them had particularly bad acne and both had the red faces associated with the phenomenon known as Asian flush. They both glared in my direction as they left, but I immediately assumed they were looking at the woman who sat behind me. I ordered another drink as my food arrived. The fish and chips were superb washed down with the beer and I thanked the barman as he took the empty plate. At that moment the woman returned to the bar near me. She nodded at the barman to indicate she needed another drink. While he made himself busy and without turning to face me, she spoke.

"Sorry for snapping at you earlier," she said.

"No problem," I replied. "I didn't know what was going on is all."

"Hmmm," she said. "Put it this way. We have a few professional differences".

The barman returned with her fresh mug of beer as she was speaking, and I realised that she would soon return to her table behind me.

"Jason Green, pleased to meet you," I said holding out my hand.

She turned and looked me in the eye.

"Gabriella Bonjiovanni," she said as she shook my hand. "Likewise."

With that, she took her beer and returned to her seat behind me. I lit a cigarette and ordered another beer not wanting to push my luck by turning around and talking to her again. Instead, I sat quietly listening to the music and watching the punters as they came and went. I could feel her presence behind me humming like electricity. It was ten minutes later that I heard the chair scrape on the floor behind me. She had finished her beer and was obviously leaving and heading towards the doorway. I felt the urge to say something, but her back was turned, and she was on her way, taking long confident strides as she went. Suddenly she turned and looked me in the eye again.

"Good night, Mr. Green," she said.

I replied without thinking and immediately regretted it.

"Good night, Mrs Bonjiovanni."

She stopped suddenly, turned and raised her left eyebrow in a disapproving manner.

"Miss Bonjiovanni!" she said sternly.

With that, she left, and I sat dumbstruck as I watched her cross the concrete apron outside and disappear into the darkness of the trees at the car park. I drummed my fingers on the bar counter as I heard the old Land Rover start and watched the lights reverse out. I ordered another beer and sat quietly for the next half hour. My mind was numb with exhaustion, but the encounter had been enough to rejuvenate me. When I was done, I paid my bill and thanked the owner Charlie as I left.

The moon had risen, and the night was quiet apart from the constant crashing of the waves to my right as I walked toward the car park. As I moved through the trees and into the darkness of the car park my foot caught on a thick concrete slab and I almost tripped. Through the gloom, I saw a heavy steel trap door in the centre of the slab. It was clearly some kind of underground tank. I shook my head and moved on. The streetlights on the beach road cast a warm yellow glow onto the road up to my hotel. Ahead of me, I saw a lone young man leaning against a lamp post casually smoking a cigarette. He was short and thin, with his hair styled into short dreadlocks. As I walked past him, he murmured something to me in Portuguese.

"No Portuguese. English only" I said as I walked past him.

"Okay, okay," he said. "Cocaine, acid, ecstasy?"

Without looking back, I held up my right hand.

"No, thank you," I said as I walked off.

"Anytime, I'm here boss," he said.

I ignored him and continued my walk. The villa was refreshingly cool, and I immediately went upstairs and took a shower after which I lay on the bed to think. I tried to plan my movements for the following day, but my mind repeatedly went to the woman. *Gabriella Bonjiovanni...Miss Gabriella Bonjiovanni no less.*

# 15

## Chapter Fifteen: Ceramica

I awoke at 6.00 a.m. sharp and for a moment I was confused as to where I was. I sat on the edge of the bed, stretched, and glanced at the pack of cigarettes on the table. Feeling slightly dehydrated from the travel and the beer I poured a glass of water and opened the upstairs doors to look out from the veranda. The morning was humid and misty and beyond the trees, the grey sea churned and frothed as the waves rolled in. Being a Monday, the beach was deserted so I quickly got dressed, locked the villa and headed out for a run. The guard only woke when he heard me pass him at the gate and I walked across the empty road to the sea wall. A section of the wall had fallen away further up the road, so I ran up and crossed the beach to the hard sand from there. I ran north at a steady pace for fifteen minutes by which time my left foot was too painful to continue. Panting heavily, I sat on the sand and looked out to sea. On the horizon were two huge supertankers and to my right, I saw several smaller ships leaving the port. *That's where the ivory leaves Africa.* I took my left shoe off and sat there massaging my foot for ten minutes until I felt strong enough to make the return run. The sun had begun to burn the mist away by the time I walked down the path to my villa. I turned on the television, opened my laptop, and headed upstairs for a shower. After I was dressed, I made a cup of coffee and sat outside to smoke my first cigarette. Afterwards, I spent ten minutes dealing with emails by which time I was starving hungry. I locked the villa and walked up to the reception to find some breakfast. It was served from a buffet on a raised open veranda under a terracotta tiled roof with a view of the ocean. I chose a table at the far end nearest the sea and after eating I sat with a cup of coffee to plan the day.

I had read Hannes' report on the Mozambique operation in detail. The process was relatively simple. The ivory would travel into Zimbabwe on trucks from the copper belt in Northern Zambia. It would then arrive in Beira on the same haulage trucks having been smuggled over the border from Zimbabwe at either Forbes border post or Espungabera further south. The ivory deliveries would take place under the cover of darkness after which the trucks would continue with their legitimate loads of raw copper ingots. Once delivered it would be packed into containers of hardwood for export to China. The company was sending out at least one full-size container of hardwood per week. Each container was thought to have at least 100 kg of ivory concealed within. Any problems at the port of Beira would be quickly dealt with using a bribe known locally as a 'suborno'. Imperial Dragon LDA was situated in an industrial area called Ceramica which was conveniently located on the main highway between Beira and the border with Zimbabwe. Apart from a few grainy photographs of the entrance to the facility, there was only written witness information on their operations. I decided I would keep it simple. Find the premises and take more photographs as evidence. I would also study the comings and goings there to see if there was any more, I could add to the report.

Anything I could do to disrupt the process in the short time I had in Mozambique would also be an option. I was fully prepared to see the Port Authority if necessary and if that was to come to nothing the revised report would still be delivered on time. As I stared out to sea my mind drifted back to the unexpected meeting with Gabriella Bonjiovanni. I shook my head as I finished the coffee and lit a cigarette. *Concentrate, Green. It's time to go.* The sun had burned the mist away and the day was starting to get hotter. I nodded my thanks to the chef behind the buffet and made my way back to the villa.

I packed my day bag with the equipment I thought I might need and left the cool of the villa. By the time I reached the vehicle, there were beads of sweat on my forehead and I sat and waited for the air conditioner to kick in as I typed into the Satnav. There was no record of Imperial Dragon LDA on the Satnav so instead I typed in the word 'Ceramica'. Immediately it showed a large area centred around the main highway as the report had said. I would have to go there and do my best to find the place. With that, I put my sunglasses on, reversed and drove out of the hotel turning left at the beach road.

Soon enough I left the pleasant leafy suburb of Macuti and entered the chaos of the city once again. Although the roads were quieter than the previous day, I found myself cursing on more than a few occasions at the appalling state of the roads and the random auto rickshaw and pedestrian traffic. In the bright light of the morning, the true state of decay of the buildings was even more apparent as I weaved through the chaos.

Eventually, I left the city and joined the new highway I had driven the previous day. The traffic was moving faster, and I soon passed under the flyover that marked the turn-off to the airport. On either side of the road, set in between pools of stagnant water. were thousands of shacks and makeshift shops. All of them were set up haphazardly and selling everything imaginable. After five minutes the landscape opened and dropped away to empty waterlogged fields with scattered palm trees. After five minutes of relatively open road, I saw the first factories on the horizon. I glanced at the Satnav which confirmed I was approaching the industrial area of Ceramica. As I approached, I noticed a side road that ran parallel to the highway. I veered off to the left and slowed down to join it. The surface of the dirt road was rough and uneven and there were large sections that were under shallow pools of water. On either side of the highway were a series of industrial units and open yards. Some were modern and newly built while others were abandoned, overgrown with grass and full of broken trucks and rusting metal. There were workshops, truck parks, and container storage facilities side by side with giant grain storage silos and processing plants. In between these were the ever-present 'bancas' or bars and makeshift shops. I lit a cigarette and slowly navigated the road keeping an eye on either side for any sign of the words 'Imperial Dragon'.

Many of the open yards were stacked with huge five-metre-long logs of hardwood and as I drove, I noticed several heavy trucks arriving loaded with the wood. Eventually, the factories thinned out as I entered what I thought must have been the outskirts of Ceramica and I thought I might have to cross the highway to look at the factories on the other side. Up ahead was a huge yard surrounded by a tall wall built from rough concrete blocks with razor wire on top. The yard stretched away at least 150 metres to the left and the entire length was stacked at least four metres high with giant hardwood logs. As I drove closer, I saw the unmistakable dragon emblem stencilled on the sawn end of each log. It was the same emblem I had seen on the tarpaulin in Zambia at Mayuni's camp.

*Bingo*. Soon enough I reached the corner of the massive yard and I drove slowly parallel with the front wall. Every inch of space behind the facade was stacked high with mature logs and I calculated there must have been many thousands of cubic metres of wood within. The front wall stretched for a good 150 metres before I came to a huge sliding gate at the far corner of the yard. Painted onto the concrete wall to the left of the gate were the words 'Imperial Dragon Trading Mozambique LDA' To the right of that was the familiar emblem of the dragon. I slowed the vehicle as I passed but the gate was clad with sheet metal, so it was impossible to see inside. Outside the gate on the far side was a small dilapidated wooden guard house. The area around it was covered in litter and surrounded by overflowing rubbish bins. A sleepy-looking young man sat inside it clearly sweltering in the heat. Through the gloom of the interior, I could clearly see a rifle leant against the wood in the corner. I craned my neck for a look as I passed the gate, but it was no good. It was clear that whoever was conducting business on the inside wanted it to remain private. Up ahead on either side of the dirt road were a series of shacks and makeshift shops. One of them had a small sign outside which read 'Banca Miguel' There was a pile of beer crates outside and a few cheap plastic tables and chairs under a roof of dried reeds. I parked the vehicle nearby and got out playing the tourist with my camera around my neck. Distorted music blared from a speaker inside the shack. Apart from myself, the only other patron was a thin elderly black man wearing a tatty Bob Marley t-shirt. Both he and the man I assumed was the owner were surprised to see me arrive and take a seat in the shade at a nearby table. The owner delivered a quart-sized bottle of Manica and a raw egg to the man in the t-shirt. I watched as he poured some beer into a glass and then proceeded to crack the egg into it. The man downed the concoction in one gulp then sat back to relax. *A beer omelette?* The owner approached me and said something in Portuguese I couldn't understand.

"Coca-Cola," I said holding up a single finger.

The man nodded and went off into the shack to get my drink. From where I sat, I could clearly see the sliding gate at the entrance to Imperial Dragon Trading. I lifted the camera and adjusted the zoom lens to get a clear picture of the gate and the sign. Not wanting my interest to be too obvious I snapped off a few pictures of the surrounding area as well.

I lit a cigarette as my drink was delivered and sat there watching patiently. It was ten minutes later that I saw a heavily laden haulage truck making its way up the slip road towards me. It was loaded high with giant hardwood logs and its progress was painfully slow as it negotiated the puddles and ridges of the dirt road. The young man whom I had seen in the guard house had obviously heard it approaching and got out to look. The driver of the truck hooted and the guard responded with a wave. Immediately he walked to the gate, unlocked it and began to slide it open. Clearly, the gate was heavy, and he took a good minute of heaving to get it fully open. I realised this would probably be my only opportunity to get a picture of the inside of the yard, so I got up and started walking towards the gate on the far side of the slip road. The truck took a wide turn as it neared the gate to line itself up to enter the yard. The guard busied himself giving hand signals to the driver so he could enter safely. From where I stood, I could see the yard was literally overflowing with thousands upon thousands of cubic metres of wood. Once the truck was in the yard the driver turned left and it gave me even more of a view. In the centre of the yard was a cheaply built factory unit outside which were two dusty-looking cars and a heavy-duty forklift. Behind the factory was a stack of thirty-foot shipping containers. Beyond these were what looked like two small cottages or accommodation blocks. I assumed they were for housing as there were air conditioners on the front walls and a satellite dish on the roof of each building. There were heavy metal gates on the two doors and thick bars on the windows. Behind the accommodation blocks were two large fuel tanks raised on a steel stand. I lifted the camera and snapped off a few pictures. It was then I saw the two Chinese men. I recognized them immediately as the same men I had seen at Charlie's Pub the previous day. I had not noticed them at first as they had been standing behind the truck as it entered the yard. Both men were dressed the same as they had been with jeans and tight T-shirts. Both wore sunglasses and on their belts were holsters with side arms. Upon seeing me with the camera they both started running towards me gesticulating and shouting in Chinese. It was very clear they did not appreciate the intrusion. They both stopped at the gate and shouted at the hapless guard to close it immediately. I raised my right hand and shook my head.

"Sorry!" I shouted.

They were clearly angry and red in the face as the gate was pulled closed. They turned around and sauntered back towards the factory unit satisfied they had sent me packing. I walked back to my vehicle and started the engine. I turned in my seat and looked back at the closed yard as I waited for the air conditioner to cool the cab. My pictures were good, but I felt I needed more. I drove further up the dirt road for a few hundred metres until I saw the point where it merged with the highway. To the left was a rough track that appeared to go off into the swampy bush. There were tyre tracks on it so I assumed it would be passable. I turned left and drove down the road slowly.

On either side were fields and ditches most of which were waterlogged. The going was slow but eventually, the track wound its way around a hillock and started gaining height. The surface was drier, and I was able to increase my speed gradually. I stopped near a small village of mud huts roughly a kilometre from the main highway. A group of small children approached the vehicle clearly excited to see a stranger in their midst. Their excitement grew when I took the drone out of my bag and placed it on the roof of the vehicle. After linking it to the controller and checking the battery was full, I sent it up to three hundred feet. Although I could just see it as a speck in the sky above, I could not hear a thing and I felt confident I could send it over the Imperial Dragon yard undetected. Using the screen on the controller as a guide I sent it towards the highway, and it was soon completely out of sight. When I saw the highway below on the screen, I stopped the drone and moved it to the right. Sure enough, the yard came into view, and I began taking pictures and videos in 4K resolution. It took less than two minutes to get the pictures I wanted and when I was finished, I pressed the 'home' button to bring the aircraft back. The group of children around the car were beside themselves with excitement as I guided the drone down and caught it with my right hand. I showed it to them before putting it back in my bag and leaving the village.

The journey back to the main highway was slow but I made it eventually and turned back towards Beira. From the road, I could just see the logs from the truck being offloaded by the forklift beyond the high wall and the razor wire. With the gate now firmly closed I pulled over and snapped a few photographs of the front of the yard. Satisfied I had enough I pulled off and headed back to the city. It was approaching lunchtime when I finally made it through the utter confusion of the city traffic and entered the peaceful and orderly suburb of Macuti.

As I was making my way up the beach road, I noticed a freshly painted building to my right with a sign that read 'Yacht Club'. I pulled into the car park, grabbed my bag, locked the vehicle and walked in. There was a small cover charge to enter which I paid at the reception, but the staff were welcoming and pleasant. The main area of the club was a long room with a bar counter that ran the length of the rear and faced the sea. The frontage was fitted with huge sliding glass doors that looked out onto a spotless verandah and beach. Although the building was old, the room was modern, breezy, and bright with a tiled floor and colourful furniture. I took a seat at a table in the shade outside and sat with the warm sea breeze blowing over me. There were a few patrons, mostly white businessmen, sitting nearby who were already getting stuck into pints of beer. After ordering one myself I opened my laptop and inserted the SD card from the drone. Even from three hundred feet the pictures that I had captured showed an astonishing amount of hardwood within the yard. Every square metre of available space was stacked high with the massive logs. As I had seen from the gate there was a factory unit in the centre of the yard with a stack of shipping containers behind. I zoomed into one of the pictures and I could clearly see the raised fuel storage tanks behind the small accommodation block.

I spent a few minutes studying and saving the pictures I had taken from the gate as well. Along with the aerial shots I had a clear idea of the layout of the yard. The waiter arrived with my beer, and I ordered an Eisbein and chips for lunch. I closed the laptop, sat back and stared out to sea as I smoked. As far as I could see the operation was simple. The chemicals, including the cyanide, would arrive in containers and be distributed regionally from the factory unit in the yard. The ivory would arrive at night and be stored in either the factory or the accommodation block. From there it would be packed in the containers along with the standard legal loads of hardwood for export to China. Product in, product out. Simple. All this business, the legitimate and the illegal would take place behind the high walls and razor wire of the Imperial Dragon yard. *Impressive operation*. My mind went back to the Chinese men I had seen at Charlie's Pub the previous night and their negative interaction with Gabriella Bongiovanni. The very same men I had seen at the yard earlier. *What was that all about?* My thoughts drifted as I remembered her red-hot anger and her unquestionable beauty. The image of her upper body showing through her white cotton shirt with the light behind it and the feel of her cool dry hand in mine. As I crushed out the cigarette, I shook my head and reprimanded myself for my idle daydreaming. *Concentrate Green.* The food was superb, and I washed it down with another ice-cold Manica. The waiter brought the cash machine and after paying for my lunch I sat and thought about what I needed to do that afternoon. My thoughts went to my flat and my work back in London. It had been a long time since I had left and there were a lot of emails to attend to. The freelance nature of my work afforded me the flexibility to come and go as I pleased but there would certainly be questions from the insurance firm. I glanced at my watch and was surprised to see it was almost 2:30 p.m. I packed the laptop and the camera and walked back through the bright interior of the Yacht Club and out to the vehicle. The steering wheel was too hot to touch at first as the vehicle had been parked in direct sunlight. When the cab had cooled sufficiently, I reversed and headed up the ocean road towards my hotel. As I drove past Charlie's Pub, I glanced at the car park looking for the old open-top Land Rover of Gabriella Bonjiovanni. There were a few modern 4 by 4 vehicles but hers was not there. *Concentrate Green.* I parked the vehicle at the hotel and walked through the ferocious afternoon sun to my villa. I spent the next hour dealing with various emails and after making a phone call to the insurance company in London I opened the front door to sit outside and smoke. The afternoon had cooled down somewhat and there was a steady breeze blowing through the Casuarinas and the Palms in front of me. I decided I would return to Ceramica that night and watch the yard from the safety of the nearby bar. It would surely stay open as long as there were punters, and I was interested to see if any deliveries would take place after dark. Still, my mind kept returning to Gabriella Bonjiovanni and her argument with the Chinese men from the Imperial Dragon yard. *What was her connection? What was their argument about? Was she there for the same reason I was?* I sat there for a good half hour smoking and pondering the many questions in my mind. It was past 4:00 p.m. when I went back inside the villa and took a shower.

I left the volume on the television turned up as I shaved and listened to the mundane repetitive news and weather from Europe. It felt as though I was a million miles away from all of it. *Not such a bad thing Green.* After dressing I grabbed my bag, locked the front door, and headed up the path to the vehicle. I was hungry and there were only two options I knew of for dinner. Charlie's Pub or the Yacht Club. As I drove down the beach road, I noticed the young drug dealer I had met the previous night had taken his usual position under the streetlight. I glanced at him briefly then continued to the car park at Charlie's Pub. The wheels of the vehicle crunched on the sand as I parked under an overhanging Bougainvillea bush. I walked past the ablution block and crossed the concrete floor of the alfresco area. There was a group of white men sitting with scantily clad local women near the drop-off to the sea. A waiter was delivering pints of beer and bottles of wine to them as I passed, and I heard the raucous laughter from the table. *Looks like a party*. I glanced around the pub as I walked in. Apart from a group of youngsters in the far corner and the owner, Charlie, who was sitting in his usual spot by the bar, there was no one there. No Gabriella Bonjiovanni and no Imperial Dragon men. *Disappointing*. The television was tuned to a music channel and there was some godawful 80's video playing.

"Evening, Charlie," I said as I nodded to the barman for a pint of Manica.

"Oh, how's it, Jason," he replied. "How are you today?"

"Good thanks," I replied as I took my beer and headed to the far left of the bar where I had been the previous night.

As I sat down, I heard the opening chords of 'We Built This City' by Starship. I shook my head and drank a full half pint of the beer. It was thirty minutes later when I saw the old open-top Land Rover pull into the car park under the trees. Gabriella Bonjiovanni wore clean white cotton shorts and a khaki bush shirt with the sleeves rolled up. She strode across the concrete floor confidently with her long, powerful, suntanned legs. On her feet, she wore the same veldskoen bush shoes. She cast a brief disapproving glance at the table of revellers sitting outside near the drop-off. It was only when she walked into the pub that I saw the smear of grease across her forehead. Her dark curly hair was damp with sweat as well.

"Don't you say a word, Charlie!" she scolded, holding up her hands which were also covered in grease.

Charlie turned on his bar stool to look at her.

"Not again!" he said with a laugh.

"Yes...Again!" she said with a bright smile.

Her perfectly white teeth were in stark contrast to the olive skin of her face.

"The starter motor, this time!"

She glanced around the pub quickly and our eyes met for a split second.

"Order me a beer, Charlie. I'm going to wash up" she said before turning back and walking off to the ablution blocks.

Her broad shoulders were still but her firm shapely buttocks swayed gracefully, as she walked, and she held her greasy hands at a dainty angle away from her spotless shorts. *Gorgeous and can fix a Land Rover too.* In my mind, it was a confirmation of sorts. The woman was tough, but she was also very much a lady. I ordered another beer from the barman while she was gone. She returned bright-eyed and fresh-faced, and she pulled up a bar stool near Charlie. She drank deeply from her beer and wiped her mouth with the back of her hand. They both engaged in a conversation I assumed was about Land Rover engines although I could not hear what was said. It was clear they were fond of each other although the relationship was purely platonic. Although I tried to mind my own business our eyes met on a few occasions and the effect it had on me was electrifying. *Pull yourself together Green*. Ten minutes later Gabriella Bonjiovanni stood and gave Charlie a friendly kiss on the cheek. Carrying her beer, she walked over to where I was sitting, and I was instantly aware of her expensive perfume.

"Good evening, Mr Green," she said pulling up a nearby bar stool, "How are you today?"

"Hello Miss Bonjiovanni, I'm well thanks. I see you've had some car trouble."

"Yes," she sighed. "Unfortunately, it's a regular occurrence but I love the old girl."

"Looks like a Series 2 short wheelbase. Late sixties?"

"Bang on Mr Green!" she said with a bright smile "You know your Land Rovers."

"No not really," I replied with a smile, "I prefer something a little more reliable and please call me Jason."

She turned to look at me and raised her eyebrows in mock outrage.

"Jason, you are treading on dangerous ground. Us Land Rover purists would be outraged if you suggested any other vehicle. Be warned. And you may call me Gabby."

We both laughed as we drank our beers.

"So, Jason," she said with an inquisitive look. "What brings you to the bright lights of Beira? It's not exactly a tourist city."

"Well, I was on holiday in Zimbabwe and got involved in an accident that put me in hospital for a while. Anyway, I'm all fixed up now, so I guess I'm just taking a break before I go back to London. And you?"

"Oh, I'm a journalist," she said nonchalantly as she motioned to the barman for a menu "Based in London as well. Satellite News Network. We are here doing a feature on the logging industry and the deforestation of Mozambique. Been here three months now."

Immediately my mind flashed back to her angry interaction with the Chinese men from Imperial Dragon the previous evening. *There's your connection Green.*

"You said *We* ....?"

"Yes, I'm here with my crew," she said as the barman handed out the menus. "There are three of us in total, but my male colleagues prefer the bars and clubs downtown. Let's just say the women there are a little more .... friendly."

"Ah, I see," I said as I opened my menu.

Gabriella Bonjiovanni pulled a pair of horn-rimmed reading glasses from the top left pocket of her khaki shirt and placed them halfway down her nose. I watched her as she scanned the menu and for a moment, she reminded me of a bossy librarian. Albeit a very beautiful one.

"Can you recommend anything?" I asked as I browsed the choices on the menu.

"This is Mozambique Jason...," she said as she turned a page, "It's all good..."

"Okay," I said. "Well, I'm going to have the pizza".

"Good idea," she said still looking at the menu, "I think I'll have the same."

"Would you like to join me," I blurted out and instantly regretted it.

She turned and looked me in the eye with the reading glasses perched on the end of her nose and for a split second, I thought I might have over-stepped the boundary.

"Sure," she said as she closed her menu, "but right now I need another beer. What about you?"

"Why not?" I said with relief before draining my glass.

It took twenty minutes for the food to arrive after we ordered. We spent the time casually chatting at the bar about the city of Beira and Land Rovers. I was eager to find out more about her work, but I decided I would wait a bit and create a better rapport with her first. When the pizzas arrived, we took a nearby table, and I ordered a bottle of

South African red wine to wash it down with. I was fully aware she was highly intelligent and fiery to boot so I kept the conversation light. After the waiter cleared the table, I sat back and lit a cigarette. Gabby sat back as well, looking content, and fiddled with the base of her glass.

"Tell me more about your work, Gabby. Must be interesting?"

She looked up from her wine glass and screwed her eyes up slightly as if she was scrutinizing both me and my motives. In that moment she was both frightening and beautiful. She took a deep breath and relaxed.

"There isn't really a lot to tell Jason. I'm an investigative reporter for a television news channel. My assignments take my crew and me around the world. The normal time frame for a good feature is between two and four months. A lot of my work is on YouTube if you search for it."

"Fascinating," I said as I sipped some more wine.

"And what about you Jason Green?" she said with a dreamy half smile "What's your story? What do you do?"

"Me?" I said. "Well, I'm afraid my work is fairly boring. I'm in insurance. Freelance work with a few firms in London."

She looked me in the eye and nodded slowly.

"I think there is more to you, Mr Green. What is your accent? Yours is not a London accent," she said.

"I was born in Zimbabwe. Rhodesia back then. I left after the war." I replied openly.

"I have a distant connection with Zimbabwe too," she said, "My grandfather was killed during the construction of the Kariba dam. He was one of the Italian construction workers stationed there at the time. His body is actually still in the wall. Never recovered."

"Wow," I said, "I had heard that a few people were buried in that wall during the pouring of the concrete."

"Hmmm," she said as she glanced towards the door and took a sip of wine.

"You seemed very upset with those two Chinese men last night," I said.

She turned her face back towards me and looked me in the eye once again.

"Mozambique is a huge country, Jason," she said firmly. "Do you know the eastern seaboard of this country is roughly the same size as that of America?"

"I know it's a big country but..."

"Well, it is," she interrupted, "and up until recently this huge country was almost entirely covered in ancient hardwood forests. Those men from last night are some of the main players in the deforestation and export of this wood to China. The country is being raped as I speak."

*They export a lot more than that Gabby*, I thought. She sighed and went on.

"In the past three months, my crew and I have had more than a few run-ins with those men. They, and the others are violent. They operate with impunity here and it is all aided by massive corruption at all levels of government. It is a multi-million-dollar operation, Jason. Soon this country will be a wasteland and only a few individuals will have anything to show for it. We are witnessing an environmental disaster unfold and I am here to document and expose it."

"I see," I said. "Sorry if I seemed to be prying." Which I was. It was clear she was extremely passionate about her work.

"No, it's okay," she said as she picked up the bill for the food and began writing on the back of it with the pen the waiter had left on the table.

"Our report is almost complete. Another month and it will be done," she said pushing the piece of paper towards me. "If you'd like to see it, come past my place tomorrow morning for coffee and I'll show you."

I glanced down at the paper to see she had written an address on it.

"Now if you'll excuse me, I have to go," she said standing up. "Thanks for the dinner, Jason."

"A pleasure, Gabby," I replied slightly surprised at her sudden exit. "I'll try and swing by tomorrow."

She turned away and left, only stopping briefly to kiss Charlie on the cheek. I watched as she disappeared into the darkness of the trees near the car park, and I wondered if there would be another problem with the starter motor on the old Land Rover. To my disappointment, it started on the first attempt, and I watched the lights as she reversed out the entrance. I glanced at my watch and saw that it was just past 8:00 p.m. *Too early to go to Ceramica Green. One more beer.* I returned to my seat at the bar and ordered a fresh drink.

I heard the opening chords of 'You Give Love a Bad Name' by Bon Jovi playing on the television. A few other punters had drifted in during dinner, but the pub was generally quiet. I looked at the paper in my hand and saw her address was in a suburb by the name of Manga. I folded and pocketed it as the beer arrived. *Well, it makes sense now Green. The connection with Imperial Dragon and the other smaller logging concerns. Her connection to Africa through her grandfather. You have your answers.* I turned in my seat, lit a cigarette and stared out through the breeze blocks at the reflection of the moon on the ocean.

My mind was spinning. Meeting Miss Gabriella Bonjiovanni had thrown me off course completely. *Concentrate, Green.*

It was 8.40 pm when I settled my bill at the bar, thanked Charlie and made my way out towards the car park. The table of revellers out near the drop-off was in full party mode and the women were screeching with laughter as the drinks were delivered. I walked into the darkness of the car park and crouched slightly to pass underneath the overhanging Bougainvillea bush. Once again, I almost tripped on the hidden concrete slab to the right of my vehicle. *Fucking hell.*

It took a moment for my eyes to adjust to the gloom and once again I saw the heavy steel trapdoor in the centre of the slab. *Charlie really needs to put a light up around here.* I thought as I fumbled in my pockets for my keys. The streets of Macuti were quiet and soon enough I drove into the city. Although the traffic was easier there were still many thousands of pedestrians to contend with and it was 9.00 pm by the time I got onto the highway and was able to pick up speed. The road-side bars were thronged with punters many of whom stumbled across the road randomly and on more than one occasion I had to swerve to dodge them. Before long I reached the outskirts of Ceramica and veered left onto the rough service road that led to the Imperial Dragon yard. The vehicle lurched through the potholes and pools of stagnant water as I drove through the darkness. Soon enough I reached the far corner of the Imperial Dragon premises. The interior of the yard was clearly lit by the yellow glow of the spotlights I had seen earlier and the deadly razor wire at the top of the high walls glinted in the moonlight. I approached the gate and the guard house slowly, driving in second gear and I saw a man sitting on a small wooden chair near a fire nearby. The full beam of my headlights was, clearly, bothering him and he lifted his hand to shield his eyes. Near his chair were three empty brown bottles and the rifle I had seen earlier was leaning against the gate. As I got closer, I saw one of the dogs I had seen earlier was chained to a metal ring on the wall of the guard house. It lay in the filthy sand fast asleep and completely unconcerned by my approaching vehicle. As I passed the huge steel-clad gate, I had a good look at the guard. He was much older than the man who had been there during the day and I could see his eyes were bloodshot from drink. The lights were still on at Banca Miguel, and I parked the vehicle nearby and walked in. Apart from two emaciated and incredibly drunk women, the place was empty. Distorted music blared from the speakers and the place smelt of urine. The owner was clearly surprised to see me again and I took the same table I had sat at earlier and ordered a Manica. I fitted the night vision lens to the camera as I waited for my beer and zoomed in on the guard. There was nothing to see that I hadn't witnessed as I had driven up. The man sat on the chair with his back to me occasionally drinking from one of the bottles. I sat there and tolerated the music for another twenty minutes. Eventually, the two women staggered out and headed off into the darkness behind the bar. I watched as the owner began tidying up and collecting the empty bottles and plastic cups that were strewn on the floor. It looked to me that it was very nearly closing time at Banca Miguel. It was exactly 10.00 p.m. when I saw the old guard gather his empty bottles and stand up from his chair. With a heavy limp, he began to walk towards the bar where I sat. He blinked his bloodshot eyes as they adjusted to the light as he walked in, and he stared at me briefly with a confused look on his face. Clearly, the sight of a white man at Banca Miguel was an uncommon occurrence. The man was clearly drunk and unsteady on his feet and he almost stumbled as he crossed the filthy floor to the bar counter. There was a brief conversation that I could not hear, above the music, but the owner took the empty bottles and replaced them with full ones.

I pretended to look at my phone as he walked past my table and returned to his chair and fire near the gate. I sat, waiting, and watching for what seemed an eternity. It was 11:30 and two beers later when I finally decided to leave. The owner had been constantly glancing at his watch and I had the distinct feeling he wanted to close up and go home for the night. There had been no traffic either in or out of the Imperial Dragon yard and the old guard sat as he had been all night drinking his beer and tending to the fire. I paid my bill to the owner of the bar and walked back to the vehicle. It was as I was about to turn the key in the ignition that I saw the lights of a vehicle approaching in the rear-view mirror. I turned in my seat to see the old guard had hurriedly stood and was in the process of hiding his bottles in the guard house. I quickly got out of the vehicle and moved off into the darkness of a nearby shack with my camera. As the lights of the approaching vehicle got closer, I realized it was not a haulage truck but a small passenger car. The driver turned, faced the gate, and hooted repeatedly as the old guard fumbled to unlock the padlock and chain that secured it. The vehicle was a cream-coloured Toyota with the emblem of a dragon on the driver's door. *Easy to remember*. I zoomed in and snapped a few photographs of the car and the driver. His window was open, and his muscled arm hung over the door. I instantly recognized him as one of the Chinese men I had seen at Charlie's and earlier in the day at the yard. There was no mistaking the pock-marked skin of his face. He shouted something incomprehensible and spat at the guard who by then was struggling to slide open the heavy gate on its wheels. I knew that relations between Chinese nationals and Africans were not good but spitting at employees was a bit much. As soon as it was open the vehicle disappeared inside, and the guard began the heavy task of closing and locking it once again. *So, the men clearly live in the yard as you suspected Green.* I moved back to the comfort of the vehicle and sat for another twenty minutes watching the gate in the rear-view mirror. With the gate locked once again, the old man had retrieved his beers from the guard house, taken his seat and resumed drinking and tending the fire. I looked back towards Banca Miguel and saw the owner had locked up and turned off the lights. The night was quiet, still, and warm and I was tired. I glanced at my watch and saw it was just after midnight. *Time to go Green.* I fired the motor and drove slowly through the puddles and dips until I reached the merge with the main highway. After making a U-turn, I drove slowly past the Imperial Dragon yard. The spotlights cast an eerie yellow glow over the massive piles of logs and the smoke from the old man's fire drifted up in curling tendrils. The journey back to the hotel in Beira took only twenty minutes and the streets were quiet for once. The only person I saw in the quiet suburb of Macuti was the ever-present young drug dealer leaning against the streetlight near the beach. Our eyes met briefly as I drove past him and headed to the gate of the hotel. The villa was pleasantly, cool and I stood for five minutes under the shower with my eyes closed, as I thought through the events of the day. I had learned a lot and the pictures and videos I had taken would no doubt be valuable for Hannes' report. I realized after talking to Gabby that the organization I was following was far bigger and infinitely more powerful than I had ever imagined.

I lay back on the pillow with my hands behind my head and stared at the stucco plaster of the ceiling. My mind drifted into random thoughts as I fell asleep and in my dream, I saw a terrified Gabriella Bonjiovanni running through the streets of some nameless city. Chasing her from behind was a giant fire-breathing dragon and I was completely unable to help her.

# 16

## Chapter Sixteen: Gabriella Bonjiovanni

I awoke at 7:00 a.m. feeling refreshed and relaxed for the first time since leaving London. I sat on the side of the bed, stretched and walked to the arched window to open the curtains. The day was misty, overcast and still and I instantly felt the extreme humidity as I opened the window. I walked downstairs and made a cup of coffee while watching the early news on the television. Wearing nothing but my shorts I opened the front doors and sat outside on the veranda to smoke the first cigarette of the day. The street, below, was quiet and the only sound was the steady crashing of the waves beyond the trees. I sat staring blankly out to sea battling to get my thoughts together as I smoked and drank the coffee. *Maybe it's time to take a break, Green. You've been running hard for a while now. Maybe take a day to relax.* By the time I drained the cup and crushed out the cigarette I was sweating so I headed upstairs for a shower. After dressing I turned the television off and left the villa from the back door.

The oppressive humidity appeared to have set in for the day and the staff had set up standing fans on the breakfast deck for the comfort of the guests. After eating I sat back with another cup of coffee and thought about the day ahead. A small part of me was beginning to doubt my reasons for being there. *Maybe you've done enough Green? There really is no point going back to the Imperial yard in Ceramica. Maybe it's time to simply deliver the report and get back to reality?* I shook my head as I realized that returning to the dreary routine of London frightened me more than anything. I pulled the piece of paper from my pocket with the address Gabriella Bonjiovanni had written on the previous night. I stared at it as I lit a cigarette. *You know you're going there, Green.* I thought. *You know it.* The clouds were thick overhead as I walked down the pathway back to my villa. By the time I had responded to my emails and browsed the news it was 9.30 am. *Good a time as any I suppose.* I grabbed my bag, locked the villa and headed up the path to the vehicle. It came as a surprise to find the Satnav recognized the exact address she had written. I reversed the vehicle and headed out through the gate with a wave from the guard who was visibly sweating at his post. It seemed the oppressive muggy conditions had kept a lot of people indoors that day and the suburb of Macuti was fairly quiet. This was not the case as I entered the familiar pandemonium of the city. The route took me through the city and up the new highway towards the airport. It was at the turn-off to the airport that I took a left and entered the suburb of Manga. The road was worse than anything I had experienced in Beira so far. Each side was bustling with people, strewn with litter and the surface non-existent. There were great pools of stagnant water with rusted metal poles sticking out of them warning the motorists of their depth. The makeshift shops and rotten buildings grew out of the mess randomly in amongst the palm trees. At one stage I wondered if Gabby had written the correct address as I found it hard to believe she would reside in such a place. I passed a fishmonger's shop on the right-hand side and saw customers strapping cardboard slabs of frozen fish onto the backs of their motorcycles.

The sign outside showed that they sold all manner of seafood including prawns, lobster, and crab. The interior was bright, fully tiled and looked clean, in stark contrast to the surrounding area. Once again, I was reminded of the reality that both the poor and the rich lived side by side in the city of Beira. It was two hundred metres further down the road that the Satnav indicated I should turn right. The road was wider and less crowded, with trees and walled properties on each side. The surface was better, and I was able to pick up speed and engage third gear as I drove. It was two minutes later that the Satnav told me I had arrived at my destination. On the right-hand side was a tall wall painted in a rustic red colour. The top was covered by a roll of razor wire and in the corner nearest me was a steel-clad gate. From the vehicle, I could see the interior was filled with mature trees. I turned in and pulled up to the gate. Immediately I saw a black face peer through the gap in the steel cladding. The man, whom I assumed was a guard, was obviously expecting me and began to unlock a padlock on the chain that secured the gate. The gate swung open on each side to reveal a lush, manicured tropical garden with a brick-paved driveway. Thick green grass grew on each side and ornamental bananas stood side by side with giant Strelitzias along the wall. The house, which was set thirty metres in, was an old single-storey colonial design that had been renovated lovingly with fresh paint and teak window frames. Further down the driveway was a giant Cashew tree that overhung the house and a single carport. The old short wheelbase Land Rover was parked underneath the shade cloth of the carport. I nodded at the guard as I drove in and parked behind the old vehicle. Once again, the humidity hit me like a brick wall as I grabbed my bag and opened the door. I looked back at the guard who had locked the gate behind me.

"Alem, alem!" he called in Portuguese, pointing further into the garden beyond the house.

I made my way around the vehicles and along the wall of the house which was decorated with African masks and old wooden carvings. Beyond the house, the landscaped garden stretched away through palm trees to reveal a sparkling blue swimming pool with an entertainment area and brick barbecue with rustic wrought iron furniture. All around were large, carefully placed Shona sculptures in stone and cascading terracotta pot plants with glistening Bromeliads and succulents. It was when I had rounded the house and walked onto a tiled patio with more furniture when I first heard it. There was no doubt it was Gabriella Bonjiovanni who was grunting and yelling. The terrible noise was accompanied by a repetitive slapping and thudding sound as if she was being severely beaten. Instantly the hairs on the back of my neck stood up with alarm and the adrenalin flowed in my arms and legs. *What the fuck?* My eyes darted around for the source of the noise for a split second before I realised it was coming from around the far side of the house near the boundary wall. Without thinking I dashed across the tiled surface of the patio and rounded the corner of the house to confront the situation. I came around at speed and almost slipped on the grass before coming to a stop. Gabriella Bonjiovanni stood barefoot with her legs apart and her fists raised ready to attack.

Her faded grey vest was soaked with sweat, and she wore a pair of small blue running shorts. Hanging in front of her from the overhead branch of another Cashew tree was an old brown leather punch bag. Its surface had been patched over the years and it was lumpy and heavy looking. As I caught my breath, she landed a heavy right-hand blow to the centre of the bag. Upon seeing me she steadied the bag, and her face broke into a bright smile. Her dark curly hair was soaking wet, and her entire body glowed with sweat.

"Oh," she said panting. "It's you. Good morning, Mr. Green."

"Jesus!" I replied "You gave me a fright. I thought you were being attacked for a moment."

Gabriella Bonjiovanni raised a single eyebrow in mock disdain before landing a savage kick to the side of the punching bag with the bare foot of her right leg. She was both powerful and lightning-fast and the blow landed with a loud meaty crack.

"Nope," she said gaily as she grabbed a small towel from a nearby chair "Just my morning routine."

She wiped the sweat from her face as she walked past me.

"It's very warm today," she said. "Come inside for some juice."

She walked in front of me tall and confident before opening a large glass sliding door to the sitting room. It was a relief to step into the air-conditioned interior and I closed the door behind me.

"Have a look around, take a seat, make yourself at home," she said motioning towards the furniture. "I'm going to take a quick shower. Two minutes."

"Thanks," I replied as she walked off down a corridor.

The room was airy and spacious with polished terracotta tiles on the floor and quality wooden desks and cupboards. There were African-style reed blinds on the windows and mud cloth coverings on the seats and tables. At the far side was a counter around which was an open plan kitchen. In the far corner was a pile of lighting and sound equipment and on the nearby desk was a laptop computer. I took a seat on a couch near a low coffee table and picked up a magazine as I waited. The flat-screen television nearby was tuned into Satellite News Network with the volume on low.

Two minutes later, as promised, Gabriella Bonjiovanni emerged from the corridor. Although her hair was still wet, she looked cool and refreshed and I saw the glow of health in her cheeks. She was barefoot and wore a fresh pair of khaki shorts and a faded light blue t-shirt with the word 'Juventus' printed on the front.

"Would you like a juice?" she asked. "Fresh pineapple."

"Sure, thanks," I replied as I turned a page of the magazine.

She spoke with her back to me as she opened the fridge and poured the drinks into tall glasses.

"Our report isn't ready yet. We still have some filming and a lot of editing to do but I can show what we have so far. Give you a rough idea of what's going on here."

"That would be interesting. I'd like to see that. Where are the rest of your crew? Do they stay here as well?" I asked.

"No," she replied. "They are set up in the house next door. I think they're working on the edit today."

She walked through and I stood up and thanked her as she handed me a glass of ice-cold juice. She put her own glass down on the coffee table near me and turned around to fetch her laptop from the desk. She returned carrying the computer, sat down next to me on the couch, and placed it on the table in front of us. I could smell the soap on her skin and the shampoo in her hair. Once again, I realised the simple experience of being in close proximity to her was astonishing. It was as if she literally radiated her strength, intelligence and beauty.

"Now then," she said as she pulled the spectacles from her pocket and placed them halfway down her nose.

Using the mouse pad, she minimised a couple of open windows leaving an open media file on the screen.

"Here we are, and remember, Jason, this is raw."

"Yup. Go ahead," I said as she pushed the play button.

What followed was a full half-hour, professional television exposé of the hardwood timber export industry in Mozambique.

Gabriella Bonjiovanni was the face and voice of the documentary that swept the entire country from north to south. The footage included hidden camera pieces of suspect individuals, expansive drone shots of vast tracts of decimated forests and spoken word pieces done by Gabby herself in multiple locations around the country. There was footage of hundreds of containers of wood being loaded onto ships bound for China. All of this had dramatic music in the background and titles throughout. To me, it resembled, if not bettered, most of the features and articles doing the rounds on the major news channels at the time. Although Gabby tried to remain impartial during the segments where she spoke directly to the camera, there was no mistaking the passion in her voice and eyes as she worked. Although unfinished, it was a slick and polished piece of filmmaking which exposed the staggering scale of the industry. Halfway through the viewing she shifted in her seat beside me and our legs made contact where we sat on the couch. I had no idea if it was intentional on her part, but I made no effort to move and neither did she. The sudden contact was like an electric shock, and I found myself having to fight an overwhelming urge to run my fingers across her back with my right hand. Instead, I made a fixed effort to hold my concentration on the film as it played. When the final titles rolled up the screen I sat back with the glass of juice and shook my head.

"Wow, impressive work," I said. "I honestly had no idea of the scale of it."

She turned and looked me in the eye and for a moment I was convinced there was a strong and palpable mutual attraction between us. Her dark, exquisite eyes searched my face, and she bit her bottom lip softly as if weighing up this unexpected interaction. It was both confusing and intoxicating and then suddenly the moment was over.

"Yes," she said as she closed the laptop and sat back. "It's not been an easy assignment and what you see here is just the tip of the iceberg. There are ports all the way up the coast of Mozambique and this is happening daily in each of them. Like I said, it's a disaster. I hate to say it Jason, but China is raping this country, this continent and they are doing it with total impunity. Those men from Charlie's are major players but there are many more".

*Oh, I know Gabby. I know.* She put her head back and drained her glass of the remaining juice. Her eyes darted to the glass in my own hand which was nearly empty too.

"How about another one?" she said wiping her mouth with the back of her hand.

"Sure, thanks," I said passing her the glass.

With that, she stood up and walked back towards the kitchen. I watched her broad shoulders as she walked. The twin orbs of her firm buttocks swayed beneath the crisp cotton of her shorts. Her slim bare feet and her long brown legs striding across the polished tiles.

My mind was spinning from simply being in such proximity to her. I had been trained to read people, to gauge their emotions and act accordingly but at that moment I had absolutely no idea what, if anything, had just happened. *Something did happen Green.* She stood at the counter and poured the juice from the container. What was left only half filled one of the glasses, so she opened the fridge and pulled out a fresh box. She returned to the counter, and I watched as she struggled to open the sealed plastic top. After a few futile attempts, she gave up and thumped the juice box onto the countertop. Her brow was furrowed with frustration.

"Damn these containers are impossible!" she said. "I'll go find some pliers."

Without thinking I stood up and walked over to see if I could help.

"Hold on Gabby, let me try," I said.

She sighed as I walked in and she slid the box of juice towards me on the counter. I knew full well that she was fiercely independent, and I wondered if my offer of assistance had angered her. The box of juice was ice cold and covered in drops of condensation. I picked up a tea towel from near the sink and dried the cap. The plastic seal cracked on the first attempt, and I slid the open box back across the counter towards her without a word. She raised her left eyebrow and gave me a half smile as I stood next to her at the counter.

"Very impressive Mr Green!" she said loudly.

Immediately, all the seriousness of the morning dissipated, and I found myself laughing as she removed the now loose top from the box. She began to pour the juice but had to stop when she began laughing. It was a light, gay sound like the tinkling of bone china at a tea party. Soon enough she shook her head and began pouring the juice once again. I looked at her from the side. Her dark hair was still slightly wet and hung in curls around her face as she filled the glass. Without thinking I raised my right hand behind her and touched the small of her back lightly with my fingertips. The muscles of her back were hard and raised and although she must have felt it, she made no move to stop me. It was only when both glasses were filled that she placed the juice box on the counter, closed her eyes and sighed deeply with both hands on the countertop. At that moment I had no idea what to expect. The memory of her vicious assault on the punching bag was still fresh in my mind and I half expected her to turn and slap me in the face, or worse. Without opening her eyes or turning to face me she slowly leant into me as my hand travelled around her waist. Once again, I smelt the shampoo in her hair as she slowly lifted her face to mine. Suddenly her right arm shot around my neck, and she pulled my head towards hers. Her lips were moist and soft, and her mouth tasted of toothpaste and pineapple juice.

Her tongue flicked and probed against my own and her breathing quickened, and she fumbled as she tried to untuck my shirt. My own hands moved under her t-shirt and ran up her bare back. Her skin was cool and smooth, and I could feel her heart beating as I pulled her closer to me. Her back arched and I felt her firm breasts against my chest. She pulled at my shirt frantically until it was free and then paused to lift it over my head before tossing it on the floor. Her breathing was heavy and frenetic as she ran her hands over my back, pulling me towards her as we kissed. With my left hand holding her close I ran my right hand up under the front of her t-shirt and held her full but firm breast. She gasped as I squeezed her nipple, and she reached behind her neck to lift her own shirt over her head. Her nipples were dark brown and perfectly formed and she pulled my head down to them and moaned as I sucked them. With my right hand, I rubbed her shorts between her legs to find she was hot and wet and with each movement she gasped loudly. Before I knew it her khaki shorts dropped to the floor leaving her wearing nothing but a white G-string. I cupped her hard, tanned buttocks in my hands, lifted her onto the counter and kissed her again. She leant back and inadvertently knocked both glasses of juice off the counter to smash on the tiled floor behind. Gabriella Bonjiovanni leaned back with her elbows on the counter and closed her eyes with her head slightly turned. Her damp hair hung over her broad shoulders and her tanned breasts rose and fell with each breath. I gently pulled the G-string from her waist and let it fall onto the floor. Slowly I got down on one knee and parted her legs. Starting at her knee I kissed her left inner leg moving forward slowly. It was when I was only five inches away, that she sat forward, grabbed my head, and pulled me towards her. She held my head in place by holding on to my hair as my tongue darted in, out and around her. Her moans grew louder and louder until her body shook and her powerful thighs tightened around my head squeezing with such force that I had to physically pry them apart with my hands. Seconds later, her entire body began to convulse, and I stood and pulled her back towards me to kiss her. With my left hand, I unbuckled my belt and dropped my trousers to the ground.

"Hurry.........hurry!" she said panting uncontrollably.

Gently I pushed her back, so she once again rested on her elbows. I gripped her waist and shifted her body slightly to allow me to enter her. Her body felt molten hot, tight, and wet around me as I pushed myself inside her.

"Oh My God....," she said to herself as her head sagged back exposing the tendons in her neck.

I held her legs up by the back of her knees and moved with a deliberately gentle motion until she gasped once again and sat up wrapping her arms around my neck.

"Bedroom......bedroom....now," she panted in my ear.

With her arms around my neck and with our bodies still linked, I lifted her body up by her waist and buttocks and turned to carry her down the corridor behind me. Carefully I let her down onto the white Egyptian cotton duvet and continued but this time harder and faster. Within a minute she pushed my left shoulder and manoeuvred her body around until I lay on my back with her sitting on top of me. I cupped her breasts which hung above me and looked up to her face, but her eyes were screwed shut in intense concentration. Faster and faster, she rode in a primal, almost animal rhythm, until I could control myself no longer.

"Gabby ... stop," I said.

"No!" she cried, and I knew from the shuddering vibration inside her that she too was in full orgasm.

It was as if we were swept over by an avalanche. Wave after wave of powerful, all-consuming spasms swirled and enveloped us until our breath finally slowed and Gabriella Bonjiovanni lay still on top of me. I could feel the small, random contractions of her body on my own like a gentle massage. I drew my arms around her and squeezed her against me tightly. I knew at that moment I would never want to let her go.

It was a full ten minutes later that she sleepily shifted from her position and lay with her head on my right shoulder.

"Well, well Mr Green, that was unexpected," she said with a hint of mischievous humour.

"It certainly was," I replied.

She sighed and ran her hand across my chest.

"I need to get away," she said dreamily. "This assignment has really affected me. More so than any other I have been on."

"I hear you," I replied, "Beira isn't really a holiday destination, is it?"

"Well," she replied thoughtfully, it does have its charms and some good people. But no, it's not really a holiday town at all."

"Where would you like to go, Gabby?" I asked as I traced a finger up her bare back.

"Hmm," she mused "I would really like to get down to Vilanculos. I hear it's beautiful and it's only five hundred kilometres from here."

"I've never heard of it," I said "But the idea of getting away sounds good to me. I've had a torrid time myself. What with the accident."

She lifted herself onto her left elbow and looked me in the eye.

"You mentioned that. What happened Jason?"

I had to think quickly. Our reasons for being in Beira were too similar and I certainly didn't want to let her know that I was watching the very same men she had confronted at Charlie's.

"I was on a trip in the Zambezi Valley in Zimbabwe," I said. "There was a problem with my boat, and I ended up getting attacked by a crocodile. I spent a month recovering in a hospital in Lusaka."

I lifted my left leg to show her the scarring.

"Oh my God!" she said sitting up to look closer, "that's insane!"

"It was pretty gruesome." I said as I gently pulled her back onto my shoulder, "Anyway, it's healed up well. Now tell me about Vilanculos. If you can get some time off, we can go. I have nothing keeping me here and a road trip sounds good. Just not in your Land Rover."

She lifted her head and frowned at me with mock horror.

"Mr Green!" she said. "How dare you bad mouth my beautiful old girl?"

I smiled at her as she sat up once again with her legs crossed on the bed. Her breasts hung full and round with her dark nipples pointing at a slightly upward angle.

"My crew will be busy with this edit for the next five days or so," she said seriously, "Are you serious about this road trip, Jason?"

"I've never been more serious, Gabby. Like I said, it's been a tough few weeks and a break with you sounds really good."

"Let me go get my laptop. We can take a look."

She leapt from the bed with youthful exuberance and walked shamelessly naked out of the room and down the corridor towards the lounge. It was clear she was completely confident in her own skin. *And for good reason*. She returned with the computer and sat once again cross-legged on the bed.

"Now then." she said as she moved her finger on the mouse pad "Let's have a look at Vilanculos."

I lifted myself up and rested on my elbow to see the screen. It turned out Vilanculos was a small coastal town in the Inhambane province of Mozambique. It is the gateway to the Bazaruto Archipelago of islands which is a national park. Preserved by civil war for decades from the ravages of tourism and development, the town and surrounding islands were relatively unspoilt and from the pictures I saw it looked like a veritable paradise. Endless deserted white beaches surrounded by crystal clear azure waters that were perfect for scuba diving and deep-sea fishing. We browsed several local hotels until we found one with private villas set among the trees above the best beach in town.

"That looks good," I said.

"That looks amazing!" she replied.

"So, call them now Gabby," I said lying back on the pillow.

"Now?" she said, "When do you want to go?"

"I want to go today. As soon as possible," I said.

"Are you serious Jason? We just, up sticks and go today?"

I reached over and ran my hand down her bare suntanned waist.

"Call them, Gabby. Book it. Let's go today..."

"Ha!" she cried in delight as she reached over to the bedside table for her phone "Okay!"

I lay and listened as she made the call to the resort. It turned out that it was a quiet time of year for tourists and several villas were free.

When asked how many nights the booking was for, she glanced at me for confirmation.

"Oh, I think four or five nights," she said into the phone.

I nodded, to confirm and the booking was made. Gabby hung up and clapped her hands three times with glee.

"I will need to go and tell my crew."

"All I need is to go to my hotel and pick up my bag and we can go," I said.

She lay down next to me once again and looked me in the eye.

"Not so fast, Mr. Green," she whispered as she ran her hand down my chest, over my stomach and under the sheet.

# 17

# Chapter Seventeen: Road Trip

After a quick shower we dressed, and I waited in the lounge while Gabby went next door to tell her colleagues about our trip. She returned with a spring in her step and disappeared into the bedroom to pack her bag. She came out a few minutes later pulling her bags and we both walked out into the sweltering heat of the car park. I put her bags in the back and started the vehicle while she had a quick word with the guard at the gate. The drive through the city was slow but the chaotic traffic did nothing to dampen our spirits and the drive was filled with conversation and laughter. Gabby walked with me to my villa and waited in the lounge while I packed my own bag. After a quick conversation with the manager, I loaded the vehicle and we drove back through the gates and headed towards the highway. It was only as we left the city and entered the industrial area of Ceramica that Gabby became quiet and began to point out the many hardwood storage yards.

"Look Jason," she said. "Look at all that wood...millions of cubic metres."

"Yes, I know," I said truthfully.

It was when we approached the Imperial Dragon yard on the left-hand side that she fell silent, and I watched as she turned her head to stare at the entrance as we passed it. I felt a pang of personal guilt at my own knowledge of what was transpiring behind its tall concrete walls and razor wire. Thirty seconds later we left Ceramica and the flat landscape opened up in front of us. The jovial mood returned as I engaged fifth gear and the cheerful conversation resumed. The road was good, and we passed through numerous low-lying towns and villages before crossing the Pungwe River. My mind went back many years to when I had crossed the very same river on foot with Hannes Kriel. The surrounding landscape was flat, green and waterlogged and it was only after forty-five minutes that the road began to gain altitude and the hills appeared on the horizon. It was exactly one and a half hours after leaving the city of Beira that we arrived at the small trading post of Inchope. The sides of the road were lined with traders selling everything from second-hand clothes to fridges and cookers. Loud music blared from the shopfronts and vendors hustled with giant bowls of fruit and bread for the business of the truckers. I almost missed the small, faded road sign on the left that indicated the turn-off to the capital city of Maputo. We took the turning and soon enough left the bustling disarray of the small town. The road was a single-lane highway that looked like it hadn't been maintained in a while and before long we came across a sign that showed it was exactly four hundred kilometres to Vilanculos.

"That's not too bad," I said, "four hundred kilometres."

"No problem," she said with a smile.

The sun-faded road twisted through the overgrown green bush and headed downwards through the hills. There was much less traffic and there was a distinct feeling of isolation as I took the bends. Soon enough we came across a small town by the name of Muda and I stopped the vehicle at a nearby 'banca' to get some cold drinks. The afternoon sun was fierce on my shoulders as I crossed the hardened red soil on the roadside and walked into the shade of the shop. The owner was surprised to see a white face but clearly understood my pointed requests for cold bottled water, Cokes, and beers. Gabby helped me offload my shopping and put it behind the passenger seat into a cooler box she had brought. She kept two ice-cold Manica beers up front which hissed as she opened them. I put the vehicle into gear and sped off.

"Cheers Mr. Green," she said with a mischievous smile as she handed me a can.

"Cheers to you Miss Bonjiovanni," I replied as I took it.

The cold beer tasted good and for the first time in ages, I felt relaxed and upbeat. The horrors, of the past weeks were fading and I felt a certain exhilaration and excitement at the prospect of heading into parts unknown. Gabby, looking breezy and carefree, took her shoes off and put her bare feet up on the left-hand side of the dashboard near the air conditioning vent. She gazed out through her sunglasses at the landscape with a half-smile as she sipped her beer. I glanced at her and in that moment, I felt like I had known her for years. *Life is good Green. Life is good.* The conversation only stopped when Gabby decided to turn the radio on and find a station. She settled on L.M. Radio broadcasting out of Maputo. The tunes were upbeat old, easy-listening classics and at times we both sang along and laughed at each other's singing skills. The casual, laid-back atmosphere continued for an hour and a half as we dropped altitude once again and bottomed out at a large one-street town by the name of Muxungue. Along with the usual bancas and shops, the road was lined with thousands upon thousands of pineapples. It was obvious there was a plantation nearby. I pulled the vehicle over to the left-hand side of the road and immediately it was surrounded by vendors vying for a sale. I bought a pineapple similar in size to a football along with four tubular bags of roasted cashew nuts. Gabby placed the huge fruit on the back seat as I edged through the sea of disappointed vendors and drove back onto the tarmac. It was when we were leaving the town that the soldier stepped into the road. He wore the grey camouflage of the Mozambican army and carried an AK47 assault rifle. He stood in the centre of the road and calmly waved me down as I approached.

"What now?" I said under my breath.

"I have no idea," Gabby replied.

The young man saluted and smiled as I stopped and opened my window.

"Boa tarde senhor," he said with a smile.

"Good afternoon," I said.

"Oh, sorry sir," he said in perfect English, "I am asking for a lift to the Save River please?"

"How far is that?" I asked.

"It is exactly one hundred kilometres, sir," he replied.

I glanced at Gabby who smiled and raised her eyebrows.

"Sure," I said, "jump in the back."

"Obrigado senhor," he replied gratefully as he opened the door behind me and sat down.

I watched the young man in the rear-view mirror as he placed his rifle carefully against the seat and pulled out his cell phone. He sat in polite silence as we left the small town and entered the low-lying scrubby bush once again. Almost immediately the surface of the road deteriorated. Large potholes began to appear here and there and then more frequently. Some of them were small and shallow but many were massive and deep with sharp edges that would rip a wheel from an axle if hit at any great speed. This slowed us down significantly as I wove the vehicle around them. At some points, the road completely disappeared, and I was left to drive a stony undulating mess through the bush. I learned later that this section of road was until recently a hotbed of Renamo rebel activity. The militant political movement had attacked several vehicles in the previous years, and this was soon evident when we passed a shot-up and burned bus on the side of the road. Unlike the rest of the country, there were few dwellings or huts there. The trees were taller and the bush thicker. Our progress was painfully slow, and it was a good two hours later when we finally crested a hill and saw the massive concrete structure of the suspension bridge below.

"Ah, we have arrived sir," said the soldier behind me, "if you could drop me just before the bridge, please."

"No problem," I said as I approached.

We dropped him at a small building on the left with some other soldiers who were stationed there guarding the bridge. He thanked us, smiled, and saluted in gratitude. The sun was setting, and it cast a yellow glow over the expansive waters of the river below. The sand banks on either side cut random abstract shapes into the waters.

"It's beautiful," said Gabby as she gazed out of the window.

"It certainly is," I said, "and not too long from here."

After a brief stop for fuel, we set off again into the now fading light. The road was as bad as it had been before the bridge, and it was a challenge to avoid the headlights of the heavy haulage trucks and buses that thundered in the opposite direction. Still, it did nothing to dampen the mood and the conversation and laughter continued through the darkness. The road began to improve slightly and soon we came across the turn-off to the tiny coastal fishing village of Inhassoro. In the headlights, I saw the many signs for the various luxury lodges and small hotels that catered to the tourists.

"I have seen pictures of that place," said Gabby as we passed. "It looks good too."

"It's a pity we're arriving so late," I said. "But I guess all will be revealed tomorrow morning."

"Hmm," she said, "I can't wait. But I'm enjoying the drive anyway."

I turned and looked at her with a smile.

"Me too, Gabby," I said.

It was forty minutes later when we came across the turn-off to Vilanculos on the left-hand side. There was a fair amount of human traffic milling around the buildings and shacks on either side of the road in the darkness. I took the corner and soon we left the settlement and entered the darkness once again. The road surface was better, and I was able to get some speed as we drove.

"It's not far from here Jason," said Gabby as she looked at a map on her phone. "I'll tell you when we're approaching the turn-off."

Lights and buildings began to appear out of the darkness as we approached the outskirts of Vilanculos.

There were a few concrete speed humps in the road which I had to slow down to pass. Soon enough we came across a blue sign on the right that read 'Sand Dollar Lodge 8 KM' with an arrow.

"This is it...." said Gabby "We're almost there."

I took the corner onto a sandy dirt road and drove in third gear through the darkness. Hundreds of palm trees lined the road in the headlights as we travelled. I opened the window and smelt the ocean in the warm air. The road turned and undulated through the groves of palm trees until we came to another sign for the lodge. I took a left turn and drove until I reached a guard house with a large sliding gate. On it was a sign with the name of the lodge. A guard came forward with a clipboard. He was clearly expecting us, and we were signed in instantly. He told us the reception was closed but the manager was at the restaurant and was expecting us. We drove through manicured gardens of palms and cashew nut trees until we saw what we assumed was the restaurant. The building was thatched with heavy reeds in true Mozambique style and was situated behind a white wall with an arched entrance. We heard soft music playing from the bar as we walked through. To our left was a large expanse of dark wooden decking that surrounded a sparkling blue swimming pool cleverly lit with underwater lights. Although we could not see it, there was a steady breeze from the ocean below and the mature cashew nut trees that the decking surrounded were decorated with fairy lights.

"Wow," said Gabby as she took it all in.

We walked into the bar area and were greeted by a smartly dressed elderly barman with a name tag on his shirt that read 'Alphonse'.

"Welcome to Sand Dollar Lodge," he said. "We usually prepare a welcoming cocktail for our guests. Shall I prepare two?"

I glanced at Gabby who nodded enthusiastically.

"Why not?" I said as we took our barstools. "Thanks, Alphonse."

Soon after we were given our colourful drinks, we were approached by a cheerful young Zimbabwean woman with short blonde hair. She introduced herself as the manager and welcomed us as well. She told us one of the guards would direct us to our 'Casa' when we were ready and to walk back to the restaurant which was situated behind the bar for dinner. She handed me a key and said goodnight.

By the time we had finished our drinks a few other guests had made their way into the bar and pool area. The atmosphere was tranquil with the mellow lighting, the soft music and the smell of salt on the breeze. We found the guard waiting for us beyond the arch in the car park and he walked in front of the vehicle carrying a truncheon as we drove slowly to our lodgings. The 'Casa' turned out to be a massive Indonesian-style thatched building with raised wooden floors and an open-plan kitchen/lounge. We entered through the back door and Gabby walked around happily opening wooden window shutters and doors as I unpacked the vehicle.

"This is amazing!" she said from the veranda as I walked in with her bags. "Look at this, Jason!"

Far away from the smog and smoke of the city, the moon had risen over the Bazaruto Archipelago. I walked onto the veranda to see a short stretch of manicured lawn that led to the drop-off to the beach. Below were clumps of rustling palm trees and beyond the pale silver sand I could see the ocean stretch away towards the islands.

"It certainly beats Beira," I said as I ran my hand lightly up her back.

"Hmm," she said softly before turning to look at me, "I'm starving, let's go have some dinner."

We walked slowly through the trees and past the lawns on the flat sandy road back to the restaurant. Not wanting to be confined indoors we opted for an outside table on the decking near the pool. That night we dined on baked crab followed by prawns in a cream sauce with a a bottle of white wine to wash it down. Gabby's voracious appetite was matched only by her fervour in the bedroom when we returned to our Casa. It was when she was finally asleep, and I could only hear the whirring of the fan above the bed and her soft breathing on my neck that I got up and opened the wooden shutter doors that led from the bedroom to the veranda. With a towel around my waist, I sat on the bannister, lit a cigarette and stared out onto the calm moonlit ocean. In the swathe of moonlight that cut across the water, I saw the distant shape of a dhow that had been anchored for the night on a sandbank. I felt content and peaceful for the first time in ages. *Life is good Green. In fact, right now it couldn't be better. Relax and enjoy yourself.* At that moment I had absolutely no idea how dreadfully wrong I was.

# 18

## Chapter Eighteen: The Bazaruto Archipelago

I awoke to the sound of the birds in the trees nearby. It took a while to remember where I was and when I glanced to my right, I saw that Gabby had gone. With the overhead fan still whirring above me I got up on to one elbow and looked around. Her bag was open where I had left it near the dressing table. *Maybe in the shower?*

"Gabby?" I said feeling a little confused.

I heard footsteps on the wooden floor coming from the lounge followed by the squeak of the door being pushed open. Gabby wore a dark blue sarong over her naked body. Her curly hair was still tussled from sleep, but the brilliant white of her smile was in stark contrast to her tanned skin. In her hands, she held two steaming mugs of coffee.

"Good morning, Mr. Green," she said as she handed me a mug. "You are not going to believe this. Come and see..."

I watched as she walked to the bedroom doors, unlocked them, and swung them open. The sudden influx of daylight caused me to blink a few times. She walked to the edge of the veranda and placed her mug on the bannister. She turned back to face me and raised both arms in the air in a gesture of delight.

"Well....Come on!" she said impatiently.

I got up, wrapped a towel around my waist and followed her out carrying my mug. It was only when I reached the doors that I saw the truly staggering beauty that was spread out before me. Thick green grass surrounded the Casa and stretched out for twenty metres to the drop off which was steep and covered with red and yellow Bougainvillea bushes. On either side of the building were mature cashew trees with grey lichen growing on the bark of their thick trunks. Beyond the drop-off, at the sea level, was a wide grassy glade on which stood a long stretch of mature palm trees heavy with fronds and coconuts. Beyond that, the perfectly yellow sand undulated and stretched out to calm channels of crystal-clear water with colours that changed from sparkling jade to deep turquoise according to the varying depths of the water. With the tide out the channels extended away into the distance until their colour became a solid dark blue as the ocean became deeper towards the distant islands. The cloudless azure sky was perfectly clear, and a gentle constant breeze blew inland. To the left, a group of tourists rode down the beach on an early morning horse safari while to the right a group of three brightly painted dhows lay on the sand being readied for a day of fishing.

"My, my," I said sipping my coffee. "Will you take a look at that?"

Gabby stood at my side, put her right arm around my waist and kissed my cheek. We stood drinking coffee and admiring the view for five minutes until I felt the nipple of her naked breast harden under her sarong on my side.

"It's beautiful, Jason," she whispered as she slowly pulled me back towards the bedroom.

An hour later and after a shower I sat under the thatched shade of the veranda and checked my emails on my laptop while Gabby busied herself inside. Thankfully there was nothing of much importance and I closed it to watch the view instead. Gabby appeared through the front doors carrying a heaped plate of freshly cut pineapple. Her hair was wet, and she wore the same blue sarong with what looked like a bikini underneath. On her slender, tanned feet she wore light leather thong sandals and I realised this was the first time I had seen her without her veldskoens and socks. The fruit was crisp, juicy, and cold as I had put it in the fridge when we had arrived.

"This is like pure sugar," I said after finishing a thick piece.

"Mm, delicious," she replied with a mouth full of fruit before covering her mouth and laughing with embarrassment.

That morning we took a drive into the small town of Vilanculos. The sandy road took us past the tiny airport and through a charming suburb of thatched huts and palm trees until we reached the actual town itself. The main street ran parallel to the coast, and we drove in the baking heat until we reached the harbour. With the tide still out, we drove around the entire curved length of it and made mental notes of the many fancy hotels and restaurants. Unlike Beira, this was a tourist destination and many of them came from all over the world for the renowned fishing, diving, and beaches.

After a good bit of sightseeing, we ended up at a small shopping mall opposite a supermarket. Gabby went shopping in the mall while I went to pick up some supplies in the supermarket. We met twenty minutes later at a trendy cafe at the edge of the mall and sat down for some iced tea. Gabby had purchased a white cotton beach frock which she eagerly pulled out to show me. The owner of the cafe approached us and introduced himself. He was a rakishly thin old English hippy by the name of Sebastian. His long, white, wispy hair and beard clashed with his shrivelled skin which was tanned to the colour of polished mahogany. The man was friendly and at the end of our conversation, he handed us a few brochures for restaurants and activities in and around the town.

I was immediately interested in a brochure advertising a place near the harbour by the name of Baobab Grill and Pub. The glossy flyer showed it was open seven days a week and the pictures of the food were enough to convince Gabby immediately.

"Let's go now," she said decisively.

The restaurant was situated on the beach within the harbour. The drive down to the car park was steep and sandy but we made it without any problems. Being a popular venue several vendors had set up small stalls and displays on the beach nearby. Gabby stopped and picked up an ankle bracelet made from tiny white shells and bark string which she tied on her right ankle immediately. We walked through the thick sand to the restaurant which was set under a wavy concrete roof with tables and umbrellas at the front. We took a table in the shade near the bar and ordered ice-cold beers to cool us down. For lunch, we shared a crab salad followed by catch of the day with chips and garlic sauce. We sat in the breeze drinking beer and watched as the tide came in and the far-reaching sands of the harbour began to fill with crystal clear blue water. To our left, a group of young tourists were kite surfing in the shallow channels nearby. They shouted with glee as the brightly coloured kites sped across the perfectly blue sky. I pulled the brochures from my pocket and spread them on the table in front of me. Gabby's attention was drawn to one by the name of 'Dugong Dhow Safaris' The picture on the front showed a perfectly white and completely deserted beach fringed with leaning palm trees. On offer were either day trips or two-night stays on the nearby Benguerra Island.

"Look at this Jason," she said with a look of awe. "Can we go?"

I picked up the brochure which included directions to the location of the company offices. According to the map they were situated not far from where we sat.

"Sure," I said, "no harm in looking. Let's finish our beers and go visit them."

For the first time ever, Gabby held my hand as we walked across the sand back to the vehicle. I looked at her briefly and she smiled back from behind her sunglasses. This was a very different side to Gabriella Bonjiovanni the hard-nosed and fearless journalist. This was the feminine, carefree, and joyous side I had always suspected was hidden beneath her hard exterior. The drive to the offices of the dhow safari company took us around the harbour to a turn-off near the port authority. The road was rough and sandy but eventually, we arrived and parked under a rusted sign that read 'Dugong Dhow Safaris' We were greeted by the manager, a young South African man with short ginger hair by the name of Dave. Obviously surprised by our sudden arrival he immediately showed us into his air-conditioned office and opened a file of pictures for us to browse while he told us what was on offer. Gabby was particularly taken by the idea of a two-night stay at their remote camp on Benguerra island. The entire trip was catered for apart from alcohol which was the responsibility of the clients.

The pictures in the file, of both the location and the accommodation were nothing short of spectacular and when we had finished looking at them, I sat back and looked at Gabby.

"Well, Gabby," I said. "What do you think?"

"Oh, I'm definitely keen if you are," she replied nervously biting her lower lip.

"Okay Dave," I said to the man, "I would like to book the two-night trip for both of us tomorrow morning. Can you do it?"

"Certainly," he said glancing at his laptop, "by the look of things there'll be perfect sailing conditions and weather."

I shook hands with him after finalising a few things and agreeing to meet at the same offices at 8:00 a.m. the following morning. The drive back through town and out to Sand Dollar Lodge was filled with excited conversation from Gabby. Her one concern was that we already had a booking, and it would be a waste of money to simply leave for the island for two nights. I explained that I was not concerned about that in the slightest and that I was happy to have the original booking as a backup in the event we were unhappy with the trip. She nodded in agreement and then turned to stare out of the passenger window as we passed a grove of palm trees.

"I can't believe it!" she said loudly.

"What?" I asked.

"We're going to the islands, Jason!" she replied even louder.

It was 2.30 p.m. by the time we arrived back at our casa. I filled the cooler box Gabby had brought with cold water and beer and we both took a walk to the steps that led down the drop-off to the grassy glade on the beach. I placed two towels in the shade of a clump of palm trees and we lay there, sipping drinks and staring out at the ocean until we both fell asleep. It was 5.00 p.m. when I awoke to the sound of a motorboat landing on the beach nearby. Three sunburnt men alighted carrying their catch of Barracuda and Yellowfin Tuna. They passed nearby and made their way up the steps. Gabby awoke with a lazy yawn and with the sun now making its way down behind us she removed her sarong and announced it was time for a swim. Her bikini was bright white against her tanned body. I removed my shirt and followed her to the water line. The clear water felt like a tepid bath and the sand squeaked under our feet as we walked through the shallows to the nearest deep channel.

Gabby lay on her back in the water and closed her eyes in a state of deep relaxation. Further down the beach to my left, a group of tourists started playing 'Three Little Birds' by Bob Marley. Treading water, I stared back at the stretch of coastline with its fringe of palm trees bathed in the golden glow of the setting sun. *Life is good, Green. Enjoy the ride.* My dream-like state was suddenly destroyed by Gabby who had mischievously slipped under the water behind me. She surfaced suddenly from behind and pushed my head underwater. When I surfaced, blinking and coughing, she was laughing gaily at her prank.

"You!" I said vengefully "I'm gonna get you..."

Gabby yelled playfully as the chase began. She swam at surprising speed with long elegant strokes but soon gave up and I pulled her back to me by her ankle. I tasted the salt on her wet lips as we kissed in the chest-deep water. That night Gabby wore a long white and blue summer dress. We took the same table near the pool under the fairy lights of the cashew tree. The thick white tablecloth was weighed down against the breeze by small pewter coconuts on clips. The whites of her eyes were perfectly clear in the candlelight and her face glowed with health. We dined on small cast iron pots of creamy mussels with crunchy Mozambican bread followed by crayfish in garlic and parsley butter. The Chenin Blanc from Stellenbosch was crisp and cold and was stored in a silver ice bucket as we ate. The quiet relaxation of the evening was only disrupted by the frenetic activity in the bedroom of our casa later. That night I never woke or slipped out for a quiet cigarette. My body and mind were totally relaxed, and I slept soundly until I heard the birds at 6:00 a.m. the following morning. I carefully pulled my right arm from under Gabby's neck and walked quietly over the decking floor to let myself out onto the veranda. The early morning sun was starting to burn away the few clouds that had gathered on the horizon overnight and the breeze was cool. I placed my cigarettes on the bannister and walked through the main doors to the kitchen to boil the kettle for coffee. When it was ready, I sat once again on the bannister to smoke and stare out at the distant islands. A few minutes later, I heard the door squeak and turned to see Gabby wrapped in a towel and yawning as she walked out. Her hair was tousled from slumber, and she smiled as she walked up behind me and wrapped her arms around my waist.

"I can't believe we're going there today," she said looking over my shoulders towards the islands. "By the way, where's *my* coffee?"

I packed the vehicle after another breakfast of sliced pineapple. We arrived at the dhow safaris office at 7:45 am to find the manager, Dave waiting for us with his crew. They loaded my wine, beer and fruit into an old pick-up truck which left for the boat while Gabby and I were given a few last-minute tips on where we were going and what to expect.

That done we took the short walk up the sandy road towards the beach. The old wooden dhow was 30 feet long and painted bright yellow. Near the bows, painted in blue letters, was the name Celeste. We waded through the shallows and boarded using a set of wooden steps that had been lowered from the side of the waiting vessel.

"Well, it looks like you're all set," said Dave. "Have a lovely time."

We thanked him as the crew pulled in the anchor and started the tiny outboard motor at the stern. The crew consisted of a captain, a deckhand, and a cook. The captain introduced himself as Horatio and welcomed us aboard in passable English. The small engine groaned and sputtered under the strain as we glided across the smooth surface of the water and stared back at the coastline. It was when we were roughly eight hundred metres out that the engine was cut and the giant triangular sail was raised. Gabby and I sat in the centre of the boat on a flat bench and watched the palm trees and buildings behind us grow ever more distant. I glanced at her briefly and noticed she was smiling to herself behind her sunglasses. Near the stern of the boat was a large wooden box filled with beach sand. The cook busied himself lighting a small charcoal fire within the box and placed a metal grill over the flames and coals. He filled an old enamel kettle with fresh water and placed it on the grill to boil.

"The cook is making coffee, sir," said the captain. "Would you like some?"

"Yes please," Gabby and I replied in unison.

Five minutes later the coffee was served in bright blue plastic mugs with a plate of biscuits. With the mainland now far on the horizon, Gabby and I both turned to face the bows and sat drinking our coffee, talking and staring ahead at the distant islands. The old canvas sail bellied above, and the sun sparkled on the surface of the water as we glided forward silently at a steady speed. The crew behind us chatted happily in Portuguese as they drank their coffee and I put my left arm around Gabby's waist. It was an hour later when the sun had started to really burn that I spotted the first dolphin. It sped alongside the boat with its glistening dark grey body occasionally rising before being joined by three others. Gabby was thrilled and snapped numerous photographs with her camera. Ahead of us, in the distance to the right, was the low-lying smaller island of Margaruque while on the left were the tall dunes of the much larger Benguerra. The captain made the turn to port and set a course for the centre of the larger island. The looming land mass grew in size as we approached, and we saw the thick belt of palm trees and greenery that rimmed the stark white dunes. Ten minutes later we rounded a long stretch of sharp black coralline rocks and entered an enclosed lagoon. The captain dropped the sail and suddenly all was silent until the small engine was started once again. The tiny motor gurgled and spluttered as we made our way along the natural wall of rock at the deepest point of the lagoon.

I glanced over the right-hand side of the boat and clearly saw the sand floor of the bay five metres below. The boat travelled for a further fifty metres and then turned left towards the perfectly white beach. The captain cut the motor and the boat drifted until I heard the sand crunch beneath the wooden hull. Suddenly there was a flurry of activity as the boat was swung around until it lay parallel to the beach. Ropes were thrown, anchors dropped, and trunks of supplies were readied for offloading. Behind us, at the top of the bay, an old man appeared from the green belt at the foot of the dunes. He wore tattered blue overalls that were bleached almost white by the baking sun. Around his waist, he wore a leather belt attached to which was a long rubber truncheon. He waved and called to his colleagues on the boat.

"Now we have arrived sir," said the captain. "That is the camp guard, Armando."

Gabby and I climbed over the side of the dhow and stepped directly into the ankle-deep shallows. The reflection of the morning sun off the water and the sand was blinding even from behind sunglasses. The crew and the guard began unloading bags and trunks under the captain's orders. I walked up the beach with Gabby to the highest point before the green belt and looked around. Apart from the crew, there was not a single building or human being in sight. Horatio, the captain, walked up to us with a smile and spoke.

"I will now show you to the camp," he said. "If you would like to follow me. The crew will bring everything and I'm sure you would like some shade."

Gabby and I followed him up the beach for fifty metres towards the area where the rock wall met the sand at the top of the lagoon. The captain paused and pointed towards a clearing in the green belt of foliage and palm trees at the base of the dunes.

"There is our camp," he said proudly. "Follow me please."

I was initially disappointed at what I saw as a deserted and incredibly ramshackle set of huts and shacks, but I held my tongue as we followed on. To the left at the front was a pole and thatch structure under which stood two bench tables. At the centre, a little further back was a large A-frame building with simple reed mats as frontage. To the right at the front was another smaller pole and thatch structure under which hung two hammocks.

"Is that it?" I murmured under my breath.

"Wait, Jason," whispered Gabby. "Let's have a closer look."

We arrived in the shade of the building to the right and stood near the hammocks.

"Please wait here," said Horatio. "I will get your welcome drinks."

The captain disappeared down a pathway behind the border of banana and palm trees. I stood and took another look around.

"Well," I said to Gabby. "It's rustic, I'll give it that".

Gabby laughed as she discarded her sandals and flopped into one of the hammocks. She lifted her sunglasses and peered out at the dazzling sand and ocean in front of her.

"Sure, it is," she said as the hammock swung gently. "It's also absolutely perfect."

Sensing my protestations were getting me nowhere, I too removed my shoes and lay back in the hammock next to hers. A steady breeze blew in from the sea and I leant my head back and took a deep breath. *Relax, Green.* The captain returned carrying a blue plastic bag and a deadly-looking machete. I watched as he passed us and placed the bag on one of the tables under the thatched structure to our right. He removed a fresh green coconut from the bag and began deftly hacking at it with the blade until he had totally removed the top. He then took a straw from the same bag and walked over to present the drink to Gabby. She thanked him as she took it and sipped from the straw.

"Delicious!" she exclaimed. "And cold too."

"Yes madam," said the captain. "Our cook and the guard have a kitchen nearby with a paraffin freezer."

The captain walked off and began hacking at a second coconut which he presented to me. As Gabby had said, the milk was sweet, cold and delicious. We lay there silently swinging in our hammocks in the shade as we sipped the cool liquid. Soon enough the guard appeared carrying our bags.

"If you are ready, I will show you your room now," said the captain.

Gabby and I got up and followed the two men back towards the A-frame building to the rear carrying our coconuts. In a matter of seconds, the simple reed mats at the front were rolled up and secured revealing a rustic and spartan interior. To the rear of the room stood a double bed with a mosquito net hanging above it. Nearer the front was a low coffee table fashioned from old driftwood surrounded by simple wooden chairs with blue canvas cushions. I looked around the interior hoping to find a fan or some electrical points. There were none.

I watched as our bags were placed on a side table near the bed. Gabby, seemingly unperturbed, followed the captain to a door at the rear of the building.

"And here is the shower and toilet," he said proudly as he swung the door open.

"This is great!" said Gabby enthusiastically "Jason, come and have a look."

I followed the two of them into the darkness and cool of the interior and poked my head around the door to the 'bathroom'. In fact, it was an open-air, reed enclosure set at the edge of the green belt at the foot of the dunes. The floor was covered with shiny blue ceramic tiles and to the rear was a simple sink and toilet. Above, in the centre of the space was a rusted shower rose with a single tap for what I assumed was cold water. Privacy was assured by the reed walls and the thick foliage that surrounded it. From what I had seen the place was rudimentary and unsophisticated, but it was clean. More important was the fact that Gabby seemed delighted with it. My eyes adjusted to the darkness as I walked back through the room, and I saw that the bed looked comfortable, and the building was cleverly placed to get a constant breeze from the ocean. I stood at the front of the building and turned to face Gabby.

"So," I said. "What do you think?"

"I think it's fantastic," she said with a bright smile.

I looked out to see the deckhand and the cook battling to carry the trunks of supplies over the sand.

"They are going to the kitchen," said the captain. "It is situated a little further up the beach near their quarters. Of course, your camp is totally secure and private, but they are there for you if you need them. For now, the cook will prepare your breakfast which will be served here."

He pointed towards the two bench tables in the sand beneath the thatched structure at the right of the clearing.

"Well," he said, "I hope you enjoy your stay. I will be leaving soon with the deckhand and will return at around 10.00 a.m. the day after tomorrow."

Gabby and I thanked the man and returned to our hammocks in the shade. We waved as the deckhand walked past to return to the anchored dhow in the lagoon. Apart from the rustle of the palm fronds above and the occasional squawk of a seagull, all was silent. Once again, I was overcome by an extreme sense of isolation. *Not a bad place to be isolated, Green*. I put my head back and closed my eyes to savour the moment and I must have dozed off at some point.

I was woken by the clink of cutlery on the nearby tables. The cook and the guard had arrived with trays of food and drinks and Gabby was quietly helping them set one of the tables. She looked up at me and smiled.

"Oh, you're awake!" she said "Come...breakfast."

I rolled out of the hammock, stretched, and realised I was ravenously hungry. I walked barefoot over to the table to find a glorious spread of food and drink that had been laid out for us. There was a jug of iced pineapple juice, bowls of chilled fruit salad, a rack of toast and ham and cheese omelettes. Gabby and I ate while we discussed our plans for the day. The guard and cook appeared once again when we were drinking our coffee. One of them lugged a cooler filled with drinks while the other carried a trunk loaded with snorkelling equipment. I lit a cigarette while Gabby went to the room to fetch a hat and some sunblock. It was decided that there would be no plan at all that day, and we would simply take a walk on the beach and explore. I put the drone, my camera and some snorkelling equipment in a small bag and we set off heading past the lagoon and into the unknown. Gabby wore the loose white cotton beach dress she had bought in the mall in Vilanculos with a wide-brimmed straw hat. The sun was high in the cloudless sky and its reflection was blinding as we walked past the now-deserted lagoon and rounded a bend in the beach. We walked on the hard sand nearest the water and as we took the corner the vista opened, and the beach stretched and curved away to the horizon. The green belt of foliage and bushes on our right gave way to colossal, silken sand dunes and there was not a single human footprint as far as the eye could see.

"This is just incredible," whispered Gabby. "There's just no one here."

I shook my head in disbelief as I looked around.

"I know," I said. "I didn't think such places existed anymore."

We walked up the hard sand in silence, the only sound being the soft crunch under our bare feet. Ahead of us dozens of ghost crabs scuttled comically into the water as we approached. Being on the western side of the island the still water stretched away in magnificent, translucent turquoise, underlaid with dark coral reefs. I knew that eventually, the beach would lead around to the heavy waves and unprotected waters of the western boundary but that was well out of sight from where we were. Gabby pointed out the absence of any great amounts of plastic trash normally associated with the beaches and islands of the northern hemisphere. She also mentioned the fact that the archipelago had been 'protected' by decades of brutal civil war.

"This place," she said quietly "This country, is a physical jewel."

Further up the beach, we came across a huge, dead tree half buried in the sand. Its thick sun-baked limbs and branches were bone white and protruded from the sand like the hand of a giant skeleton. By then the heat in the direct sunshine had become unbearable. Gabby and I dumped our bags and headed gratefully for the shallows. The water was almost too warm, so we swam a good thirty metres out to a deeper channel to cool off. We bobbed and floated there for fifteen minutes until it was decided it was time to return to the shade and comfort of the camp. As we walked through the shallows, I noticed a white object concealed in the sand. I reached into the water to retrieve it and immediately recognized it as a sand dollar or pansy shell. The thin, delicate white disc was bigger than my hand and the organic, petal-like pattern in its centre fascinated Gabby who took numerous photographs of it before I returned it to the sea. It was a full half hour later when we finally returned, dripping with sweat, to the camp. I waited at the bench tables in the shade for Gabby who went for a cold shower and a change of clothes. I did the same and when I emerged, I found her swinging on her hammock in the shade drinking an ice-cold beer.

"Join me, Mr Green!" she said with a smile.

"Thank you, Miss Bonjiovanni," I replied as I pulled my own beer from the cooler, "I believe I will."

I slumped back into the hammock and the can opened with a hiss. The beer was bitingly cold and extremely welcome after the furnace of the beach. Gabby and I spent the next hour in light-hearted conversation until the cook appeared from the path in the jungle to our left. A late lunch of crumbed fish fillets was served with chips and salad. Gabby and I took our time eating before making our way back to the hammocks with fresh beers. Within fifteen minutes we had both fallen asleep. I awoke at 3.15pm. as the sun had started its descent towards the mainland. Leaving Gabby to sleep I got up, lit a cigarette, and walked barefoot out onto the beach. The tide was in and the lagoon to the right was full. I walked quietly back to the dining area and opened the trunk of snorkelling equipment. I placed two pairs of fins and two masks on the bench table and opened a fresh beer. My idle relaxation was disturbed by a sudden cacophony of birdsong from the nearby jungle. With the heat of the day subsiding a pair of Olive Bee-Eaters were defending their tree from a Green Coucal.

I looked around me at the picture postcard scene of tranquil beauty and I realised that I had finally broken away from the horrors of the recent weeks. The birds had woken Gabby who yawned as she got up out of her hammock.

"Hello, sleepy head," I said as I sipped my beer.

"Mm hello," she replied sleepily as she raised her arms and stretched her tall frame "Oh! Are we going snorkelling?"

"I thought we might," I replied. "While there's still enough sunlight."

A few minutes later we went out onto the beach and down towards the lagoon. It turned out she was an experienced diver and we both took to the water together and finned across to the natural rock wall that enclosed the bay. Although the clarity of the water was excellent there was very little sea life or coral within the lagoon. Using underwater signals, I told Gabby to follow me to the mouth of the lagoon so we could follow the rock wall in the open sea. It took some minutes to reach the opening but as soon as we had rounded the wall we were instantly rewarded. Suddenly the underwater vista exploded into vibrant colour and life. The sharp rock wall descended at a steep angle to a depth of around six metres after which it flattened out to sand. Ten metres out from there the sand dropped off into a great dark blue unknown. Great clumps of orange clubbed finger coral clung to the stone wall and we were suddenly surrounded by scores of curious, almost translucent, needlefish that swam up fearlessly and peered through the lenses of our masks. Below us, great schools of bright yellow and black angel fish, pennant fish, pyramid and millet seed butterfly fish swayed and waved in the fronds and clumps of weed. In all my years of sport diving, I had never seen such visibility and clarity in open water. The subtle undercurrent meant that there was no need to kick our fins. Instead, we hung motionless in the water and allowed the current to carry us slowly along the wall. At one stage I had to guide Gabby away from a crevice in the rock as there was a particularly angry-looking Moray eel poking its head out and baring its teeth as we passed. Huge clumps of mushroom coral gave way to bright green stag horn forests interspersed with delicate gardens of ancient plate formations. Below us, a group of parrot fish crunched away at a large dome of grooved brain coral and the sound was clearly heard by both Gabby and me. The spectacle was as overwhelming as it was unexpected. At one stage Gabby suddenly grabbed and shook my arm. Slightly alarmed and expecting to see a shark I looked to where she was pointing only to witness a giant sea turtle swimming away to the depths in what looked like slow motion. Gabby dived repeatedly, sometimes to over four metres, to more closely inspect items of interest. Her slim body glided through the depths effortlessly as if she was completely comfortable in the alien environment. The myriad of colour and life continued as we drifted along past giant elk horn formations and glittering shoals of bright orange clownfish. It was fifteen minutes later when we finally reached the end of the rock wall and entered the shallows at the head of the lagoon. We removed our fins and stood in the warm knee-deep water. When Gabby removed her mask and snorkel it left a temporary red line where the pressure had pressed the mask on her face.

"Oh my God!" she panted "I have never seen anything like it!"

"No," I replied "Me neither. It was amazing."

We took a slow walk along the beach back to camp with Gabby in animated conversation describing and reliving what we had just witnessed. We sat in the shade at one of the bench tables and drank cold beer until the sun had made its way down the sky over the distant mainland.

"I'm going to take a shower," said Gabby with a satisfied sigh, "wash the salt from my hair."

"I'll go in right after you," I replied.

I watched her walk into the darkened interior of the bedroom, lit a cigarette and turned on my seat to look out towards Margaruque Island. The slowly setting sun had turned the dunes to a burnt orange colour and the ocean was beginning to take on the same hue. Gabby returned after a few minutes wearing a yellow sarong around her waist and her bikini top. I followed suit and took a quick shower and changed my clothes. Although the water was cold, it felt good to wash the salt from my skin and hair. I walked back out to find Gabby had set up a small blue-tooth speaker and was playing Cuban music from her phone. I rummaged through the cooler and pulled out a bottle of wine with two glasses. Not wanting to stray too far from the music we took a seat on a towel on the beach to watch the sunset. The sea was a solid slab of orange with light horizontal brushes of gunmetal grey that stretched out to infinity. On the horizon near the island of Margaruque, a dhow set sail and its black outline was stark against the warm glow of the ocean. It was completely dark, and the moon had not yet risen by the time the guard and the cook arrived with the gas lamps. They hung two of them from the poles of the roof of our room and placed another three around the outside living area. The yellow glow and quiet roar of the lamps lent an atmosphere of homely warmth to the area which the music complimented. The cook approached us and asked what we would like for dinner. There was a choice of crumbed calamari, lobster, or prawns. Gabby and I both chose the calamari and the cook set off to prepare dinner as the guard arrived. At first, we were puzzled as he carried a large, rusted piece of flat sheet metal that he placed on the sand not far from where we sat. He returned soon after with a wheelbarrow of driftwood and began to build a fire. It crackled and glowed and sent tiny sparks into the air to join the blanket of stars above that were completely free of any light pollution or smog. A fine dinner was served later on one of the bench tables and I regularly filled our glasses with chilled wine from the cooler. Afterwards Gabby and I retired to our seats on the beach near the fire. We watched as the moon rose and slowly climbed up the sky. It was 9.15 when the table was cleared behind us and the guard and cook both came to say goodnight. We thanked them and watched as they made their way up the beach back to their quarters. Later that night Gabby and I took a walk to the lagoon. The moon had turned the surface of the water into a sheet of pure molten silver. We stripped off our clothes and swam naked in the warm still water. It was when we were about to get out that I stopped her in the shoulder-high water and pulled her gently towards me. Once again, I tasted the salt on her lips, as we kissed, and she soon found the reason I had held her back. Our intertwined bodies ground against each other under the water in a rhythm as ancient as the earth. Later that night, when Gabby was asleep, I got up and walked out to sit on the bench table to have a cigarette. The air was cool, the night was silent, and I was content. The next day was a carbon copy of the previous. We spent the morning exploring the south side of the island collecting coconuts and snorkelling the reefs.

A lot of photographs were taken, and I flew the drone taking numerous videos and stills from all altitudes. We returned to the camp in the heat of the day to eat lunch and rest only to venture out again as the afternoon cooled off. The private paradise we found ourselves in was as pristine and untouched as the brochure had shown. That afternoon we climbed the highest dune on the island and saw whales through the zoom lenses of our cameras in the rough open waters of the eastern coast.

The night was spent with much laughter, merriment and music and it was midnight when we finally lay down in bed exhausted and more than a little tipsy. It was a bittersweet moment when the captain arrived the following day to take us back to the mainland, but the sadness was tempered by the knowledge that we were returning to the luxury and facilities of Sand Dollar Lodge. The trip back to Vilanculos was quick and smooth thanks to the brisk wind that filled the sail of the bright yellow dhow 'Celeste'. That night we took a drive to town and had dinner at one of the fancy hotels we had spotted on our first day. The food was, of course, excellent and it was 9.45 pm when we finally returned to the bar at Sand Dollar Lodge for a nightcap. Later that evening, at around midnight, I carefully pulled my right arm from around Gabby's neck and walked out to the veranda to smoke a cigarette. I sat on the wooden bannister and looked out at the lights of a distant ship beyond the islands. There had been something troubling me for the past few days. Something I had been avoiding but was eating away at my conscience. Even more so that night given the fact we were due to return to Beira and reality the following day. *You need to tell her Green. You need to tell her everything. Tell her about Hannes. The reason you are in Mozambique. The reason you were in Zimbabwe. You need to tell her how you got the scars on your body. Tell her about Dixon Mayuni. You need to tell her about Imperial Dragon and the ivory. There's no doubt you've fallen for her Green so don't be a fucking idiot. Do you want a future with her? Tell her. Tell her how you feel. Tell her everything or you might lose her.* I flicked the cigarette butt out onto the grass and watched as the glowing tip broke up and died.

"Yup," I whispered to myself, "that's what I'll do."

# 19

## Chapter Nineteen: The Gathering Storm

I awoke at 6.30am. feeling fresh and rejuvenated. I slipped out quietly through the bedroom door and boiled the kettle for coffee. When it was ready, I opened the lounge doors and sat on one of the veranda chairs to smoke. The night had brought in a layer of clouds that hung in the sky like dirty smog and I could no longer see the islands on the horizon. Ten minutes later I heard the squeak of the bedroom door and Gabby stepped out wearing nothing but an old t-shirt.

"Oh," she said sleepily. "Where has the sun gone?"

"I'm sure it will burn through the clouds soon enough," I replied. "Coffee?"

"Yes, please," she said as she took the chair next to mine.

We sat in silence as we drank our coffee and looked out to sea. I had the distinct feeling that something was not quite right with Gabby, and this was confirmed when she sighed, and I turned to look at her. She sat with her legs up on the cushion clutching her coffee mug with both hands and her eyes welled with tears.

"Hey," I said putting my hand on her shoulder, "what's wrong?"

She sniffed and wiped her eyes with the back of her right hand.

"I'm sorry," she said clearly embarrassed, "it's just I don't want to leave this place. I don't want to go back to reality. Work and all that shit."

"I know...," I said as I rubbed her back, "me neither. But hey! We'll have a nice drive back, now we know what to expect from the road and we'll do something fun tonight. How does that sound?"

She leaned her head briefly on my arm then turned and flashed her bright smile at me once again.

"That sounds fine."

After a shower and more coffee, we walked to the restaurant for a cooked breakfast. The sun broke through the clouds as we ate on the decking and the mood lightened. I packed the vehicle, and we left the small town of Vilanculos at exactly 9.00 a.m. The short distance to the main Maputo road was well-tarred and free of potholes and soon enough we took the right turn heading north towards Beira. In the light of day, the main road was in even worse shape than I remembered. Huge sections simply didn't exist anymore and those that did were peppered with deep sharp holes.

That and the fact there were a lot of heavy haulage trucks and passenger buses travelling the same route slowed us down significantly. Gabby and I accepted we were in for the long haul, so we passed the time listening to music and chatting about the island trip. It was a full two hours later when we finally reached the Save Bridge.

"This is where we dropped the soldier isn't it?" she said.

"That's right," I replied "And if my memory serves me well, we have another two hours of bad road before it improves..."

"Oh well," she said as she handed me a bottle of water from the cooler "I guess we'll just take it easy."

The sun burned overhead as I negotiated what was left of the dusty road and it was just under two hours later when we reached the small, isolated plantation town of Muxungue. Crowds of vendors surrounded the vehicle when I stopped at a service station so Gabby could pick up some snacks from the kiosk. I ignored them and kept the engine running to keep the interior of the cab cool with the air conditioning. Soon after we had cleared the town the road improved, and I was finally able to drive at speed. The landscape changed as we gained altitude and far in the distance, I saw the hills of Inchope where we would eventually make the turn towards the coast and the city of Beira. Gabby seemed content, eating snacks, chatting and flicking between her own music and the radio station she had found when we had driven down. I, however, found myself agonizing about how and when I would tell her my story. On more than a few occasions, I resorted to simply smiling and nodding when she spoke as I grappled with the mechanics of how to go about it. Another thing that worried me was how she might react when I told her. *She's a journalist Green. For fuck sake, she's been covering atrocities, injustices, and wars for her job all over the world! She'll appreciate your honesty and hell it might even work in your favour. You love this woman Green, and you want some kind of future with her. Fucking tell her! Tell her everything.* The journey continued with me delaying the inevitable confession until we reached the bustling trading post of Inchope. I glanced at my watch as I took the right turn onto the new motorway. It was 3.00 p.m. and I knew we were only one and a half hours from Beira.

"Gabby, I need to talk to you," I said.

Sensing this was serious she removed her sunglasses, turned the music off and looked at me.

"Sure," she said soberly. "Go ahead."

I started from the very beginning leaving absolutely nothing out. I told her about the article in the news I had seen back in London all that time ago. I told her of my history with Johannes Kriel during the war and his achievements in the world of conservation and anti-poaching thereafter. I told her about the guilt I had felt upon hearing of his death and the fact that at the time it had been treated with suspicion because of the nature of his work. I recounted my journey from London to Harare for the funeral and the bizarre encounter with his widow when she had entrusted me with the hard drive that contained the report that she believed was the reason he had been murdered. I went on to tell her how I had accessed the files on the hard drive and the moment I realised the importance of the information on it. I described the night when the men who I believed to be government agents broke into my room in Harare to retrieve the dummy hard drive which I had switched with the real one. I narrated my journey to the Zambezi Valley and my ill-fated encounter with Dixon Mayuni and his band of poachers. I told her, in detail, of my escape and how I had been injured by the spike through my foot, the bullet wound, and the crocodile attack. Gabby maintained her composure throughout and sat stony-faced, taking it all in as she listened. I went on to explain the appalling conditions of the Kariba Hospital and my eventual transfer to the Mercer clinic in Lusaka, Zambia. She shook her head in disbelief as I described the long journey to recovery at the bush camp on the outskirts of Lusaka.

"Are you okay, Gabby?" I asked.

"I'm listening, Jason," she said softly. "Carry on please."

I was sure she was taking the story well and the truth about my injuries would invoke some measure of sympathy from her that might carry through to the end of my confession.

"Okay," I said.

I spent a good ten minutes describing the highly organized poaching operations of Mayuni in the Zambezi Valley and went on to recount my journey back there to punish him. I was totally honest about leaving him tied up in the river for the crocodiles although I neglected to mention cutting his Achilles tendons. Making no mention yet of Imperial Dragon Trading I went on to describe how the ivory and other illegal wildlife products were smuggled through Zimbabwe on haulage trucks from the copper belt in Zambia.

"And this ivory ends up where?" she asked.

"Well," I said, "ultimately it ends up in China of course, but it leaves Africa in shipping containers from here in Mozambique".

"From where exactly in Mozambique Jason?" she said.

"From Beira Gabby," I said. "It leaves here hidden in containers of hardwood. It's smuggled out, bribes are paid, and it sails away to China."

She turned to me with a look of shocked disbelief in her eyes. The fingers of her right hand began drumming silently on her leg and this worried me. It was then that I noticed a road sign that showed we were only sixty kilometres from Beira. My story had taken a long time to tell and we had covered a lot of distance during the telling of it. Gabby's naturally enquiring journalistic mind kicked in and she began to fire question after question at me. I fielded each of them with total honesty and openness and went on to tell her how the entire operation was shrouded under the veil of legitimate business and that the people in charge of these businesses were hugely wealthy, powerful, and politically connected. I stressed the ultimate importance of Hannes' report and the fact that it was due to be presented at the conference on illegal wildlife trade in Geneva later that year. I explained its ramifications and the good that would result in its being made public. Still, the questions came one after the next and with increasing intensity. It was when we were approaching the industrial area of Ceramica that we passed the first haulage truck loaded with hardwood. I watched as her body tensed with anger at the sight of it.

"You say that the focus of this report of yours is on one company in particular," she said.

"That's right," I replied.

"And that company is?"

"The company involved in the export of the ivory is Imperial Dragon Trading," I said, "owned by the millionaire Chinese businessman Charles Tang."

She nodded to herself and then turned to stare out of the left passenger window in silence. The tension was palpable, and I could have cut the atmosphere with a knife.

"Gabby I."

She held her right hand up and stopped me from speaking.

"Just a minute Jason," she said. "I need to just take this all in for a minute."

"Sure," I replied.

I felt a wave of relief wash over me at the fact that I had finally told her my true story. I knew everything was now out in the open and the dirty washing had been cleaned and hung out to dry. *It's done, Green. Everything has been told. Now you can move on with a clear conscience.* Gabby remained silent and stared out of the window as we drove through the industrial area of Ceramica. It was some minutes before she spoke.

"I don't fucking believe it," she said shaking her head.

"It's true Gabby," I said.

"Oh, I know it's true Jason," she said raising her voice, "I know it's fucking true. What I can't believe is you! All along you've had an agenda here. A very serious agenda at that. I've been diligently working on this logging story for months now and you waltz in and lie to me saying you were involved in an accident in Zimbabwe, and you had come to Beira to chill out..."

"Gabby," I said. "What I said wasn't untrue...I have been wanting to tell you about this for ages, the real reason I am here, I just hadn't found the right opportunity until now."

Gradually I saw the fiery Italian temper build in her. As she spoke, she began to gesticulate with her hands in exasperation.

"We have been talking for over a week Jason! Jesus Christ! We've just been on holiday for four nights together and only now do you decide to actually be honest with me! I can't fucking believe it!" she yelled.

"Gabby," I said. "Your reason for being here is as important as mine. I had no idea who you were or what you were doing here when I met you. It just happened to turn out that our reasons for being here are linked. It's crazy I know but I had no control over that. I had absolutely no idea. I'm sorry."

There was no doubt she was incandescent with anger, and I decided to shut my mouth for a while. By then we were approaching the slums on the outskirts of the city of Beira.

"Jason," she said quietly "I would appreciate it if you would drop me at home."

"Gabby I," I said before she interrupted me.

"Please Jason," she said with finality holding up her right hand, "I'm tired, I have work to do and quite frankly I need to be alone to get my head around all of this."

"Okay," I said, "of course, I'll drop you at home."

From there on we drove in an uncomfortable silence until I took the right turn and entered the filth and chaos of the suburb of Manga. So late in the afternoon, the pedestrian traffic was heavy, and I found it infuriatingly slow after the speed of the motorway. The atmosphere in the cab did nothing to improve the situation either. Eventually, we passed the fish shop, and I took the right turn onto the road that led to Gabby's house. I pulled up to the gate, turned the engine off and got out to help her with her bags. At that moment the guard opened the gate and walked up to assist as well. Gabby handed him the cooler and told him to take it into the house. I reached into the back seat and grabbed her bag which she immediately took from me. It was clear she wanted to be left at the gate and needed no help.

"Thanks," she said quietly as she walked towards the gate.

"Gabby..." I called after her in desperation "The world brought us together. Can you see that?"

She stopped in her tracks and turned to face me.

"Ya," she said nodding "I can see that."

It was obvious she was upset but for a split second, I saw some kind of understanding in her eyes. It was as if she knew I was right. She turned and walked down the driveway and into the lush tropical garden. *Leave her for a while Green. The news must have come as a big shock. Give her a bit of time and she will come around. You did the right thing.* The drive out of Manga and through the city to Macuti was painfully slow and I lost my temper on more than a few occasions with the traffic.

Eventually, I arrived at the coastal road and drove up to my hotel. I parked the vehicle, grabbed my bags, and took the walk to my villa. The humidity, of the late afternoon was oppressive and I was sweating by the time I opened the back door. I tossed my bag onto a chair, turned the television on and slumped onto the couch. I spent the next hour flicking through channels and watching repeats on the news. Bored and frustrated I walked onto the veranda to smoke a cigarette. My melancholy was aggravated by the low clouds that hung over the sea and blocked the evening view. Feeling hungry I began to weigh up my options for dinner. Either way I would be eating alone and the only two places I knew of were the yacht club and Charlie's. I crushed out the cigarette and headed inside for a shower. It was 7.15 and dark outside when I had dressed and was ready to leave. I picked up my keys and walked to the back door of the villa. It was then I noticed the glossy flyer on the tiled floor. Someone had obviously just done a mail drop as I had not noticed it when I arrived. I picked it up and had a look.

The flyer was in Portuguese on one side and English on the other and was advertising a pizza delivery service in Beira. *Fuck it Green. Order in. You're in no mood for company and probably tired as well. Get a pizza delivered and relax.* With my mind made up I walked back into the lounge, sat down, and called the number on the flyer. It was answered immediately and the person on the phone spoke fluent English as well. I made the order, gave them the address, and hung up. It was then I noticed Gabby's number on my phone. I stared at it for a while, wondering whether to send her a message or not. I toyed with the idea for a minute before I decided it would be wise to leave her alone for the night. With my mind made up I opened my laptop, checked my emails, and browsed the news sites.

The pizza arrived forty minutes later, and I tipped the driver who was accompanied to my door by the security guard from the hotel. I spent the next three hours channel-hopping on the television and browsing the drone footage and photographs from the island. There was one photograph that I found to be exceptional. I had taken it on arrival at the island and it featured Gabby standing ankle-deep in the water next to the dhow 'Celeste'. The contrast in colours with the bright yellow painted boat, the pure white sand, the turquoise water, and the extremely photogenic Gabby was a firm favourite of mine and I set it as the screen saver on my computer. It was 11:30 p.m. when I fell asleep briefly on the couch. I awoke feeling annoyed and decided to have a last cigarette before turning in for the night. Great clouds of warm damp mist rolled in from the sea and I could barely see the street from where I stood on the veranda. Ten minutes later I lay down on the bed and closed my eyes. That night I dreamed of our time on the island and the happiness we had shared. Flashing images of the laughter and the music and the swimming in our secluded lagoon. But like the trip to the island, my dream came to an end only to be replaced by a re-run of the bizarre, unsettling dream I had before. Gabriella Bonjiovanni was running in terror through the streets of some gloomy dystopian city. Chasing her from behind was a giant, grotesque, fire-breathing dragon. I tried to move, to call after her to warn her, but I was unable to and as much as I tried, my voice made no sound at all. Despite the dream, I awoke at 6.45 pm the next day feeling refreshed and upbeat. After a long shower, I walked downstairs to make a cup of coffee and have a cigarette. Gone was the oppressive heat and misty humidity of the previous night and the horizon of the sea was clearly visible in the early morning sun. After watching the news headlines and checking my emails I took a leisurely walk up to the restaurant for breakfast. The morning was cool, and the staff were cheerful at the buffet. After eating I ordered a coffee, sat down, and lit a cigarette. My thoughts went to Gabby, and I began to browse my phone for florists in Beira. I smiled to myself as I imagined her reaction to finding me at her gate clutching a bunch of roses. *You'd probably get a slap Green but hey, why not?* It was then I noticed the two men arrive. One of them was tall, thin, and very scruffy with wild unkempt hair and a beard to match. He had the dark complexion and hooked aquiline nose of a continental European. The other man was much shorter and smartly dressed, with short-cropped blonde hair and rimless spectacles. Both men appeared flustered and impatient as they spoke to one of the members of staff behind the bain-marie.

I put them out of my mind and went back to browsing my phone. It was then, out of the corner of my eye, that I saw the staff member point me out and the two men approached me.

"Sorry to disturb you," said the shorter man in a German accent "Are you Mr. Jason Green?"

"I am," I replied, "what can I do for you?"

"Oh, thank God," said the visibly relieved man. "We are looking for Gabby. She is our colleague; we work with her. Where is she?"

"What are you talking about?" I said feeling annoyed "I dropped her at her house in Manga just after 5.00 p.m. yesterday."

"Yes." said the man as a frown formed on his forehead "She came to see us next door at about 6.30 and told us what a wonderful time she had. She was very happy."

"And...?" I said.

"Well, the guard said she went out again at around 7.00 p.m.," he said, "and she hasn't returned."

## 20

# Chapter Twenty: Dark Horizons

"I think we better go and discuss this in my villa," I said.

The two men followed me down the path through the garden to the back of the villa. I opened the door and showed them into the lounge before formally introducing myself and learning their names. The tall scruffy man's name was Alec while the shorter German man was Klaus. Both of them showed me their press cards before taking a seat.

"You say she went out at around 7.00 p.m.?"

"Yes," said Klaus "The guard wasn't a hundred per cent certain, but he said right around 7.00."

"And she used which vehicle?" I asked.

"Her Land Rover," said Alec in a Spanish accent.

"Well," I said, "that vehicle is a piece of shit. It's broken down a few times, hasn't it?"

"Yes, it has," said Klaus. "But she is pretty good at getting it running again."

"Another thing," said Alec. "She was last online at 11.00 pm last night."

I picked up my phone and looked at her details. He was right.

"Last seen at 11.04 pm," I said. "There is obviously a perfectly innocent explanation for this. I'm assuming the vehicle broke down and she took a hotel. She more than likely forgot her 'phone charger and this would explain why she is offline."

"Yes," said Klaus. "But this is most unlike Gabriella. We've worked together as a team for three years now. It's most unusual."

"Well," I said, "I suggest we go to Charlie's right away as I'm assuming that's where she went. You follow me in your vehicle, okay?"

"Sure," said Klaus.

"Right," I said as I grabbed my keys and bag. "Let's go."

I locked the door, and the two men followed me up to the car park. I reversed, engaged first gear, and nodded at them in their vehicle as I approached the gate. The road was quiet as I took the right turn for the short drive down the beach road to Charlie's. *I wouldn't worry about it, Green. There's obviously a perfectly good reason. More than likely that fucking Land Rover. She'll be in a hotel.* I pulled into the deserted car park in a cloud of dust and waited for the two to arrive. They arrived soon after and parked near the Bougainvillea bush.

"The place looks empty," I said as they followed me up the path towards the restaurant.

"Maybe too early?" said Alec behind me.

We rounded the corner to find a guard sitting at one of the outside tables drinking tea. Clearly surprised to see us he stood up immediately and began answering questions in Portuguese from Alec. I stood waiting impatiently as they spoke.

"Charlie and the rest of the staff arrive at 10.00 a.m.," said Alec eventually.

"Do you have his phone number?" I asked.

Alec got the number from the guard, and I typed it into my phone and saved it.

"Well," I said to the two men, "it's only an hour till they arrive. I suggest we meet back here then."

"Yes," said Klaus. "We can do that."

We exchanged and saved each other's phone numbers.

"Right," I said as I turned and made my way back down the path, "see you then."

I lit a cigarette as I started and reversed the vehicle. *Now then. Which route would Gabby use to get here?* I decided she would more than likely use the most direct route through the city. I headed off driving slowly and looking down alleyways and side roads as I drove. At each stop, I checked my phone to see if she had come back online. The early morning traffic was easier than usual and before long I was through the city and on the motorway heading for the Manga turn-off. There was no sign at all of the old Land Rover. By the time I reached the fish shop in Manga, I decided there was no point in continuing and I pulled up on the side of the road to try to call her number. The call went straight to voice mail, and I heard her voice.

"Hi this is Gabriella, I'm not able to take your call right now but leave a message and I'll get back to you."

"Fuck," I said under my breath as I reversed and headed back towards the motorway.

I glanced at my watch to see it was 9.35 p.m. *Head back to Charlie's, Green. Go talk to him.* I kept my eyes peeled on the way back as I had done before. There was no sign of the Land Rover. I kept glancing at my phone, willing it to ring, but to no avail. The city traffic had become congested, and it was 10.05 p.m. by the time I pulled into the car park. The waiters had arrived for the day and were preparing the outside tables as I walked in. Charlie sat in his usual spot near the bar drinking coffee and watching tennis on the television. He turned and smiled pleasantly as I walked in.

"Oh, hello Jason," he said casually.

"Morning Charlie," I said. "Have you seen Gabby?"

"Gabby?" he said with a frown "She was here last night. Was telling me about your trip and how good it was. Why do you ask?"

"She's missing," I said. "Her crew came to my hotel this morning looking for her. I dropped her off at her house just after 5.00 yesterday."

Charlie frowned and looked down at his coffee.

"Must be her vehicle," he said. "It's always breaking down."

"Yes," I said, "That's what I thought. What time did she leave?"

"I can tell you exactly what time she left," he said.

Charlie spoke to the barman in Portuguese who promptly handed him a stack of till slips from the previous night.

"Now then," he said as he browsed through them, "yes. This is it. She paid her bill at exactly 10.54 p.m. using cash and then she left. I remember it clearly because we spent the whole night chatting and I wanted to pay for her pizza. She refused."

"So, you were with her the whole evening?" I asked.

"Yes," he said, "we had a great laugh."

"And nothing unusual happened?" I said.

"Not at all," he replied thoughtfully. "Well, apart from a bit of a run-in with those two Chinese blokes."

Suddenly, despite the growing heat and humidity, I felt a cold chill run through my bones. Keeping it to myself I nodded in understanding as Alec and Klaus walked in.

"Any news?" I asked them.

"No," said Alec "Still nothing. Her phone goes straight to voice mail."

The four of us sat for five minutes discussing the situation. I explained the fact that Charlie had the exact time she had left recorded on the till slip and that he was the last person to see her. Charlie told us that he had locked up and left at around 11.20 pm and had turned left down the beach road towards his house.

"And you saw nothing at all on your way home?" I asked.

"No," he replied "Not a thing. But it was very misty last night."

"I think maybe we should report this to the police now," said Klaus in his German accent.

"No," I said. "It's too early for that. I think we all go looking for now and we wait for her to call one of us. When she does, we all let each other know immediately. If we don't have a result by say 2.00 p.m. we all meet and take it from there."

"Ya," said Charlie. "That sounds good. We don't want to involve the police and to be perfectly honest they're useless anyway."

It was decided that we would all go out searching individually and if she was not found, or not turned up by 2:00 pm we would meet again at the Yacht Club.

For the next three hours, I drove the streets of the city incessantly. From the filthy back alleys of the rotten skyscrapers to the sprawling port and the nearby industrial sites. Every fifteen minutes I stopped to call Gabby's number but every time it went back to the infuriating voice mail.

Twice I received phone calls from Alec and every time the phone rang my heart jumped in my chest anticipating some good news. It turned out he was simply checking if I had heard anything to which I reminded him that I would call immediately if I did. The feeling of dread I had sensed when Charlie had told me of her confrontation with the men from Imperial Dragon would not leave me either. Time and time again I tried to put it out of my mind as a normal occurrence. After all, I had witnessed the same the very first night, I had met her. *She's a tough one Green. She can certainly look after herself. You know that.* It was exactly 2:00 p.m. when I pulled into the car park of the Yacht Club and parked. I walked in to find Charlie, Alec, Klaus and another older man I didn't recognize huddled around a table talking quietly amongst themselves. My chair scraped on the tiled floor as I pulled it out and sat down. The man was quickly introduced as Rodrigo, a local fixer. Fluent in Portuguese and well-connected in Mozambique, he had worked with visiting television crews and journalists for over twenty years. All of the men spoke in English in hushed tones with worried expressions. We dismissed the waiter and discussed the situation for ten minutes.

"Our protocol says we must first inform the local police and then report to head office that one of the crew is missing," said Klaus with a deep frown on his forehead.

"In that case I agree," I said looking at Rodrigo. "Do you have contacts in the police?"

"I do," he replied in perfect English. "Mainly in Maputo. But if this is to go to the local police, of course, I will make some calls."

"Well then I think we should do that immediately," I said as I stood up. "Let's go. I'll follow you."

The afternoon was sweltering as we crossed the road to the car park. Charlie took the lead in his car and the three vehicles headed north up the beach road in convoy. The Macuti police station was situated in a ramshackle old colonial building with peeling paint near the lighthouse. We parked in the shade of a row of Casuarinas and walked into the charge office together. To the centre of the room was a long wooden counter that was deeply worn with decades of use. Behind that, to the right, was a group of prisoners sitting handcuffed on the floor against the wall. Their filthy clothes, bare feet and terrified expressions bore testimony to the appalling conditions of the Mozambican holding cells. Loud Latino music blared from a radio in an office at the rear.

The room was dark, dirty, and unbearably hot. Above us the single neon light gave off a loud incessant buzzing sound and behind the counter a young policeman sat, half asleep, leaning back in an old office chair. Clearly surprised to see us, the officer stood up slowly and walked to the opposite side of the counter. His sweaty face was a caricature of lazy arrogance and it appeared he was trying to impress the prisoners. Swallowing our impatience, Klaus, Charlie, and I took a seat on an old wooden bench near the windows while Rodrigo and Alec spoke to the man in Portuguese.

It wasn't long before tempers began to flare and a shouting match began amongst the three men. Feeling angry and frustrated I stood up to confront them.

"What the fuck is going on here?" I said loudly.

Alec turned to me with a film of sweat on his face.

"They say they cannot investigate anything until the person has been missing for at least twenty-four hours," he said.

"Wait, wait please gentlemen," said Rodrigo holding his hands up in frustration. "Please, wait outside and let me deal with this."

Reluctantly I walked out followed closely by Alec, Klaus and Charlie. I lit a cigarette in the shade and began pacing the overgrown garden.

"Useless," said Charlie under his breath.

It was ten minutes later when Rodrigo finally emerged wiping the sweat from his face with a tattered old handkerchief.

"Okay," he said. "They have taken the report, but they will only act on it at 7.00 p.m. this evening. I told them we would return then. If anyone has any photographs that will be of assistance."

"I have plenty," I said, "and I'm not wasting any more time here. I'll meet you all here at 7.00 pm tonight. Until then, if anyone hears anything, we contact each other as agreed. Is everyone clear?"

They grunted in understanding, and I walked out of the garden back towards my vehicle. I had expected a poor reaction from the police but what I had just witnessed was more than the typical arrogance and incompetence one would expect from an African police force. I spent the next four hours relentlessly driving the maddening streets of the city and the surrounding suburbs. I stopped the vehicle every fifteen minutes to try to call Gabby's phone but as before it went straight to voice mail. It was with a profound sense of despair and hopelessness that I cropped and printed off some of my pictures of Gabby in the manager's office of my hotel. I placed them on the passenger seat of the vehicle and as I was about to turn the key in the ignition, I turned to look at the picture on top of the pile. *Where are you my darling Gabby? Where are you?* I arrived at the police station at 7.00 pm. on the dot to find the other three waiting in the car park as arranged. Their sullen expressions were enough to convince me they too had made no headway in their search.

Thankfully there was a senior policeman present who dealt with the report and spoke with Alec and Rodrigo at length while the rest of us waited in the twilight outside. They emerged half an hour later and it was decided we would meet at the Yacht Club to discuss the way forward. The mood was lugubrious as we took our table and ordered much-needed drinks. Klaus informed us that he had alerted the head office of Satellite News Network that Gabby was missing. They had been on the phone every half hour since and were in the process of informing the Italian embassy in Maputo. We were told by Rodrigo that the police might want to interview us all separately the following day and that they would contact us individually in that event. After half an hour of bleak, hushed conversation, the others left to go home, and I was left at the table with Charlie. Although he attempted to remain upbeat I knew he was as worried as I was.

"I know I've only known her for three months, Jason but we've become really good mates. I just don't know what to do," he said sombrely as he stared into his beer.

"I know, Charlie," I said, "I know."

"Would you like to come to the pub for some dinner?" he asked.

"Thanks, mate but no," I said. "I don't have much of an appetite and to tell you the truth I'm exhausted."

"I have to get back," he said as he finished his beer, "you'll call me if you hear anything?"

"Of course, I will Charlie. You'll be the first." I assured him.

I watched as he made his way towards the exit, and I signalled to a waiter for another beer and a menu. The bright lights of the interior of the building were stinging my eyes so I made my way out to sit in the breeze and listen to the waves. I yawned as I browsed the menu and, in the end, I ordered a simple starter of crab cakes as I wasn't feeling hungry at all. The mist began to roll in from the sea as it had done the previous night, as I sat smoking and staring out into nothingness. The food, although superb, did nothing for me and I pushed the plate away after eating only half. In my mind, I felt the black mists of depression and despair gathering steadily as I ordered another pint of Manica. Time and time again I looked at my phone expecting a different result, but it was always the same. It was 10.00 pm and quite a few beers later by the time I settled my bill and left the Yacht Club. The drive to my hotel took me up the beach road past Charlie's which seemed to be winding down for the night as there were only a few cars parked. The humid fog that rolled inland from the ocean made the driving visibility difficult and the only person I saw on the street was the familiar drug dealer who stood in his usual spot under the halo of the streetlamp.

I parked the vehicle and walked down to my villa in a state of dazed exhaustion. My attempts at normalcy by turning on the television and attempting to check emails were futile and I ended up on the veranda smoking a cigarette I didn't want and staring into space. Eventually, I locked the door and headed upstairs for a shower. I stood, swaying slightly under the jets of water and closed my eyes. When I was done, I dried myself off and lay on the bed with a towel around my waist. In my mind, I ran over a hundred different possible scenarios. None of which made any sense. Once again, I felt a terrible sense of hopelessness and anguish. This combined with my exhaustion and soon I slipped into a troubled and restless sleep. On three occasions I awoke, confused and sweating heavily, before once again slipping back into unconsciousness.

It was 7:26 a.m. when I finally woke to the morning light coming through the vertical blinds. For a moment I had forgotten the events of the previous day, but they all came crashing home after a few seconds. I wrapped a towel around my waist and walked downstairs nursing a slight headache from the beer and stress. Before making coffee, I checked my phone in case Gabby, or anyone had made contact or sent a message. There was nothing. *Jesus Green. What the fuck?* Knowing I would have to kick myself into action again, and needing to rid myself of the creeping hangover, I went back upstairs and pulled on some shorts and a t-shirt for a run. The morning sky was clear and there was no breeze as I walked through the gate and crossed the road to the beach. By the time I had covered three kilometres on the hard sand, my head was pounding, my foot throbbing and my mouth was dry. I sat on the sand, cupped my forehead, and closed my eyes. *Today is the day. She'll turn up. You'll find her Green. Think positive for fuck sake.* I ran harder on the way back to the hotel and by the time I walked into my villa, I was dripping with sweat and panting heavily. I took a cold shower, brushed my teeth and walked downstairs to make a coffee and smoke my first cigarette. As I walked out to the veranda, I picked up a pen and some paper to make some kind of plan of action for the day. I stared at the paper as I smoked and drank the coffee, but in the end, I wrote nothing at all. *There's no fucking point. How about 'Find Gabby'* It was 8.45 am. when I locked up and walked to the restaurant deck for breakfast. When I had eaten, I called Klaus and got an update from him on the situation. There had been no change and there was no news other than that an official from the Italian Embassy was due to fly into Beira on the afternoon flight from Maputo.

"What the hell is he gonna do?" I asked.

"I'm not sure," he replied morosely, "perhaps he will work with the police".

I told him I thought it would be a good idea for us all to meet at lunchtime to update each other. He agreed and promised to stay in touch throughout the morning. I hung up and called Charlie who sounded weak and exhausted when he too confirmed he had heard nothing.

It was 9:30 a.m. when I finally left the hotel and stopped the vehicle in the driveway as I decided which way to turn. *It doesn't make a difference Green. What matters is that you are not going to give up. Get to it. Find her.* Once again, I spent the morning searching every corner of the sprawling city. The densely populated slums in the wetlands to the west of the city were particularly hard to drive through and on two occasions I had to engage four-wheel drive to navigate the mud. Like clockwork, I called Gabby's number at least twice every hour. It was at 12.45 p.m. as I was buying a bottle of water from a roadside shack that my phone rang. My heart jumped a beat in anticipation of some good news until I saw the caller ID was Alec.

"Hello, Alec," I said hopefully. "Have you had any news?"

"No," he said solemnly, "I'm sorry I haven't. The police called Rodrigo and said they need to interview us all. They asked if we could go in at 2.00 p.m. today. I told them we would be there."

"That's fine," I said. "I'll be there."

I made my way slowly through the mud and litter of the slums back towards the city and finally reached the tarred road. The lunchtime traffic was heavy, and the sun burned through the windscreen in a spirited fight with the air conditioning. Eventually, after much frustration, I made it through the traffic and arrived in the shade of the Casuarinas outside Macuti Police Station. Rodrigo, Alec and Klaus were waiting in the shade near the entrance. All three of them looked drained and morose as I approached.

"Right," I said. "Let's get this done as quickly as possible."

The heat in the charge office was unbearable so I waited outside while Rodrigo went in to see the officer in charge. After a few minutes, I was summoned by Rodrigo who accompanied me as an interpreter to the office of the station boss. The old wooden floors creaked as we entered the dimly lit office. The officer in charge was a huge man with a bald head the size of a cannonball. He sat in an office chair behind his desk and his body looked like it would burst out of his uniform at any time. The overhead fan only served to move the hot air around and the man wiped the sweat from his face with a cloth as he signalled us to take our seats opposite his desk. The interview took twenty minutes during which the big man shuffled papers and wrote the occasional scrawled note on a sheet of paper. Rodrigo translated everything and we stopped only once to photocopy my passport on an antiquated machine in the next-door office. The questions were exactly what I had expected, and it was a great relief when they were finally concluded, and I walked out of the charge office to the relatively cooler air outside.

"How was it?" asked Klaus.

"Routine, red tape, bullshit," I replied as I lit a cigarette. "I don't expect much from that bunch. Anyway, I'm out of here. Good luck."

It was exactly 4.00 p.m. when I got the call from Alec. I was in the city centre having done a round trip through the north of the city and was making my way to the port area.

"What news?" I said.

"The police have found the vehicle," he replied. "It was hidden behind a building in Macuti. Not far from Charlie's."

"No sign of Gabby at all?" I said impatiently.

"No," he said quietly. "I'm afraid not."

"Right," I said. "Meet me at the police station. I'll be there in twenty minutes."

The disappointment was crushing, and this was only made worse when we arrived at the location of the Land Rover forty-five minutes later in the company of a junior policeman. The vehicle sat in a filthy alleyway on concrete blocks with all four wheels missing. Also stolen were the battery and carburettor. There had been an attempt to remove the engine, but the thieves had been unsuccessful probably due to a lack of tools. A vagrant who lived in a nearby shack had been picked up by the police and was in the process of being interviewed at the station. As I stared at the broken old vehicle, I felt a cold chill run down my spine despite the appalling heat. *This is not looking good Green*. It was 6.00 pm when the vagrant was released having been lightly beaten by the investigating officers. The man was in his seventies and was a toothless alcoholic who lived on cheap rum and home-brewed spirit. He had told the police officers he had not seen who had parked the vehicle nor who had stolen the parts from it. The man was known to the police mainly for public drunkenness and they told us they had no reason to doubt what he had said. A tow truck had been dispatched to pick it up and take it to the central police station for fingerprinting. A meeting was arranged for 7.00 pm. that night at Charlie's and attending would be the official from the Italian Embassy in Maputo. Klaus told me that his main concern was that Gabby may have been kidnapped. Although this sort of thing had happened only twice in Beira it was relatively common in the capital city of Maputo. My exhausted mind was spinning with possibilities as I took a shower back at my hotel. The sun had set when I pulled up and parked near the bougainvillaea tree at Charlie's.

Waiting inside at a corner table were my four companions and a man whom I assumed was the official from the Italian consulate. Wearing a light cream suit and sporting spiky gelled hair he was introduced simply as Mr Bianchi. I shook his hand, ordered a beer from a waiter and took a seat. I sat and listened as the man spouted various scenarios and theories to explain Gabby's sudden disappearance. One of these was the possibility of kidnapping although this was vigorously argued against due to the lack of any ransom demands. There had been constant communication with Satellite News Network and a blanket hush order on Gabby's disappearance had been given for the time being. I had to bite my tongue as the man attempted to dominate and steer the discussion and it appeared to me, that he was more concerned with his expensive clothes and his suntan rather than the very serious situation we had found ourselves in. It was an hour and three drinks later when I finally spoke.

"Gentlemen," I said angrily, "this conversation is going nowhere. Please excuse me."

I walked to the stool at the bar I had sat on the first night I arrived in Beira and ordered a fresh beer. I turned once to look at the gathered men and caught Charlie glancing at me from his seat. His face was pale and there were black smears beneath his tired eyes. He nodded at me once before I turned to face the bar and lit a cigarette. *My God what a fuck up, Green*. It was twenty minutes later when the solemn-looking group approached me to let me know they were leaving and to say goodnight. The four men left together leaving Charlie who took his usual spot at the bar in front of the television. He stared at it blankly with unseeing eyes as he twisted his beer glass on the surface of the bar. Fully aware I needed to eat but feeling no hunger at all I paged through the menu. I settled on the calamari and handed the menu back to the barman as I gave him my order.

It was as I was eating that the two Chinese men from Imperial Dragon walked in and took their usual place at the far end of the bar. I watched them where they sat, and the waiter delivered their drinks. They huddled close together in conversation wearing their trademark tight t-shirts revealing their muscular tattooed arms. Once again, I felt a cold shiver run down my neck and spine as I watched them. Their demeanour was unchanged from before but some unknown feeling deep inside told me that something was different. I watched them as I wiped my mouth with the serviette and took a sip of beer. Although they appeared calm on the surface, the man with the pockmarked face glanced around repeatedly and his eyes darted from person to person. *He's fucking nervous Green. The man is scared*. The men stayed for one drink only and then left after paying cash at the bar. By then I had had a skin full of beer and that combined with the exhaustion began to make me feel sluggish.

"One more please," I said to the barman. "I'll be back shortly."

Feeling the call of nature, I got up and walked towards the entrance to make my way to the ablution block across the concrete patio outside.

"Sorry about earlier, Charlie," I said as I walked past the dejected-looking figure in front of the television, "I couldn't listen to that Bianchi idiot anymore."

"I know Jason," he replied. "I felt the same."

"Back in a minute," I said as I walked out of the door.

The moon had turned the waves to my right into a seething grey slush as I passed the outside tables and walked down the short path to the gent's toilet block. I stood at the urinal swaying slightly as I relieved myself. It was at that moment that the automatic flush mechanism kicked in and water began to flow from many holes on the chrome pipe above the sheet metal of the urinal. As I gazed out towards the trees through the staggered air vents, I became aware of an unusual smell. I quickly put it out of my mind as I zipped up and walked to the hand basin. The strange smell returned when I leaned over and opened the tap to wash my hands, but I thought nothing of it and the smell soon disappeared when I began to lather the sweet-smelling soap between my fingers. The fresh air on the walk back to the bar made me slightly dizzy and I debated whether to have the beer I had ordered. *Not gonna make much of a difference Green.* After grabbing it I walked around to the front of the bar and sat in silence next to Charlie as I drank. The situation was such that no words were necessary and there was some comfort in the mindless drivel on the screen. Fifteen minutes later the events of the day and the beer had caught up with me and I stood to leave.

"I'm out of here, Charlie," I said. "See you tomorrow."

"Cheers, Jason," he replied quietly.

I crossed the concrete outside and walked into the dark area near the bougainvillaea tree where I had parked the vehicle. It was when I took the right turn to reach the vehicle that I stumbled once again in the darkness on the hidden concrete slab on the sand beneath the tree. I fell forward only breaking my fall by grabbing the side of the vehicle.

"For fuck sake!" I shouted as I pulled out the keys.

The drive back to the hotel was uneventful and once again the only person I saw was the familiar drug dealer who was in his usual spot leaning on the lamppost near the beach. I only realised how drunk I was when I stood swaying under the shower in my villa. Afterwards, I filled a tall glass of water and lay back on the bed. My mind was in an acute state of confusion, fear and worry and it was only a few minutes before I fell into a deep but troubled sleep.

It was 7:30 a.m. when I finally woke. I rubbed my eyes and frowned as I looked at my watch. The events of the previous evening came back to me as I drank from the glass of water. My head was pounding with the hangover from the beer, and I quietly cursed myself as I got up and sat on the edge of the bed. With my elbows on my knees, I closed my eyes and rested my head in my hands. I thought of the man from the embassy in his trendy suit and his outlandish theories. Then there was the memory of the broken Land Rover in the alleyway. Finally came the vision of the two Chinese men from Imperial Dragon. Although they had tried to give the impression that everything was normal, I couldn't put the nervous darting eyes of the man with the scarred face out of my mind. *You could be wrong Green. You might just be paranoid. You need to keep your fucking head straight Green. Getting pissed isn't gonna help find her.*

The twenty-minute run up the beach did nothing for my pounding head and I swallowed three paracetamol tablets with my coffee when I returned dripping with sweat and regret. The first cigarette of the day tasted like shit, and I stared out at the sea beyond the Casuarinas as I smoked. By the time I had showered it was too late for breakfast, so I decided to watch the news and check my emails until Charlie's opened at 10:00 am. I realised I hadn't been eating properly in the past few days and I was starving. As usual, I checked my phone automatically every few minutes but there was not even a message or call from the crew. The smiling image of Gabby standing in front of the boat on the island was still showing on my laptop and it pained me to minimise it. It was 9.45 am by the time I was ready to leave and after a few calls to Klaus and Charlie, I locked the villa and headed up the path to the vehicle. The heat of the day had set in, and the steering wheel burned to the touch as I started the engine and reversed. Charlie arrived as I parked at the pub and we both walked in together and ordered coffee from the barman who was cleaning up and tallying receipts from the previous day. The rest of the staff busied themselves sweeping the floors and setting up tables while Charlie turned on the television and I browsed the menu. We were sitting in comfortable silence and halfway through our coffees when I first heard the commotion near the ablution blocks. At least three men were shouting at each other. Charlie and I turned on our barstools to see one of the waiters sprinting towards us across the concrete floor outside. The young man burst into the cool interior of the bar with wide terrified eyes and almost slipped as he reached the smooth floor at the door. Immediately he broke into a rapid outburst in Portuguese directed at Charlie who sat listening and firing quick questions back at the man. Not understanding a word my eyes flicked between the frightened man and Charlie as I waited to find out what all the fuss was about. It was then I saw Charlie's jaw drop and the small China cup of coffee fall from his hand and smash on the polished floor below. When he turned to look at me, I saw the colour had completely drained from his face and there was true fear in his eyes.

"You better come with me, Jason. We have a serious problem" he said with a shaky voice as he stood up.

"What is it, Charlie?" I said placing my cup on the bar counter, "What's going on?"

"Please Jason, he said. "Please just come with me. They have found something."

I followed Charlie and the man, out into the sunlight and I noticed that Charlie's legs were shaking uncontrollably as he walked. The waiter led from the front and repeatedly turned to look at us as he walked. We followed him past the toilet blocks and into the car park where we turned right. It was then I saw the rest of the staff standing in the shade under the Bougainvillea around the concrete slab I had tripped over the previous night. As we approached, I noticed that although the steel trap door in the centre of the slab was closed, the thick wire normally used to secure it had been removed and was lying on the concrete surface nearby. I also became aware of the smell. It was the same putrid stench I had noticed in the toilets the previous night. It was the smell of death. I felt a cold sliding sensation in my stomach as we approached.

"They said the water was smelling bad," said Charlie, "so they opened the storage tank to have a look."

The waiting men were silent as we came closer, and Charlie and I stopped in our tracks when we arrived at the heavy steel trap door.

"I can't do this Jason," said Charlie. "Please open it."

I leaned over and grabbed the handle. As I lifted it the hinges to the right squeaked loudly and the heavy steel thudded onto the concrete as I dropped it open. Daylight filled the gloomy interior of the huge subterranean tank and floating face down in the water, a metre below ground level was a body. Although the exposed skin of the arms and neck had turned white in death there was no mistaking the identity. The white shirt and khaki shorts were a giveaway. At that precise moment, the bottom fell out of my world. The body was that of Gabriella Bonjiovanni.

# 21

## Chapter Twenty One: Cyclone

I staggered backwards and almost lost my footing once again at the edge of the slab. Charlie stumbled to the left and vomited loudly near the passenger door of his car. The smell was overpowering and instantly there was a swarm of green and blue flies humming in the air above the trap door. My mind and body were completely numbed from the shock but in some faraway corner of my mind I knew I had to preserve what was left of her dignity from the awful buzzing of the flies. I stepped forward and slammed the heavy steel door shut. By that stage, Charlie had dropped to his knees in the sand and was coughing and spitting yellow bile into the pool of vomit below. I walked over and helped him to his feet.

"We need to call the police now, Charlie," I said.

It was as if my voice was not my own but some distant narrator who still had some vestige of sanity.

"Stay here!" I shouted at the men who had made the discovery. "Don't touch a fucking thing."

The men nodded in understanding as I led Charlie away from the scene and back towards the bar. Once again everything appeared distant from me. The sound of the waves crashing to my left and the crunch of the sand beneath my shoes on the concrete surface near the bar seemed quieter than normal. Through the shock and confusion, I sat Charlie down at a table and made a call to Rodrigo.

"We have found a body," I recall saying, "yes, it's Gabby. Yes, she's dead. Get here as soon as you can."

Charlie too regained some modicum of composure and made a call to the officer in charge of Macuti police station. He also instructed the guard to close the entrance and allow no one inside except the police and the crew. I watched his pale face as he spoke on the phone and a terrible feeling of helplessness came over me. I wanted to open the tank, go in and retrieve her. To bring her out of that dark, dank tomb and restore some kind of dignity for her. *That is a job for the police, Green and you may well be destroying critical evidence if you do.* It was only ten minutes before the police arrived. There were eight of them in total who arrived in an unmarked open pick-up truck soon followed by the officer in charge who arrived in his own vehicle. There was a good half hour of confusion and shouting as I insisted that the tank remain closed until the arrival of the actual homicide unit of the police and the fire service who would retrieve the body. Like before, the events seemed distant to me, almost mechanical, as if they were a dream and there was a strange buzzing sound in my ears.

It was 11.45 a.m. when the homicide unit finally arrived. They were followed soon after by the fire service in a bright yellow truck equipped with ladders and a hoist. By then a large crowd had gathered at the perimeter fence and were jostling among themselves for a peek at what was going on. One of the homicide officers sent an armed policeman to disperse the crowd and keep them at bay by guarding the fence. Thankfully the homicide unit set up a barrier of plastic sheeting around the water tank so the operation to remove the body would be done in private. By then the crew had arrived along with Bianchi from the Italian Embassy. Still sharply dressed he quickly lost some of the colour from his tanned face when he approached the water tank. He left soon after and joined the rest of the crew in the bar area. The sense of loss and shock was palpable amongst the crew who sat huddled together drinking coffee while making call after call, on their mobiles. I sat on the periphery feeling strangely disassociated from proceedings and keeping to myself. Every ten minutes I went with Charlie to check on the retrieval of the body. It was just after 1:00 p.m. when the hoist was positioned and with the assistance of a police diver, the body was finally lifted from the tank. Although Charlie could not bear to witness this I stood and watched proceedings from inside the wall of plastic sheeting that surrounded the tank. The image burned a hole in my mind. There was massive bruising to the side of her face, but thankfully, her eyes were closed, and the police were quick to cover the body once it was laid down on the concrete surface of the slab. Soon after, a government ambulance drove up and an aluminium body box was brought in. I watched as Gabby's body was lifted and carefully put in the box. The strange feeling of detachment continued as I watched the dented lid as it was placed on the box. I stepped backwards out of the line of plastic and stood at the corner of the ablution blocks in the shade of the overhanging Bougainvillea tree. It was as I lit a cigarette that I saw the vehicle. The cream Toyota sedan approached from the left on the sand road driving slowly as it came. On the driver's door, clear as day, was the emblem of a dragon. It was the same car I had photographed that night outside the Imperial Dragon yard in Ceramica. There was no doubt. I backed further into the shade of the tree for cover and watched as it drew parallel with the armed policeman at the perimeter fence. It was then I saw the tinted window open slightly and the pock-marked face of the driver peer out. He turned and spoke to his colleague in the passenger seat briefly before closing the window and accelerating. The vehicle passed out of my line of vision and was gone. *What the fuck?* I stood in stunned silence as I absorbed what I had just seen. Slowly the reality of the events of the morning began to clear in my mind and I started seeing the bigger picture. I knew my brain was in a state of shock but the sight of the two Chinese men had the effect of awakening me somewhat. *That is no coincidence, Green.* I crushed out the cigarette and emerged from the shade of the tree as the body box was loaded into the government ambulance and the plastic sheeting barrier was removed. By that time there were at least twenty homicide and uniformed policemen hovering around taking notes and speaking to the staff. The armed policeman was still doing a good job keeping the hordes of curious onlookers away.

The officer in charge signalled me to follow him into the bar where Charlie, the crew and Bianchi were waiting. As I walked towards the outside seating area, I turned to see the government ambulance trundling over the sand towards the exit. *That's it, Green. She's gone.* The briefing from the senior policeman was translated for me by Rodrigo who sat next to me mumbling as the man spoke. The speech was disrupted constantly by phone calls and messages on the crew's mobiles, and it was a full half hour before it was over. It was 2:30 p.m. when the police finally departed the scene, and we were left to deal with the aftermath. Klaus, Alec, and Rodrigo paced the interior on their phones while Bianchi sat, seemingly composed, drinking cappuccinos and typing on a tablet computer. Charlie sat in a state of fearful confusion, and it was only when I ordered two double whiskies and took him to one side that he finally calmed down. A local plumbing company was called to drain and scrub the interior of the water tank and the staff were instructed to flush all cisterns and boilers with seawater in the meantime. The bar and restaurant were officially closed for the day and finally, it was decided that we would all meet at the Yacht Club at 7.00 pm that night. The last of the whisky burned my throat as I drained the glass and put my hand on Charlie's shoulder.

"I'll see you later, Charlie," I said. "I'm gonna take a walk up the beach to my hotel. I need to clear my head. I'll pick up my vehicle on the way to the Yacht Club later."

"Okay Jason," he said in a weak voice.

"You gonna be alright?" I asked.

"I will," he replied. "I'm sorry."

The old man looked at me with tears in his eyes and I squeezed his shoulder.

"I'll see you later mate," I said.

My mind was spinning as I walked out into the afternoon sun past the parked vehicles and the now abandoned water tank. The security guard nodded at me grimly as I left the gate and made my way up the sandy road that ran parallel to the beach. Most of the crowd of onlookers who had gathered earlier had left with the police and the road ahead was clear. To my right, a row of mature Casuarinas grew from the mounds of yellow sand and the ocean stretched out to the horizon beyond. I fought to gather my thoughts as I walked onto the tar road and up to the pedestrian walkway near the sea wall. Ahead of me the street life and traffic carried on as if nothing had happened. Across the street, to my left, a group of small children laughed and kicked a rusty tin can around like a football. To my right, on the beach, a young couple sat leaning into each other listening to music from a small portable radio.

It was as if no one knew that my world had changed forever and I was left alone with my thoughts and memories. The sun moved steadily down to my left and I gazed at the pebbles in the concrete walkway below as I walked. It was some minutes later when I lifted my eyes to see the familiar figure of the drug dealer, I had met that first night in Beira. He stood leaning against the lamp post in his usual position ahead of me. Our eyes met as I approached him, and he nodded at me in recognition.

"Hi," he said as I passed him.

"Hello," I said quietly without thinking.

It was when I was five metres past him that he spoke again.

"I saw what happened," he said quietly.

I stopped in my tracks and turned to face him.

"What are you talking about?" I said through gritted teeth.

"I was here that night," he said in perfect English. "It was very misty, but I saw what happened".

I looked into the young man's eyes and through his bravado I saw fear. I had seen it a thousand times before. Realising I might spook him I forced myself to be calm and reasonable. I relaxed my jaw, sauntered back towards him and leant casually on the sea wall nearby.

"So, what did you see?" I said quietly.

"The two men," he replied, "the Chinese men. They were waiting over there in their car."

He pointed up the tree-lined avenue that led to the city centre.

"They parked their car in a dark place, but I could see them waiting there. They were smoking cigarettes," he said proudly.

"Waiting for what?" I said keeping my voice low.

"They were waiting for the woman," he replied. "I think they were going to follow her, but her car stopped just before. There was smoke coming from the engine. It's a very old car."

Suddenly I felt a tingling sensation in my arms and legs and the periphery of my vision began to turn red. I forced myself to remain calm and control my voice.

"Cigarette?" I said pulling the pack from my pocket and putting one in my mouth.

The young man looked at me suspiciously at first then took the offered smoke. I lit them both cupping the lighter from the wind. I leant back on the sea wall and blew a plume of smoke into the breeze.

"What happened then?" I asked.

"Are you a policeman?" the man asked cautiously.

"No, of course not," I replied. "But I am interested and if you tell me the truth, I will pay you."

He smiled and a look of pride came over his face.

"Those Chinese men," he said. "They thought they were alone, but I was hiding behind this wall. It was very misty that night."

"And what happened then?" I asked.

"There was a fight," he said. "They beat her and took her in their car."

"What time was this?" I asked.

"It was 11.00 pm," he replied. "I checked my watch. The Chinese men came back two hours later and towed that Land Rover away."

"And where was the woman?" I said.

"The woman was not there when they came back," he replied, as he took a drag on the cigarette, "but the Chinese men came back from that direction."

The young man pointed back towards Charlie's pub.

"I think those men killed her," he said.

I gritted my teeth again and swallowed in an attempt to stay focused.

"If I show you a picture of their car, do you think you can identify it?" I said.

"Of course," he said with a smirk. "I know this car very well."

I reached into my pocket and pulled out a $50.00 note. The man's eyes lit up as he took it.

"Have you told anyone else about what you saw?" I asked. "The police?"

The young man laughed again.

"In my business, it's best not to talk to the police," he replied, "you understand?"

"Of course," I said. "What is your name?"

"Domingo," he replied.

"Wait here, Domingo," I said calmly. "I'll be back in five minutes and there will be more money."

"I am always here," he replied happily.

My arms and legs were buzzing with adrenalin as I took the short walk back to Charlie's. More importantly, my brain was functioning again after the shocking events of the day and a plan was forming in my mind. I nodded at the security guard as I entered the car park and quickly unlocked the vehicle. I opened the laptop and downloaded six images of similar Toyota models to the one from Imperial Dragon. In my mind, I knew the drug dealer would identify the correct vehicle, but I needed to be certain. I reversed in a cloud of dust and drove at speed through the gate and back up to the sea wall. Domingo was waiting as promised and I parked on the opposite side of the road and signalled him to come over. Once he was sitting in the passenger seat, I opened the laptop and spoke.

"Now I am going to show you some images of various cars," I said. "I want you to look at them all carefully and tell me which was the one you saw that night. If you get it right, I will pay you. Okay?"

"No problem," he replied with a smirk.

I began to bring up the images one by one leaving my own photograph of the Imperial Dragon vehicle till last.

"That is the car I saw," he said triumphantly pointing at the screen as I brought my own picture up, "I know that car very well. There is a lizard on the door. Look."

I nodded as I closed the laptop and smiled at his simplistic description of the dragon emblem. I pulled another $50.00 note from my pocket and handed it to him.

"Thank you, sir," he said gratefully.

"There is one more thing I need from you Domingo," I said quietly.

"Yes, sir," he said obediently. "What is it?"

"Sleeping pills," I said. "I need a pack of strong sleeping pills. Can you help?"

"Yes, I can get them no problem," he replied.

"How long will it take?" I asked.

"I can have them for you in an hour or less," he said confidently.

"Right," I said. "I will be back soon and there will be another $50.00 for you when I return. Understood?"

"Yes, no problem. I will get them."

"Another thing," I said. "Where is the nearest hardware shop?"

"Less than one kilometre up there on the left," he said pointing up the avenue that led to the city.

"Thank you, Domingo," I said. "Hurry up and get those pills, please. I have your money and I will be back soon."

"Yes, sir," he replied.

The young man got out of the vehicle and closed the door. I pulled off making the left turn up the familiar avenue and drove slowly, keeping my eyes peeled for the hardware shop.

The shop turned out to be a large builder's merchant's outlet with a yard to the front. Although the salesman spoke no English, I found what I was looking for and emerged twenty minutes later with two heavy plastic bags of supplies. The sun was moving down the sky behind me as I took the drive down the avenue back to the beach road. As promised Domingo was standing expectantly in his usual spot. He approached the driver's window as I parked and with a furtive look around, he produced a small box of prescription pills from his pocket.

"10 mg Zopiclone," I said as I read the name on the box.

"The strongest ones you can buy sir," he said.

"Thank you, Domingo," I said as I pulled another $50.00 note out and handed it to him.

I left the young man standing in the dust as I pulled away and drove north up the beach road towards my hotel. I pulled into the car park, turned the engine off and stared ahead blankly in thought. *Things are moving too fast Green. Take some time out to think.* I locked the car and walked calmly back through the gate and across the road to the sea wall. Fifty metres up the beach I crossed onto the sand and walked north to a secluded spot near the water line. The setting sun warmed my back, and the early evening breeze blew in as I sat down, lit a cigarette, and stared out to sea. I sat, deep in thought, for five minutes as I pondered the events of the day and my planned response. *What you are about to do is all well and good Green, but it's not enough. No fucking way is it enough. You must crush the head of the snake.*

"Or the dragon for that matter," I said to myself under my breath.

With my mind made up I pushed the end of the cigarette into the sand and stood up. It was twilight by the time I unlocked my villa and walked in. Using a plate and a teaspoon, I crushed ten of the tablets into a fine powder which I stored in a folded sheet of writing paper. I spent the next half hour booking the flights online for the following day and it was 6.25 by the time I stepped into the shower. It was with an unusual sense of calm that I shaved and dressed for the evening. It was as if the shock and grief had been sidelined somehow by the knowledge of what I was about to do. I took a slow drive down the beach road to the Yacht Club waving at Domingo as I passed. It was with great disappointment that I noticed Bianchi had joined the crew and Charlie at a corner table in the Yacht Club. I ordered a beer, pulled up a seat next to Charlie and sat down. The mood was bleak, and I spent the next fifteen minutes biting my tongue as Bianchi pontificated about due process, diplomacy and crime scene procedures.

Rodrigo and Alec listened with exasperation while Klaus and Charlie stared into space. Choosing the right moment, I leaned over and whispered discreetly in Charlie's ear.

"If I listen to another minute of this man talking, I'm going to fucking kill him," I said. "Join me if you like. I'm going to get a table for myself."

The old man nodded at me gratefully as I stood up.

"Excuse me, gentlemen," I said as I picked up my beer glass.

I chose a table in the centre of the room near the bar and sat down. A waiter appeared and handed me a menu. I ordered another beer and browsed the dinner selection. I realised that I hadn't eaten properly in days and my appetite had returned with a vengeance. I ordered an Eisbein with chips when the waiter returned with my beer. Charlie arrived soon after and pulled up a chair.

"Jesus," he said quietly. "That Bianchi character is a nightmare. Not surprised you left."

Charlie ordered the fish and chips and we settled into a quiet conversation purposely avoiding the obvious subject. I knew the old man had been deeply traumatised by the events of the past few days, so I kept it light and open. Despite what had happened he ate his dinner enthusiastically and I saw the glimmer of a spark in his tired eyes. *He'll be all right, Green*. Despite repeated glances from the crew, I sat alone with Charlie until we had finished dinner and the waiter had cleared the table. By then it was 8.30 and I needed to get moving.

"Well mate," I said. "Sorry to abandon you, but I am tired, and I need to go."

"Ya me too," he said. "Thanks for the dinner, Jason."

"Pleasure. Take care of yourself," I said as I stood up.

He glanced at me and for a split second, I thought he might have suspected that I would not be seeing him again.

"You too," he said as he glanced over at the crew, "See you tomorrow."

I turned and walked towards the door with a sense of relief knowing that I would be long gone by that time the following day. I opened the driver's window of the cab as I got into the vehicle.

The night air was warm but less humid than usual and I turned to look at the supplies I had bought earlier that were stashed in the foot well of the back seat. After starting the engine and switching on the lights I paused to think one final time about what I was about to do.

"Right," I said to myself under my breath, "let's do this."

22

# Chapter Twenty Two: Rage

The traffic in the city centre had thinned out by that time and it only took fifteen minutes to reach the highway. Apart from a few drunken stragglers the road to Ceramica was clear and I arrived in the dark industrial suburb twenty minutes later. I pulled off to the left and drove slowly up the undulating sand road that led up to the Imperial Dragon yard. Before long I had reached it and I saw the towering piles of hardwood logs above the razor wire at the top of the wall to my left. The security guard and his dog were in their usual place near the guard house at the gate. The old man held his hand up to his eyes to shield the glare of my headlights as I approached. The sand crunched under the tyres as I passed the huge steel sliding gate and made my way up to Banca Miguel. I parked the vehicle in the darkness thirty metres behind the bar making sure that no one would see it if they approached. Satisfied it was well hidden I locked it and walked back towards the bar. The scene was much as I remembered it from the previous time with loud distorted music blaring from a broken speaker behind the bar and the smell of urine in the air. There was only one patron apart from myself. A young man in overalls sat on the opposite side of the dimly lit space sipping a beer and playing with his phone. I approached the barman who recognised me with a nod and a half smile. The selection of drinks was limited but using hand gestures I ordered a Manica beer and a plastic half bottle of cheap rum. The barman gave me a thumbs up and indicated for me to take a seat. I took the same table I had sat at before which gave me a view of the gate to the Imperial Dragon yard. The drinks were delivered, and I watched as the old guard stood and collected a bottle from the guard house. He stood in the dim light of his fire and drank the contents before replacing it with a fresh one. *That's right old fellow. Drink up.* The old man sat down once again near his dog and continued his vigil. I took a sip of my beer and looked around. It was getting late and there was little chance of any more punters arriving. The barman appeared carrying a plate of fried chicken and delivered it to the young man in the overalls on the opposite side of the bar. The two men engaged in a conversation after which the barman disappeared to what I imagined was the kitchen area to the rear. He returned with an empty cardboard takeaway carton into which he placed the young man's food. I called the barman over when he was done and attempted to ask about ordering some food.

"Chicken," I said pointing at the young man who was getting up to leave. "Do you have Chicken?"

"Frango?" the man replied.

"Yes," I said holding up my index finger, "One."

The barman looked at his watch as if to imply it was too late to order food. I pulled a $10.00 note from my pocket and placed it on the grubby table.

"Por favor," I said hopefully.

The barman nodded at me and shouted something in Portuguese to whoever was in charge of the kitchen.

"Obrigado," I said as he walked off back to the bar.

It was 10.00 pm when the food finally arrived. The barman had packed it in a takeaway carton, and I thanked him as I handed him the money. The bar was empty apart from myself and I sensed that things were winding down for the night. The old guard at the gate was drinking steadily as he sat at his small fire in the darkness. I opened the half bottle of rum I had purchased earlier and brought the neck of the bottle to my nose to smell it. The words 'rocket fuel' came to mind as I lowered the bottle and emptied a tot of the noxious liquid onto the sandy floor beneath me. As the barman sat browsing his phone behind the counter, I removed the folded paper with the crushed sleeping pills from my pocket. I unfolded the paper and examined the contents under the table. The white powder sat as I had left it in a neat pile in the centre of the sheet. Carefully I tipped the folded sheet of paper into the open top of the bottle and the powder ran and dropped cleanly into the dark brown liquid. I replaced the bottle top and shook the bottle thoroughly beneath the table. With the barman still distracted by his phone, I held the bottle up to the dim light above. The powder had dissolved completely into the lethal brown spirit. *Good. Now we play the waiting game.*

The repetitive distorted music began to annoy me until fifteen minutes later when I saw the headlights of the car approaching from down the sandy road. Immediately the guard got to his feet and began the process of unlocking and opening the heavy sliding gate to the Imperial Dragon yard. *Bingo.* The cream Toyota pulled up to the gate as it had done before, and I saw the emblem of the dragon on the door clearly in the moonlight. My stomach tightened and the buzzing feeling of adrenalin returned to my arms and legs as I waited for the driver's window to open. *Control Green. Control.* This time the window remained closed, and the guard was left to heave the huge gate open on its wheels. I watched as the car entered the yard and the guard dutifully pulled the gate closed and locked it. The arrival of the car was his cue as the old man immediately collected his empty bottles from the guard house and made his way towards where I sat in the bar. He barely noticed me as he crossed the floor in the dim light and placed the bottles on the bar counter. After a quick exchange of coins, the old man pocketed three full bottles and began walking back towards his post. I whistled to get his attention and he turned to look at me with bloodshot eyes. I held the half bottle of rum in the air and shook my head as if to say I didn't want it and he could have it. The old man glanced briefly at the barman who shrugged and went back to browsing his phone. He shuffled over to my table and took the bottle without hesitation.

"Obrigado," he said before turning and walking back to his post.

The man had opened the bottle and drunk at least a quarter by the time he took his seat near the fire at the gate. The guard dog slept soundly nearby the whole time. I sat sipping my beer slowly and watching as the old man drank from the bottle steadily. Eventually, the music was turned off and the barman appeared to be closing for the night. I finished my beer and with a quick wave to the barman, I stood and walked back to the parked vehicle in the darkness.

I watched as the outside area of the bar was closed by the barman who dropped reed mats from the tin roof effectively sealing the bar off. The lights went out and all was quiet. Staying in the darkness I walked back towards the sliding gate to get a better view of the guard. He sat in his usual position smoking and occasionally drinking from the half bottle of rum. *Anytime now Green. Anytime.* In the moonlight, I noticed a large empty paint tin that had been left outside the bar. I had no idea how long I would have to wait, and it offered a good vantage point from which to watch the proceedings. I sat down on it and leaned back against the rough wooden pole that held the roof. It was five minutes later that the old man fell off his chair. Thankfully he fell to the side and not forward into the embers of his fire. He made no effort to break his fall and simply slumped to the side and lay there completely unconscious. The dog lifted his head to look at the unusual scene but thought nothing more of it and went back to sleep. *He's out Green. He won't wake up for a good while.* I lit a cigarette and sat watching and listening. The night was warm, still, and quiet, the moon lit the scene with a ghostly grey palette. Satisfied the coast was clear and the old man was truly unconscious I crushed out the cigarette and stood up. I walked back into the dark area where I had parked the vehicle and collected the box of takeaway chicken I had purchased earlier. I approached the sleeping man slowly and steadily and it was when I was within five metres that the dog awoke. The Alsatian cross sat up and growled quietly as I squatted down on my haunches and whistled softly to show I was not a threat. I placed the takeaway carton on the sandy soil and pulled out a leg of fried chicken. Immediately, the growling stopped, and the dog's ears went back onto his head as he smelt the food. I tossed the leg towards the dog who scoffed it down immediately. I noticed then that the dog's collar was attached to a rope which in turn was attached to a pole in the ground nearby. I crept forward and saw the dog's tail wagging in eager anticipation of more food. I got to my feet, walked over to the dog, and patted its head as I fed it another piece of chicken. It was a simple process to untie the rope from the collar and I watched and listened to the old man snoring on the ground as I did so. Freed from its restraints, the dog sat happily and watched as I walked over to the old man and felt in the pocket of his jacket for the keys. I found them on a steel ring along with a bunch of others and I pocketed them immediately. Next, I pulled the sleeping man into a sitting position and lifted him onto my right shoulder using a fireman's lift. His tattered clothes smelled strongly of wood smoke and beer and his slight frame was not difficult to lift. The dog followed faithfully as I carried the man along the outside of the wall until I had passed the Imperial Dragon yard and entered the safety of the dark bushy area beyond.

I carried him a further forty metres into the bush before carefully lying him down on his side so he would not choke in the event he was to vomit during the night. Again, the dog sat happily nearby waiting for more food. I left it chewing on a fresh chicken thigh while lying next to its sleeping master.

Quietly I crept along the front of the wall back towards the huge sliding gate. I poked my head briefly into the guard house where I saw the old .303 rifle leaning in the corner where I had seen it before. *Good*. The chained gate was extremely heavy, but I managed to push it open slightly leaving a gap of six inches through which I could investigate the yard. The overhead spotlights cast a murky yellow glow over the many thousands of cubic metres of hardwood logs that surrounded the interior. Although the lights of the factory unit in the centre were off, I could see the two accommodation blocks behind to the right. There was a light in what I imagined to be the bathroom of the one building while the other was in complete darkness. *They're fast asleep too*. I whistled softly to get the attention of the second guard dog I knew was inside. A similar breed to the one I had just fed it responded immediately and ran at speed towards the gate from a dark area between the housing units. I tossed a piece of chicken through the gap before it arrived at the gate and as expected it stopped instantly to wolf it down. By the time I had fed it a second piece through the gap I had gained its complete trust and I set about finding the key to the lock on the chain. I found it on the third attempt, and I carefully unlocked the gate and slid it open far enough for the dog to get out. With the promise of more food, the dog followed me out and as it ate, I slid the gate closed once again. I squatted down and ruffled its head as I fed it another piece. The scrawny hound followed me happily as I made my way along the wall and back to the sleeping guard in the bush beyond. I left both dogs feasting on the last of the chicken while their master snored nearby. I stopped briefly at the parked vehicle and retrieved the equipment I had bought at the builder's yard earlier. I placed the two short lengths of heavy chain and the two padlocks into my bag and zipped it closed.

The scene inside the Imperial Dragon yard was all quiet and as I had left it when I had enticed the second dog out. I took the ancient Lee Enfield .303 rifle from the guard house and checked the breach and the small magazine in the light of the fire. It was fully loaded. *Good. Time to go.*

Leaving the gate-chain and lock in the sand near the front I pushed the gate open quietly and slipped inside. After pulling the gate closed, I crept into a dark area to my right and squatted down near the wall of logs to watch and listen. The light of the housing unit to the right was still on and all was quiet in the yard. I knew the basic layout of the yard from the aerial photographs I had taken with the drone, but my immediate focus was on securing the two single entrances to the housing units. Crouching low and keeping close to the wall of logs to my right I crept forward clutching the rifle as I went. The darkened factory unit loomed large to my left as I made my way steadily toward the centre of the yard. My heart pounded loudly in my chest and the tingling feeling of adrenalin made my arms and legs feel like coiled springs. I stopped and steadied my breathing when I made it parallel to the two cottages. Parked behind the first building was the forklift I had seen before.

A large log of hardwood was still in its forks from when the stacking work had stopped. I cursed the overhead spotlights that would expose me as I crossed the open yard in front of the houses. *Nothing you can do about that Green. It's quiet anyway.* The soft sandy soil underfoot made no sound as I padded across the open area to the corner of the first building. I stood panting quietly with my back to the wall, clutching the rifle and waited. The night was still and hot and I wiped the sweat from my eyes as I listened for any activity from within the first house. There was not a sound.

Parked nearby was the Toyota sedan with the dragon logo on the driver's door. The window had been left open and I stepped forward a few metres to look inside the cab. As I had hoped, the keys were in the ignition. I stepped back and stood against the wall to wait and listen. Satisfied my movements had been unheard I took the bag from my back, leaned the rifle against the wall and squatted on my haunches to open the bag. The heavy chain came out almost silently as did the padlock. Leaving the bag and the rifle I crawled forward to the wrought iron security gate that hung in front of the door. I knew from the photographs it was the only entrance to the building and I needed to make sure the building's occupant would have no way out when he finally learned what was happening. It was a painfully slow process but eventually, I managed to thread the chain silently through the security gate and around the bracket that was cemented into the wall. The giant padlock closed in the links of the chain with a dull click effectively making a prisoner of the man inside the building. I crawled back to where I had left the bag and the rifle and sat with my back to the wall to rest and listen. Feeling certain I had gone unheard I removed the second chain and padlock from the bag and crawled back past the locked door towards the far corner of the building. I repeated the process on the second building silently and returned to where I had left the bag and the rifle. My entire body was wet with sweat, and I was panting lightly as I leaned back onto the wall to rest. *You're halfway there Green*. The moon was rising steadily in the night sky and the air was still and humid.

I stood up, put the bag on my back and lifted the rifle. I crept silently to the great wall of logs to my left and made my way in the shadows around the rear of the two cottages. As I had seen in the aerial photographs there were no back doors to the cheaply built dwellings and the two windows to the rear of each building were secured with heavy burglar bars. As in the photographs, to the centre of the rear of the two structures were the two raised fuel tanks. They stood twenty feet away from the buildings on a tall steel stand with an access ladder in the centre. The two cylindrical tanks could hold five thousand litres each of petrol and the height of the tanks would ensure enough pressure to fill a vehicle with the force of gravity alone. After making sure the coast was clear I placed the bag and the rifle in the shadows near the logs and made my way towards the two tanks. I felt naked and completely exposed in the glare of the overhead spotlights but there was no other way. I needed to know how much fuel they contained. I climbed the steel rungs of the ladder until I reached the top twelve feet above the ground. Each tank had a filling port that was sealed with a steel trapdoor and a rubber gasket to prevent any leakages.

I flipped the latch and lifted the trapdoor to the tank on my right and immediately saw it was full to the brim. The pungent smell of petrol filled my nostrils as I closed the tank and shifted my body to inspect the second one. Although the fuel level was slightly less than the first, I was confident there were at least four thousand litres making a total of roughly nine thousand litres in the two tanks. *More than enough Green*. After a quick look around, I descended the ladder passing the two steel pipes that met in the centre where the thick black hose was curled. The nozzle at the end of the hose was like any at a regular filling station. I carefully lifted the nozzle from where it hung on a hook and slowly unravelled the thick black hose. There were still many loops by the time I had pulled it off to ten metres. I knew for sure then that I could get the nozzle to the back windows of both cottages easily. *Good*. I placed the nozzle in the sand at my feet and retreated silently to the darkness near the wall of logs to my left. I squatted down and looked at the scene in front of me in final preparation for my plan. In my mind, there was only one weak link. *Those men are armed, Green. You know that. The padlocks are heavy, but they could quite easily shoot them up and get out. Too much of a risk. You need to block those doors*. There were only two options available to me. The Toyota sedan and the forklift. Moving either would surely raise the alarm so I needed it to be quick and efficient. I stayed in my position and weighed up the various scenarios and how they might play out. A few minutes later, with my mind made up. I got to my feet and picked up the rifle leaving the bag on the ground. Staying in the shadows I moved back towards the front of the dwellings and paused for a moment before my big move. There would be a series of events that needed to follow each other seamlessly for my plan to succeed. I crept forward in the light towards the parked Toyota. The door opened with a quiet click, and I slipped into the driver's seat placing the rifle butt in the foot well of the passenger seat. The interior of the cab smelled of body odour and spilt beer. Ten metres in front of me stood the burglar bars of the door with the heavy chain and padlock lying just in front of it. With my right hand, I turned the key in the ignition and the lights of the dashboard lit up. *Right Green. Here we go*. The starter motor noisily turned, and I pressed my right foot down hard on the accelerator. Almost immediately a light in the building in front of me was turned on. Still, the motor did not start and quickly I turned the key to the left so I could try again. *Fuck!* Within seconds, the door opened, and I saw the man with the pock-marked face staring out at me with a mixture of anger and confusion on his face. He wore nothing but a pair of boxer shorts and upon seeing my face he began to scream obscenities in what I imagined was Cantonese. I turned the key once again and the starter motor groaned as it spun in an effort to fire the engine. The man disappeared into the building and returned immediately with a set of keys. Still shouting, he unlocked the gate and forced it forward with all his weight. The chain at the foot of the burglar bars clanked noisily and the man stood back and looked at his feet in shock. The man gripped the bars with both hands and began screaming even louder in an attempt to raise the alarm to the man in the next building as he shook the steel gate with all his strength.

It was then I saw the lights in the second building turn on and I knew my plan was rapidly falling apart. *Fuck!* The scene in front of me was quickly turning into one of chaos and I knew that I would have only seconds before I had to move. As expected, the man with the pock-marked face in front of me gave up wrenching at the security gate and disappeared from the doorway. *He's going for the gun Green, fucking move now!* At that moment, the engine fired, and I revved it until it screamed. I jammed the gear stick into first and let the clutch out. The vehicle jumped forward in a cloud of dust and sand as the man returned to the doorway with gun in hand. My last vision was the sight of him standing there with the gun pointed directly at my face. The impact of the car hitting the gate coincided with the gunfire and I ducked as the windscreen in front of me turned white as the glass shattered. With the car now stalled and up against the burglar bars I reached to my left to grab the rifle as the bullets slammed into the windscreen above. With my ears whistling I rolled out of the still open door and came to rest with my back against the wall. I wiped at my right temple with my hand and it came back bloodied. A piece of glass from the windscreen had nicked the skin and as with all head injuries, it was bleeding profusely.

"I kill you man!" the pock-marked man screamed in English from behind the bars nearby, "I fucking kill you!"

By then the man in the next building was also shouting rapid questions. I heard him rattling the security gate noisily as he attempted to escape. Carrying the rifle in my right hand I crawled to my left towards the corner of the building, and I heard the window above me smash as I went. The screaming continued as I made my way to the safety of the corner of the building. Knowing I was completely out of the range of fire I stood up and aimed the nearest tower light. The old rifle kicked my shoulder, and the powerful spotlight blew turning the middle of the yard dark. I repeated the process shooting out the remaining two spotlights to the front of the yard and plunging the area into darkness. *Move fast, Green. The other one will try to shoot his way out as well.* I walked around the side of the building stopping once to shoot the three remaining tower lights. To the left of the two fuel tanks, the forklift stood in the moonlight. I ran across the sand and climbed into the seat. Unlike the car, the forklift started on the first attempt and within seconds I was trundling along past the back of the second building with the giant log in the forks in front of me. I made the turn left as the back window smashed and I heard the gunshots firing wildly from the back of the second building. I made the last turn as the two men were frantically yelling at each other in Cantonese. As expected, the man in the second building was firing into the chain and lock on the ground outside his cottage and I saw the small puffs of sand and dust in the moonlight. I stopped the forklift and pushed the lever to the right of the dashboard upwards. The huge log rolled forward off the forks and thudded heavily onto the sandy ground. It came to rest three inches from the iron bars of the door effectively blocking any exit from the building. I turned the engine of the forklift off and walked back around the side of the building to look at the situation. I found the electrical circuit box that supplied the two buildings with power and with a flick of a switch, the inside lights went out. The panicked shouting continued as I made my way around the building and walked towards the two fuel tanks.

Hidden by the cover of the darkness I lifted the heavy nozzle and began pulling the thick hose from where it lay in the sand. I backed up towards the first building and the nearest window which I assumed was the bathroom. With my back to the wall, I held the nozzle and squeezed it to check the flow of petrol. Within seconds half a litre of fuel had gushed from the nozzle onto the sand below and the handle clicked in the locked open position. I clicked the handle again and the flow stopped. *Good*. I turned and put my right hand and the nozzle through the burglar bars of the small window and smashed the glass. Immediately there was more shouting from within, and I quickly locked the handle into the flow position. I could hear the liquid splashing on the tiled floor inside the building and with my back to the wall, I fed more of the hose in. By the time the man inside had found his cell phone and turned on the torch, there were at least three hundred litres of petrol on his floor. His rabid screaming began to tone down and there was a note of real fear in his voice.

"Why?" he cried in English. "Why you do this, man?"

I stood panting with my back to the wall and listened to the petrol splashing on the tiles inside. *You know why.* When I was certain there was at least a thousand litres of the liquid covering the floors of the entire building I pulled the hose out and clicked the nozzle into the shut position. The voice of the man trapped inside had become shaky, almost whimpering and I was certain he was talking to the man in the next building on his cell phone. Feeling certain he would no longer risk using his firearm I left the hose and nozzle on the ground where I had been standing and walked up to the tanks to unravel more of the hose. After doing so I walked back to where the nozzle lay in the sand, picked it up and began dragging the hose towards the back windows of the second building. As I had done before I stood with my back to the wall and using the heavy nozzle, I put my hand between the heavy burglar bars and smashed the small bathroom window. Immediately there was loud shrieking from within followed by two gunshots. In the periphery of my vision, I could see the man shining a torch at the window from the inside. I clicked the nozzle into the open position and fed it through the smashed window. *Feel free to use your gun now pal. Your decision.* As I expected there was no further gunfire from the man inside. Instead, there was a long low wail as he realized what was happening. At one stage the man stepped forward and pushed the gushing nozzle back through the window. It clattered and splashed petrol in the burglar bars to my left. I pulled the hose out quickly and clicked the nozzle to stop the flow. Turning to my right I smashed the larger window which I assumed was for the bedroom. I opened the nozzle to flow and fed the hose into the room. This time there was no splashing sound of petrol on tiles but rather a dull patter of liquid falling onto padded material. *Maybe the bed? Fine by me.* Realizing that throwing the nozzle out of the windows was not going to work, the man inside instead tried to stem the flow of fuel by slamming the adjacent doors closed. To be sure there would be enough to completely cover the interior floors, I stopped and changed windows once again until I was certain there were at least a thousand litres in the house.

The man inside began crying and praying and I heard him throwing himself against the security door repeatedly. His escape attempts were futile and soon enough he gave up.

"Why sir?" he said mournfully. "Please stop."

"Go to Hell," I said through gritted teeth.

Satisfied I had done enough I pulled the hose from the window and leaving the nozzle open, I walked back towards the first house. The petrol left a thick dark stain on the sandy soil behind me as I walked. Being careful to make sure none of the fuel splashed onto my body I dragged the hose and nozzle to the space between the two buildings. I stood back and watched the flow of fuel as it gushed from the nozzle creating a wide pool with thick rivulets that spread forward towards the factory and left towards the wood piles. Next, I retrieved my bag from where I had left it. By then the river of petrol had reached the wall of logs nearby and was pooling beneath them. I took the old rifle from my shoulder and pushed it into a gap between the logs. *No need for that anymore, Green.* I walked back towards the factory unit to have a look at the scene. By the time I arrived the river of petrol had reached the back doors and was beginning to run around the building to the left. *Good.* I hopped over the streaming liquid and made my way around the front of the second building. As I rounded the corner, I saw that the petrol had formed a stream that ran as far as the far wood pile on the left-hand side of the yard. By the time I walked back towards the factory the two Chinese men were both standing in the blocked doorways of their cottages. They watched me as I walked in the moonlight past them. The man in the building on the left held on to the bars of his security door and sobbed uncontrollably while the other attempted to reason with me.

"No do this please!" he called desperately. "No do this, Sir."

I ignored him completely and walked towards the wall of logs ahead of me. I had no way of telling but I was certain that at least five thousand litres of petrol had spread throughout the yard from where I stood and still it flowed in a narrow stream towards me near the wall of logs. I pulled the packet of sparklers from the bag and removed one. From my pocket, I took the packet of cigarettes and lit one as I took a last look at the yard. *Pray this works, Green.* I carefully pushed the sparkler through the body of the lit cigarette and twisted it in the air to make sure it was stuck fast. In the moonlight ahead I could see the dark stream of petrol in the sand as it got closer and closer to where I stood. *Hurry up, Green.* I squatted down on my haunches and pushed the wire end of the sparkler into the end of one of the giant logs between the bark and the inner wood. It stuck fast and to make sure I flicked the end of the sparkler.

The makeshift incendiary device wobbled but the wire was firmly rooted in the wood. I gauged that the rivulet of petrol would reach the point where I was within a minute or two and the sparkler would ignite soon afterwards. Satisfied I had done all I could I grabbed the bag, stood up and walked back towards the gate. The lights from the distant factories glowed yellow as I pulled the heavy gate closed behind me and reached down to pick up the chain and the lock. I checked my pocket for the keys before locking the gate and leaving it as I had found it. My right temple was sticky with dried blood, and I dabbed it gingerly with my sleeve as I took the walk past Banca Miguel towards the vehicle. I threw my bag in the passenger seat, closed the door and lit a fresh cigarette. It crossed my mind briefly to leave the scene immediately but instead, I walked around the back of the vehicle and leant on the cab to wait and watch. *You need to be sure Green. You need to be very sure.* The night was still and quiet, the only sound being that of the cicadas in the nearby bushy area where the guard slept. The seconds passed with agonising slowness, and I glanced at my watch frequently as I waited. My mouth was dry, my head ached, and the cigarette tasted terrible. It was only half-smoked when I crushed it out impatiently. The seeds of doubt were beginning to grow in my mind, and I wondered if the cigarette had extinguished by itself or perhaps the stream of petrol had failed to reach the sparkler. It was as I was pacing back and forth along the length of the vehicle that the explosion came. Nothing could have prepared me for the incredible force of the blast. In a split second, the night sky lit up like late afternoon sunlight and it was as if my vision shifted a few inches from the shock wave. The almighty boom that followed shook the very ground I stood on and left my ears whistling and aching from the sudden spike in air pressure. Colossal raging flames engulfed the wood piles at the perimeter of the yard immediately after as the scene in front of me rapidly began to resemble a vision of hell.

"Jesus!" I said out loud as I stared at the pandemonium.

At that moment I felt a rush of air along with a loud whooshing sound followed by an almighty thump. Once again, the ground shook under my feet. The top half of one of the fuel tanks had been split along its centre weld by the force of the explosion and had been blown sky-high. It landed in a fiery dusty heap not five metres from where I stood. Jagged, twisted pieces of steel jutted out from the smoking mass. It had been a close shave indeed. *Time to go Green*. I got into the driver's seat, started the engine, and revved it hard. I pulled away in a cloud of dust and headed up the dirt road towards where it met the motorway. The tyres squealed on the tarmac as I made the 'U-turn to head back to the city. By the time I was parallel with the flames the entire Imperial Dragon yard had been transformed into one huge raging inferno. I watched as the factory unit at the centre of the yard collapsed in a shower of sparks and there were yet more explosions from what I imagined would have been the chemicals, vehicles and the gas bottles from the workshop and kitchens. Giant spinning tornadoes of flames spun and licked the night sky reaching sixty feet into the air.

An unusual sense of morbid curiosity forced me to slow the vehicle and stare at the raging pillars of fire and even from the highway I could feel the glowing heat on my face and right arm.

"Yes," I said to myself under my breath. "Burn you fuckers. Burn."

# 23

## Chapter Twenty Three: Hong Kong

The lunchtime flight from Beira to Johannesburg took exactly one hour and fifty minutes. I used the time to reflect on the events of the previous night. By the time I returned to my hotel, I was filthy and exhausted. I had stood under the shower for twenty minutes and washed away the blood and the memories of the explosion and the fire. Afterwards, I lay on the bed and contemplated the great unknown that would be Hong Kong and Charles Tang. Sleep had come quickly, and I awoke at 6:00 a.m. and used the next two and a half hours to download as much information as I could about Mr. Charles Tang and his company, Imperial Dragon Trading. I had avoided the crew and Charlie on purpose choosing to call them instead. They knew nothing of my plans, and I was happy to leave it that way. I checked out of the hotel at 10:00 a.m. and after getting the vehicle valeted at a nearby car wash, I took the drive up to Ceramica to see what was left of the Imperial Dragon complex. The entire inside of the yard and most of the perimeter wall had been completely obliterated leaving an enormous smouldering mess of twisted metal, collapsed buildings and ash. I drove slowly past the small crowd of onlookers, police officers and firemen who stood with their hands on their hips as they stared at the almost dystopian scene of destruction in front of them. Three kilometres further up the highway I turned back to drive to the airport. I stopped at a nearby shack to buy a bottle of water and chanced my luck that the owner would speak English.

"What happened there?" I asked the man.

"Big fire boss," he replied gesturing towards the sky with his hands, "no survivors."

I thanked the man, got back into the vehicle, and drove to the airport feeling mildly satisfied. After returning the vehicle to the car hire company I checked in and waited in the departure lounge for my flight. On the plane, I read up as much as I could of the saved information on Mr. Charles Tang until the battery on my laptop died. Eventually, the plane started to lose height and I saw the yellow glow of the huge mine dumps of the city of Johannesburg in the distance. My table at the coffee shop at Johannesburg airport had expansive views over the runway and there was a power point nearby. I used the free internet to further my research into the flamboyant businessman and his extensive empire. Charles Tang was a forty-nine-year-old Chinese national. Educated at first in Hong Kong and later in England, he had fallen foul of the authorities in Oxford after having been caught in possession of a substantial amount of cocaine. Having narrowly escaped a prison sentence and having been expelled from Oxford University, he had returned to China to join his father's company which at the time was a small but successful import and export concern operating from a factory in Zhuhai, mainland China. Charles Tang's father had died under mysterious circumstances in the late 90's leaving the company in the hands of his ambitious young son.

At the time, his death was put down to food poisoning but there had been a subsequent police investigation into foul play by Charles Tang, but nothing was ever proved. The young man had re-branded the company and expanded rapidly, penetrating global markets, particularly in Southern Africa. Over the years since his father's death, he had built a huge factory complex across the water from Hong Kong in Zhuhai China and set up a large chemical manufacturing plant. A lover of social media, Charles Tang was in no way shy of flaunting his massive wealth and the internet was awash with pictures of him wearing expensive jewellery, watches and driving flashy cars. With a global Twitter following of over 150,000 people, many suspected the ban on social media in China to be one of the reasons he now lived in Hong Kong. His penthouse apartment atop the massive Highcliffe building near Happy Valley was rumoured to have cost over $80 million. The building was the tallest residential skyscraper in Hong Kong. Never married, the man was well known for throwing lavish parties wherever he travelled and was often pictured in the company of minor celebrities and rap artists. There was, however, a dark side to Mr Charles Tang. He was known for having a violent temper and for being extremely ruthless and competitive in business. Any man who had accumulated such sudden wealth and power was bound to have met a few obstacles on his way up. There were rumours and whispers of his association with the Triads. Powerful Chinese criminal syndicates operating in China, Hong Kong, Macau, and Taiwan. There were also reports on his suspected involvement and financing of the blood diamond trade in central and southern Africa. However, none of these allegations had ever been proven and Charles Tang continued with his business and his extravagant lifestyle, flipping between his homes in Hong Kong, Paris, and New York and on his super yacht which was moored in the Marina of The Royal Yacht Club in Victoria Harbour, Hong Kong. I sat back from my reading and thought. *But I have my proof Mr Tang and we have an appointment.* I looked up from my computer screen across the runway to see the giant Cathay Pacific aircraft that would take me to Hong Kong had just landed. I watched as it taxied across the apron in the setting sun and parked near an air bridge to my right. I glanced at my watch and saw that there were only two and a half hours until my flight. I waved at one of the cabin staff, ordered another cup of coffee and continued with my research. It was four hours later, while I was sitting at forty thousand feet staring out of the window of the aircraft into the night sky, that the events of the past days finally caught up with me. I realised I had been in a state of shock since the discovery of Gabby's body, and I had largely been acting on and driven by, some sort of mechanical instinct. My mind and body were completely exhausted, and I knew I needed to rest. I reclined the seat, put the pillow against the side of the plane and fell into a deep, dreamless sleep. It was eleven hours later when I awoke feeling dehydrated, stiff, and sore from the slumber. Through the window the sun was rising, casting a silver swathe of light across the South China Sea. I stepped past the two passengers who were sleeping next to me and walked up to the galley to stretch and drink some water. The crew were getting ready to serve breakfast, so I downed half a bottle of water and returned to my seat.

After the morning meal was served, I sat and stared out of the window and took a moment for some introspection. Physically I was fine, apart from a slightly tender head, but I was more concerned with my state of mind. *Is what you plan to do rational Green? Would it not be better to simply deliver the report and be done with this now?* I sipped my coffee and thought long and hard. I thought of my old friend Hannes Kriel and his violent death at the hands of Dixon Mayuni. I thought of the raw fear in his widow's face at the funeral service and the suffering of his children. My mind went back to the guest house in Harare and how I had been pistol-whipped and left bloodied on the bed. I recalled the awful pain and fear on the night I had been impaled by a spike through my foot, shot in the back and left for dead in the Zambezi River. Then there was the humiliation and agony of my recovery in the government hospital in Kariba and afterwards in Lusaka. And then there was Mozambique. I closed my eyes and smiled as I recalled the idyllic image of Gabby grinning as she stood near the dhow on the beach at Benguera Island. This picture was soon replaced by the horrific memory of her lifeless body floating face down in the dark, dank, lonely interior of a steel water storage tank. I opened my eyes and stared into the golden rays of the rising sun. *No. What you are doing is not irrational at all Green. This man. This man and his organisation have caused so much death and suffering. You said it on the beach in Beira. Crush the head of the snake. Crush the head of the snake. Imperial Dragon is the snake and Charles Tang is the head of that snake. Fuck the consequences. Crush the head of the snake.* An hour later the jet finally descended through the clouds, and I saw the steep lush green hills and the many thousands of skyscrapers that make up the huge metropolis of Hong Kong. The morning light painted the waters of the Pearl River Estuary in gunmetal grey as we landed on the man-made island of Hong Kong International Airport. I made my way through the crowds to the immigration desks and was relieved to find that there was no visa required for British passport holders. I was quickly processed and on my way to the baggage reclaim. The scale of the vast modern airport terminal was strangely alien to me. I put it down to having spent so much time in Africa and having become used to being in open spaces. I collected my bags and walked through the green route without even a glance from the officials. Desperate for a cigarette I made a beeline for the nearest exit and stood in the cool morning air to smoke. The vast airport boasted a nine-hole golf course and a five-star hotel within the grounds, and I watched as a group of men tee-d off in the distance. I knew from my research that the quickest way to get into the city was the airport express so after I was done smoking, I made my way back inside the arrivals hall to buy an Octopus card and head to the train. The process was easy and the directions to the train were well signposted. Within ten minutes I had boarded the train, stashed my bags in the luggage storage area and settled into a comfortable seat. Within a minute the train set off and soon I was speeding past flyovers, roads, and bridges on my way to Tsing Yi and Kowloon station. The morning sun broke through the clouds, and I stared out of the window to my left as the lush green vegetation alternated with glimpses of the sea beyond.

Soon enough the landscape became more urban, and the train passed container yards and docks before entering the tunnel that marked the approach to Tsing YI station. A group of local passengers sitting near me spoke in polite, hushed Cantonese while behind me an elderly American couple argued loudly over a street map. The scene reminded me of the London underground only it seemed cleaner and more efficient. The train stopped briefly at Tsing Yi station where a few people disembarked before we set off again. Eventually, the train exited the tunnel and instantly I was surrounded by hundreds of skyscrapers that jutted out of the hilly landscape like knitting needles. The train sped through a maze of flyovers and bridges before leaving Tsing Yi Island and heading over the water towards Kowloon. The calm movement of people and the muted lighting in the vast interior of the station reminded me of a scene from a science fiction film. From there it was only a few minutes underground to Hong Kong Central Station where the train terminated. The video screen in the carriage showed a clip of smart-looking young people collecting their bags and leaving the train. A recorded woman's voice came over the speakers and said a few words in Cantonese followed by English. "Hong Kong. Doors will open on the right. Please take all your baggage with you. Thank you for using the airport express." The entire journey had taken exactly twenty-four minutes to the second. I collected my bags and walked out into the enormous station.

It took me some time to make my way through the maze of shiny, well-lit passageways to the central hub. Every single wall was covered with giant screens advertising everything from designer brands to fast food. Although the place was busy there were clearly defined walkways and escalators, and the crowds went quietly about their journeys through the spotlessly clean environment. Feeling the need for a cigarette I made my way to the nearest escalator and headed up to ground level. The signs and advertising were in both Cantonese and English and this was reflected in the mix of cultures, with both locals and Westerners making their way down to the station on the opposite side of the escalator. I emerged onto a busy street surrounded by some of the tallest buildings I had ever seen. The streets were packed with double-decker buses and red coloured taxis while the pavements bustled with people of every description. The hissing of brakes and the honking of horns mixing with the music from the shops and the chatter of the people created a typical big city buzz and my nostrils were filled with the aromas of both Chinese and Western foods. Under my feet, I felt the rumble of the underground trains and the pneumatic drills of a nearby construction site as the twenty-four-hour machine that was Hong Kong ground on. I walked through the crowds towards a nearby newsstand where I stood and hailed a taxi. Immediately one of the red taxis I had seen pulled up and I dumped my bags in the back seat.

"Holiday Inn Golden Mile please," I said to the driver as I sat down.

"Sure sir," he replied politely. "Please put your seat belt on. I must ask by law."

I complied and we pulled out into the controlled chaos of the Hong Kong traffic. The shops on either side were a confusing mix of expensive brand names, local noodle houses and Western fast-food outlets. Above the street hung hundreds of brightly coloured neon signs that flashed their messages even in broad daylight. The scene was confusing and chaotic with an underlying semblance of order. The driver weaved skilfully through the traffic and before long we had arrived. I paid him and got out of the cab with my bags. The surrounding buildings were tightly packed and incredibly tall. It was as if space was at a serious premium and the emphasis was on building up rather than out. The Hotel was no exception. With a floor area of one small single block, it had to be at least sixty floors tall. The reception area was clean, modern, and typical of any Holiday Inn worldwide. Not knowing how long I would be there I paid for one week's accommodation in advance using my credit card. My room was situated on the 47th floor of the building and for the first time since leaving the train station, I could see a horizon. I stood at the windows and gazed out at the spectacular vista of the city dropping steeply down to the waters of Victoria Harbour below. I pulled my laptop and the hard drive from my bag, set them up on the desk in front of the window and got to work.

My plan was to send a package to my lawyer in London. The package would contain a single letter along with a second package containing the hard drive. The initial letter would be a series of instructions on what to do with the second package if I did not return to collect it from him within two weeks. There was no doubt in my mind that what I was planning to do would be extremely dangerous and there would be a very good chance that I would fail. The consequences of that failure would mean me losing either my freedom, my life or both. I needed to be sure that even in the event of my death, the hard drive, and the crucial information it contained would be delivered to the Conference on Illegal Wildlife Trade as Hannes had intended. I needed to be certain that his life's work would not be wasted, and the truth be known. As for Gabby's life, my reasons for being there were personal. The letter I typed contained instructions for the second package to be held in safekeeping for two weeks. If I did not collect it, the letter instructed that he open the package and follow the second set of instructions within. This entailed shipping the hard drive along with a personal letter from myself to a certain Dr Helmut Schmidt, programme chairman of the conference in Geneva. It took an hour to find the various addresses and write all three letters. Once done I saved them onto a flash stick and sat staring out of the window drinking coffee. *This is where it ends Green. One way or another.* I called reception from the phone on the desk and asked for some information on the hotel's business centre and the nearest branch of FedEx. An hour later I had printed and signed the letters, shipped them by priority courier to my lawyer in London and returned to the desk in my room. *Now then, Green. Let's see about Mr Charles Tang.*

# 24

## Chapter Twenty Four: All Aboard

The extravagant lifestyle of Charles Tang was well documented and available for anyone to see should they wish. The internet was awash with thousands of pictures and status updates from various social media platforms. That very morning, he had posted a picture of his breakfast from the deck of his yacht with the hashtag '#lifeonthewater'. I browsed the internet for pictures of the yacht and before long I had established that it was a British-made vessel from a company known as Ocean Seeker. The company had been established thirty years previously and had been supplying super yachts to the rich and famous ever since. Charles Tang had chosen the '131' model. With a full length of forty metres and a width of ten, the huge vessel had accommodation for up to twelve guests and nine permanent staff members. With its sleek exterior, tinted windows and four decks, the magnificent vessel would not look out of place in the marinas of Monaco or the Bahamas. Charles Tang had also seen fit to have his trademark dragon logo painted on the bows along with the name 'Dragon of The Seas'. *Easy to find Green.* It was as I sat there that Charles Tang posted a live status update on his Facebook page along with a picture. Once again it appeared to have been taken from the deck of the yacht and was accompanied by the hashtags '#lifeonthewater #hongkongsunnyday'. I smiled to myself as I stared at the image.

"I see you now, Mr Tang," I said under my breath. "I know where you are."

I spent the next hour browsing the Ocean Seeker 131 model on the manufacturer's website and familiarised myself with the interior layout of the vessel. This was made especially easy as there was a fully interactive 360-degree video tour. By the time I was done, I had a comprehensive map in my mind of all four decks from the engine room to the bows and I was confident I could navigate the interior with ease. From my suitcase, I took the hunting knife and removed it from its leather sheath. I sat back in my chair and stared out at the vast cityscape as it sloped toward the waters of Victoria Harbour. The glare of the sun glinted on its polished blade as I turned it in my hand. *Well, Green, there's no time like the present. Get on with it*. Into my bag, I packed the drone, the camera with its lenses and the hunting knife. I chose dark jeans and a light cotton shirt which I wore with the sleeves rolled up. Five minutes later I emerged from the building and stood on the busy sidewalk. The afternoon sun had descended past the buildings behind me and there was a slight tinge of pollution in the air from the massive factories across the water in mainland China. I smoked a cigarette in the cool shade before stepping onto the tarmac to hail a taxi. Within a minute a red cab pulled off the busy street and I took my seat in the back.

"I'd like to go to The Royal Yacht Club please," I said.

"Certainly sir," the driver said as he glanced at me in the rear-view mirror.

The taxi pulled out and joined the steady stream of traffic and soon we had merged onto a flyover that met a raised highway which headed down towards the waters of Victoria harbour. The driver moved on to the inside lane and soon we were speeding past the surrounding buildings. The city was fast and slick and although it struck me as being extremely modern it was clear the city planners had taken the time to ensure there were parks and green spaces in between the skyscrapers. Five minutes later we had descended to sea level and the driver took an exit to the left and merged with a seafront road with a long promenade on the right. We drove slowly past the restaurants and bars until I saw the familiar nautical shape of the Royal Yacht Club building with its rounded frontage ahead. To the right was the boundary of the marina and a series of long paved piers stretched out into the water with the boats of the great and good of Hong Kong moored on either side. The driver pulled up near the entrance and I paid him and left a tip. I crossed the street and stood at the painted steel rail at the water's edge. It seemed to me that the bigger yachts were moored further out, and the smaller boats kept closer to the land. This would afford the wealthier owners a better view of both the city and harbour. I took the camera from its bag, attached the zoom lens, and hung it around my neck in an effort to look like a tourist. Instead of heading directly into the yacht club, I decided to backtrack and take a stroll along the promenade to see if I could spot The Dragon of The Seas. I walked in the cool afternoon sunshine for two hundred metres until I had reached the boundary of the marina. I stopped regularly to look through the camera and zoom into the larger vessels further out to sea, but my vision was obscured by the fact that I was trying to look from sea level and there were hundreds of smaller boats in between. Ahead of me was a break in the railing and a concrete staircase that led down to a jetty. Bobbing in the water below were several sampans or water taxis. The rickety-looking small wooden boats with brightly coloured tarpaulin roofs waited in an orderly queue for passengers and tourists. Standing at the top of the stairway was a short Chinese man who called to the passing tourists.

"Sampan tours cheap," he repeated. "Harbour tours!"

I walked up to him and nodded.

"What time do you close?" I said.

"We no close sir," he replied. "Twenty-four hours. Hong Kong by night very beautiful. You want a tour, sir?"

"Maybe later," I said as I leant on the railing and lit a cigarette.

I brought the camera to my eyes and zoomed in once again towards the bigger boats in the marina. It was still no good. I needed some height.

I glanced towards the white rounded facade of the Royal Yacht Club building and noticed a raised veranda at the front. *That'll do it.* I walked casually back up the promenade towards the building and entered through the large brass and glass rear doors. The interior of the building was in grand old colonial style with plush red carpets and wood-panelled walls adorned with shields and awards of every description. Overhead fans spun silently above and there was an air of grace and old-world charm about the foyer. I was greeted by a polite young man sitting at an ornate desk in a black suit who stood up, welcomed me, and asked if I was a member. I explained that I was just a visiting tourist to which he happily pulled out a card machine. The day visitor fee was the equivalent of $50.00 which I paid with my credit card.

"Welcome to The Royal Hong Kong Yacht Club, sir," he said with a bow and a welcoming sweep of his left hand.

I thanked him and walked into the darkened interior of the building only to emerge in a tiled courtyard filled with tropical plants and a water fountain in the centre. Thick white pillars surrounded the space and there were tables and wicker chairs placed around the perimeter. I walked through the courtyard and up a set of stairs where there were several doors. There was a billiards room to the right and a bar to the left. I heard the murmur of conversation and the clinking of glasses in the bar, so I followed on through. The huge, darkened room had polished ebony floors with glass cabinets of trophies to the right and a plush bar counter with a padded black leather front to the left. Antique diving helmets and ship's bells were on display and the wood-panelled walls were covered with more shields and faded black and white photographs in expensive frames. At the far end of the bar, a group of men sat on barstools drinking Scotch whisky and talking in hushed tones. Beyond that were the heavy ebony doors that opened onto the veranda I had seen from the promenade. I walked past the men and stepped out onto the large half-circle of the veranda. The space was tastefully decorated with palms in pots and tables with crisp white cotton tablecloths and old colonial wicker chairs. Beyond that, the marina stretched out into the harbour and to the right was a stunning view of the city as it climbed the green hills towards The Peak. To my left, a group of ladies sat and drank tea from China cups and a silver tea service. A plate of scones with cream and strawberry jam sat in the centre of the table. The scene was one of classic colonial grandeur and it came as no surprise that Charles Tang had chosen this place to moor his yacht. I took a seat at a vacant table near the railing with a view of the marina. An old fan spun slowly, overhead and I sat back in the comfortable chair to wait for service. Soon enough I was approached by a waiter who took my order for a coffee. Stretching out into the harbour in front of me were four concrete piers. Hundreds of pleasure boats of all descriptions lined the piers, but it was the bigger vessels at the far end of the marina that interested me. I lifted the camera to my eyes and zoomed in on the yachts at the far side of the marina.

I found The Dragon of The Seas moored at the furthest end of the second pier. There was no mistaking its super modern sleek lines and the garish dragon emblem on the port bow. I felt my arms and legs tingle as I saw it. Although it was at least 150 metres away I could clearly see there were people on the middle stern deck. *I see you now Mr Tang. My appointment with you is soon*. The coffee arrived after I had taken a few photographs of the giant vessel. I thanked the waiter and sat pondering my next move. I needed to get closer to the yacht to see what kind of access I could get later that night. When I had finished the coffee, I paid the waiter and walked down a set of stairs to the front of the veranda and onto the pathways that led to the individual piers. The path wound through a small lush tropical garden before meeting the access road where supplies would be brought to the many boats in the marina. I walked onto pier number two and ambled slowly along the concrete surface past the myriad of boats on either side. As I had noticed from the promenade the boats grew bigger and more expensive the further out the mooring was. The sun had passed behind the peak and the day was cooling rapidly by the time I reached the chain cordon at the 100-metre point. A sign in Cantonese and English clearly stated that access beyond that point was for owners and invited guests only. I noticed a marina security guard in a white company uniform casually patrolling the opposite pier. It would have been easy enough to step under the chain, but I resisted the temptation and instead played the tourist snapping pictures of the city and the harbour from where I stood. The vessels that lined the pier beyond the chain moved from the realm of average pleasure cruisers to actual super yachts with permanent crew members. It was in no way unusual that the Royal Yacht Club had seen fit to provide added security and privacy for the wealthy owners. I leant against a nearby balustrade, stared at the city and lit a cigarette. To my left, I could see the end of the pier but my line of sight towards The Dragon of The Seas was obscured by the other boats. *Damn it!* I knew that the man I had come to see was less than fifty metres from where I stood and there was nothing, I could do about it. I crushed the cigarette out on the balustrade and dumped the butt in a nearby dustbin as I walked back towards the Yacht Club. Instead of walking back into the main building I turned left and made my way around the front left of the building back towards the promenade. I passed a marina security guard at a stone arch gateway who saluted as I walked out of the premises back onto the public street. I walked for a hundred metres until just before the sampan rank then stopped and took the bag from my shoulder. It took less than two minutes to set up the drone and by the time I had got it to a hundred feet above I had gathered a crowd of enthusiastic young children who clamoured to see what I was doing. Keeping the altitude, I flew out across the sea until I was sure the aircraft was in line with the pier ends of the marina. I turned the drone left and sure enough the screen showed a clear view of the super yachts that were parked there. It took only thirty seconds until the drone hovered above The Dragon of The Seas and I adjusted the gimbal, so the camera faced downwards. The live 4K image on the controller showed the huge yacht in stunning high definition and I quickly took a series of photographs and videos.

Not wanting to draw too much attention to myself I took the drone up to two hundred feet and performed a few fly-byes of the marina but always returning to the end of pier two. I left the video running continuously. Satisfied I had enough footage and being unable to see the drone in my line of sight, I pressed the home button and waited anxiously for the buzzing sound of its return. The sound came a minute later, so I brought the aircraft down and caught it safely in my right hand out of reach of the excited children who had gathered. After briefly showing them the drone, I packed it in my bag and walked off past the sampan rank towards the line of bars and restaurants on the waterfront. I chose a small quaint bar by the name of Sammy's on the opposite side of the road to the promenade. The inside walls and ceilings were completely covered with banknotes from every country on the planet and rock music played quietly on the sound system. The owner welcomed me and offered me a table outside with a view of the harbour. I sat down and ordered a pint of beer. While I waited, I took the SD card from the drone and inserted it into the camera. The pictures and video footage of Charles Tang's superyacht were better than I expected. Apart from a thick purple rope barrier at the stern of the boat, the boarding ramp was open for access and without security. I paused the video as my beer arrived and thanked the waiter who placed the frosted glass in front of me on a bar mat. The video of the last fly-by was particularly impressive as I marvelled at what essentially was a palace on the water. It was in the last few seconds of the video that I saw the man step out from the lower deck of the boat and point at the drone. I paused the video and zoomed into the picture to take a closer look at the man. He wore dark sunglasses, a white t-shirt and jeans and his moon-shaped face was frozen in a grimace of annoyance at the intrusion above. I could tell the man was not Charles Tang from the many photographs I had studied but there was also no doubt that he was armed. The shoulder holster was clearly visible over his shirt. The man was carrying a gun. It was a stark reminder that what I was planning would be extremely dangerous. *This will not be a walk in the park, Green.* I put the camera on the table and stared out towards the harbour as I sipped the ice-cold beer. The harbour was busy with commercial shipping, junks and sampans as the captains rushed to moor before the sun went down. Already the famous light show, from the cityscape to my right had begun and the buildings glowed in multiple colours in the dusk. I sat staring out at the water as I pondered my next move. By the time I had finished the beer it was dark, but a plan had formed in my mind. I paid the bill and crossed the road to hail a taxi back to my hotel. The motorway was fast, but the inner city was jammed with traffic, and it was 7.45 pm by the time I sat at the desk and opened my laptop on the 47th floor of my hotel. I took some time to research the Highcliffe building, Charles Tang's primary residence in Hong Kong. Completed four years previously it was one of the most sought-after addresses in the city. I had no doubt that security would be tight and simply entering the building would be difficult let alone making it to the penthouse suites. Feeling slightly frustrated I paced the room wishing for a cigarette and occasionally staring out at the fantastic lights of the city and the harbour. Standing on the corner of the desk was a pamphlet with the menu for room service.

I picked up the telephone and ordered a fillet steak with all the trimmings to be delivered to my room. It was at exactly 8.15 p.m. as I waited for the food that Charles Tang posted a live status update on his Facebook page. The picture was of a table spread with exotic food and champagne and once again appeared to have been taken from the deck of The Dragon of The Seas. The hashtag that accompanied the picture read '#partyintheharbour'. My mind was made up. I knew then exactly what I was going to do. *Tonight's the night, Green. You are going aboard that ship.*

There was a knock on the door and a young staff member rolled a trolley of food in. I tipped him and closed the door as he left. I sat at the desk with the magnificent view over the city as I ate, occasionally glancing at the computer screen. I left my credit cards and wallet on the desk and left the hotel at 9.20 p.m. carrying only the bag containing the camera, the hunting knife, and some cash. Although the inner-city traffic had lightened it still took twenty minutes to reach the highway that led to the harbour. The blinding illuminations and multiple advertising screens on the buildings flashed their confusing messages and gave the impression of some post-apocalyptic futurist urban jungle. As before, the traffic on the highway was faster and soon enough we reached the waterfront road near the Royal Yacht Club. I told the driver to pull over and paid him, then made my back towards Sammy's Bar. The owner recognised me from earlier and signalled for me to take the same table outside at the front. There was a loud group of English tourists celebrating inside and cajoling one of their party to sing karaoke, so I was glad of my solitary spot outside. I sat in the cool evening air with the ever-changing lights on the buildings of the city to my right. I ordered coffee instead of beer and settled in for a long night. I sat for the next two hours watching the harbour, drinking coffee, and occasionally checking my phone for any status updates from the social media of Charles Tang. There were none and I could only hope that his own party was proceeding as well as the one inside Sammy's Bar which grew louder by the hour. It was 12.15 a.m. when the English party group finally stumbled out of the doors and made their way up the promenade to the right. They made their way to the sampan rank and dropped out of sight as they descended the steps to the waiting boats. I could only assume that they were going for a tour of the harbour or heading to one of the boats in the marina to sleep. The caffeine and the burning desire to exact my revenge coursed through my veins and carried me through to closing time at 2:00 a.m. By then the street was quiet and only the occasional local walked past the bar on their way home. I paid my bill and left a tip for the tired-looking waiter who locked the doors on his way back inside.

Wispy clouds drifted past the moon above as I walked quietly up the road under the trees on the opposite side of the promenade as the multi-coloured lights of the city blinked at me silently. Far out in the harbour, an unseen cargo ship sounded its horn, and I crossed the deserted street and walked towards a bench to take a seat and smoke. The short rasp of the disposable lighter igniting sounded loud in my ears, and I stared out at the black water with the occasional distant blinking lights of the junks and the ships. I was totally alone. I sat back on the bench and drew the smoke deeply from the cigarette. *This is it, Green. It's time. One way or another all of this is going to end tonight.*

It was on the dot of 2:30 a.m. that I stood up and walked back down the promenade towards the sampan rank. The concrete steps leading down to the water were well-lit and although three boats were waiting, the scene was quiet apart from the squeaking of the rubber that lined their hulls as they bobbed on the water. I walked down to the water line and knocked on a nearby lamppost. The hollow metal sound rang loud in the night. Immediately an old man who had been sleeping on the deck of the small boat sat up from the darkened space and spoke a confused line in Cantonese. Upon seeing I was a Westerner he changed to English.

"Harbour tour or sampan taxi sir?" he said rubbing his eyes.

"Taxi only," I said with a slurred voice feigning drunkenness, "I need to get back to my boat."

It turned out that due to the number of bars and restaurants on the waterfront, my request was not uncommon. The old man immediately stood up and beckoned me forward so I could step onto the boat.

"No problem, sir," he said yawning, "but late time, double fare."

"I don't care," I said as I gripped the railing and stepped into the wooden hull. "Just take me to my boat."

The small motor gurgled and spluttered as the old man untied the bow of the boat and skilfully pushed it away from the landing and out into the black water. By the time he had turned the boat towards the harbour the drivers of the other two waiting sampans had moved forward and moored at the landing.

"Pier number one at the marina," I said over the sound of the motor.

Leaving the old man at the rear sitting by the motor I walked to the bow of the sampan and sat on the wooden bench seat. Soon enough we were out in the open water, and I could see the lights from the boats on Pier One.

"There!" I shouted pointing towards the larger boats at the end of the pier, "Go there."

Three minutes later we were close enough to the pier to see the various landing spots between the boats. I chose one situated between two of the larger vessels near the end of the pier.

Although standard deck lights were glowing on the two yachts there was no sign of any cabin lights, so I assumed the boats were empty.

"Yes," I said to the old man as he slowed the engine to an idle and we drifted towards an aluminium gangway. "Stop here."

The old man stepped forward and stopped the drift of the old sampan by gripping the railing on the gangway. I handed him a bundle of notes and pulled myself onto the gangway.

"Thanks," I said as he pushed the boat away and restarted the tiny motor.

I crouched down in the darkness and watched as the sampan puttered away in the moonlight until I could no longer hear the motor. Apart from the gentle lapping of the water on the hulls of the giant yachts on either side of me, there was no sound. I had made it safely to the cordoned area of Pier One. I crept slowly up the gangway and stepped onto the concrete surface of the pier to look around. There was not a soul in sight and apart from the occasional creak of a rope or slop of water, all was quiet.

The Dragon of The Seas was moored at the furthest end of the opposite pier, so I slowly made my way up to get in line with it. I made it to the end of Pier One and sat on a steel bollard in the shadow of the giant cruiser to my left. Across the water a hundred feet away from where I sat The Dragon of The Seas floated silently in its mooring. The sharp point of its sleek raised bows towered above me ominously in the moonlight. I paused to watch and listen for a few minutes before opening the bag, pulling the camera out and zooming in for a closer look. As far as I could see Charles Tang's party was over and there was no sign of any human activity on board apart from a few interior lights. Still, the memory of the picture of the armed man I had taken with the drone weighed heavily on my mind. There was no way I would attempt to board the yacht conventionally. I stood up to take a look around and noticed the tiny fibreglass rowing boat floating in between the two massive yachts behind me. I assumed it would be used by the deckhands to clean the hulls of the yachts while they were moored. A steel ladder ran down the side of the concrete pier which would allow access. I turned and climbed down the ladder into the dark shadows between the two huge yachts. As I had expected, there were cleaning products, mops, and cloths inside the small boat but more importantly, there were a pair of oars. I stepped off the ladder and into the tiny unstable craft which wobbled uncertainly at first. After checking my balance, I untied the rope that was attached to the ladder and quietly rowed out into the water in between the two yachts. It took a full five minutes of rowing through the darkness of the open water between the two piers but eventually, I pulled up along the starboard side of The Dragon of The Seas. I stopped and held on to the heavy chain of the submerged anchor and listened. Apart from the gentle lapping of the water on the hull, everything was silent. Once again, I felt the tingling sensation in my arms and legs - it was as if things were happening in slow motion around me.

I pulled the tiny rowing boat along the hull of the giant yacht until I was dead centre and within reach of the lower gunwale. Once again, I paused to listen for any sound on board the yacht. There was nothing. My intentions were to get aboard without alerting anyone and to make my way to the master stateroom on the second deck. I threaded the rope through a sunken ring in the hull and secured the rowing boat with a quick-release knot. Next, I took the bag from my back, removed the hunting knife in its sheath and attached it to my belt. Leaving the bag in the rowing boat I paused once again to look around and listen for the slightest sound or movement aboard the yacht. Everything was quiet. I stood up in the tiny dinghy and gripped the railing of the lower gunwale with my right hand. At that moment, before I committed, I closed my eyes and hung my head in thought. *This is it Green. It's do or die. Get the job done and get the fuck out of here.* With a final look around, I pulled myself up onto the second deck and reached for the railing above. The sole of my right shoe squeaked quietly as it gripped the edge, but I stepped over the tubular polished steel railing and stood on the synthetic wooden deck silently. Finally, I was aboard The Dragon of The Seas and within touching distance of Mr. Charles Tang. From memory, I knew that the corridor leading to the entrance to the master stateroom was only accessible from the main lounge and dining area. To get to the lounge I needed to move around the outside and enter from above the swim board near the entrance ramp at the stern. I removed the hunting knife from the sheath and gripped the handle tightly in my right hand. My shoes made no sound as I crept down the narrow walkway toward the rear sun deck. Any evidence of the party that had happened earlier that evening had been cleared away by the staff and the tables and seats were spotless. I knew I was dangerously exposed in the mellow lighting of the sun deck, so I moved quickly to open the entrance to the foyer and the main lounge. The heavy door opened with a light click and I stepped onto the thick cream-coloured carpet of the interior. Although the lounge area was brightly lit, I was grateful that the curtains had been closed over the huge bay windows to either side of the room. They would at least save me from any scrutiny from the pier. The furnishings were plush and expensive while the surfaces and tables were all fashioned from heavy pink marble. I crept forward and crouched behind the first double couch. Ahead of me was the sitting area and the polished wood veneer walls of the corridor to the dining area. The only sound was the quiet whisper of the air conditioning and the pounding of my heart in my chest. I waited there, knife in hand, for a minute to see if there was any movement or if I had triggered any silent alarm. Satisfied that I hadn't, I rose to my feet again and padded across the carpet towards the relative darkness of the corridor. With my back to the polished wall, I inched forward and poked my head around the edge to look inside the dining room. The heavy marble table had seats for eight people. On the centre of the table, mounted on a plinth of ebony, was a huge elephant tusk intricately and minutely carved with an old Chinese village scene. I glanced at it briefly and wondered from which part of Africa it had been poached. Ahead of me was another corridor with a brightly lit spiral staircase to the left.

I knew it led up to the bridge lounge and pilot house, then down to the lower corridor and guest cabins. Its vellum-covered walls, thick carpeting and chrome handrail shone in the bright light of the stairway. Beyond that was the entrance to the master stateroom where I was hoping Charles Tang lay asleep. I glanced around quickly to make sure the coast was clear before crossing the room. *So far so good Green. Control, speed, and silence. Then get out.* I crossed the dining room quietly, pausing only briefly to check the stairway. Despite the air conditioning, I was sweating profusely, and I stood with my back to the wall beyond the stairwell and wiped my face with my left sleeve. Directly in front of me was the doorway to the master stateroom and I stood for a moment to breathe and mentally prepare myself for what I might find inside. My mouth was dry and once again I was aware of the pounding in my chest. I stood and stared at the chromed handle of the door. *Now Green! Fucking do it now!* I leant forward and with my left hand, I gently turned the handle. The last thing I remember was the dull click as the door opened. The savage blow came from behind and connected with the back of my head. It cracked my teeth and turned my vision into a series of bursting white explosions. My body crashed into the heavy door, and I fell forward onto the thick carpet unconscious.

I became vaguely aware of being searched and pulled around by my hands and feet. It seemed there was a lot of shouting in Cantonese and general confusion around me, but I continued to drift in and out of consciousness. After some time, the shouting died down and I felt my body being lifted onto a seat and my hands being tied behind my back. There was more shouting, screaming even and a series of blows to the side of my face. I slowly became aware of the terrible throbbing pain in my skull, and I could hear myself moaning softly. My senses returned fully when a bucket of iced water was thrown in my face. I blinked my eyes repeatedly and looked around to see that I was sitting in the dining room of the yacht at the far end of the table. In front of me were four men who stared at me with enraged faces. At the far end of the table was the unmistakable face of Charles Tang. He sat in a royal blue silk dressing gown and drummed his fingers continuously on the marble surface. I recognised the man sitting nearest to me as the one I had seen in the drone photograph. In his right hand, he held a Chinese-made Norinco 54 pistol which was pointed at my chest. I had no idea who the other two were, but their eyes burned with nervous fury as they stared at me. I realised also that the thick metallic taste in my mouth was blood and I gagged slightly as I swallowed it. I blinked again and stared at the man I had come to kill.

"Who are you and what do you want here?" said Tang in perfect English.

Although he was a big man his voice was high-pitched and strained. It reminded me of an overgrown chipmunk. I blinked and smiled at him not knowing what to say.

"Liko!" shouted Tang to which the moon-faced man with the gun stood and slapped me with ferocious strength on the side of my face.

The blow sounded like gunfire, and I sat there stunned and once again became aware of the taste of blood in my mouth. I lifted my face and stared once again at Mr Charles Tang. His fists were now clenched and shaking with rage.

"I will only ask you one more time," he said. "Who are you and what do you want here on my boat?"

"My name is Green," I said quietly, "and I want to kill you."

The three men nearest me exploded into animated shouted conversation in Cantonese as they pointed at me and each other. The pandemonium only stopped when Charles Tang slapped his meaty hand on the table with a crack.

"Anjing! Silence," he screamed at his subordinates.

I looked around at the red faces of the three chastened men who now sat staring at me.

"Ah, I see," said Tang with a look of smug satisfaction on his face. "You are the man who has been causing problems and disrupting my business operations in Africa no?"

His mispronunciation of the word 'business' sounded like he was saying 'bithineh' and his 'R's were replaced by 'W's.

"That's right, Mr Tang," I said. "The report that you tried so hard to stop. The report that you killed for is now on its way to London and will be presented to the authorities. It's over for you."

Charles Tang stared at me and slowly his face broke into a grin like a Cheshire cat. His laughter started as a chuckle but soon exploded into great whooping bursts of raucous mirth. His subordinates around me joined in nervously but moon face Liko kept the gun pointed at my chest. The bizarre spectacle only stopped when Charles Tang once again slapped his hand on the marble surface of the table.

"I know all about you, Mr. Gween," he said in his theatrical voice as he stood up from his seat.

He walked slowly towards me around the table to the left.

"And I know about your Italian woman. The reporter. She was very troublesome as well Mr Gween."

Moon face Liko held the pistol to my chest forcing it into my ribs as Tang approached. He put his meaty hands on the table in front of me and brought his face close to mine. I smelled the whisky on his breath and his thick, purplish lips wobbled as he spoke.

"She screamed your name as she died, Mr. Gween," said Tang. "Do you know that?"

A sudden bolt of rage hit me, and I felt an uncontrollable urge to lunge forward and bite the small stubby nose off. The pistol jammed into my ribs prevented that so instead I spat a huge gob of blood and saliva into the face of Charles Tang. He retreated with a shriek and wiped his face with the sleeve of his silk dressing gown. Immediately there was another savage blow to the side of my head from Liko. It took some seconds for me to regain my composure.

"Fuck you!" I said through gritted teeth. "You're going down, Tang."

Charles Tang broke into high-pitched laughter once again and his thugs followed suit.

"No, Mr Gween," he said. "It is you who are going down. Deep, deep down."

Charles Tang walked back towards the curtains and pulled them to one side. He turned and looked at me then looked at the diamond-encrusted Rolex on his left wrist.

"Liko!" he shouted to which Moon face instantly turned to face him.

He barked a series of orders in Cantonese that I could not understand but I managed to catch the word 'Zhuhai' which was repeated constantly. The two other men stood up and grabbed me by each arm while Liko kept the gun pointed at me. They dragged me towards the corridor and manhandled me down the stairwell. My legs felt weak and the last I heard of Charles Tang was a faint farewell.

"Goodbye Mr. Gween," he said.

The two men forced me past the guest cabins and back towards a bulkhead that marked the entrance to the engine room. Liko opened the door, and the two men shoved me into the cavernous utilitarian space. The overhead neon lights cast a blueish tinge over the massive engine and Liko stepped over a giant pipe to open a small oval-shaped steel door to the right. The two men physically threw me into the dark interior and I crashed into a series of unseen metal shelves as the door was closed behind me. I sat on the steel floor in the stuffy darkness and began to tease the bindings on my wrists behind my back.

The darkness was absolute, so I closed my eyes and gritted my teeth as the throbbing in my head pounded away. The rope that bound my wrists felt like thick marine nylon and after five minutes of pulling, I finally managed to untie one of the many knots. The rest came undone more easily and soon I was sitting, rubbing my numbed hands together to get the blood flowing once again. It was when I finally stood up in the cramped space that I heard the massive engine rumble into life through the door. Charles Tang was on the move. There was no doubt in my mind that he was taking The Dragon of The Seas to Zhuhai across the water in mainland China. I had heard him say the name a few times. I took his ominous warning that it would be me who was going down, to mean that he would kill me and dump my body in the sea on the way. I ran my hands against the steel walls of the compartment until I found the light switch. The sudden glare of the single bulb caused me to blink a few times. The tiny storage room measured two metres long by one metre wide with steel shelving all around. There was also a storage space above the steel door with a thick rail to prevent anything from falling during travel. The shelves were neatly packed with spare cushions and mattresses for the many sun decks and lounges on the yacht. I tried the heavy handle of the door only to find it was locked and would not budge a bit. *There must be a way.* I switched the light off once again and lay down on the floor with my hands behind me in the same position that I had landed. With as much force as possible, I began kicking at the steel door repeatedly. The noise rang through the hull as steel clashed with steel and soon enough, I heard the door unlock. The blue glare of the engine room lights filled the space and the furious moon face of Liko stared down at me.

"Anjing!!" he screamed at me pointing the pistol in my face.

I thought his eyes would pop out of his head. The door slammed again leaving the room dark. I stood up and flicked the switch of the light to look around. By then the vibrations and the rumbling of the giant engine had changed pitch and there was a slight sensation of movement in the hull. I knew then that the giant yacht was leaving its mooring and getting underway. With a renewed sense of urgency, I began pulling at the mattresses and cushions on the shelves to see if there was anything I could use to my advantage. It was behind a pile of tattered cushions on the bottom shelf that I found the glass bottle of clear turpentine. I popped the cork, and the pungent smell of the cleaning spirit filled my nostrils. I felt my pockets and noticed that during the body search, although they had removed everything else, they had failed to find my cigarette lighter. I brought it out and flicked it to check it still worked. The flame flickered in front of my eyes. I felt the hull tilt slightly and heard the revs of the massive engine increase. I knew then we had left the marina and were on our way. *Hurry Green!* I got down on my haunches and began tearing at the cushions that lay scattered around my feet. They were filled with a fluffy fibrous material that was pure white in colour. Within a minute I had amassed a substantial pile of the stuff which I packed in the far corner of the room under one of the steel shelves.

I stood up and pulled the mattresses from the storage recess above the door and then looked at the ceiling. The smoke alarm and the fire sprinkler were positioned near each other in the centre of the ceiling. Even if the sprinkler activated, its spray would be unable to reach the cushion stuffing where I had placed it under the shelf. I stepped onto the second shelf on the left and gripped the railing above the door. The position offered a great vantage point from which to kick at the door from a height. With my plan finalised I jumped back onto the floor and pulled the cork from the bottle of turpentine. I poured the contents liberally over the fluffy cushion stuffing I had placed under the shelf. The choking fumes filled the tiny space. Outside, in the engine room, the revs of the giant engine increased again, and I knew we were now out in the open water of the harbour. *Do it now before it's too late, Green!* I took a moment to hyperventilate then crouched down and lit the soaking pile of cushion stuffing with the lighter. It immediately burst into an intense blue flame and started belching thick clouds of noxious black smoke. Holding my breath, I turned around and climbed onto the second shelf and gripped the railing above the door. The fire alarm activated as I took my position and immediately there was the sound of a loud siren throughout the ship accompanied by the fierce spray of the fire sprinklers. The pile of cushion stuffing under the shelf burned on unaffected and continued to produce choking clouds of thick black smoke. I reached down and flicked the light switch off and then began kicking at the door repeatedly with my right foot.

"Fire!!" I screamed as my foot pounded the steel door "Fire!"

My eyes began to burn from the smoke in the darkness so I screwed them shut and continued kicking. On the deck above I heard the panicked sound of running footfalls. The invisible acrid smoke cut at my throat and for a few seconds, I thought I might fall from the railing. Finally, I heard the door being opened and I readied myself for the swing. The blueish light of the engine room filled the blackened room and holding the railing above the door, I swung my feet outwards and kicked blindly as hard as I could with both feet. The blow connected with the centre of Liko's chest and sent him sprawling backwards over the thick steel pipe behind him. We both landed simultaneously on the deck, and I heard the loud clatter of the pistol on the floor next to me. The force of the blow had knocked it out of his hand. I picked up the pistol and raised it as Liko recovered and launched himself at me with a winded snarl. His fingers were like claws and his moon face was almost purple with rage. The sound of the shot hurt my ears in the confined space. The bullet hit him just under his left eye and I saw his face collapse as the body slumped and fell onto the steel deck. By then I was soaking wet from the sprinklers and the fire alarm was loud enough to pierce my ears. The blue lights in the engine room were now flashing along with the red emergency fire alarm light. Still, the engine held its revs and there was a definite feeling of movement in the hull. I leapt over the dead body of Liko and ran down the lower corridor to the stairwell.

I stood with my back to the wall nearby and readied myself for the climb. With a quick wipe of my eyes from the water of the sprinklers, I spun around and pointed the gun up the stairs holding it with both hands. There was no one in sight and the water dripped down the padded cream vellum walls in torrents. I climbed the spiral staircase steadily with the gun held in readiness in front of me. Suddenly there was panicked shouting and the thud of footfalls nearby. One of the other men who had taken me below flew around the top entrance to the stairs and gripped the polished chrome bannister. The look of shock on his face as he saw me was priceless. The bullet slammed into his solar plexus and his dying body tumbled towards me. I grabbed the man's shirt with my left hand and threw him noisily down the stairs behind me. Above me, there were more shouts and confusion and I realised I would soon be totally outnumbered. *Fucking get out now Green!* I made it to the second deck in the soaking wet and flashing lights and pointed the gun down the corridor towards the dining area. Running towards me from the lounge were two men I did not recognise. I let off a single round and the two men immediately ducked behind one of the couches. I heard a wail of pain as I backed away looking over my shoulder for any other attackers. In the darkness of the narrow corridor, I saw the exit door to the lower port gunwale on my right. I opened the door and stepped out into the cool fresh air. With the gun still in hand I leapt over the polished chrome rail and fell blindly into the vast blackness of the ocean below. My body slammed into the water, and I was tossed around like a rag doll while submerged for a good thirty seconds. My head finally broke the surface in the creamy churning wake of the giant yacht as it powered away in the moonlight. I put the gun in my belt and began to tread water all the while dreading the captain would turn around and attempt to find me. Thankfully he didn't and I can only put it down to the death and confusion aboard.

It was only when the Dragon of The Seas was a pinprick of light on the horizon that I finally gave some thought to my predicament. I turned in the water and saw the lights of

Hong Kong city twinkling behind me. There was no way I could tell how far out from land I was, but I became aware of a powerful current that tugged at my arms and legs. I breathed a sigh of relief as I realised it was slowly pulling me back towards the lights. I lay on my back, stared at the stars above and allowed my body to relax and float. It was half an hour later when the throbbing in my head gradually began to mingle with the steady thud of a nearby motor. I turned in the water to see my body had been carried a good distance and boats of the Royal Yacht Club Marina were clearly in view in the moonlight to my left. Behind me about fifty metres away was a sampan. Its hanging yellow lights swung in the choppy water as it chugged slowly towards the sampan rank, I had used earlier. I yelled repeatedly until I heard a reply from the driver and saw the tiny boat change course and make its way towards me. Two minutes later I was dragged aboard the ancient wooden boat by a frightened-looking young man who spoke no English at all. Looking like a drowned rat, I sat on the wooden bench seat and wearily pointed at the sampan rank.

"Take me there, please," I said quietly.

# 25

# Chapter Twenty Five: Tower of Ivory

The crawl space between the two massive industrial cooling towers was dark, cramped, and dirty. I glanced at my watch to see it had just gone 11.00 p.m. I had been sitting there for seven full hours on the 74th floor of the massive Highcliffe building. Above me, on the roof of the giant skyscraper, was the helicopter pad for the wealthy residents of the building who couldn't be bothered with the city traffic. The two windowless floors where I was hiding were part of an area usually reserved for service staff and workmen. They were filled with giant water tanks and a complicated maze of pipework. There were massive lift cable wheels and access doors, backup generators, lightning conductors and other nameless machines that kept the tallest residential building in Hong Kong running smoothly. There had been a lot of time to reflect on the events of the previous days. After being dropped at the sampan rank by the frightened young man who had pulled me from the harbour, I had made my way quickly down the promenade and as far away from the Royal Yacht Club as possible. Freezing cold, wet, and exhausted I eventually hailed a taxi as the sun began to rise over the city. The driver had initially been reluctant to allow me into the cab and I couldn't blame him either as I was looking decidedly the worse for wear at the time. Eventually, I made it back to the hotel and instructed the driver to wait while I went to my room, changed my clothes, and checked out. After a quick stop at a cash machine, I instructed the driver to take a long drive through the city. I had spent the time craning my neck and watching behind the vehicle to make sure there was no one following us. There was a good chance that Charles Tang would believe I was dead, but I needed to be sure. After twenty minutes I told the driver to drop me at The Langley Hotel near Cherry Street Park. Having changed and smartened up my appearance I managed to check in under a false name without a problem. The throbbing in my head had worsened and after a quick shower, I had flopped onto my bed on the 23rd floor and passed out.

I awoke with what felt like a massive hangover at 3:00 p.m. that afternoon. After ordering room service I sat at the window and stripped the Norinco pistol I had taken from Liko. The cheap Chinese copy of the Russian Tokarev weapon was easy to clean and there were still twelve rounds in the magazine. I spent the next two days holed up in my hotel room recovering and studying the layout and history of the Highcliffe building. It came as no surprise that Charles Tang had been absent from social media for that period but eventually, he surfaced with a tweet announcing that after a 'minor setback' he had returned to Hong Kong. The tweet was accompanied by the hashtag '#backtowork'. During those two days, I had also done some research into the better-known residents of the Highcliffe building. Of particular interest to me was the widowed wife of millionaire Greek shipping magnate Aspostolis Stouyannides.

Still active in her late seventies, Elizabeth Stouyannides was a high profile, art collector with a well-publicised history of big spending at the local Hong Kong branches of Christie's and Sotheby's. Being somewhat old-fashioned, her telephone number was still listed in the local directory. Posing as a junior manager at Christie's I had called to inform her that I would be hand-delivering a new sales catalogue sometime later that week. I politely told her that I looked forward to meeting her and that I would call again before my visit. The well-spoken old lady thanked me and said she would wait for my call. With my access to the skyscraper now in the bag, I ventured out to purchase some new clothes, a briefcase and to have a few fake business cards printed. The dark pinstripe suit had cost the equivalent of £600.00, but I saw it as a worthy investment - it certainly looked the part. The local print shop had no qualms about copying the Christie's logo and it took only ten minutes to print and cut 100 high-quality cards. After that, it had simply been a waiting game to see where and when Charles Tang turned up. I had used the time in the hotel gym and the indoor swimming pool while constantly checking his social media for long-awaited updates. His tweet was accompanied by a picture taken that morning from the balcony of his residence in the Highcliffe building. I was fully aware that given the incident on the yacht, Charles Tang would more than likely have beefed up his personal security. It was a risk I was prepared to take and the twelve bullets in the magazine of the pistol were acceptable security to me. I called Elizabeth Stouyannides immediately after seeing the post and told her I would be visiting at around 4:00 p.m. that day to deliver the new brochure. She was most gracious in her response and said she hoped I would stay for tea as well. I asked her to please call security at the reception of the building and inform them that I would be visiting her at around 4:00 p.m. She said she would do so immediately.

Wearing the new suit with the business cards in my top pocket I left the Langley Hotel at 3.00 pm that afternoon. In the briefcase were my lock-picking set, the gun and two bottles of water. I told the cab driver to head to the suburb of Happy Valley and twenty minutes later the car crested the hill that marked the boundary of the wealthy suburb and I saw the colossal, towering structure of the Highcliffe building in the valley below. After paying the taxi I strode confidently into the massive, marbled reception area of the building and announced my arrival and my appointment with Mrs Stouyannides. The young, uniformed guard inspected the business card I presented to him, checked his computer screen, and nodded in acknowledgement.

"Do you know the apartment, sir?" he asked politely.

"Yes, I do. No need to call her" I said as I walked towards the lifts. "I just spoke to her. Thank you."

The plush lift sped up to the 50th floor where I knew Mrs Stouyannides had her apartment. I stepped into the wide corridor of the elliptical-shaped building and immediately turned right to where I knew from my research the fire escape stairwell to be.

I was sweating profusely by the time I had climbed to the 72nd floor of the building but I couldn't help taking a quick look round the door of the emergency stairwell. The space was identical to the 50th floor and it appeared all quiet. I was acutely aware that there would be no guarantee that Charles Tang would be in his flat and his social media posts simply be a ruse or a trap, but that was a risk I was prepared to take. I made a quick call to inform Mrs Stouyannides that I had run into some delays and to offer my sincere apologies that I would need to re-schedule my visit. She accepted my apology graciously. It came as a surprise to find the giant service space on the last two top floors of the building was unlocked. Being late in the day I was not expecting any workmen, but I had chosen the dark, cramped crawl space between the cooling towers as a final precaution. After so many hours the constant hum and clatter of machinery and circuit boards was no longer bothering me but rather the aching in my joints and the discomfort of being cramped up sitting on the bare concrete floor. I checked my phone every half hour on the dot for any updates from Charles Tang, but it appeared he had gone quiet.

The seeds of doubt slowly began to creep into my mind and as I waited, I began to wonder if I had indeed set myself up for an elaborate trap. *But then how does he know you are even alive Green? Sure, he is a powerful man in Hong Kong, but could he have traced you to the Holiday Inn? And if so, what then?* These fears, doubts and self-reassurances spun through my mind as the hours passed until finally at 2.30am I stood up and stretched my aching bones. *Time to go. Get it done this time!* Placing the gun in my belt and the lock pick set in my pocket I walked to the doors of the service area. The stairwell above and below was deathly quiet as I closed the doors behind me and walked downstairs. I left my jacket and the briefcase behind the emergency exit door and stepped through.

The foyer area of the 72nd floor was as I had seen it earlier that day. There was not a soul in sight and the only sound was that of my breathing. From my research of the layout of the building, I knew exactly where the entrance to the apartment was. I walked silently to the grand double doors and tried the handles. As I had expected, they were locked. With a final look around, I pulled the lock pick set from my pocket and kneeled to set to work. Within two minutes I had opened the door and I stepped into the dim lights of the foyer of Charles Tang's penthouse apartment. I pulled the gun from my belt and crept in silently closing the door behind me. Although the lighting was dimmed, I could clearly see the layout of the room and the wide windows with the lights of the city below. The furnishings were in keeping with the prestigious address and similar to those aboard The Dragon of The Seas. I knew from my research that the apartment had four bedrooms that were situated down a corridor to the right. With the gun raised I walked slowly through the lounge and dining area towards the darkened corridor ahead. It was as I stepped off the tiled floor and onto the carpeting of the corridor that I heard the television. What sounded to me like a vintage Chinese musical was playing in the furthest room on the left. *The Mikado?* The door had been left slightly ajar and I could see the changing purple tinge of the screen within the room. *Get this over and done with quickly Green!* Every sense was heightened as I crept down the passage slowly towards the door. I reached the door and looked inside to see a giant circular bed on the far side of the room to the right.

Bunched up in the centre of the bed was what looked like a sleeping body. The television, which was out of sight to the left-hand side of the room, continued to blare the high-pitched racket of the movie while the figure under the sheets on the bed lay motionless. Suddenly I felt a cold sliding sensation in my stomach. *This is too easy, Green.* With the gun pointed at the sleeping figure I slowly pushed the door and looked around. To the right of the room was a large ornate marble desk complete with ivory carvings, a heavy glass paperweight and a large silver ornamental dagger with an eight-inch filigree blade. To the centre of the table was a series of lines of white powder with a rolled-up bank note nearby. *Cocaine?* It seemed to me that Mr Tang might have developed some bad habits. The ceiling of the room was completely covered with mirrors which reflected a confusing array of images from the television screen along with the reflections of the lights of the en-suite bathroom to the right. I glanced at the ceiling again to see there was also the reflection of another set of screens. Feeling puzzled I craned my neck to look at the left-hand side of the room. In the corner, on the far side, was yet another flat-screen television but this was not for watching movies. The screen was divided into eight sections. Each section showed a live feed of a different room in the apartment. Charles Tang had installed an elaborate closed-circuit security system. I glanced back at the sleeping figure on the bed. *Who cares Green? Kill the fucker and get out!* The screeching high-pitched singing grated at my nerves as I stepped onto the thick white shag carpeting of the room. The sleeping figure lay under the sheets facing the wide widows at the far side of the room. I needed to be certain that it was Charles Tang I was about to kill. With the gun still trained on the bed, I stepped forward until I was level with the foot of it. It was at that moment that I heard the click of the revolver and the manic giggling behind me that reminded me of a skulking hyena.

"You are very persistent, Mr Green!" said Charles Tang as he stepped out of the shadows of the dressing room behind me.

Realising my dreadful mistake, I leapt forward and to my right to get cover behind the bed. At the same time, I swung the gun around to shoot but it was too late. Charles Tang had fired the .38 Special. The heavy bullet slammed into the side of the barrel of my own gun, and I felt my wrist strain as the weapon was violently ripped from my right hand. I landed behind the giant bed and rolled into a flat position to shield myself from the bullets I knew were coming my way.

"Bastard!" screamed Tang in his high-pitched chipmunk voice as he emptied the chambers of the revolver.

The bullets slammed into the mattress and crunched into the plaster of the wall behind me. One, two, three, four, five shots, I counted until there was only the manic clicking of the trigger of the empty gun. It only took me a split second to realise I had not been hit and for a moment I was puzzled to see the dust and the duck-down feathers of the pillows as they settled around where I lay. I jumped to my feet to see Charles Tang standing in nothing but his underwear in the centre of the room. His entire right shoulder and half of his chest were covered with an elaborate multi-coloured tattoo of a snarling dragon. His face was contorted with rage and his body shook like a pneumatic drill as he repeatedly pulled the trigger. Knowing the gun was empty, I launched myself towards him.

"Bastard!" he screamed as he threw the useless weapon to the side and ran towards me.

Our bodies met with an almighty thump at the foot of the massive bed, and it soon became apparent that either his rage or the drugs had given him some kind of superhuman strength. The iron grip of his right hand closed around my neck and although I rained blow after blow to either side of his face with my clenched fists, he forced me back until my body slammed into the wall near the window behind me. It was only when I felt myself passing out that it occurred to me that his groin was unprotected. I brought my right knee up between his legs with enough force to bring his feet off the ground briefly. Charles Tang let out a loud and continuous cawing sound and finally, his grip on my neck weakened slightly. It gave me enough leeway to force him backwards and we both stumbled and fell rolling onto the thick carpet intertwined in a mutual death grip. Charles Tang began to scratch and punch blindly at my face all the while snarling like a caged animal. It seemed the blows I was landing had absolutely no effect on him at all. My strength began to wane by the time my back hit the leg of the table near the entrance door. Charles Tang fought on like a rabid dog and eventually managed to get on top of me. Out of the blue, he landed two heavy punches on my left temple, and I knew then I was losing the battle. With the same superhuman strength he lifted me by my shirt to a standing position and I looked into his maniacal eyes.

"Bastard!!" he screamed in my face.

With a final burst of strength, I head-butted Charles Tang squarely in the nose and heard the cartilage break. The blow stunned him briefly and the big man's legs collapsed under him. He sat on the carpet with his hands behind him as a torrent of blood flowed from his ruined nose. I staggered backwards wheezing heavily as I tried to catch my breath. My misguided sense of security was all too brief. Charles Tang kicked at my lower legs and hooked his foot behind my ankles. My legs lifted into the air and my back slammed heavily onto the surface of the marble table behind me.

I lay there winded and confused as Charles Tang sprang to his feet once again and held me down by my shirt on the table. I saw the deranged fires of madness in his eyes above me from where I lay as his right hand lifted the heavy glass paperweight high above his head ready to smash my skull. He never saw my right hand which had found the thick carved ivory handle of the silver ornamental dagger that lay on the table nearby. I gripped it hard and brought it up towards his head with as much force as I could. The razor-sharp point of the filigree blade pierced the flesh under his chin, travelled through his tongue, and embedded itself an inch deep into the roof of his mouth. Charles Tang's eyes opened wide, and the heavy paperweight fell from his right hand and smashed into the table near my head. Still bent over, the big man released me and took a step backwards from where I lay on the table.

"Hmmmmmmm," A long, unusual sound emanated from deep in his throat.

The shrill piercing voices from the opera on the giant television to my left reached a crescendo as I lifted myself from the table and stood over the hunched figure in front of me. I lifted his head slightly by his ears and looked into his wide mad eyes. His thick purplish lips were quivering uncontrollably. I tightened my grip on his ears and brought the knee of my right leg up as hard as I could under his chin. My knee hit the pommel of the dagger with great force and the long blade travelled through the roof of Charles Tang's mouth. It passed through the temporal lobe of his brain and came to rest in the roof of his skull. As if by some strange muscular spasm, the big man stood bolt upright and raised his arms in a cruciform position. I stood and watched as his eyes rolled back in his head. His body fell straight back with a dull thud and Charles Tang lay dead on the carpet of his penthouse apartment in the Highcliffe building of Happy Valley, Hong Kong.

# 26

# Chapter Twenty Six: Geneva, Switzerland, Five Days Later

The bright morning sunshine reflected harshly off the blue waters of Lake Geneva. In the distance, I saw the famous Jet d'Eau water fountain that shot a solid column of water 140 metres into the sky above the lake. Beyond that, the distant snow-capped Alps cut a jagged black-and-white line against the perfectly blue sky. Having removed the hard drive of Charles Tang's security system I had left the Highcliffe building quietly and without incident. I left Hong Kong that evening and flew back to London via Dubai. After spending two days holed up in my flat, I ventured out to my lawyer's office in Soho and retrieved the package I had sent from Hong Kong. The day after that I had flown to Switzerland and booked into a suite for one night on the 4th floor of the Hotel Metropole. I poured a cup of coffee and sat at the desk near the window where my laptop computer was set up. There were four hours to kill until my flight back to London, so I decided to use the time to catch up with some work. I had been feeling somewhat dazed and detached from reality since leaving Hong Kong. This feeling stayed with me as I delivered Hannes' report to Dr. Schmidt at the offices of the World Wildlife Fund in the city. Our meeting had been short and although he had accepted the hard drive with polite gratitude, I could see he was a busy man and had more pressing business to attend to. After the appointment, I had spent the late afternoon wandering the streets aimlessly before ending up in a bar near the waterfront. The feeling of blank disassociation was still with me, and I drummed my fingers on the table as I sipped the coffee and stared out at the view. The shrill electronic ring of the telephone in front of me woke me from my daydream and I lifted the receiver.

"Hello," I said quietly.

"Good morning, Mr Green this is the front desk," said the male voice in a French accent "We have Dr Helmut Schmidt here at reception."

"Yes?" I said feeling somewhat puzzled.

"He sends his sincere apologies for having arrived without an appointment," said the man "but he would like to see you as a matter of urgency."

"Um, sure," I replied. "Please send him up."

"Thank you, Mr. Green, I will send him up right away," said the voice.

I stood up from the desk and removed my bag from the table in the centre of the room to tidy up. *What is this all about I wonder?* The sharp knock on the door came two minutes later. I opened it to find a very dishevelled Dr. Helmut Schmidt standing there panting from his climb up the stairs. His long grey hair was all awry and I could see the eyes behind the tiny rimless spectacles were tired and bloodshot. In his left hand, he clutched a thick file.

"Mr. Green!" he said loudly as he shook my hand vigorously "Oh, Mr. Green, I'm so glad I caught you. I got the name of the hotel from the reception at my offices. Please accept my sincere apologies for arriving without an appointment but I *had* to see you urgently."

"No problem at all," I said feeling slightly bemused. "Please come in."

The portly man walked in and sat down on a chair at the table with his back to the window. His tweed suit was creased and ruffled around his shoulders and arms. He placed the file carefully on the table in front of him.

"Would you like some coffee, Dr Schmidt?" I asked.

"Thank you but no, Mr Green," he replied watching me intently. "No, if you don't mind, I will just sit with you for a few minutes."

I sat down on the chair opposite and waited for him to speak.

"Mr Green," he said. "I have been up all night along with a staff of eight people."

He tapped a pudgy finger on the thick file on the table.

"This report you delivered to my offices yesterday afternoon is what kept us up."

"Right...?" I said still feeling somewhat puzzled.

"Mr Green," he said sitting forward in his chair, "This report is without a doubt, the single most damning expose ever seen in the history of the WWF. This report, when made public at our forthcoming conference, will expose and crush some of the most powerful poaching syndicates in the world. It will result in hundreds, if not thousands of international prosecutions. Not only that, Mr Green. It will demonstrate the collusion and corruption of countless government officials in the countries mentioned in it. In other words, it is priceless. Mr Green, on behalf of the WWF, I would like to thank you for bringing it to us."

"Thank you, Dr. Schmidt," I said, "but you are aware that the majority of this report is the work of the late Johannes Kriel."

"Yes," he replied, "yes Mr Green I am aware of that. To tell you the truth we never expected to receive it since hearing of his death."

I tapped my finger softly on the arm of the chair not knowing what to say. The portly man sat forward again his thick grey moustache bristling. His bloodshot blue eyes stared at me through the spectacles.

"Mr Green," he said, "forgive me for pressing you on a subject you seem reticent to discuss. But I have a distinct feeling that you may have been through some personal hardships in getting this report to us. Would I be correct in thinking that?"

I looked at the old man sitting in front of me. My eyes wandered to the view of the distant mountains and then settled on the screen of the laptop on the desk behind him. The smiling face of Gabriela Bonjiovanni standing near the dhow on the island looked back at me. Suddenly the shocking and vivid memories of the past months came crashing into my consciousness. It was as if a giant dam had burst, and I had been hit by an all-consuming wall of flood water. The sudden rush of emotion was both unexpected and frightening and I felt the tears welling up in my eyes. I blinked and cleared my throat before I spoke.

"There were a few problems Dr. Schmidt." I said quietly "Nothing serious..."

The End

Dear reader. I'm guessing if you are seeing this, you will have finished this book.

I really hope you enjoyed it! If so, I would like to ask you to kindly take a minute to leave a review on Amazon and Goodreads.

Reviews REALLY help me reach new readers.

You can find the other books in the series at this link: https://geni.us/QCVsT24

Feel free to follow me on my Facebook page which you can find at this link: https://www.facebook.com/gordonwallisauthor

Thank you once again and rest assured, Jason Green will return soon!

Cheers, Gordon.

Printed in Great Britain
by Amazon

33604094R00169